THE AMAZING JUDGMENT

The world-weary Lord Hildyard, Marquis of Esholt, is on a yachting tour with a group of friends, including his kept lover, Pauline Owston. When Hildyard spies an apparently uninhabited island, he slips off the ship in search of adventure. What he finds is the exotic woman-child, Bertha, and her guardian, Stanley Owston, estranged husband of Pauline. Before the yachting party returns, Hildyard discovers himself in love with Bertha, and vows to return for her. But when the Owstons are dramatically reunited, Stanley confesses to his wife that Bertha is the daughter whom she has not seen in twelve years. Will Hildyard ever find the love he seeks, or is his love for Bertha now doomed beyond hope?

MR. LAXWORTHY'S ADVENTURES

For Mr. John T. Laxworthy, detection is a serious game, and all of Europe is his playground. In a series of 12 adventures, Laxworthy travels with a well-padded wallet and two sporting companions, following only his instincts and the scent of money to be made. Along the way, he nabs an international burglar, exposes a cross-dressing murderer, foils a plot to steal battleship plans, and even helps a respected criminal opponent recover 40,000 pounds owed him by an unscrupulous London banker. Laxworthy is an amateur sleuth and an adventurer: urbane, clever, and oh-so-British. You'll cheer him on as he always gets his man – and, in the end, even his woman.

The Amazing Judgment

...

Mr. Laxworthy's Adventures

...

E. Phillips Oppenheim

Introduction by Daniel Paul Morrison

Stark House Press • Eureka California

THE AMAZING JUDGMENT / MR. LAXWORTHY'S ADVENTURES

Published by Stark House Press
1315 H Street
Eureka, CA 95501, USA
griffinskye3@sbcglobal.net
www.starkhousepress.com

The Amazing Judgment originally published by Downey, London, 1897.

Mr. Laxworthy's Adventures originally published by Cassell, London, 1913.

ISBN: 1-933586-27-3
ISBN 13: 978-1-933586-27-4

Cover design and layout by Mark Shepard, SHEPGRAPHICS.COM
Proofreading by Rick Ollerman

*The publisher would like to thank Daniel Paul Morrison for making
this book happen, and Rick Ollerman for making it happen correctly.*

First Stark House Press Edition: December 2009

REPRINT EDITION

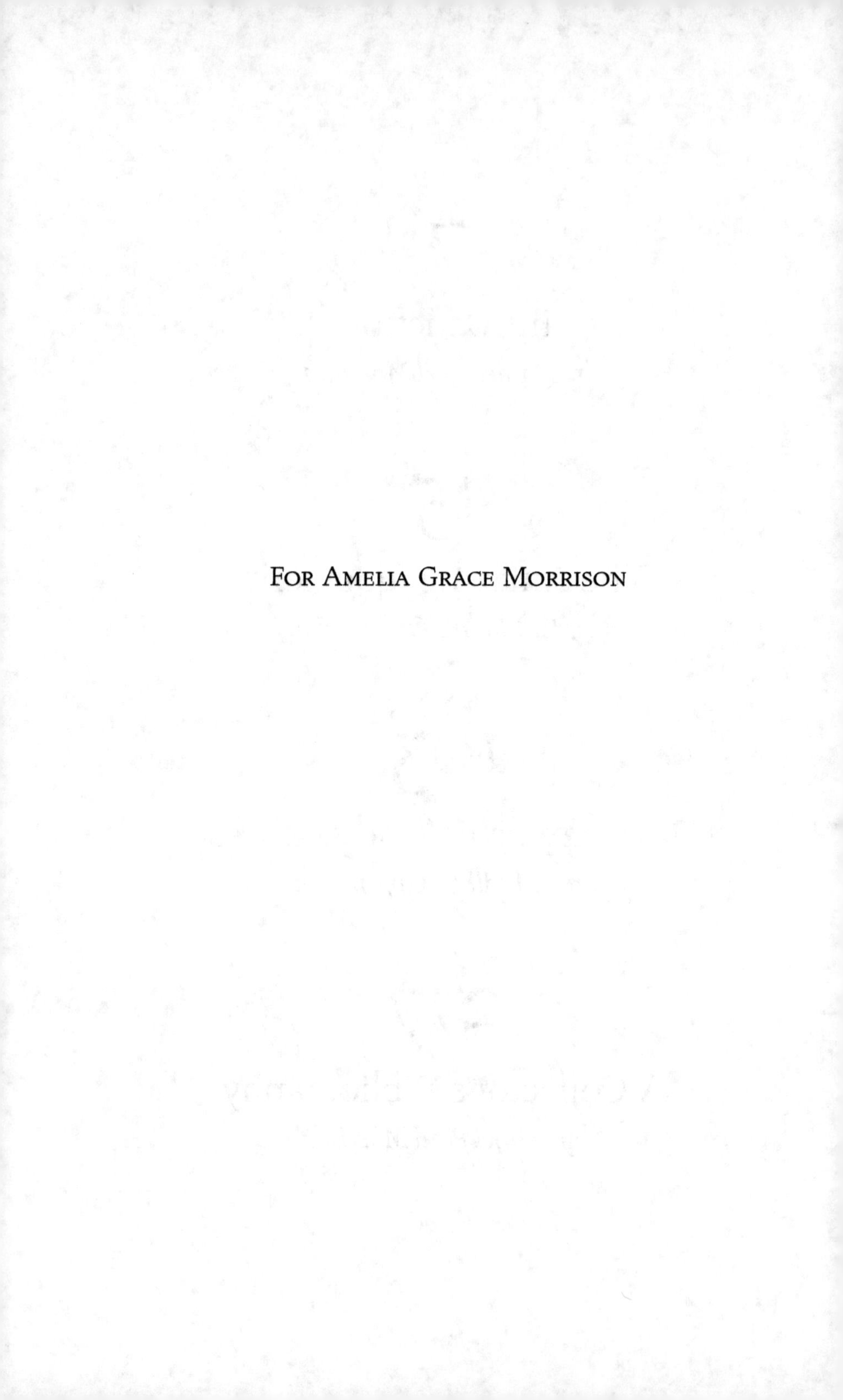

For Amelia Grace Morrison

Introduction

...

Daniel Paul Morrison

RESURRECTING THE RAREST OPPENHEIM

My first glimpse of *The Amazing Judgment* came by mail. About a year ago, a package containing a photocopy of a photocopy of the actual book landed on my doorstep.

For more than a decade, I had searched for this book. Along the way, I amassed more than 500 Oppenheim items: books, magazines, autographs, letters, photographs, movie stills, posters and advertisements. I even have two of his golfing trophies!

But in all my searching, I never caught sight, however distant or faint, of a copy of *The Amazing Judgment.*

E. Phillips Oppenheim is an attractive author for book collectors for two reasons. First, he published lots of titles – more than 150 distinct books – offering plenty of game for book hunting safaris. And, second, his books are inexpensive – most cost less than $10; only a few go for more than $100.

But there is a catch: one Oppenheim title, *The Amazing Judgment,* just can't be found. Not anywhere; not at any price.

By resurrecting Oppenheim's rarest book, Stark House Press has given collectors their first realistic chance of assembling a complete set of Oppenheim volumes.

How rare is rare?

Published in 1897 by Downey & Co. Ltd. in London, *The Amazing Judgment* is, without a doubt, Oppenheim's rarest title. But how rare is rare?

At present, there are three known copies of *The Amazing Judgment.* Compare that with the 48 known copies of the Gutenberg Bible and the whopping 228 copies of Shakespeare's First Folio.

Two copies survive because of British copyright law. When *The Amazing Judgment* first appeared, British publishers were required to deposit copies of all new works with the British Museum in London and with the Advocates' Library in Edinburgh.

The second-generation photocopy I received through the mail was made from the original copyright deposit volume on the shelf at the British Museum.

The third copy, and the only one known to have been bought by a collector, is now part of the Albert Borowitz Collection at Kent State University in Ohio.

With the exception of Borowitz, heavyweight collectors and top-shelf antiquarian book dealers have all looked for this book without success.

One of the greatest Oppenheim collectors was the late Wray D. Brown. He pursued Oppenheim volumes for nearly four decades. His collection, now part of the Mercantile Library at the University of Missouri in St. Louis, would be complete if it weren't for the hole left by *The Amazing Judgment.*

Otto Penzler, the granddaddy of mystery book collectors, also reports being stumped by *The Amazing Judgment.*

Penzler is the long-time owner of the Mysterious Bookshop in New York City, editor and publisher of *The Armchair Detective,* publisher of the Mysterious Books imprint, and editor of many mystery anthologies. No one has better mystery book collecting credentials.

Penzler's own Oppenheim collection once contained more than 200 American and British first editions. When asked about *The Amazing Judgment,* Penzler replied, "That title remained a frustration for me after 40 years of collecting. Had I seen one, I'd have bought it."

Inquiries with long-established bookshops in the United Kingdom – where *The Amazing Judgment* would be most likely to surface – produced the same result. All reported they had never seen a copy. One seasoned dealer doubted the book ever existed.

How rare is *The Amazing Judgment?* Very rare!

Reconstructing the text

Though it was nothing more than a hand-me-down photocopy of the British Museum's example of *The Amazing Judgment,* I was thrilled by the package I received in the mail.

I quickly read the long-lost book and began to transcribe the text, hoping one day to see the book republished.

But then there were problems.

Years ago, the British Museum volume had been badly rebound. Pages were trimmed and the gutter – the fold where the pages meet in the middle of the book – was so tight that a clear photocopy was impossible. Words and parts of sentences were missing!

I pressed on with my work, noting the lacunae and making educated guesses to fill in the missing bits. All the while, I was nagged by the possibility that my transcription might have errors.

Then I discovered a copy of *The Amazing Judgment* in its original cardstock covers in the Albert Borowitz Collection at Kent State University.

Albert Borowitz, an expert on Jack the Ripper, is a Harvard-trained lawyer and the author of numerous books and articles on crime and crime literature. The son of an important book collector, Borowitz began collecting crime literature more than 50 years ago. In 1989, Borowitz began to donate his extensive collection to Kent State University.

There are now more than 12,000-volume in the Albert Borowitz Collection, housed behind double-locked doors in the archives and special collections department, up on the eleventh floor of the main KSU library.

Before making an eight-hour drive to Ohio, I called ahead and got an appointment with a special collections librarian. Once there, I was allowed to examine the Borowitz copy of *The Amazing Judgment*. By checking my transcription against the Borowitz volume, I was able to iron out the problems presented by the British Museum book.

A question of provenance

How did Borowitz acquire a copy of *The Amazing Judgment* when so many other collectors and dealers failed to so much as see one? Where did the treasure surface?

When asked, Borowitz said he had no idea that he had such a rare item among his Oppenheim volumes and couldn't say where he got his copy of *The Amazing Judgment*. He recalled having acquired a large lot of Oppenheim volumes on one occasion and speculated that perhaps *The Amazing Judgment* was part of that lot.

The auction records and receipts that are part of the Albert Borowitz Collection show no record of this particular book having been bought.

For Borowitz, whose collecting interests tend toward true crime in general and Jack the Ripper in particular, the mystery novels of E. Phillips Oppenheim seem to have been a minor sidelight. Of his 12,000-volume collection at Kent State, only 150 are by Oppenheim.

We can conclude that the rarest Oppenheim title fell into Borowitz's hands by simple good fortune, from some source now lost to memory.

Whatever its provenance, we are fortunate that a copy of *The Amazing Judgment* in its original state is now available in a university library.

Why so rare?

Finding and resurrecting this book raises a couple of questions. Why is this book so rare? And how could a best-selling author like Oppenheim have produced such a rare book?

Two factors primarily contribute to the rarity of any given book: 1) the number of copies printed and sold, and 2) the fragility of those copies.

Number of copies. A book can be rare if few copies were made. Typically, an author's first work is the rarest for the simple reason that press runs for unknown authors tend to be small.

The first edition of *The Philosopher's Stone*, the first in the popular Harry Potter series, fetches fantastic prices today. That's because in 1997 a mere 500 copies were printed of the first edition of the first book by the then-unknown J. K. Rowling.

But *The Amazing Judgment* wasn't Oppenheim's first book.

In fact, it was his tenth or eleventh work and a couple of his earlier books – *A Monk of Cruta* and *A Daughter of the Marionis*, for example – were popular and are still easy to find.[i]

Given the healthy sales of his previous books, it would make little sense for Oppenheim's publisher to have produced only a short run of *The Amazing Judgment*.

Another possibility is that the book was issued by a small publisher with limited output.

But, in fact, *The Amazing Judgment* was published by a large, general interest publishing house. In the year *The Amazing Judgment* appeared, the catalog of Downey & Co. lists more than 240 different titles. Downey published popular novels for adults and juveniles, reprints of literary classics, histories, biographies, and a few large picture books.

A small press run seems unlikely and alone can't account for the rarity of *The Amazing Judgment*.

Fragility. A book can be rare if few copies survive the ravages of time. A well-made book – one printed on good paper and bound in a strong binding – can last for centuries. But beginning in the nineteenth century, some books were produced cheaply, designed to be read and thrown away. Without a doubt, *The Amazing Judgment* was such a book.

The original book, which has roughly the same dimensions as the book in your hands, sold for just one shilling – one-sixth the price of Downey's first-tier, hardback novels.

The book was issued in flimsy pictorial cardstock covers. A full-page advertisement for Brooke's Monkey Brand Soap on the back cover allowed the publisher to sell the book more cheaply. This was the kind of book sold to travelers by railway station newspaper vendors.

The Amazing Judgment was a fragile book. Its chances for survival down through the years were slim. But plenty of similar books from that period do survive.

Two perfect examples are *Expiation*, Oppenheim's first novel, and *His Father's Crime*, a pirated edition of *The Mystery of Bernard Brown* – both published as flimsy paperbacks.

Oppenheim's inaugural work was published in London by John and Robert Maxwell in 1887. In my years of collecting Oppenheim, only once have I seen this book offered for sale – and at the hefty price of $1,300. As a pirated book, *His Father's Crime* is less interesting to some collectors, but

---

[i] Depending on whether or not *The Wooing of Fortune* is a real or a phantom title. I suspect it is a phantom title, making *The Amazing Judgment* Oppenheim's tenth outing.

I have a particular relish for such contraband. *His Father's Crime* was published in New York by Street and Smith as number 112 in their Adventure Library series. I have seen this book for sale more than once and picked up my copy for a pittance.

In sum, we can't attribute the rarity of *The Amazing Judgment* solely to the fact that it was published as a cheap paperback.

The books

A real mystery remains regarding the excessive rarity of *The Amazing Judgment.* Maybe one day you will solve that mystery.

In the meantime, you have in your hand a delightful volume which pairs the elusive *The Amazing Judgment* with the charming *Mr. Laxworthy's Adventures.*

Oppenheim's rarest book begins with the air of a supernatural thriller – spooky, weird and disorienting. But as the story progresses, the reader encounters most of the genres mastered by Oppenheim, including mystery, adventure and romance.

Published when Oppenheim was 31 years old, *The Amazing Judgment* reveals a budding author reaching for his settled voice. Present here are many of the motifs that appear again and again in Oppenheim's later books: mistaken and hidden identities, exotic romance, recovery of a stolen birthright, smoldering resentment and righteous revenge, and, as ever, a believable and well-resolved ending.

Though long lost, this work is unmistakably from the pen of Oppenheim.

Mystery writers often create detectives who appear in story after story, book after book. Conan Doyle's Sherlock Holmes and Arthur Morrison's Martin Hewitt were familiar fixtures in the mystery literature early in Oppenheim's career.

Mr. Laxworthy could have been Oppenheim's answer to Holmes or Hewitt.

A wealthy, amateur detective, Laxworthy travels restlessly across Europe with two younger companions, ever in search of new sensations, adventures and profits. He operates with equal facility on both sides of the law, bravely rescuing friendless victims and gleefully fleecing unsavory criminals. To all appearances, Laxworthy is an unremarkable British gentleman with fastidious habits and an aversion to drafts. His unassuming exterior camouflages his clever detective mind and devilish mercenary motives. Uncanny powers of observation, flawless memory and clear logic solve the puzzles. Steely nerves and a bit of jiu-jitsu get Laxworthy and his companions into and out of a string of entertaining and lucrative adventures.

Mr. Laxworthy's Adventures can be read as a series of short stories or as an episodic novel. It was first published in London by Cassell and Company in May 1913. This Stark House Press edition is its first publication in the United States.[ii]

With very few exceptions, Oppenheim books were published roughly simultaneously on both sides of the Atlantic. For example, *The Mischief-Maker* was published in Boston by Little Brown in March 1913 and in London by Hodder and Stoughton in August 1913. It is not clear why *Mr. Laxworthy's Adventures* was never published by Little Brown – Oppenheim's US publisher for more than 40 years. Yet another mystery.

What is clear, however, is that you can now read two rare Oppenheim gems. I hope you enjoy reading them half as much I enjoyed bringing them to light.

Daniel Paul Morrison
Willow Grove, Pennsylvania
October 2009

[ii] There might be an earlier US publication. The Library of Congress catalog lists *The Peculiar Gifts of Mr. John T. Laxworthy* but notes that its copy is missing. This title is not listed in OCLC or the NUC. The twelve Laxworthy stories were serialized under this title in *Popular Magazine* from May 15, 1912 through November 1, 1912. *Popular Magazine* was a cheap, story magazine and generally not the first-run publisher of serialized stories. It is likely *The Peculiar Gifts of Mr. John T. Laxworthy* appeared earlier in another magazine or newspaper. The LOC item might be a fan-assembled chapbook of clippings. I have such a chapbook containing the whole of *Miss Brown of X.Y.O.* assembled from newspaper clippings.

The Amazing Judgment

...

E. Phillips Oppenheim

BOOK I

CHAPTER I

A white-winged ship sailed out on the sunlit ocean into a dense sheet of drifting mist. The world of sunshine and blue sky and murmuring waters seemed to have faded into chaos. In a very few moments the decks were wet and slimy, and a damp chilliness hung about the air. The pleasant warmth of the afternoon was gone. Gay voices were sunk into whispers. A sailor who had been polishing some brass work to the tune of "Nancy Lee" whistled no more. The thick twilight seemed to have fallen upon them like a mantle of silence. It was a metamorphosis so sudden and complete as to possess for one of the little company at least a significance almost allegorical.

A woman who was lying in a low deck-chair under a canvas awning, clad in the lightest and daintiest of summer gowns, began to shiver. She looked around her and back again into her host's face with a slight uplifting of the eyebrows.

"This is one of the delights of yachting, I suppose, Hildyard?" she remarked. "Have you any idea how long it is going to last? I am getting chilly."

He stooped down, and drew the rug, which had fallen away from her feet, up to her throat.

"Only a few minutes," he answered. "It is really on a heat mist, and we should pass through it directly. Seems pretty thick, though: would you like to go down? It isn't exactly pleasant, I must admit."

She shook her head slightly. She was so well wrapped up that there was little else of her to be seen now.

"Not for worlds! I am quite comfortable with this rug around me."

"It is almost like a London fog," he said disconsolately. "Our view has gone altogether."

"I am not sure that I regret it—for a moment or two. To see nothing at all is rather a relief, after seeing so much day by day."

He looked at her doubtfully. Presently she continued,—

"An ocean view is too expansive for my tastes. It suggests infinity, and infinity—no end of disagreeable things. On the whole, I prefer Bond Street. It is wearisome to be made to think. Don't you think so? But then you are rather a dreamer, aren't you? You like to lose yourself. I don't."

"I am afraid that this cruise has bored you," he said quietly.

"No; I think not," she answered deliberately. "I have great hopes of being able to say that I have enjoyed it—so far as my capacity for enjoyment goes, of course!"

"There is nothing—"

"No; there is nothing else in the world which you could have done," she interrupted thoughtfully. "You have been very good indeed. The only thing is, that I am afraid I am not a very satisfactory person to be good to. I do not enjoy things as I ought. I suppose it is my unfortunate disposition. How dreary it looks up on the bridge; and why doesn't Captain Henderson put on his oil-skins? He will be soaked. Aren't you glad that you are not there instead?"

He glanced upwards. His captain, a stalwart, middle-aged man, was standing like a carved figure, his hands grasping the rail in front of him, and his eyes fastened upon the vessel's bows. Two extra men had been sent forward, and the throb of the machinery had slackened. They were going at half speed. Oscillation seemed to be completely suspended. The sea was as smooth as glass.

"Yes; I think it is just as well that Henderson is there," he answered; "especially as we are rather out of the beaten track. Nothing but fishing smacks ever come into these waters."

"And how far are we from land?"

"There should be some uninhabited islands close about here. Henderson is on the lookout for them now. See, it is lifting a little already. It will be all over in a minute or two. Do have another peach."

She shook her head. A somewhat elaborate tea equipage was by her side, and several silver bowls filled with fruit. A steward was waiting a few yards away.

"Nothing more, thank you. Yes, I think it is getting lighter. How quiet every one is! It is like the silence before—shall I make you nervous, if I say—disaster?"

He did not answer her. He had moved a few steps forward, and was gazing steadfastly across the vessel's bows. Suddenly the stillness was broken by a hoarse shout from one of the look-out men, echoed promptly by the other.

"Land on the starboard bow! Land to starboard!"

"Land on the starboard bow it is."

A brief order was thundered from the bridge. Then the captain looked down.

"It's the outside island of the group, my lord!" he cried, with his hand to his hat. "We're clear by half a mile."

The yacht had altered her course slightly, and was going now at full speed. Every one was standing up. The woman, for whose sake this cruise and many other things had been planned, threw aside her rug, and leaned over the white railing. With an involuntary movement, she suffered her hand to rest upon her companion's arm. They stood there watching together.

Suddenly the mist lifted. The veil of grey, floating shadows melted into thin air. Before them was a glassy, waveless stretch of sunlit ocean whose lack of colour was atoned for by phosphorescent streaks of multicoloured light. Exactly opposite was the land.

It was an island rising high out of the sea, and shaped something like a sugar-loaf. Its cliffs and summit were fringed with stunted pines and firs. Here and there only was a patch of green—standing out with a peculiar vividness of bright colour from amongst the darker background of trees and rocks. There were no cattle, nor indeed was there any sign of life, or any dwelling-house. To all appearance the place was uninhabited, and uncultivated. The little strip of beach was piled up with mighty masses of rocks of huge size and terrible shapes. Amongst them, the sea-gulls in countless numbers screamed and circled, darting in and out of the drifting mist which lay behind them, like phantom birds. At one moment their wings flashed like little streaks of silver lightening, as they flew round and round in the sunlight; then they vanished into chaos, only to reappear again and again crossing the broad path of the sun's rays, and catching once more upon their slowly flapping wings the glory of the sudden, white light. Their hoarse cries struck a weird, almost unearthly note in the deep silence.

"What a desolation of desolations!" she exclaimed, with a little shiver. "Almost lonely enough for you, my friend, when you have the blues, and cultivate misanthropy. What do you say? Would you like to try it? It would be a pleasant little retreat for you, and I almost think that you would be undisturbed!"

Her companion did not answer. It was rude of him, but he was evidently deeply preoccupied. He was standing motionless by her side, his arms folded upon the rail, and his eyes full of a curious expression, steadfastly fixed upon the island. She tightened her grasp upon his arm. She looked into his face, and she was full of wonder.

"My dear Hildyard, what is the matter with you?" she exclaimed. "You look positively tragic! One would think that you were face to face with the modern ghost—the ghost of our sins, you know. If there is anything of that sort walking upon the waters, I am going down. Whatever are you looking at?"

He did not even glance towards her. There was a distinct shade of pallor creeping through the bronze sunburn of his cheeks. He did not answer her, but stretched out his right hand towards the island. She followed his shaking finger, and uttered a little cry.

They had passed a promontory jutting out into the sea from the northern end of the island, and before them, on the sheer edge of a great, bare rock, a large cross of fire flared up into the clear sky. For a moment every one seemed to be dumb with the wonder of it. The faint ripple of conversation from behind them had ceased. Even the sailors stood still at their work. Then there was a little murmur. The woman drew a deep breath of relief, and laughed softly.

"What an illusion!" she exclaimed. "It was the sun, of course. For a moment I thought that we had found another wonder of the world!"

He looked over her shoulder half doubtfully. The long, slanting rays of the dying sun lay across the ocean like broad bars of red gold stretching to the feet of the piled-up rocks, and touching with fire the sea-stained stone. Even while they watched, the light died out. Slowly the sun sank down into a bed of angry clouds. Cold and grey the cross stretched out its naked arms against the colourless background of sky and air. The woman, looking up at her companion, wondered at his unchanged expression.

"Hildyard!" she repeated, with a note of impatience in her soft, languid tones. "What on earth is the matter with you? Why don't you talk to me? You stand there as though you had been transformed into—something wooden. You are very stupid, and you don't amuse me at all. I shall go and ask Mr. Pearmain to tell me a story."

"I will tell you a better one myself directly," he answered lightly. "Please forgive me, and don't go. Besides, Pearmain wouldn't thank you to be interrupted. He is telling Lady Bergamot the plot of his next novel. Just a moment!"

He drew a silver whistle from his pocket, and blew it. The chief mate was by his side in a moment.

"Johnson, do you know anything about that island?" he asked.

"Nothing, my lord," the man answered doubtfully. "The group is down in the chart as barren and uninhabited."

"You don't know how that cross got there, then?"

"No, my lord—no more do any of the others on board. We've been passing the question round. I should say myself, that it was a natural cross. There's a terrible sea running upon that beach, and I've seen rocks twisted into some queer shapes."

"Captain!"

The captain looked down from the bridge.

"Yes, my lord."

"Johnson seems to think that that might be a natural cross over on the rocks there. What is your opinion?"

"Very like it is, my lord. It would be an odd thing if any one had troubled to build on such a desolate spot, and no shipwreck or anything that I ever heard of, to call for it. I should call it a natural cross myself."

The captain resumed his walk upon the bridge, and the chief mate departed about his duties. The man and the woman were alone again. She went back to her seat, and he drew a camp stool to her side. She was still watching him curiously.

"Hildyard," she said, "I am prepared to hear something thrilling. You have a look in your eyes as though you had seen more than we saw upon that island. Perhaps you are one of those favoured individuals who possess—what is it they call it?—second sight. Tell me about it. I insist!"

He hesitated, and then he obeyed her. He generally obeyed her. It had become a habit with him.

"Well, it is rather a coincidence," he said deliberately, choosing a cigarette from his case, and lighting it. "Pardon me. You won't smoke before dinner, I know. Always gives me an appetite."

"I don't want to hear about your appetite, Hildyard, I want to hear about the island. You needn't be afraid. I'm not going to laugh at you. I'm immensely impressed!"

"Quite sure? Well, here goes!"

He blew the smoke away from his cigarette, and became suddenly serious. His eyes were fixed upon the dim, white line where sea and sky seemed to touch. His voice was sunk almost to a whisper. He had the air of a man talking to himself.

"Last night I had a dream. I saw myself upon the rocky beach of just such an island as that. I was alone amidst the roar of the surf, and the crying of the sea birds. I was another man, and yet I was the same man. I felt, and I suffered! I was searching ever for something which I could not find. We are always doing that every day of our lives; only instead of being in Piccadilly—I was there. My hands were stretched out toward the ocean. I am not sure that I was not praying—but if so, it was in an unknown tongue, and to an unknown God!"

"Hildyard, are you serious? You are raving!"

"I am perfectly well aware of it. Please let me finish, though. I want to photograph my impressions—verbally, of course. Some day I am going to write another novel, and weave this in. It is excellent material. Last night, as I was saying, I saw it all! The cross was there, the island was there, I was there! Centuries ago, Pauline, there was an ancestor of mine who fought in the Crusades. He joined the Saracens for the love of an infidel woman, and he spat upon the Cross. It was bad form, especially in those days, but he did it. I think he was hung up by his heels afterwards, or crucified—I am not sure which, but it is immaterial. The point of the thing is this, that since then, for generation after generation, the cross has been a token of woe to all my family. Whenever it has appeared—in any exceptional way, of course—some great change has followed, generally a death, or disaster of some sort. Please don't look so incredulous. That is the worst of you modern women! You will believe nothing! I don't think I will go on!"

"You will go on at once!" she commanded. "Don't you see that I am deeply interested?"

He looked at her lazily, and flicked the ash off his cigarette.

"Well, I was going to give you a few proofs," he continued. "These things are in the family archives, and they must not be doubted. Sir Hugh, who fought at Cressy, saw a golden cross in the sky, and fell with a French sword cleaving his heart. A century or so later Sir Francis was riding out to join Monmouth, when he saw a cross—some of his followers declared that it was a gallows—on the top of Dunkerry Beacon, and like a wise man he rode home again, and saved his neck. My great grandfather, who broke his neck in an Irish steeplechase, sobbed out with his last breath, that the winning post had turned into a cross. There are many others. Last night I saw them all. One by one they flitted into my cabin, and when I stretched out my hand—quite in a friendly way—they vanished through the port-hole. It was tremendously aggravating. And then I saw myself upon the rock, always searching, waiting, with the cross before my face. It was my warning."

"Your warning. From what?"

"I could not tell. Only I seemed to see the story of my life written across the sky in letters of fire, and it was like the lives of all other men—it was evil. I looked in vain for a single deed that was not selfish, a single impulse that was not vicious. Pauline, I think that we men of to-day have fallen upon evil times. We have no duties, we have no scope to develop even such stuff as sent our forefathers to Palestine. We are, as Pearmain would say, an 'effete and scentless blossom upon the tree of Life!' That dinner bell is a distinct interposition of fate. In a few moments I should have been preaching. We must hurry."

"Hildyard, I believe that you are half in earnest."

He looked down at her, and laughed.

"You are always right!" he said. "I am."

CHAPTER II

Dinner was a rather long affair on board the *Sea King* but it was drawing toward a close at last. The softly-shaded electric lights flashed upon silver and cut glass bowls of hot-house fruits and delicately fashioned vases of wonderful flowers. The wine in the glasses had become red. The light through the portholes was growing dim.

The woman who sat on her host's right hand leaned over and whispered in his ear.

"Hildyard, why cannot you always be so light-hearted? To-night you are charming. You make me think—of days—when we were both younger."

He laughed gaily, and, lifting his glass to his lips, bowed to her.

"I have not always you on my right hand," he answered. "Lady Bergamot, don't go, please," he added, looking further down the table, "I have ordered coffee to be served here to-night. It is cold on deck, and the flavour of the cigarettes is lost."

Lady Bergamot, who had half risen, sat down again readily.

"By all means, dear host," she said. "For my part, I think you are all too anxious to rush up on deck. I am quite comfortable here. What do you say, Mr. Pearmain?"

"I am more than comfortable, I am happy," remarked the man who sat by her side. "At the same time, one must be reminded occasionally that we are not in London! Hildyard has brought his cuisine, his cellar, his servants, and all the luxuries of Esholt House. If we did not see the sea now and then, we should find it hard to realize that we are supposed to be roughing it upon a yachting cruise. At the same time, I prefer getting through what measure of exercise is necessary during the morning. There seems to me something crude in leaving such an atmosphere as this for the dark draughtiness of the open deck. Parker! a glass of Benedictine."

"You are a sybarite, sir," laughed Lady Bergamot, with a shrug of her shapely shoulders. "You know quite well that you would never have left Pall Mall if there had been the least chance of your having to rough it."

"A sybarite," he repeated musingly. "I do not quite know what you mean to imply, but the word sounds pleasant enough. I will plead guilty. If sybaritism is a sin, I have a very charming partner."

There was a little lurch. Morton Pearmain, the man who had been talking, bent forward and looked through the porthole.

"I do not know much about navigation," he remarked, "but it seems to me that we are altering our course. The engines are slacking, aren't they, Hildyard?"

"I have not the least idea," his host answered carelessly. "Henderson is like me— a saving man! Perhaps he is running a sail up. The breeze seems to have freshened since we came down."

Pearmain shrugged his shoulders.

"I should have said that we had altered our course altogether," he declared. "Shows how much I know about it! As we are now," he added, dropping his voice, "I am willing to sail the Antarctic Ocean. There go the engines again."

"Never mind the engines," laughed Hildyard, filling his glass, "and, whatever you do, don't go bothering Henderson with questions. He doesn't like it. Tell Lady Bergamot that story you told me this afternoon about Fanny Dussein and old Catherall."

Pearmain put up his eyeglass, and twisted his thin, black moustache doubtfully.

"Isn't it—just a little—? That was in confidence, you know! I don't fancy that I ought to repeat it."

"Tell me at once!" Lady Bergamot ordered firmly.

It was very late indeed before everyone went on deck. When at last they left the saloon, and the women had gone for their wraps, Hildyard made his way alone into the captain's room.

"Have you managed it?" he asked.

Captain Henderson rose from his chair and set down his pipe.

"Yes, my lord! We have swung right round, and we're within three miles of the island again now. She's away on the lee bow yonder. I'm giving her all the berth I can, and running half speed, but I shall have to bring her to within half an hour."

Hildyard looked thoughtfully away into the darkness.

"I daresay that will do," he answered. "The boat will be ready at midnight, I suppose?"

"The boat is ready now, my lord."

"And you understand that, if possible, I don't want a soul to know that I have left the ship."

"No one will know, my lord, unless your guests discover it for themselves."

He nodded, and stepped back on to the deck. Through the shadows came the little group of laughing men and women, the red tips of their cigarettes glowing like fireflies in the darkness. Pauline came to him, and took his arm. The others passed on.

They stood together looking over the side. A bank of low, thick clouds obscured the moon. The white-topped waves rose and fell upon a sea as black as ink. They watched the eddies go swirling by the side, and the phosphorescent light gleam upon the water.

"May I consider myself a more privileged person than Mr. Pearmain?" she asked abruptly.

"Naturally!"

"I want to ask you a question, then. Is it true that our course has been changed?"

"Who says so?"

"No one. I only asked. I am curious."

There was a moment's pause. He was annoyed that she should have suspected what he had studiously endeavoured to keep secret.

"Yes, we have come round a little," he admitted reluctantly.

She tried to peer through the darkness. Her eyes were very bright and very steady, but she could not see anything.

"How far are we from the island?"

"Only a mile or two," he answered. "There it is."

He pointed over the ship's side, glancing round first to be sure that they were alone. Once more she tried to see through the floating shadows. She gazed until her eyes ached with the strain, but she could see nothing.

"Listen!" she said softly. She held her breath. From far away behind that wall of darkness, there came a dull, threatening roar.

"It is the surf on the beach," he whispered. "I am afraid that the others will hear it."

She glanced for a moment over her shoulder. Her lips were parted in a fine disdain.

"Oh, they will not notice it," she answered. "Lady Bergamot is too absorbed in Mr. Pearmain's stories. Hildyard, why are those people here? What made you bring them?"

He looked at her in genuine surprise.

"The inconsequence of woman!" he exclaimed lightly. "Why, you yourself told me whom to ask. I think you added that a six weeks' cruise alone with me would be insupportable."

"I was a fool," she said quietly. "I did not know what I wanted. We are like that sometimes, you know. We say things that we do not mean, and we suffer for it."

"I am sorry," he began awkwardly. "I—"

"Never mind. It was my own fault. I was a fool. It was exactly from those people and their associations I desired to escape for a little while. I fancy that I am beginning to find the air of the demi-monde a little enervating."

He looked at her curiously. This was a new phase to him.

"Not exactly that, is it?" he said quietly. "Lady Bergamot is quite respectable."

Their eyes met for a moment. He looked away.

"Because she has not been found out," she answered drily.

He ignored her little speech.

"Besides, you occupy a place by yourself," he reminded her. "You have attained a special immortality, you are the most beautiful woman in England."

"Many men have told me so, and a few newspapers," she answered quietly. "There is nothing in the world I am more weary of hearing. It makes me feel like a—pagan."

"We are all pagans," he murmured.

"Not altogether. Lately I have been subject to fits—of what do you think?—of morality. I am beginning to wonder whether it might not have been better for me to have been a little less beautiful, and a little more honest! But never mind. I do not want to talk of that, to-night. I want to ask you something."

"Yes?"

"Are you going on that island?"

"Yes."

"When?"

"As soon as you people have gone to your cabins."

"Why?"

"I really have not the remotest idea. I have an inclination to go, and it is so long now since I had an inclination to do anything in particular, that I am going to gratify it."

"It is only a barren island. There is nothing to see there. I would rather that you did not go. I do not want you to leave the ship. Please, don't."

He looked at her in amazement. Her soft, brilliant eyes were raised to his. She was in earnest. He had known her only as a brilliant woman of the world, a creature at once imperious and capricious. She offered herself to him at that moment in a new light.

"My dear Pauline!" he exclaimed. "You bewilder me. If I feel like going— why on earth not? I am actually experiencing the luxury of a genuine, unadulterated curiosity. It would be a sin not to indulge it."

"Then, for my sake, please sin."

"I must have a reason," he declared. "The luxury is too rare a one to be parted with lightly. Besides, it is so easily gratified. There is not the faintest shadow of danger or difficulty in any way. Why do you wish me to give it up?"

"I have no reason," she answered. "Perhaps I have a superstition. I only know that I do not want you to go upon that island."

His face changed. His manner was no longer artificial. He was suddenly very serious.

"I do not think that I have refused you many things, Pauline," he said, "but this is not a matter of choice with me at all. I cannot hope to make you understand quite how I feel about it, but I am forced to go. I must go. I should not care to make that confession to anyone else in the world, but you have it."

"Nothing could keep you way, then—nothing?" she whispered in his ear.

"Nothing upon the earth, or under the earth," he answered gravely. "If you really wish to do me a kindness, you will go to the others, and try and get them below early. The sooner I can leave, the quicker I shall be back again. I should like to be here to breakfast with you."

They were behind one of the boats, and she lifted her face to his.

"Kiss me, Hildyard."

He bent down and obeyed her, stretching out his arm to draw her closer to him. But she was gone. In the distance he heard her slow, musical voice mingling with the others. Then all sound died gradually away. They had gone below.

CHAPTER III

The night passed. Through the glimmering air stole the wan, grey light of the coming day. Afar in the east the dun-coloured clouds grew gorgeous, stained with the splendour of the unrisen sun. On the horizon the glass-like water caught the earliest beams, and glistened and gleamed like a belt of silver. Now the light came travelling over the water, and a soft breeze stole rippling over its surface. The mists, which had been riding upon the ocean, faded away into thin air. A deep blue stole into the sky. The morning had come.

With the first breaking of the clouds Pauline had come on deck. She had heard the boat put away from the yacht's side soon after midnight, and ever since then she had sat in her cabin, waiting and listening. Hour by hour the long night had stolen away. The boat had not returned.

She had changed her evening gown for a plain serge suit, and bareheaded she stood out in the bows, watching. There was no longer any attempt at concealment as to their whereabouts. The engines had stopped, and they were riding at anchor. Barely a mile away, the little island, with its pine-topped hill, and cloud of seagulls, rose out of the blue sea. She leaned over the rail heedless of the wind which swept through her glorious hair, or of the curious but covert glances of the seamen as they passed to and fro. She was waiting for the return of the yacht's boat with an admixture of sensations which would have defied any attempt at analysis.

At last it came, a mere speck upon the waters, gradually taking to itself shape as the long regular strokes of the rowers brought it nearer and nearer. There was a glass in her hand. Three times she raised it, three times she laid it down again. Soon the time for its use had gone by. She could see distinctly without it. The cushioned seat was vacant.

She half closed her eyes, and for a moment she felt faint. A curious premonition had suggested this thing to her from the first. Yet, now that it had happened, it was none the less a shock. She had the reputation of being a woman without heart. For the first time she doubted it. She had doubted it since last night.

She was an actress, and her art came to her aid. She received the note the first mate brought her, with just the proper amount of surprise. He held one in his hand for each of the other guests, and one for the captain.

She stood apart behind a boat, and tore open the envelope. It was written on heavy cream note paper without crest or monogram, and apparently with a quill pen:—

"PAULINE,—I am not going to inflict upon you all the conventional lies which I am compelled to invent for Lady Bergamot and Pearmain. The bald fact is that I am going to stay here for a little while, and you must go. I was right after all! I have found another phase of life here, and it interests me.

"This world is a very odd place, Pauline, for those who look upon it as you and I do. Since last night I have undergone a metamorphosis. In a sense I am a changed man. I am possessed of a new range of sensations, a new field of ideas, a new personality. I have gained a new experience! You will think that I am mad. I am sure of it! Farewell!

"If I should miss the first night of the new play—success. Adieu. We shall meet again in London. There is no fear of my turning anchorite. My madness is only of the midsummer order. London is like a great magnet to its parasites and wanderers. It will draw me back again. But for a while, adieu.

"HILDYARD.

"I have written to Ayres. He will attend to any business matters for you during my absence. Henderson will land you wherever you like. Afterwards he will return for me. I do not expect to be here longer than a week."

She crushed the letter up in her hand, and turned her sightless eyes to the little island. She stood there without movement—almost without realization. Her sensations were numbed. The throb of the engines recommencing their deep steady action, the hurtling of the waters rushing away from the bows, and the clanking of ropes and staples, filled the quiet morning air. The spray leaped up into her face. The outline of the island grew fainter and fainter. Soon it was only a dim blue haze.

A murmur of voices brought her to herself. She set her teeth together. The rustle of skirts and the faint odour of violet powder were in the air.

"My dear Pauline, whatever do you think of this?" cried Lady Bergamot, waving her letter in her hand. "Most outrageous, I call it. The man must be altogether out of his senses."

Pauline shrugged her shoulders, and laughed lightly.

"Hildyard was always peculiar," she answered. "I suppose he has discovered a colony of Communists, or smugglers, or something, and is going to join them. For a man who professes to be so weary of life, he always struck me as being remarkably anxious to try it all round!"

"But to leave us without a word, without any more explanation than this!" exclaimed Lady Bergamot, gazing at her brief note. "I never heard of such conduct. It is outrageous!"

"At any rate, we have the yacht," remarked Pauline. "We ought to be grateful that he did not insist on our staying there with him. Let us talk it over at breakfast."

They crossed the deck—Pauline, graceful, self-possessed, and smiling.

Lady Bergamot, who was disappointed, touched Morton Pearmain on the arm.

"How well she bears it," she whispered.

"She is an actress," he remarked drily.

CHAPTER IV

Soon after midnight, the heavy banks of clouds which had darkened the sky, rolled slowly away. The air became clear, and the moonlight lay upon the earth like a cloth of gold. Hildyard, standing upon the summit of the pine-topped hill in the centre of the little island, could see every stone that lay upon it.

He paused to take breath, for he had found no footpath, and the way had been a difficult and a rough one. Far below him, shapely, like a beautiful, living creature upon the moonlit sea, rode his yacht, tugging gently at her anchor. Nearer in, the men who had brought him here were sitting on the side of the boat, which they had dragged into a sheltered little cove, smoking and talking softly to themselves. Between him and them was a patch of open country, a mass of thick undergrowth, and a steep rugged pile of rocks, up which he had clambered. He looked at all these things lingeringly. As yet he had not even glanced downwards to see what lay upon the other side of the island. He was even conscious of a certain reluctance to do so. But, by-and-by, when he had regained his breath, he moved slowly away from the tree against which he had been leaning, and turning round, walked a few steps forward.

His heart gave a quick, unaccustomed beat, and he set his teeth close together. He had quite made up his mind that the island was inhabited. He told himself he had known it from the very first. Yet, now that the proof was here, it came almost as a shock, for there was no longer any doubt abut it. The sloping land before him was cultivated, and cattle were browsing in a meadow to his left. A little distance down there was a long building covered with some sort of creeping shrubs. In an inlet of the sea were anchored several boats and a small sailing yacht.

Steadily he made his way downwards. In a few minutes he found himself before a wicket gate. It opened at his touch, and he found himself in a trimly kept garden.

The house was now directly in front of him. It was only one story high, and so embosomed with flowing shrubs, that it was impossible to tell whether it was of wood or stone. He kept steadily on. Another gate by the side of the house opened at his touch, and he found himself in front of the place.

Here, for the first time, he paused. Before him was a smooth lawn starred with clumps of creamy-hued rhododendrons, and beds of blossoming flowers. About twenty yards ahead a plantation of pine trees ran down sheer to the water's edge. Through the red trunks he could catch glimpses of the gleaming moonlit sea. By his side was the house with windows opening on to the lawn from every room.

A curious instinct of drowsiness stole into his senses. The perfume of many sweet flowers hung heavily upon the bosom of the pine-scented night wind. He walked quietly along by the side of the yew hedge, and after a moment's hesitation flung himself down upon the short turf in the shadow of the plantation. Then he laughed softly, and brought out his cigarette case.

"I think that I must be a little mad," he said, carefully extinguishing the match with his heel. "I feel as though I am on the eve of an adventure—a real adventure—something psychological and supernatural. I remember I felt like it once before—when Pauline—Bah!"

He broke off abruptly. He looked away from the house, along the path by which he had come, to the top of the hill and beyond. His face darkened. A flood of half-formed thoughts rushed into his brain. He swept them away. They belonged to what had gone before. To-night was to make history for him. The past was inevitable, the future was his own. The present was sufficiently absorbing. If indeed there were in store for him anything akin to a new sensation, he would enter upon it untrammelled by any sense of obligation to what lay behind. The moral status of the man, naturally robust, had become enervated and vitiated by the hot-house culture of his environment. He recognized only the paramount necessity for novelty and experience.

Presently he took up the thread of his musings again.

"After all, I am a fool," he murmured. "Probably a dog will bark soon, or someone will see me from the windows—it is quite light enough, and I shall get kicked out, which, by the bye, is exactly what I deserve. It is an odd place, though. I should rather like to know who lives here."

Raising himself upon his elbow, he gazed at the long, low outline of the house now directly in front of him. All the windows save one were dark. From that one came a faint gleam of light as though a heavily shaded lamp were burning in the room. He watched it steadily and yet, strange to say, with very little actual curiosity. A sense of dreamy yet pleasurable anticipation had crept over him, associated somehow with the delicate colouring of his surroundings, and the aromatic perfume of the still night air. He was so far an epicurean that danger of all sort seemed lessened to him, almost annihilated by an environment so exquisite. In such a mood as this he was content to die—at any rate, he did not fear death. The superstitious awe of that gloomy cross, and its possible message to him, which had penetrated for the moment the armour of his habitual nonchalance, had passed away.

He lay there steeped in a sort of *nirvana* of sensuous repose. From far below came the murmuring of the softly breaking waves upon the shore. Now and then, a breath of the night wind rustled amongst the pines above him. From the house there came no sound.

Suddenly his lethargy passed away. Bewildered, yet delighted, he rose to his feet, and gazed around him astonished. The very air seemed quivering and throbbing with strains of the most entrancing music—music that thrilled every sense of the man, and found its way into his heart. He held his breath and listened, drawing himself back amongst the shadows. It was coming towards him, nearer, and nearer, and nearer. Ah! it was no spirit after all, then.

A girl tall and slim, and with a stream of black hair floating over her shoulders, stood for a moment on the threshold of the lamplit room, and then came slowly toward him. She was playing the violin as she walked, bending over it so that he could scarcely see her face, and playing as he had never heard it played before. A loose white robe hung from her shoulders and trailed behind her on the grass, and her footsteps were so light and so exquisitely graceful, that she seemed to be gliding over the lawn into his arms. But before she reached him she stopped.

Her music came to an end with a weird little burst of melody—like the end of an elfin chorus. She raised her head, and glanced cautiously towards the house. There was no movement nor any sign of life. Reassured, she stooped and gathered up her skirts in the hand which held the violin. Bending down, she drew her bow across it again. The note of the music was changed. It was a dance she was playing, weird and quaint, sometimes plaintive, sometimes gay. After the first few bars she leaned back, and her body commenced to sway to and fro. With a deliciously graceful undulation, she stooped forward and glided away. Round and round amongst the trees she went, playing all the time and moving as she played, sometimes with the dainty Watteau-like grace of an old minuet, sometimes with all the abandon of a nautch girl dancing to the minor key of a copper instrument. And all the time her movements matched the music. She held herself one moment with all the stateliness of a duchess, at another with the bold, almost lecherous, seductiveness of a Turkish dancing girl. As he followed her, he felt his breath grow thick, and his heart beat in quick, fast throbs. He could scarcely persuade himself that she was human. She was more like one of the syrens of mythology.

With a little crash of strange minor chords, the dance and the music came suddenly to an end. After all, her wild, wanton movements seemed to have had some definite destination. She was standing in a little clear space enclosed by thickly growing pine trees except on the seaward side. The green turf was covered with a thin layer of pine needles. A rough garden seat faced the opening which seemed to look sheer down upon the sea. She shook her skirts for a moment vigorously and then sat down.

For the first time, Hildyard, who stood back a few yards amongst the shadows, saw her face clearly. She was bending forward looking down at the sea, and her features were sharply outlined against the background of moonlit space. He stood and watched her like a man turned to stone.

There was a picture by a famous French artist in a certain Bond Street gallery, which he had visited again and again with a curious persistency. The same nameless fascination which had led him to that picture some time after time, was upon him now. "A daughter of the Pharaohs!" it was called, a glorious type of dusky and regal Egyptian beauty. This girl might have been the study for it. Her clear, olive face with the mobile mouth and the dark, dreamy eyes, half closed now as though in meditation; the thick, soft coils of black hair floating loosely over her shoulders; the limbs, as lissome and shapely as the limbs of a goddess, and asserting themselves at every curve and angle of her body; the matchless grace which made repose as beautiful as movement,—they were all typified in this girl who sat gazing out upon the sea. As though to complete the picture, she twined her white hands behind her head, and leaned back, with a faint, slow smile at the corners of her lips.

The man who was watching her, after a desperate and futile attempt to persuade himself that he was dreaming, or that he had become the victim of some new hypnotic trance, abandoned all attempt to govern his sensations or to behave in any way like a rational human being. All his days he had affected cynicism and despised romance. To-night the little tenets of his life seemed all upside down. His sense of the ludicrous unreality, the impossibility of the situation, was completely overborne by the fascination which had thrilled through his nerves and pulses from the moment she had issued from her room to the accompaniment of that strange music. It was ridiculous, but it was a fact. His eyes were unnaturally bright, and his heart was beating with quick, sharp throbs. He was full of a burning desire to rush out of his ambush, to fall at her feet, to take her hands, to persuade himself by means of her living touch and the caress of her white fingers, that she was a creature of flesh and blood, a denizen of the same world as his, a woman to be loved and won. He would have gone to her without a second's hesitation, but he could not. There were weights upon his feet. His limbs were chained as though by a nightmare. He was tormented by sudden icy fear—a fear lest at his touch, at the sound of his voice, she should mock him and catch up her skirts, and float away into thin air to the sound of elfin music. So he lingered, and while he stood there came a footstep on his right. Someone was coming! She, too, heard, and turned slightly round with a smile of welcome. His heart grew thick with rage. She was waiting for someone. It might be a lover!

The footsteps passed him close at hand; footsteps as light as a woman's and yet with a sort of childish, at any rate unfeminine shuffle. A shape stepped out into the moonlight. His brain reeled; he nearly cried out. At first it seemed something altogether inhuman. He had found his way into a world of ghouls and ghosts, where the souls of men and women took strange shapes of beauty and horrible ugliness. No! he was awake! He was alive! The thing was human. The face was the face of a man, but the body—Oh God! Now he could see it plainly. He drew a little breath of relief which hissed through his teeth, and died away. The shape was human. It was horrible, but it was human!

CHAPTER V

With an unconsciousness which was in itself a fine element in the dramatic completeness of the little scene, the figures of the two, the woman and the creature, stood out clearly and sharply outlined in the still, moonlit air. He was a humpback. Underneath the little cloak he wore, the unnatural protuberance which was the stamp of his deformity showed itself plainly, defying all and any attempt at concealment. He had taken a corner seat on the rude wooden bench, and he turned a delicate, oval face towards her. She was standing a few feet away from him, humming softly to herself and looking across the sea. The man, who remained like an image behind the rhododendron shrub, held his breath. One of them would speak soon—if, indeed, it were not all a dream—if they were, as they scarcely seemed, human flesh and blood. So he held his breath and listened.

It was the creature who spoke first. The sound of so beautiful and flute-like a voice coming from him amazed the man who listened. It was scarcely raised above a whisper, and yet every syllable was clear and distinct.

"Mia Cara, your audience is ready. The curtain has rung up. What is it to be tonight?"

She looked away from the sea and laughed. It was the laugh of a woman of some southern race. Her voice, too, had a peculiar intonation in it.

"To-night I am like a wild woman!" she cried softly. "I am like the tree-tops in a storm. I am bent and tossed and restless. To-night I will be Carmen!"

She plucked a great scarlet blossom from a tree close at hand, and thrust it into her hair. The low, minor chorus of the last act floated from her lips. She caught up her skirts, and threw herself back in an attitude of complete, voluptuous abandonment.

"Play, Andrew, play!" she cried. "I am going to dance and sing. I am a gipsy, the Queen of the Gipsies! Ah!"

He snatched up the violin, and drew his bow across it fiercely. A flood of strange weird discords leaped out into the air. She dropped her skirts and covered her ears wither her hands.

"You know that I loathe Carmen," he muttered, looking at her with his coal-black eyes afire, and his thin lips quivering.

She escaped back into her former strange personality as if by magic. She shrugged her shoulders, and taking the flowers from her hair, commenced to pluck them in pieces, throwing the petals at him one by one.

"Very well! Very well! I will be anything else, any one else. Will you be

Faust to my Marguerite? or shall I be Cleopatra and cry to the sea to bring my Antony? Say Cleopatra, Andrew, if you love me. The wit and dalliance of Egypt, are in my blood to-night. I feel them bubbling up. Music, Andrew, music!

"'Give me some music, moody food of us that trade in love.'"

She was almost opposite the man who formed the little audience in this mock drama. Her face was turned towards the sea. Her arms were out-stretched, and the broad, loose sleeves of her gown falling back left them bare. The moonlight flashed upon a dull gold band upon her wrist.

"'Give me to drink mandatory,

That I might sleep out this great gap of time,

My Anthony is away!'"

He laid down the violin. His face was dark and sullen. She continued,—

"'Antony! Antony! lord of lords!

Oh, infinite virtue! comest thou smiling from

The great world's snare, uncaught?'"

She dropped her arms, and looked round at the creature. His dejection was written out in his frowning brows and moody, downcast face. She shrugged her shoulders with a gesture which was almost pettish.

"Andrew, you are very hard to please," she declared slowly. "Carmen annoys you—I may not be Cleopatra. What would you have? Shall I dance to you—sing, play, weep? I must do something. The blood in my veins is like quicksilver. It will not let me be quiet! Sometimes I think that it is only by night that I live. The daylight oppresses me. I am not gay then. I am one of Cynthia's children. I am a daughter of the night."

"You are a daughter of—Satan!"

She made him a sweeping courtesy.

"I am gratified," she said, with a mocking smile. "I did not know that I was of royal descent. I only suspected it. I am going now. You do not amuse me. Besides, you are rude."

He caught at a portion of her skirt as it floated past him, and held it in his hand. The anger was gone from his pale, dark face. His tone was full of supplication. She listened.

"Bertha, you will not go! Stay, and you shall be whom you like, what you like! Only have a little mercy on me. Remember—remember—"

She swept round upon him. His eyes drooped, and his face flushed painfully. The man who was watching stirred a little from his cramped position, and a dry twig snapped under his feet. They both heard it, and started round. They looked at one another in terror.

"He has followed us," she whispered. "He must be in the shrubs, listen-ing. Hurry away, Andrew! He is in one of his moods to-day, and he may be rough with you. Leave me to face him. I can humour him. Quick!"

Hildyard heard all. The time for concealment was over. He stepped out from his hiding-place, and stood, bareheaded, upon the edge of the little green plot. In the moonlight, with his tall shapely figure outlined against the empty air, he was very comely. From the moment of his discovery his usual *savoir faire* returned. He was quite at his ease.

"I am the guilty trespasser!" he said, bowing low. "I scarcely dare to offer you my apologies. I came here a wanderer, and I remained—because I was powerless to go away."

She looked at him with a curious mixture of coquetry and fear. But the creature who was with her had no mixed feelings. He raised his puny arms above his head, and with a little hoarse cry he went shambling along the zig-zag path toward the house. She seemed at first half inclined to follow him. Curiosity struggled for a moment with her alarm. With her skirts gathered up in her hand ready to run, she paused and stole another glance over her shoulder at the intruder. He was very handsome, far more hand-some than any man she had ever seen, and perfectly respectful. She gave a little sigh, and—she remained.

"I do not understand where you come from," she exclaimed doubtfully. "How did you land here on the island, and why have you come?"

"I came in a yacht," he answered. "It is anchored on the other side of the island. As to why I came—well, I am afraid that I can scarcely answer that question myself. At first I think that it was curiosity—the place looked so picturesque from a distance, and I wanted to see if anyone lived here. I am inclined to think now that it may be—fate!"

Through the respectful constraint of his tone there flashed a sudden wildness. The dramatic strangeness of the scene upon which he had wandered, and the beauty of the girl who stood there gazing at him like a marvellous picture, with that background of glittering sea and framework of purple and cream-coloured rhododendrons, had thrilled his whole sensuous being. He began to wonder whether he were quite sane; to have doubts as to his actual and material existence. It was some exquisite yet diseased phase of living, some strange night-world into which sleep or illness had borne him. Yet the warm blood flowed in his veins, and his heart was beating with a quickened throb. A subtle glow of pleasure, a new delight in being, was upon him. If there were indeed the waters of Lethe, let him float down them. He was very well content.

"Fate!" she repeated, still holding her skirts in one hand, and with the other idly plucking to pieces a great mass of scarlet blossoms which drooped over her dark head. "That is what our guardian is always talking about. I do not understand you. What is fate, and what had it to do with bringing you here?"

He shook his head slowly.

"I cannot tell you!" he answered slowly. "Fate is the one thing in the world which—no one understands. We admit it, and we bow before it—but we do not understand it. Tell me, who are you, and where am I? What island is this? Who lives here?"

She moved her head slowly toward the house.

"He calls it the island of Maros. I do not think that you people who live out in the world have any name for it at all. It is so small, and this is the only house upon it."

"Who is he?"

"Our guardian."

"Our guardian!" he repeated. The information sounded to him a little vague.

She looked along the silent, moonlit path along which the creature had fled.

"His, and mine."

"And you have lived here for long?"

"Ever since I can remember anything at all. Ever since I was a very little girl. So long that every week has seemed a month, and every month a year. One gets very weary," she added with a sigh. "It is my guardian and Andrew, and Andrew and my guardian, every day. Andrew is good to me in his way, but he is savage and wayward sometimes. He is not an inspiring companion. Some day it will become unendurable, and then I shall run away."

"But your education. Have you never been away to school?" he asked.

"My guardian taught me everything."

"Even your music?"

"He and Andrew. Andrew plays wonderfully upon the violin."

"But don't you ever have visitors?" he asked. "Do you mean to say that you never leave the island at all?"

She shook her head. "Never. Do you know what a misanthrope is? Well, my guardian is a misanthrope, and they are not pleasant people to live with."

He left off questioning her. Every word she uttered only added to his bewilderment.

"Tell me your name?" she asked.

"Hildyard."

"Is that all?"

"It is what I should like you to call me," he answered.

She raised her dark, brilliant eyes, and looked at him frankly.

"Hildyard," she repeated, her soft speech giving a sort of caressing intonation to the name. "Yes, I like that. What are you going to do here, Hildyard? How long are you going to stay?"

"As long as I am allowed," he answered readily. "Until you bid me go."

"You had better not be rash," she said with soft playfulness. "You might find yourself a prisoner here. I might never tell you to go away."

"You are lonely?"

"I think that there is no one in the world so lonely as I am. Andrew is often savage and fretful. He has seen and he knows so much more than I—and yet—he will not often talk to me of the books we read—or of the world, the great outside world of men and women and art. It is not living, here. It is dreaming. I wonder is it very wrong for me to want to live?"

"And your guardian?"

"Sometimes he is kind," she answered. "Sometimes I am almost afraid of him. He has not always lived like this, but he will not let me question him. I think that he has had great troubles. So you will stay, really, if he will let you?"

"Yes, I shall stay," he answered dreamily. "When I came I felt that I was going to stay. I—"

"Listen!"

She was leaning forward with her hand upraised, and her dark eyes full of fear. She had turned suddenly pale.

"He is coming!" she whispered.

He turned round, following her rapt gaze. Only a few yards away from them a man was coming down the zig-zag path. There was no time for any speech between them. The new-comer was already by their side. He did not even glance at the girl; his eyes were fixed upon her companion. Hildyard took a step forward to meet him.

"I fear that I am a flagrant trespasser," he said, acutely conscious all the while of the incongruity of this or any such conventional form of speech with the nature of his surroundings. "The island attracted me, and I landed without knowing that it was inhabited. I have already had the misfortune to alarm your ward. I am really very sorry."

The man who stood before him bowed slightly. His features were almost invisible beneath his broad-brimmed felt hat.

"You had always the reputation of doing odd things, Hildyard," he remarked drily. "I see that you still live up to it. I watched your yacht for an hour this afternoon, but I scarcely anticipated the pleasure of a visit from you. You do not appear to recognize me."

He removed his hat as he spoke, and stood bareheaded in the moonlight, a faint smile hovering round the corners of his lips. Hildyard took a quick step backwards, and a little cry escaped him. He no longer doubted but that he had stepped out of his life into a little enchanted world. He was face to face with the impossible!

CHAPTER VI

They stood for a minute motionless on the little plot of turf, clear and distinct figures in the moonlit air. The wan pallor of the new-comer's face, intensified in that white clear light, was almost corpse-like. His speech was human and natural enough.

"You are surprised to see me, of course," he said, quietly. "Quite a dramatic meeting, is it not? Come, won't you shake hands?"

Hildyard drew a deep breath, and held out his hand. He was already beginning to feel annoyed at this sudden desertion of his self-possession. The man's face had changed; it was wasted and worn almost to a shadow, but it was certainly the face of a living man. Hildyard recovered himself rapidly.

"Owston! by all that is amazing!" he exclaimed. "I thought that you were in South America, naturalizing. Ringwood said that he had heard that you were there, and I saw it in the paper only a few weeks ago. This is most extraordinary!"

The new-comer shrugged his shoulders.

"So far as the newspapers and the few hundreds of people we call the 'world' are concerned, I am in South America," he answered, grimly. "As a matter of fact, I am, as you see, here. But what brought you into this quarter of the globe?"

"Merely a desire to escape a little way out of the beaten track. I was just cruising about. I landed out of mere curiosity. My God!"

The interjection leaped from him with the sudden crispness of a pistol shot. A horrible idea—an idea filled with madness—came flashing into his brain. It was as though the little strip of soft, green turf had yawned at his feet, and disclosed a horrible precipice. Scarcely a mile of sea separated his yacht and his guests from this man. Supposing they were to miss him, were to follow him here! It was quite possible. He was a brave man, but an icy fear was at his heart. And all the while those cold, grey eyes were watching him mercilessly, as though striving to read his thoughts.

"Your nerves are not quite what they were when you kept wicket for the Varsity, Hildyard," he remarked quietly.

Hildyard shrugged his shoulders. After all, he could return by daylight or soon after. The burden rolled away. But it had been a shock.

"Our modern life scarcely admits the necessity of nerves," he answered. "The wonder to me is that we preserve any at all!"

"It is a truth which almost reconciles me to my isolation," Owston answered. "You are the first figure linked with my past whom chance has brought here. Can you give me a day or two? I can put you up after a fashion, and there is some good duck-shooting on the other side of the island."

Hildyard hesitated. Unconsciously he glanced to the place where the girl had been standing. It was empty. She had glided noiselessly away, but at that moment there floated out from somewhere amongst the shrubs a low, passionate strain of music. He listened for a moment, and the die was cast. Here was such a chance of escaping from himself and his environment for awhile as might never present itself again. Already the weariness of life seemed to have passed away. It was folly to hesitate.

"Willingly, if you are sure that you would like to have me," he answered. "I have some guests on my yacht, but I am very weary of them—as weary as I daresay they are of me. Let me write some notes and send them away."

"As you like. Come and see the home I have made for myself."

He turned, and Hildyard followed him along the zig-zag path, through the pine grove, and across the lawn to the front of the long, low dwelling-house. The front door stood open. Inside was a square hall hung with prints and curios very much after the fashion of an old English house. Owston turned the handle of the door on the left-hand side, and ushered in his guest.

He turned up the lamp, and Hildyard looked around him with curiosity. On three sides of the room there were books from the floor to the ceiling. On the fourth, high French windows opened out on the lawn. The ceiling was low, and the pine rafters had been left uncovered. A table in the centre of the room was covered with papers and volumes. The suggestions of the place were distinctly scholarly.

"This is my library," Owston said. "It is here that I am living, or attempting to live, my second life. Every one of those bookcases I made myself. I cut down the trees and sawed the planks, and fitted them together. It is the same with everything in the house, and indeed with the house itself. I have tried civilization, and it did not agree with me. I am endeavouring now to return to the primitive state of man."

"But you had some help, of course?" Hildyard interposed.

"Some manual help from my own servants. Butlin and his wife—you would remember Butlin—live in the house. Then there are three men, one to manage my little boat and the fishing, and two for the land and garden. They live down on the beach on the other side of the island. You will find paper and envelopes upon that table. Write your notes."

Hildyard sat down and wrote. His curiosity as to his surroundings had been short lived. It had passed away like a flash before the crisis with which he was standing face to face. The growth and evolution of his sensations during the last half an hour comprised a notable epoch in his life. Conscious of only one strong, vehement desire, he wrote his notes swiftly and without hesitation. By his side like a shadow stood Owston, with a curious smile upon his calm face.

Hildyard stood up, holding the sealed letters in his hand.

"I will take them down to the boat myself," he said. "I know the way. It is just on the other side of the hill."

"We will go together," Owston answered. "I shall not sleep again. We shall see the sun rise as we come back. It is one of the charms of untrammelled life that the clock has no meaning for us. Often we sleep by day and walk and work and dine by moonlight. You were surprised, perhaps, to meet my ward wandering about at long past midnight. It is nothing. The night loses its significance here. We have no restrictions. There is no need of any. Come."

They left the house together. As they passed the window from which the girl had issued a glad strain of triumphant music came dancing out through the shuttered blinds. Hildyard felt that those notes were for him, but he only set his teeth hard. A fear more terrible than the fear of death was upon him.

In single file they left the garden and climbed the hill. From its summit they could see the yacht riding at anchor, and through the twilight they could hear the voices of the sailors as they clambered about the rocks.

Hildyard paused. He spoke with precision, almost with indifference. Yet there was a good deal at stake.

"If you do not care about having your whereabouts known, you had better not come down to the boat," he suggested. "One or two of the men are Devon men, and Jones is there—the fellow from Cowes who took us for that cruise many years ago. He is my first mate now. Even if the others did not, he would probably recognize you, and sailors are great hands at gossip."

Owston nodded. "I will wait for you here," he said. "Do not hurry."

He leaned against the trunk of a pine tree, and Hildyard hastened down the steep slope. As soon as he was alone, Owston took a small folding telescope from his pocket, and looked through it long and steadily at the graceful yacht, which was gently rising and falling on the bosom of the incoming tide. No one was moving on board her. It was scarcely possible to distinguish more than her shape. The deep, shadowy twilight of the hour before dawn lay like a curtain upon land and sea. The moon's full light had gone. In the east there was a lightening of the clouds, and a faint grey shade stealing into the horizon, but as yet it travelled slowly. Owston shut up his glass with a little snap, and leaning once more against the tree, set his face seaward with a faint introspective smile upon his lips.

"Scarcely twenty minutes' swim," he said to himself, measuring the distance between the shore and the yacht with his eyes. "Perhaps half an hour with the tide coming in. Imagine me, wet and dripping, suddenly presenting myself on board, finding my way down into her cabin, and standing over her while she slept, waiting till her eyes should open and fall upon me. She would sit up; I know exactly how she would sit up, and then the terror would flash into her face, and she would cower down. And I—I—what should I do? Gods knows! Strangle her, most likely! What a situation for the modern drama! A trifle too realistic, perhaps, but thrilling—distinctly thrilling. I wonder how long my young friend is going to be?"

He lit a cigarette, and yawned several times. Soon Hildyard came back. The dawn was brightening the sky as he clambered up the hill.

"Well, is it done?" Owston inquired.

"It is done," Hildyard answered. "I am on your hands for a week. I hope you haven't begun to repent."

Owston smiled absently. He was taking a last glance at the *Sea King.*

"No, I have not repented," he said. "I am not likely to. By the by, your men are coming back with some of your things, I suppose?" he added, as they began to descend the hill.

Hildyard shook his head.

"No. I have relied altogether upon your hospitality," he answered. "I did think of it, but I was afraid that if the boat had to return some of my guests might insist upon gratifying their curiosity by coming with it, and I take it that you did not want any more trespassers upon your seclusion. I have sent word to the captain to run them straight back into the port we had arranged to land at, and then return for me. It will take them about a week."

"I am afraid that I am breaking up a pleasant party," Owston remarked, calmly.

Hildyard shrugged his shoulders. "They will enjoy it better without me," he remarked. "I have a bad habit of being easily bored, and showing it. I am like that famous Roman emperor we used to read about together. I am pining for a new experience."

"There is nothing new upon this island, or in my life here," Owston said. "I do not believe that there is anything new upon the world. If there is, civilization has made us too effete to discover it."

"I agree with you," Hildyard said. "Civilization has emasculated us. We are a nerveless race."

"You will not find anything new here," Owston repeated. "My life is simply a study in negations. I am at war with the complex. That is the text of my solitude. You will find nothing new here, but you will miss many of the things which make our modern life a species of slavery. I have no excitements, but, on the other hand, I have not enervating reactions. I am the slave of no one, not even time. I make my own days and my own nights. Worry and turmoil and emotion pass me by. As to art, I do not need it; I am face to face with nature."

"And this life contents you?" Hildyard said.

"I did not say so," Owston answered, sternly. "See how quickly the sun is breaking through the clouds."

They turned their faces eastward. The first dim shaft of morning sunlight fell upon the stone cross below, flashing along its sea-stained arms with soft brilliancy. Hildyard laid his hand upon his companion's arm, and pointed downward.

"Is that nature's work?" he asked.

"So far as I know," Owston answered. "Men's hands could scarcely have fashioned it. It was there when I came. It has all the appearance of having been there for a thousand years."

Hildyard was silent. He looked away, and they moved on. Soon his companion's clear voice sounded again in his ears.

"I am going to ask you a question, Hildyard."

"Ask me as many as you will."

"Well, I am curious to know why you have accepted my invitation. Why did you accept it without a moment's hesitation? I am a man in the eyes of your world, I suppose, dishonoured. I do not think that we ever passed beyond the ordinary terms of our relative positions into anything like intimacy. What you have heard of me since we parted can scarcely have seemed creditable to you. Therefore I am curious! If we had met in London, I should have expected to have been ignored. Yet chance brings us together here, and on my first word of invitation you desert your friends, abandon your yachting cruise, and are content to spend a lonely week upon a small island with a rabid misanthrope. You do it without hesitation, as though it were the most natural thing in the world. Is it compassion? If not, what is it?"

Hildyard glanced across the sea. The small rowing-boat was approaching the yacht's side now. For the first time he realized how completely he was cut off from the world.

"No, it is not compassion," he answered. "I am not good-natured enough for that. To be frank, it was more the offspring of a diseased craving for novelty. You offer me an asylum from my friends, of whom I am a little weary; you offer me a blank page of life under new conditions. If you lived in the London of to-day, where life is fashioned out of worn-out types and men die more of *ennui* than of heart disease, you would understand my prompt acceptance. I can assure you that I never hesitated."

They were descending the hill now by the same path which Hildyard had followed alone only a few hours ago. Freed from the sudden burden of intolerable anxiety which had sat heavily upon his shoulders for awhile, the fascination of that strange little scene in the moonlit garden reasserted itself. He seemed to hear again the low, thrilling music, to see the wonderful light of her dark eyes gleaming from her olive face, to hear the rustle of her gown as she floated through space with the matchless, effortless grace which had seemed so wonderful to him. As they drew nearer to the garden he looked eagerly forward. She was there, in a plain cream-coloured gown, moving across the lawn to meet them, with both hands full of the yellow and purple blossoms she had been plucking. Owston watched him keenly.

"Do you admire my ward?" he asked.

"Admire her! She is wonderful!" Hildyard answered. "She is a new type. I never saw anything like it, even in the streets of Cairo."

"You seem to have divined her nationality," Owston remarked. "Her father was a French officer, but her mother, who came from Cyprus, was a pure Egyptian of ancient family, descended in a direct line, poor Mallalieu used to tell me, from the Pharaohs. Mallalieu was her father, and, at one time, my friend."

Hildyard glanced toward the house.

"And—and the boy?" he asked.

"He is not a boy; he is a man," Owston answered. "He is my cousin, and almost my only relative. I will tell you more about both of them later on. See, Bertha is waving to us."

"Look!" she cried, waving her hand full of drooping yellow blossoms. "The smoke! The smoke!"

They followed her gesture. A thick line of smoke lay across the sky.

"It is the yacht," she cried. "You have sent her away, then. She has taken up her anchor. She is off."

Hildyard shaded his eyes and looked. She had swung round, and was standing out to sea. Through the deep morning stillness they could even hear the thud of her engines.

"Yes, she is off right enough," Hildyard remarked, with a little sigh of relief. "I'm on your hands for a week. By the by, Owston, if you are introducing me to your ward, call me Mr. Hildyard. I want the change to be complete. I am weary of being a lord."

The girl had joined them now. In the sunlight her strange Oriental beauty was as potent, though less fantastic, than it had seemed to him a few hours ago. Owston spoke a few words of introduction; then he left them for a moment and entered the house.

She raised her dark eyes to him. There was a gleam of trouble in them.

"So you are going to stay," she said, softly.

"Yes, I am going to stay," he answered. "You do not look glad. I hope that you do not mind having me?"

She glanced toward the window through which Owston had vanished, and back again into his face.

"For myself," she said, slowly, "it is a happiness—it will be a great happiness. Need I tell you that? For you—I do not know. I wonder! You are the first stranger who has set foot upon this island within my recollection. I do not understand it. Why did he ask you?"

"We knew one another years ago," he answered. "We have had many friends in common. There is a past in which we are both interested."

"You knew one another years ago," she repeated. "Tell me, were you great friends? He must have been much older than you."

He hesitated. There was no harm in telling her the bare facts, at any rate.

"We were at college together," he told her. "Afterwards he was my tutor. We travelled and lived together for several years."

"You parted—friends?"

"Yes."

She took one of the blossoms from her hands and thrust it into his button-hole.

"I am fanciful, perhaps," she said. "I thought that he looked at you once as he might have looked at a man whom he hated. It must have been a fancy."

"I am sure it was," he told her.

"I am too happy to have forebodings," she murmured, looking up at him with a brilliant smile. "Come, and I will show you our flower garden."

CHAPTER VII

On the summit of the southern slope which ran down to the sea skilful hands had planned and fashioned a wonderful flower garden. As Hildyard followed his guide through the iron gate, a little cry of surprise escaped him. It was so different from what he had expected.

The text of the gardener had been colour—colour, brilliant and universal. Great beds of crimson and yellow carnations filled the air with their sweet fragrance. A hedge of roses bordered the little enclosure on either side. Below, it was open to the sea; above, a great bank of flowering rhododendrons rose sheer over the hill side. There were no box-lined walks or artificial beds, nor apparently any method whatever in the reckless and luxurious distribution of the blossoming plants. Flowers had been planted apparently with the sole intent of forming one huge wave of colour. Gold-dusted snapdragon and tall hollyhocks grew up out of the beds of many-hued stocks. A sea of azure blue-bells waved their drooping heads in the morning breeze. In the far corner was a row of pink and white blossoming chestnut trees. The whole air was faint with perfume.

The last few hours had witnessed a curious evolution in Hildyard's whole sensuous nature. He gazed across the sea of colour to where the thin, black line of his yacht's smoke touched the skies. To him, her departure was typical of many things, besides being in itself an inexplicable relief. There were bonds there which he had broken—perhaps for ever. Even then he was content.

"It is a little corner of Paradise!" he declared, dreamily. "Tell me, are there lotus flowers in your garden?"

She shook her head. She was gazing seawards with her hand shading her eyes. The yacht now was no more than a speck upon the horizon.

"I wonder—will you ever regret that?" she said, with her eyes fixed upon the smoke.

"Never!" he answered.

"You would rather be here?"

"Ten thousand times! Let me sit down!"

There was a shelving bank of green turf close at hand. She moved towards it, and he threw himself on the grass by her feet, clasping his hands behind his head. She looked back towards the house, and dropped her voice.

"I wish I knew exactly why he asked you to stay here. You are quite sure that you never had any quarrel with him?"

"Absolutely! I do not see anything to wonder at in his asking me. Considering that I was here, it would have been rather inhospitable if he had not!"

Her dark eyes were troubled; there was a nameless fear in her face.

"I do not understand!" she said, slowly. "He shuts himself up, and is nervous and angry if a boat does but approach the island. Yet you come and you stay. It is by accident you come—at least, you say so, and it seems so. Yet for days he has watched from the hill yonder with his face toward the sea. Was it for you?"

He shook his head. "He could not have known that I was coming!" he answered her. "I did not know myself. It was by the merest chance that we came in sight of the island at all!"

"He knows many things!" she answered, slowly. "He knows many strange things. Yet you are here, and I am very glad. Only—"

Again she looked along the path towards the house. There was no one in sight. She listened. There was no sound save the far-off falling of the rippling waves upon the beach.

"Only be very careful!" she added, looking up at him wistfully. "You and he are as unlike as that sea as it is now and when the north winds blow and the great clouds fly across the sky. Strange things there have been in his life—strange things and sad. He does not forget them! He never will forget them. He lives here alone, and he broods upon them. Some day those who have wronged him will reap a bitter harvest. Hush, do not speak! Be careful! The flowers are of many years' growth. We have added to them year by year as we have been able. The carnations which you admire so much—"

"Bertha!"

At once he understood the sudden change in her expression and tone. He knew, too, that her sudden languor was assumed with all the graceful facility of a woman of fashion, and he was moved to wonder. Where had she learned it? A deep, quiet voice came from behind them.

"Bertha!"

This time she turned round, barely repressing a little shiver as she did. The man who saw it was perplexed. The voice was quiet and gentle, yet she certainly shivered.

The new-comer said something to her—only a word or two, but in a language altogether strange to Hildyard. She made no answer, but she rose slowly to her feet, and he heard the rustle of her gown as she disappeared. He muttered a little word between his teeth. So there was to be espionage. Then he too rose up and joined his host.

"So you have found your way, or rather my ward has shown you our little paradise!" he remarked, quietly. "This is where I sometimes find even the summer days too short!"

"I can well believe it!" Hildyard answered, absently. But he was not thinking of the garden.

"It is here that I come when I want to be perfectly sure that I do not regret Pall Mall and Piccadilly!" Owston continued. "This is the only place in the world where I have been able to read Horace and Keats with perfect satisfaction!"

"It is a poet's dreaming place!" Hildyard murmured. "I think there must be a spice of magic in the air. The languor of the lotus-eater is in my veins!"

Owston turned, and swung open again the little gate.

"Come," he said. "The odour of flowers is sweet, but it is not satisfying. There is some breakfast waiting for us. Come and see whether our Arcadian fare will tempt your appetite."

They strolled back to the house. On the lawn just outside the open window a small round table was spread in a tempting fashion. A silver coffee urn and a great jug of claret flashing purple in the sunlight stood side by side on a cloth of dazzling whiteness. There was an omelette, a dish of boiled eggs, brown bread, pats of deep yellow butter, and a glass bowl of honey. A vase of lilac, and a glass bowl of hothouse fruit upon which the bloom still lingered, gave almost an epicurean tone to the little repast; the eyes and the palate were alike to be ministered to. But Hildyard's first impulse was one of disappointment. The table was laid for two only. There was no sign of Bertha. It was evident that she was not to be present.

Nevertheless he breakfasted, and breakfasted well. With the satisfying too of so purely a physical desire as hunger, something of the glamour of his surroundings commenced to pass away. It was no enchanted island which boasted an excellent cook, an attentive though elderly man-servant, and a small dairy farm. The memory of that moonlit scene upon the lawn amongst the flowering rhododendron shrubs would always be touched by a little halo of romance, but the curious sense of unreality about it was passing away. That strange revival of an old superstition which had been kindled in him, of all men, by the sight of that lone cross with its flaming arms set against the dark background of sea-stained rocks, was already growing faint. After all, it was only a mass of twisted stone; its symbolism was an accident. It could have no meaning for him. The fact that it was indirectly responsible for his visit was already half forgotten. It was not the first time by many that he and his host had breakfasted together. So long as he could keep his thoughts from straying into one particular channel, there seemed to be nothing at all unnatural in this return to their old companionship. The bar which had come between them he had steadily ignored. There was a sort of dramatic piquancy in the situation which was in some measure fascinating. The darker side to it he set his face against. The psychological potentialities of their intercourse was curious and imminent. But for the present his thoughts were running in another groove. The soft morning air seemed full of the murmuring of a low voice. More than once during the meal he pictured her to himself as he had first seen her, floating across the shadowy lawn with supple and marvellous grace, seeming something scarcely human in the weird half lights and shadows amongst which she moved. She was very beautiful, very unlike any other woman in the world. What did he mean to do with her? Hildyard wondered, gazing across the table into his host's cold, impassive face. He could not be seriously thinking of keeping her apart from the world all her days. The thing was absurd—it was a crime. A life of cold negations for such a woman as this was a thing hideous and unnatural. In the world there was an empire before her! Yet—Hildyard looked from his host's face across the sea. It was such an empire as hers might be which had driven this man into premature middle age and rigorous exile. He was her guardian. Was he likely to send her out into the world to sow the seed of which he had reaped so bitter a harvest? The sunlight seemed suddenly dimmed—the morning breeze had become enervating. Hildyard's face was clouded.

They had finished breakfast, and were leaning back in low basket chairs with a tin box of cigarettes and a tiny flask of liquers upon the table between them. Owston, who had hitherto preserved an almost singular silence, waved the curling blue smoke from around him, and leaning forward with his keen eyes, fixed upon his guest's face.

"It is a strange chance which has brought you here, Hildyard!" he said, quietly. "You are one of the last men I should have expected to penetrate my exile. It is like what we used to call sometimes when we dabbled in fatalism, the writing of destiny."

"I am afraid that my coming here must have looked very much like taking you by storm," Hildyard remarked. "You had very little choice as to my entertainment. Tell me candidly," he continued, "would you rather have been left alone? Am I here on sufferance, or are you really content to have your seclusion broken in upon? You have only to say the word, you know, and two can play the hermit! Let me choose half a dozen books from your library, and give me a box of these cigarettes, and I can make myself perfectly happy amongst the pine trees."

Owston shook his head. "There is not the slightest need for anything of that sort," he declared. "I am honestly glad to see some one whom I can call a fellow-creature again, and I am looking forward to the week which you have promised me. Do not think that I am attempting to discount my hospitality, however, if I venture to ask you a favour."

Hildyard nodded, and watched the ash of his cigarette grow white between his fingers. There did not seem to be any need for him to say anything.

"There is a certain lady occupying a somewhat notorious position in English society—Mrs. Stanley Owston, I believe she still does me the honour to call herself. You are a man of the world, and are doubtless acquainted with her—directly or indirectly."

Hildyard emitted a volume of cigarette smoke in a thin blue line from between his compressed lips, and watched it steal upwards in the clear sunlit air. His expression was entirely nonchalant, but the faint tinge of colour had left his cheeks, and the fingers of his hand, which rested on the side of the basket chair, shook so, that he locked them in the open canes.

"Yes, I am acquainted with her," he answered, slowly.

"Exactly! Before you leave I have a question to ask concerning her. I shall not ask you, or allude to this matter again, until the eve of your departure. May I beg that until that time you eliminate from your mind the existence of that lady so far as I and my past life are concerned. I have lifted a little corner of a very dark and a very heavy curtain. Now it is dropped again. I am afraid that I have expressed myself in a somewhat roundabout fashion. You will doubtless understand me, though."

"Yes, I understand," Hildyard answered, gravely. "Until you yourself choose to open the subject, it shall be a sealed one to me. I would very much rather that you did not allude to it again. I should infinitely prefer that you ask me no questions concerning that lady."

Owston's face was turned toward the sea, and his expression was inscrutable.

"Let that pass. The time has not come yet. And now I have another thing to ask you. Many years ago I shook the dust of the world from off my feet. I made a vow, and retired with all formality. My intention was to lead an absolutely solitary life, to indulge my old delights for dreaming in beautiful places, to cultivate philosophy, to dominate sensation, to acquire indifference, to mend a broken heart. So I bought this little island and came here with my books, and my one faithful servant, Butlin, and his wife, prepared to play the hermit. But after all we are the puppets of fate, and she seems to take a malicious pleasure in thwarting our most cherished schemes. It was written that my hermithood should be but partial. By a combination of unfortunate events, I became the only possible protector of a deformed lad and a girl in pinafores."

He paused, and looked over his shoulder toward the house. Hildyard leaned forward and helped himself to another cigarette. There was no sign of life anywhere around them. In a moment or two Owston continued. A certain restraint had fallen from his tone. He was very much in earnest.

"That lad has become a man, and the girl a woman. I have brought them up in the way which seemed best to me. They are the voluntary companions of my isolation, and they are endurable to me and answer my purpose simply because their world is bounded by the seas which girt my little island. You understand me, Hildyard, I am sure! The presence of a stranger, and such a stranger as you are, must be richly suggestive to both of them of a world of which they are not denizens. I do not want their minds to dwell upon this world. I am bound to ask you therefore to hold as little converse with them as possible. I accepted my guardianship in both instances with distaste and anger, but having accepted it, I do not wish to lose them. Such as they are, they are mine. They are of my moulding—they are the fruit of my labours. They represent to me humanity. I cannot spare a single disturbing emotion of discontent or unsettlement from either of them. Their connection with myself, I repeat, both in the present and the future, is my concern only."

The eyes of the two men met for a moment. The same thought was at the heart of both of them.

"The girl—Bertha, I think you call her—is beautiful!" Hildyard said, slowly. "You cannot intend to keep her here all her life. It would be unnatural. She is made for a place in the world."

A thundercloud darkened Owston's face. He removed his cigarette from his mouth, and leaning over, answered slowly, but with a peculiar impressiveness,—

"Whilst I remain here, she remains here. Where I go, she goes. Her sex, in the person of one woman, owes me a good deal. She shall repay it."

This time it was not fancy—a clear, gay voice rang suddenly out on the breathless air. Both men looked up. Bertha, with her hands clasped behind her head, was crossing the lawn towards the cliff. As she walked she sang. Hildyard, who was but an indifferent linguist, could only guess at the meaning of the words which floated from her lips so mockingly, yet so seductively. As she moved, her feet kept time with the music—she was half dancing and half walking. A deeper shade stole over Owston's face. His brows were knitted, and he seemed annoyed at her inopportune presence. Hildyard leaned forward, watching her with rapt intentness, until she was out of sight.

"She is marvellous," he exclaimed. "I never saw any one like her in my life. She is the incarnation of orientalism. She is like the daughter of a hundred Pharaohs!"

Owston did not answer. His eyes were fixed upon the furtherest corner of the lawn, and the dark shade upon his face had deepened. Hildyard followed his gaze. Amongst the bushes the creature of last night was standing, still in his black coat and slouched hat, with his pale face turned toward the spot where the girl had disappeared. For a moment or two he remained there perfectly silent. Then with a little, gurgling cry which sounded oddly enough in the ears of the two men, he plunged into the shrubbery, taking a path in the same direction as that by which she had vanished. The bushes closed behind him. In the distance they could still hear the faint refrain of the girl's song.

CHAPTER VIII

The long summer day passed like a dream, and it was night again upon the island. Hildyard had been shown over the place, had sailed for an hour or two in a tiny skiff to the leeward of the rock, and had shared with his host an incomparable little dinner in the room which looked out upon the sea. Afterwards they had sat out upon the lawn smoking and talking until the stars had crept into the sky, and the evening breeze had swept in from the ocean. The conversation had been desultory at first, but in its course Hildyard had answered many questions about many people, and he had listened to a good deal of pent-up bitterness of spirit. They had peopled the twilight around them with the ghosts of forgotten days and faces only dimly remembered across the gulf of years. Hildyard was not in the least deceived by his host's somewhat strained attempt to pose as a cynical yet contented misanthrope. The restlessness of the man was only too readily apparent, and every now and then there flashed forth in the turn of a sentence or in the inflexion of his voice the dark lightenings of an infinite bitterness which seemed to have poisoned his very soul. All day long Hildyard had borne him company with a curious mixture of sensations. There could be no pleasure for him in this revival of an intimacy which he had grown to look upon as a thing wholly and completely passed. Yet the psychological possibilities of their renewed intercourse appealed strongly to his love of the unusual. It was in itself a little drama.

Somewhat abruptly Owston had bidden his guest good-night, and had gone off to his room at the rear of the building. Hildyard was lounging in a low chair before the open windows of his apartments. As his host's footsteps died away in the distance he gave a sigh of relief. The situation had not been without its embarrassments. It was something to be alone.

He took a cigarette from the tin box on the shelf, and lighting it, looked around with more interest than he had yet been able to bestow upon his immediate surroundings. The room which had been allotted to him was large and somewhat bare. The floor was covered with a coarsely-woven Japanese matting, and the walls, innocent of any pictures, were painted a bright creamy yellow. There was a piano in one corner and a couple of music stands. On the side remote from the door there was a camp bedstead, and a dressing case laid ready for his use. An india-rubber bath had been dragged out and placed against the wall. The room was obviously no bedroom. It had probably been extemporized into one for his use.

He pushed both windows wide open, and let in a little stream of the cool air. Then he sat down, his hands clasped behind his head, and looked thoughtfully out into the shadowy night.

The day had been a long one, full of experiences which had been novel and sensations which were a little bewildering. Life, which in the world's capital had seemed a very simple and somewhat flavourless affair, presented to him suddenly in this lonely island a complex and a difficult side. There was a certain pungent but unwholesome humour in the paradox with which he was confronted.

He blew his cigarette smoke out into the darkness and pondered. By degrees the abstract side of the question paled before the real issue. Why was he subjecting himself to this moral dilemma? Why had he chosen to become the guest of a man between whom and himself such relations were grotesquely out of place? Or, to put the matter more plainly still, why was he so feverishly anxious to remain upon the island? Why was he sitting there with a heart which beat the faster for every rustling of the breeze in the pines, and with eyes so steadfastly fixed upon a certain part of the lawn, that they had already grown accustomed to the darkness, and able to penetrate it?

He answered his own question bluntly. The spell of his last night's delight was upon him. He was waiting to see whether she would come again, listening keenly all the while for the faint throbbings of that wonderful music. All day long he had been expecting to see her—and he had been disappointed. Owston, after this morning's conversation, had not even alluded to her. There could be very little doubt that whilst he was upon the island, she was to be, in a measure, banished.

The fault was his own. It was the result of his too evident admiration. He frowned, muttered a word or two of mild blasphemy, and lit another cigarette.

Then, at a moment when he was least expecting it, came what he had been longing for. There was the sound of a cautiously opened window to the left of his, and the soft trailing of a woman's gown upon the grass. He sprang to his feet, and looked out into the night. It was Bertha!

She was crossing the lawn, a dim, shadowy figure in a flowing grey cloak, and whilst he stood there for a moment motionless, the music from the violin in her hands stole like some sweet magic through the darkness to his ears. He hesitated no longer. The memory of Owston's menacing words faded away. He was no hero, and he was utterly unaccustomed to any form of self-restraint. His sense of obligation to the man who had become his temporary host was swept away in the flood of his desire. He stepped lightly outside, and followed her across the grass.

"Bertha!" he cried softly.

She flashed a sidelong glance at him, but she did not stop playing. He walked close behind her to the rhododendron shrubbery. She did not speak to him or take any notice of him whatsoever. On the little grass plateau she paused and leaned with her back against a young fir tree, playing still, although the music grew fainter and slower every moment. He stood and watched her, fascinated against his will. Her eyes looked into his steadfastly, yet with a far-away gleam in them which puzzled him. Slower and slower grew the music, dying away at last with a quivering pathos which was almost a sob. Her white shapely fingers ceased to flash through the darkness. The hand which held the bow hung down by her side. There was silence.

"Tell me," she asked, leaning towards him with the dreamlight lingering in her eyes. "Is it like that?"

"Is what?—I do not understand," he answered, bewildered. "It is very beautiful music. I do not know anything else like it."

Her face clouded slightly. She sighed.

"I forgot. Andrew understands all that I play to him. I want to know about life—human life. Is it like that?"

He shook his head. "It is not so sad. Sometimes it is as beautiful, but then it is more joyous. Life is a symphony in a major key."

"Ah!"

There was a brief, nervous silence, then he spoke again.

"Life is beautiful when one is young. When you come into the world, for some day you must come, you will find it all out for yourself. The world is made for the young and the beautiful. Nothing else save those two things, youth and beauty, is of any account. You have them both. You have a right to make use of them. It is barbarous to keep you cooped up on this wretched island."

"If he hears you talk to me like that—if he comes and finds you here, he will kill you," she said simply.

He smiled. He had the full measure of a man's contempt for physical fear. She regarded his attitude with silent admiration.

"I am only telling you what is right and natural. Everyone would say the same. I shall tell him so myself when I leave."

"When you leave. Ah!"

"You will be sorry?"

She covered her face for a moment with her hands. Then she looked up at him.

"Why should I not be?" she said softly. "It would be strange if I were not sorry. Your coming has been like a breath from some promised land. You know where my promised land is. It is across the seas. It is where the world throbs. It is where one lives!"

"You will find your way there," he said. "You were not made to see your youth ebb away in a barren solitude. There is the fire of life in you. Some day you too will live. It is written!"

She caught a spark from the deep enthusiasm of his tone. Her eyes flashed. The light of hope was in her face.

"'It is written.' That is what I will tell myself," she repeated softly. "When the winter comes, and the sea and the sky are grey, I will say to myself, and I will believe it. Now, tell me. This morning I was wondering why he asked you to stop here. Tell me now why you consented to. There was your yacht, and you had guests—had you not? What made you send them away? It was strange that he should ask you, but it is strange too that you should want to."

A shade stole across his face. He looked across the dark sea on whose bosom the white-topped waves were rising and falling, swelling and breaking. He could almost fancy that he heard the same question in the deep, monotonous ebb and flow of the rushing tide. Why had he stayed at Stanley Owston's bidding? A phrase of that incipient fatalism which had hung like a faint cloud over his younger and more studious days, floated again into his brain. To such a question he felt that there was no definite answer. He thought of the cross, of his dream, without flippancy—almost with awe. Was it indeed possible that some force other than his own caprice had brought him here? What would be the result? He was drifting down a broad avenue—soon he would see the end. He would stand upon the high road—before him the branching of the roads, behind him the precipice. He looked into her dark, beautiful face as she leaned back against the red-barked tree, with the lines of her supple, graceful figure faintly defined under the folds of her thinly woven gown, and he felt his heart beat the quicker. She was glorious—incomparable! The Egyptian woman of Bond Street with her queenly yet seductive beauty seemed almost vulgar in comparison. Then a little shiver stole through his frame. Perhaps it was a premonition of the tragedy which waited upon his coming.

"Why did I stay?" he repeated. "I do not know. It was an instinct. Call it an inspiration."

She leaned forward towards him till her eyes gleamed like stars through the dusky twilight.

"It was I who brought you," she murmured. "I stood upon the rocks below by the great stone cross, and I played, and I played, and I played with my face to the sea, and my heart was lonely and sad, and the strings of my violin sobbed. I was playing for you, I think. I was very lonely."

She bent her head, and her white fingers flashed once more before his eyes. A low strain of music floated out upon the heavy air—music full of strange chords, and with a weird perpetual refrain. By degrees it grew louder and yet sweeter. It dawned upon him that the music was for him— she was speaking to him, calling him to her—every quivering note was charged with words. What was she saying? His heart was throbbing, the blood in his veins began to tingle, his eyes were bright. He tried to move towards her, but his feet were like lead. Dimly he began to wonder whether this girl with her great, dark eyes, and music which seemed to leap into burning, passionate life at her touch, had inherited any of the occult powers of her Egyptian ancestors. Well, if she were a sorceress, he was content to be bewitched. He was a very willing victim. The charm was in his blood.

Suddenly the music came to an abrupt end. There was a sharp screaming discord, a wild sob like the cry of a dying spirit. The violin slipped from her nerveless grasp. A string had broken in two. She buried her face in her hands and shivered. Hildyard, too, involuntarily stepped backwards. The ordinary mishap to the instrument seemed to have become transformed into something emblematic and significant. And almost at the same time a white, gleaming object, like a flash of silent lightening, passed before his dazzled eyes. He followed its downward course with fascinated horror. Only a few feet away from him a long knife was quivering in the turf. He raised his hand to his forehead, and looked at his fingers. They were covered with blood. From the bushes close by came a low, crooning cry, familiar to him since the morning, and the sound of heavy, shuffling footsteps rapidly growing fainter.

She, too, had seen it all—had seen the knife graze his forehead, and the blood upon his fingers. With a single movement of swift but effortless grace she stood before him. Her face was blanched and her eyes were dilated with horror. Stooping down, she tore a handful of soft lace from her skirt, and pressed it to his forehead, and looked at his fingers.

"Are you hurt?" she whispered.

"Not in the least," he answered, his voice trembling with a new sensation. "You broke a string, and the music came to such a strange ending, that I sprang back. It was nothing. The knife only grazed me."

Once again that low, weird cry came floating through the perfumed darkness to their ears. The girl heard it and shivered from head to foot. But he heard nothing. She was in his arms!

CHAPTER IX

They were sitting before a small, round table drawn up close to the cedars upon the lawn. The dying sunlight flashed upon the crystal wine-glasses and the silver dishes of fruit spread upon the white tablecloth. A thin blue cloud of smoke had risen over their heads from the cigars which they had just lit.

Hildyard had wheeled his chair round, and was gazing seaward. Owston, on the contrary, was interested in nothing save his guest's face. Through half closed eyes he watched it with curious and steadfast intentness.

Below, riding at anchor about half a mile out, was the *Sea King.* Early in the afternoon they had watched her bearing down upon the island, growing larger and larger from a mere white speck upon the horizon. Just before the evening meal had been served, she had swung round and prepared to lower a boat. Hildyard, who had been steeped to the lips with the pleasure of having ceased for a week to be an integral unit in the civilized world, thought of the pile of letters which were even now on their way to him, and shivered. He thought too of the wonderful sweetness of these few days of perfect naturalness, of the host of new sensations to which they had given birth, of the falling away of the old lassitude and melancholy. All these things, bewildering in themselves, seemed yet insignificant beside the internal metamorphosis in his own nature. The effeteness and languor of the palled citizen of the world had gone. The intolerable sense of age, so surely the reward of the man who hammers ceaselessly at the doors of the temple of pleasure, had taken to itself wings and flown away. More than anything, he reminded himself of one of those old Roman pilgrims who had dragged their weary limbs up to the hospital of Aesculapius, high up amongst the hills of Etruria, and in the clear, sweet air and temperateness of living, have felt the fever pass from their blood, and the wholesome vigour of youth take root once more in their limbs. It was like this with him. He had not enough of cynicism left to mock at himself.

The two men had talked very little during dinner. Hildyard, face to face with the crisis which was before him, had been abstracted and thoughtful, and Owston had humoured his guest's mood. Butlin, the factotum of the household, who waited upon them, had filled their glasses often, and the wine had been good. But their tongues had not been loosened.

It was Owston who broke through their silence at last. He leaned over the table, softly waving away the cloud of tobacco smoke from between them, and fixed his eyes steadily upon his companion.

"Lord Hildyard!"

Hildyard started. His title had become unfamiliar to him. He looked away from the sea into Owston's pale set face, and a sense of coming trouble loomed up before him.

"I have a thing to ask you, Lord Hildyard!"

Hildyard nodded. The fewer words the better so far as he was concerned.

"I have a thing to ask you," Owston repeated slowly. "I have put it off from day to day. Now that you are going I must put it off no longer. It is about the lady who was once my wife—who still, I believe, does me the honour to call herself by my name!"

Hildyard started. He had been nerving himself to meet a question on another matter. But this was serious enough.

"I gather from such papers as come within my reach," Owston continued, "that she has become a personage. She was always very beautiful. I have seen society papers which have gone so far as to call her the most beautiful woman in England. A royal prince, they say, has shared in her favours. What a compliment to my poor judgment!"

Hildyard kept his eyes fixed steadfastly upon the ground. He would have given a considerable portion of his worldly goods for an interruption of any sort. But none came. None was like to come!

"The latest news I have of her," Owston continued, deliberately knocking the ash off his cigar, "is of her success upon the stage. I learn from a prominent society paper that she has become the lessee of a London theatre, and unless the critics lie, that she really does act. You have seen her, doubtless. May I ask you for your candid opinion? I am curious."

"There is no question as to her genius," Hildyard said, in a low tone. "She is a great actress."

"You amaze me! I should have thought that she wanted nerve. But you are a judge. You must know. Pauline a great actress! How strange! And that reminds me—I have come to my question. I do not ask you to betray any confidences. The thing is perfectly well known in London. I want to know the name of the nobleman who took the 'Novelty' theatre for her, and under whose protection she is living?"

There was a dead silence. The breathless air seemed full of the dying sunlight. There was no sound to be heard on all the island. Hildyard relit his cigar, which had gone out, with fingers which visibly trembled. There were two beads of perspiration upon his forehead.

"I am not asking you to divulge any confidences," Owston continued calmly. "I believe the little arrangement I allude to is perfectly understood in London. Nor am I asking for a list of my wife's infidelities. I simply want the name of this one man. It is a matter of some interest to me."

There was another short silence. Then Hildyard turned slowly round, and looked his host in the face.

"Why do you want to know this?" he asked. "He is not the man who took your wife away from you. He may not have known even of your existence. Your wife's reputation, pardon me—as a professional beauty, was before the world long before his connection with her. It was he—or someone else—"

"These matters do not interest me," Owston said slowly. "I want an answer to my question! I want that man's name!"

The *sangfroid* of his order and training came back to Hildyard. He answered firmly and yet with a certain indifference,—

"I am sorry, but I do not feel justified in telling you this man's name. I don't like disobliging you, but the thing is impossible!"

"All I want is the name of the joint lessee of the 'Novelty' theatre," Owston repeated slowly. "Nothing more!"

"I cannot tell you!" Hildyard repeated. "As you say, you have no difficulty in finding it out. But not from me."

Owston threw his cigar away, and taking a cigarette from the tin box at his elbow, lit it. He appeared to be neither surprised nor annoyed at Hildyard's refusal to answer his question. On the contrary, the set lines about his mouth relaxed into a faint forbidding smile.

"I must say that your refusal to answer such a simple question seems to me a little ungracious, Hildyard," he remarked quietly. "I am only asking you to save me a letter to London. Any twopenny-halfpenny little society paper would furnish me with the information in its 'answers to correspondents.' I am simply asking you to spare me the humiliation of writing. You will probably change your mind before you leave the island."

Hildyard looked at him fixedly with raised eyebrows. Whatever else he may have been, he was no coward.

"I think not," he said stiffly. "I am not in the habit of changing my mind. You may—"

He broke off in his sentence. After all, an interruption had come—a most unlooked-for interruption. The garden gate had been thrown open, and was swinging upon its hinges. The deep twilight stillness was suddenly broken by the sound of alien voices. Both men looked round, and then their eyes met for a moment across the table. Hildyard was white to the lips.

"Is that a planned thing?" Owston whispered hoarsely.

"By God! No!" Hildyard answered with broken fervour.

There were no more words between them. It was the silence before the storm!

CHAPTER X

A curious little group came strolling across the lawn towards the two men. There was Lady Bergamot, with her too golden hair very much in evidence, holding her skirts in one hand, and peering out of a lorgnette which she held in the other. By her side was Morton Pearmain, tall, thin, and sallow; and a little to the right of them—the most beautiful woman in England, her eyes fixed upon Hildyard, and a wonderful smile breaking across her face.

Pale still, but with a wonderful self-possession, Hildyard rose to greet them. Owston took a single step backwards. He was now standing in the shadow of the cedars, and his features were obscured.

"Is that really you, Hildyard?" she cried gaily, but with a certain note of relief in her tone. "Why, we expected to find your bleached bones, or to discover you sitting on a rock half starved, and here you are in the very lap of luxury. You didn't mind us coming back in the yacht? We—why what is the matter?"

Hildyard did not answer. The situation was a little beyond him. And then came Stanley Owston's deep bass voice as he stepped out from the shadows.

"Will you not present me to your friends?" he asked quietly.

There was a deep silence. The eyes of the man and woman were fixed upon one another. Everyone else seemed to sink into the background. A little, low cry burst from Pauline's lips. The colour faded from her cheeks, and her eyes were dilated with horror. Her outstretched hand fell slowly to her side. Morton Pearmain dropped his eyeglass, and his lips unconsciously curved themselves into a whistle. Lady Bergamot, who also understood, was silent and shaken. Outwardly, Owston was the least disturbed of the party.

"This is very kind of you, Pauline!" he said, bowing to the little group. "I am delighted to see you. Won't you introduce me to your friends? Lady Bergamot, I believe, I have already the pleasure of knowing."

Lady Bergamot bowed stiffly.

"Mr. Owston—Morton Pearmain," she murmured. "Be civil," she added under her breath. "We're in a jolly row!"

Mr. Morton with difficulty repressed an audible whistle. Mr. Owston! The idea of there being a Mr. Owston. He was at once deeply interested in the situation.

"You are very welcome," Mr. Owston continued. "By the by, have you dined? I have only a hermit's fare to offer you, but such as it is, it can be got ready in a very short time. John!"

The man stepped out from the study window, and crossed the lawn. But by this time Lady Bergamot was herself again.

"Please do not order anything at all for us Mr. Owston," she begged. "We dined on board the yacht, just before we came."

"On board the yacht!" He glanced over his shoulder as he repeated the words. The coloured lamps were hanging out from the rigging and masthead, but the yacht itself was still visible through the gathering darkness.

"How curious!" he remarked softly. "You are all together, then? I don't remember hearing you say that you were entertaining such an interesting party, Hildyard!"

Hildyard pulled himself together. It was no good being unnerved.

"I am an unconscious host," he remarked, with an attempt at lightness. "I thought my guests had landed."

No one spoke. What was there to be said, or rather how could they say it? They had come back for Pauline's sake. It was she who had proposed and almost insisted upon their return. She had had a stupid presentiment about Hildyard's safety, which by some means or other, she had contrived to communicate to them. So they had all come back together, and this was what they had found—her husband and her lover of to-day dining together under a cedar tree. It was distinctly an awkward situation. There was humour in it, no doubt, but just at that time the humour seemed strained. Morton Pearmain, who had written a cynical novel, and professed to be a disciple of Ibsen, was the only one who found it endurable.

"Well, if you won't dine with me, you must try my grapes," Owston continued. "John, some grapes, and a couple of bottles of claret—the yellow seal. Lady Bergamot, there is a chair behind you—permit me. Mrs. Owston, I know, prefers a low seat. There, you will find that comfortable!"

The man seemed to have gained a sort of unholy mastery over the little party. He who should have been the chief sufferer, became the chief torturer. From sheer inability to do anything else, they all obeyed him.

"You have quite an Arcadian home, Mr. Owston," Morton Pearmain remarked, looking around him.

Owston shrugged his shoulders.

"It is rather like a scene from Arcadia, is it not? The place is well enough. I am quite a hermit, you know, and it suits me. Lord Hildyard's visit has been a great event. We have talked over old days and old friends, until I became almost homesick. I have heard all the news about everybody, all the latest gossip, and all the scandal. I am beginning to feel quite up to date. It has been a wonderful week for me. In a sense I think Lord Hildyard has found it wonderful too."

Ghoul-like he leaned forward and laughed at his wife through the twilight. She shivered.

"I am afraid you are a little cold," he observed. "Let me fetch you a wrap. The evenings are always a little chilly."

He glided from his chair with a word of excuse. They could see him crossing the lawn.

"Hildyard," she whispered, bending over towards him, "for God's sake, let us go. Whatever made you stay here—with him? Are you ready? Let us get away from the hateful place."

He drew apart with a frown upon his forehead.

"No, I cannot slink away like that," he answered. "I had a reason for staying. Of course I had not the least idea that you people—"

"We ought not to have come," she faltered.

He shrugged his shoulders, and was silent, brutally silent. Owston was with them again. He had come across the lawn swiftly and noiselessly in the twilight, with a shawl upon his arm. John followed closely behind with a great bowl of grapes.

"The cigarettes are at your elbow, Mr. Pearmain," he remarked. "I am sorry that you won't try my grapes. John, the grapes to Lady Bergamot."

Most of them took something—all except one woman who sat there with white, strained face, nervously clasping and unclasping her hands in the darkness. Morton Pearmain made a little conversation, the others were silent. Even Lady Bergamot, who was very much a woman of the world, found the situation beyond her.

Suddenly the soft, dreamy silence was broken. Hildyard, who knew what it meant, was galvanized at once into a state of eager and nervous unrest. The others looked around them, wondering. From behind the rhododendron shrubbery came the sound of strange, sweet music, more weird than ever tonight, striking a deep thrilling note of sorrow in the night stillness. Owston leaned back in his chair, watching his guests' faces through half closed eyes.

Gradually that single strain of minor music grew fainter and fainter. Finally it died away. The silence seemed deeper and blacker after the last sob of those few lingering chords. Everyone was a little nervous—even Morton Pearmain had let his cigarette out. Then suddenly the music came floating out again on the faintly stirring breeze, only this time in a different vein and key. It was at once seductive and sparkling, voluptuous and dreamy. Pauline alone seemed unmoved by it. She sat upright, listening with pallid lips, and eyes fixed upon Hildyard. Aware of her gaze, he yet could not keep his seat. He knew quite well that the music was for him. It was his summons—he was being called. He forgot that any one was watching him, forgot that a woman's eyes were trying to read his soul. He rose from his chair, and unchallenged he stole away into the darkness.

Soon the music ended abruptly. For the first time Pauline addressed her husband.

"Who is it?" she asked slowly.

He shrugged his shoulders. "A poor deformed little creature," he answered. "A faithful companion of mine, though, and, by the by, my ward. You shall see her."

The light of a sudden and great relief flashed into her face. She drew a quick little breath.

"I should like to see her. She plays wonderfully."

He rose and motioned her to follow him. They crossed the smooth, dark lawn, threading their way amongst the lilac bushes and the clustering laurels, until they reached a hedge of rhododendrons. With noiseless fingers he drew back the screening bushes. Then he glanced at her face with a smile at the corners of his lips.

Bertha was leaning against her favourite tree, with the back of her head against the trunk, and her white fingers flashing as she slowly drew the bow across her violin. Her yellow gown and the exquisite grace of her pose were thrown into strong relief against the background of the dark pines. The faint light of the rising moon gleamed in her dark eyes, and touched her face with a strange beauty. She was playing to him, and he was at her feet.

"It is the last scene in a modern comedy—a seven days' comedy," he whispered. "See, the curtain has fallen." He let go the bushes. "Let us go back."

They crossed the lawn in the glimmering darkness. He looked into her face and laughed softly. Suddenly her fingers gripped his arm.

"Stanley, who is that? Tell me. Who is she?"

He laughed lightly. There was something diabolical about his appearance just then.

"The comedy is certainly a French one," he declared. "It even has a savour of that Norwegian with the impossible name. You really ought to make something of it for the 'Novelty.' Thrilling situations are so scarce, and this one is unique. A mother who does not know—her own child."

She stood quite still. She was trembling from head to foot.

"It is not true. It is not true," she moaned. "That—that girl is not Mil—not my daughter!"

He shrugged his shoulders.

"Considering that you have left her to me for twelve years—a little more than twelve years, I believe, you might at least accept my word as to her identity," he remarked suavely. "She has altered, it is true—but then girls do alter between six and eighteen. Won't you take my arm? You seem a little upset."

There was a circular seat around the trunk of a cedar tree close by. She sank down upon it, and covered her face with her hands. The deep, soft stillness of the night was all around them.

"Does he know?" she asked suddenly, looking up at him.

He had lit a cigarette, and was stooping down to look at a glow-worm. At the sound of her sharp, sobbing speech he strolled up to her side.

"Well, no," he answered. "He is not particularly squeamish, but I scarcely think that he would be—where he is—if he knew that the girl was the daughter of his mistress. No! I have kept it back for a pleasant little surprise. If you like, you may tell him. I really think that he ought to know, especially as he has been using all his powers of persuasion to induce her to try a little sea air with him on board his yacht. You see, your coming back is just a trifle awkward for Hildyard. In the event of his succeeding with the girl, I am afraid you may find yourself *de trop*. Better make up your mind to stay here, and spend a week or two with me."

She gave a little gasp, and her head fell back. She had fainted. Owston watched her for a moment with a changing face. All the bitter hardness, the brutal mockery, of which he had spared her nothing, fell away from him. There was a lump in his throat, a mist before his eyes. She looked very beautiful and strangely young in the dim moonlight, some faint gleam of which had found its way through the thick, dark branches. He stooped and kissed her forehead passionately. For a moment he forgot. He was living in the past! She was the first and the only woman he had ever loved. God forgive her! God forgive them both!

The faint murmur of voices came floating out from amongst the rhododendrons. The music had ceased. It seemed to Owston that he had fallen from dreamland, from one of those bright stars, perhaps, on to the solid, pernicious earth. The wave of tenderness passed on. She was the woman who had taken his life into her hands to rend it asunder. She had borne his name and disgraced it. She had come here not for him but for her lover. A storm of sudden anger shook him. He even raised his clenched hand— his hot breath fell upon her pallid cheek. But his hand fell nerveless to his side. Her punishment was written out large in fiery letters across the pages of the future.

He set his heel into the ground, and his pale face hardened. Then he strolled away to find Lady Bergamot.

It was night once more upon the island, and night upon the sea. On the hill-top a slim, grey figure was standing with her face turned seawards. The salt wind blew in her tear-stained face, and her hair streamed behind her shoulders. Afar out in the centre of the black gulf below was a red light—the steady throb of a steamer came faintly to her ears.

"What did he mean?" she asked herself piteously. "What did he mean?"

The echo of his words was in the air. She repeated them to herself:—

"Bertha, I have forged for myself a chain, and I must wear it for awhile. Trust me, and I will come to you again! Only trust me, dear!"

Then he had gone—gone with that woman whose pale, wonderful beauty had seemed to her like a dream. She had only seen her for a moment moving across the lawn in the faint moonlight. What did it all mean? Who were these people? What had they to do with Hildyard? Her heart was hot and sad.

A cloud rolled away from the moon. The sea became dotted with millions of scintillating beams of light. By straining her eyes she could even faintly distinguish the shape of the yacht. There was a little black speck moving toward the land. She watched it eagerly. Her heart leaped. It was a boat. In a moment she heard the grating of its keel upon the beach below. A man sprang out and commenced to climb the rocks. She waved her hand to him gladly. It was Hildyard!

He sprang up to her side, and took her into his arms. His face was pale. The shadow was already upon him.

"You have come!" she whispered. "Oh! I am so thankful. I had a terrible fear when I heard the engines. I was afraid that you had forgotten."

He took her hands and held her at arm's length.

"Bertha, listen to me! You said only yesterday that you would love me if I were poor, even if I were wicked. Did you mean it?"

She looked at him with wide open eyes.

"You know I did."

"Dearest, I am wicked! Yet I hold you to your word. I have forged for myself a chain, and I must wear it a little longer. But from this night my life and love are yours! From this night I will have nothing to reproach myself with. I have a duty before me, and I must do it. It calls me away from you—it may keep me away for months, perhaps for years. But I will come back. I will find you out wherever he takes you. Will you swear to love me, to wait for me, and to believe nothing you may hear about me until I myself tell you the whole truth?"

"You have my word," she answered softly. "I shall trust you and wait for you!"

He caught her in his arms. Her face was bright again. She believed him implicitly.

"My love! Farewell!"

In a moment he tore himself away. As he sprang down the hillside the moonlight flashed upon the towering cross below. The reflection lay stretched out upon the dark waters beneath him. He looked at it and laughed.

"Henceforth," he cried, "I believe in fables!"

BOOK II

CHAPTER I

It was the brightest, smartest week of the London season, the week of the "Derby" and the "Oaks." A dull, grey morning had suddenly given place to an afternoon of brilliant sunshine, and the Park was literally crammed. The great rhododendron beds were laden with blossoms, the toilettes of the women were brilliant almost to audacity; even the servants' liveries seemed to speak of a season noted for life and colour. Under the full green-leafed trees the rows of chairs were every one filled. The broad walk was packed. An old man and a girl, curiously at variance with their surroundings, looked about in vain for a seat.

Both carried violin cases. Both were dressed in sober and somewhat shabby black. Their boots were dusty, and their clothes had seen much service. They moved along with the throng, the man quick-eyed and rest-less, with a faint satirical smile at the corners of his mouth, as though appreciating and even enjoying the anomaly of their appearance there; the girl, erect as a dart, proud yet intensely curious, entirely unconscious of it.

At last fortune favoured them. Some people rose as they passed, and left two chairs vacant. The old man secured them quickly, and sank back with a little sigh of relief, carefully stowing his violin case between his legs.

"This is shocking extravagance," he said softly, "shocking! One penny for a few minutes' rest on a cane-bottomed chair! What imprudence!"

She was looking about her eagerly, scanning the faces of all the passers-by, as though in search of some one.

His remark fell upon deaf ears.

"It is wonderful," she said. "I could never have imagined anything like it."

"Ay! it is wonderful," he answered, with a faint touch of satire in his tone. "After all, we have not wasted our substance. One penny to gaze upon the greatest show in the world. Who shall say that we have not value for our money? There they go, child, jumbled up together like the prizes and blanks in a lucky bag, and with nothing to tell the one from the other—the gold from the tinsel. There they go, princes and stock-jobbers, peers and soapmakers, bishops and music-hall caperers. And the women too. Look at them—look at them well. There is not such another medley on the earth. Peeresses and actresses, ladies of high degree and ladies of the bal-let, shoulder to shoulder, and cheek to cheek. Lord! what a pandemonium!"

She looked at him, faintly puzzled. His rhapsody was not altogether intelligible to her. There was a frown upon her high, clear forehead.

"Do you know the names of the people?"

"Of a few," he answered. "Not many. See!"

He rose to his feet half reluctantly, and bared his head. All the men around them had done the same, only with more alacrity. There was a little hush, and the flood of carriages had suddenly drawn up. A victoria plainly appointed, but with a matchless pair of dark bay horses, drove swiftly down. The girl caught a glimpse of a woman bowing.

"Who is it?" she asked breathlessly.

"The Princess," he answered. "She is the leader of English society—and here comes, by the by, a leader of a different type."

A victoria drawn by a single horse drew up almost opposite them. Bertha looked at the woman who leaned back amongst the cushions, toying with a lace sunshade, and started.

"Who is that?" she asked quickly.

"That is supposed to be the most beautiful woman in England," he answered. "Her name is Mrs. Stanley Owston. She is an actress."

Half a dozen men were at her side, hat in hand, the moment the carriage came to a standstill. The girl and her companion sat and watched them from the shadow of the tree, the man with a half cynical, half amused interest, the girl with indrawn lips, and a new light in her dark eyes.

Presently the man chanced to look at the girl. The intentness of her gaze surprised him.

"You seem interested. Have you ever seen her before?"

"Seen her before!" The girl drew a quick breath, but she did not immediately reply. The murmur of low voices and soft laughter and the brilliancy of her surroundings had passed for a moment away from the range of her sensations. In its place she saw a dark, moonlit lawn, and the low swell of the distant sea was in her ears. She saw a woman glide out of the shadows of a deep cedar tree, and raise her passionate face to his. She was pleading and he was listening. There were other voices and other figures close at hand, but unseen. Those two, the man and the woman, had seemed like the priest and the priestess of her fate. Even now that cry of appeal rang in her ears:

"Take me away, Hildyard! Take me away!"

The white, pleading face had not seemed very beautiful to her then. She had hated it. She hated it now—hated it all the more for the beauty which was beyond denial. Her unwilling eyes took in every detail of the woman's toilette, simple, but elegant and costly. She looked at the carriage with its soft cushions, and the smart men-servants, and back again at the woman's soft, cool dress, with its folds of creamy lace. Then she glanced down at her own rusty black gown. She smiled a little bitterly, and rose to her feet. The old man looked at her.

"What are you going to do?" he exclaimed. "Sit down! You will lose your seat!"

She did not answer. She did not appear to hear him. She stood with her eyes fixed upon the gay little throng before her, and the colour coming and going in her cheeks. The old man tugged at her sleeve.

"Bertha, sit down! Are you mad, child?"

Two of the men were leaving. They stepped back from the rail, and arm in arm strolled away. A third hurried after them. There was only one now left, and Mrs. Owston smilingly dismissed him, and leaned on one side as though to speak to the coachman. Bertha stepped swiftly forward, and the eyes of the two women met. The order to drive on remained unspoken. With parted lips and white cheeks, the woman in the carriage sat quite still. She was an actress, and after that first convulsive start her face gave no sign.

The girl stepped quickly to the rail. She stood there, a sufficiently curious figure in her plain black gown and home-made hat, clenching the rail with both hands, and leaning a little forward.

For a moment her courage almost failed her. The other woman was so different. She was leaning back amongst the cushions now, with her parasol gently tilted over her hat, perfectly self-possessed and cool, with her eyebrows faintly raised. All the minor details of her toilette were faultless and exquisite. Bertha had never seen anyone quite like this. She looked at her, and wondered.

"You remember me!" she said. "It was on the island! May I speak to you? I want—to ask you something!"

The woman in the carriage bent her head—a slow and unassenting gesture.

"Certainly!"

There was a moment's silence. The girl was fighting with her thoughts. It had seemed so natural to her to ask, yet she was finding it very difficult. A crowd of laughing men and women went by. The air all around seemed full of gay voices and laughter and sun-light. Only the girl in black stood there pale and nervous, a pathetic, almost a dramatic, figure in such a scene. She was like a Cassandra with a background of roses.

"You were on the island. He left with you. I want to know how to find him—where he lives? Tell me, please!"

The woman in the carriage leaned a little forward. There was a faint rustle of silken draperies as she moved.

"Why do you want to know? What is he to you?"

The girl hesitated. The words were calmly spoken, but a woman's instinct is swift and true. She felt that she had made her little effort in vain; that of all the women in the world, this one was the least likely to help her.

Her heart sank, yet she continued,—

"He promised—he said that he should return. I want him to know that I am here, that I am not going back to the island. That is all."

"I am afraid that I cannot help you," Mrs. Stanley Owston said quietly. "I can only give you some advice."

"Oh, it is no matter," the girl said wearily. "I saw you, and I thought that you might have told me. I can wait."

Mrs. Owston put out an exquisitely gloved hand, and resting it lightly upon the side of the carriage, leaned a little forward. Her voice continued nonchalant and slow, but there was a gleam in her eyes.

"I would tell you if I thought that any good could possibly come of it," she said, "but I do not think so. Are you in London alone?"

"Yes."

"Your—your guardian is not with you?"

"No."

"With whom are you living, then? What are you doing?"

"I am studying music. I am living alone. If you will not tell me what I want to know, I will go away. I am sorry I troubled you."

She made a backward movement. The woman in the carriage motioned with her parasol imperiously. Bertha hesitated.

"You say that you are living alone. Do you mean quite alone?"

"Yes."

Mrs. Owston half closed her eyes. The sun and dust were a little trying. She began to be aware of a headache.

"Quite alone!" she repeated slowly. "Then you are much better off without that address. If he were—a man of your own station in life, I would give it you. As it is, I shall not!"

"What do you mean—of my own station?" the girl asked proudly. "He is a worker too. He told me so. He writes books."

The woman looked at her steadfastly from underneath the drooping lace of her parasol.

"Did he not tell you on the island who he was?" she asked slowly. "Do you mean to say that you know nothing more of him than that?"

The girl shook her head. The eyes of the two met. The woman knew that this pale-faced girl was telling the truth.

"Will you come and see me if I give you my address?" the woman asked. "I have something to say to you. It is scarcely the place to talk much here, and I see some people coming who will want to speak to me. See, there is my address. Will you come?"

The girl did not hesitate. She leaned over and took the card.

"Yes, I shall come," she said. "I shall be sure to come!"

She stepped back swiftly, and joined her companion. A woman with several men took her place, and chatted for a minute or two, then the carriage drove off. Mrs. Owston did not glance toward her again. She was leaning back languidly amongst the cushions, with half-closed eyes as though fatigued.

Bertha watched from her seat with stony eyes. She followed the carriage until it was out of sight. Then she turned round and met her companion's steady, inquiring gaze.

"How did you know that woman?" he asked.

"I do not know her. I have only seen her once. She came to the island!"

He stooped for his violin case with a little gesture of irritation.

"You looked at one another as though you were old enemies. And, child, remember this. It is not well for you to have friends like Mrs. Stanley Owston. She is a great lady, but she is not of your world—thank God! You must not be seen with her. Later on, when you are famous, it might do you harm!"

The girl looked at him. "Is she a wicked woman?" she asked quietly.

"I do not judge her," he answered. "But at any rate, she has a reputation."

She got up and they moved off together. As they waited with a little crowd to cross at Hyde Park Corner, Mrs. Owston's victoria passed amongst the stream of carriages. She looked curiously upon the old man and the girl. Herr Dowe returned her gaze keenly from underneath his shaggy eyebrows.

"They say that she has ruined the Marquis of Esholt," he remarked. "What fools men are!"

"How old is he?" she asked.

Herr Dowe shook his head. "I have no idea. He can't be very old though. See, there is our 'bus, nearly empty. Garden seats too. What luck! Hurry, child."

"I think that he is very foolish—that Marquis," she said softly, "for she does not love him."

He looked at her sharply. "How do you know?"

She moved her violin case to her other hand. It was heavy, and they were walking fast.

"I know that she loves another man!" she answered wearily.

CHAPTER II

"Hildyard, by all that is amazing—by all that is delightful! How like a man this is."

Sunburnt and travel-stained, he stood up in her dainty little boudoir, holding out his hands. She had come over to his side expecting a warmer greeting, but something in his face had stopped her. The light died out of her eyes. A little hysterical laugh and a suspicious catching of the breath warned him of what lay behind.

"I am afraid that you have thought me unkind," he said. "Really, I am ashamed of myself, I ought to have written."

"Never mind. Sit down and tell me where you have been, what you have been doing, and all about it. It has seemed odd to get my only news of you from the papers. You have been in the Mediterranean, haven't you?"

"Some of the time," he answered. "I have had a long cruise. I wanted to make the most of it. I shall probably never get another."

"Come and tell me all about it."

He drew off his gloves and laid them on the little table by his side. Then he sat down upon the nearest lounge, and looked at her thoughtfully. He had a great deal to say, and he was wondering how to commence.

"The fact is, Pauline," he said, "I have spent a great deal of money. When we returned from our last cruise, I had an interview with Webster, my lawyer, which was—well, mutually unpleasant. My agent, Clareson, had died suddenly, and everything was in an awful muddle. We looked into affairs as well as we could, and what we saw was very bad. I made up my mind then to get to the bottom of things. Webster said it would take six months to do it, and I decided suddenly to clear right out for a time. I hated hanging about in suspense. That is why I went away without a word to any one—and with only that hurried line to you. I found a letter at Gibraltar a week ago from Webster to say that he was ready for me, and here I am. It sounds dreadfully lame, doesn't it? I can't quite explain the mood I was in when I went away. I was horribly inconsiderate, I know, but Webster had been pelting me with figures until I was half mad."

She got up, shaking out the folds of her deep orange tea-gown, and came over to him.

"Poor boy," she said lightly, bending over him, and touching his forehead with her lips. "You might have come and told me."

"It was brutal of me," he admitted frankly. "I can't explain how I felt. I can't excuse myself. It was inexcusable."

She sat down by his side.

"I am very sorry," she said, "that I have been so extravagant. Perhaps I can atone a little for it now. We are doing remarkably well at the 'Novelty,' you know, and Maddison tells me that everything is booked for months. The new play has been a wonderful success. To think that you have not seen it yet!"

There was a measure of reproach in her tone, and he felt that it was deserved. Yet in the face of what was to come the thing seemed small. He brushed it away.

"I shall see it one night this week," he said. "I am glad that it is a success. I gathered that from the papers. The lease is all right, at any rate. It was taken out in your name. I wish it could bring you in more. I must talk to Maddison. I am afraid that he is rather too liberal in his ideas to make a thoroughly successful manager."

"Is it very bad?" she asked softly. "I am so sorry."

"It is the end," he answered, with a touch of unusual gravity in his tone. "I have come to have a serious talk with you, Pauline—and to say—good-bye."

"Good-bye!" she repeated vaguely. "Are you going away again, then? Good-bye!"

He took her hands in his, and held them.

"I need not beat about the bush, Pauline," he said. "As I told you, I have just come from my lawyer. I gave him a clear six months to get to the bottom of my affairs. He has done it, and the bottom is bad. The long and short of it is that I am ruined. I am just able to pay my debts, and that is all. And you know what that must mean for us, don't you?"

"No."

"It must mean good-bye, of course. I have done all that I can for you, but I am afraid that it is not much. This house is yours, and the six thousand pounds settled upon you last October—no one can touch that, or the lease of the 'Novelty.' That belongs to you for five years, either to let or use yourself. I hope that you will use it yourself. You have got over the uphill work now. You have made your public, and they are beginning to understand that the fact of your being a very beautiful woman does not prevent your being also an artist. I should keep the lease up if I were you."

"I don't want to think about that just now," she said quietly. "I want to know about you—about us."

He looked doubtful. He began to see that she would not understand easily.

"Well, there is not much to tell. We have been spending a good deal of money it seems—one way and another, and I have dropped a lot, racing—a beastly lot when you add it all up. The rents have gone down twenty-five per cent., and even then the tenants don't pay. The coal mines on the

Clamon estate have had to be closed—they have been worked at a loss for years. The fact is, when we come to look into it, Webster has shown me that I have been spending about sixty thousand a year on an income of a little over ten. It has come to an end. That is all. I shall have to sell my Hoton estates and all my horses, and raise money by mortgaging Esholt. For five years I shall have virtually no income at all. So you see it has to come. While it has lasted life has been pleasant, has it not? Now it is over. It is inevitable. We must say good-bye!"

She drew her hands from his, folding them before her and looking at him steadily. Her face was very pale.

"I do not understand you," she said slowly. "You come to tell me such news as this, and you do not seem even sorry. One would think that the loss of all your money was the loss of some evil thing. One would think," she added deliberately, "that to lose me—to give me up, was a relief to you."

He laughed a little bitterly, but not without a note of self-consciousness. The mingled perfumes of the little chamber, the bowl of violets, the pot-pourri, and the odour of scented wood, seemed suddenly stifling. He longed to open the window. He rose abruptly to his feet and walked up and down.

"Pauline," he said, "I have lived in the constant dread of this for two years. Like all other calamities, its embrace is not so bad as the shadows which it casts before. After all, I am a man. I am young, and I am strong. I think that there is some instinct of the democracy in me. I have a desire to meet the world on even terms. In a certain way I have always felt it. Now that the time is come, I am ready. I—"

She held up her hand. He stopped at once.

"And how about me?"

He hesitated. He had feared that there might be trouble. Underlying her reserve, he could trace the portents of the coming storm. The lace hand-kerchief in her hand was twisted up into a crumpled ball. Beneath the loose folds of her gown her bosom was heaving.

"About you!" he repeated vaguely. "I have done all that I could! I—"

He stopped short. She had taken a sudden step towards him—her eyes were alight with a strange fire. A white hand flashed out from amidst the yellow lace of her broad, drooping sleeve. He did not flinch. He watched it raised to strike him. Physical pain would have been a positive relief. But the blow did not come. With a little convulsive twitching her hand fell to her side. So they looked at one another in deep, breathless silence till the storm passed by. She found her voice at last.

"I know now that the Bible is true. God made the beast first, and then man."

She sank into a chair some distance away from him, and buried her face in her hands. He stood apart, looking at her. There was nothing for him to say. He was deeply moved, and in a manner altogether unexpected, but he had wit enough to know that silence alone was possible for him. Between him and her there was suddenly fixed a deep, impassable gulf. No word that he could have spoken, no pleading, no appeal, could have found its way into her heart. And with it all, he knew that it was she who was pure and he who had sinned. She had loved; he had not. Her justification had now become her misery. He could do nothing. He was utterly and completely powerless. Her past only deepened the outrage so far as he was concerned. He stood on the great plain of brutal self-indulgence side by side with millions of his fellow-men, with his face turned upwards to the hills. But whither she had gone he had no power to follow. It was like a stain from that wonderful Indian plant which no herb or any chemist's mixture can make less black; and the stain was on his soul, not hers.

She recovered herself presently, and looked up at him. Then he saw what suffering had done for her. It was the face of another woman.

"Forgive me," she said, quietly. "You see, I am not used to this sort of thing. It is my first dismissal. No! don't interrupt me. It is all over now. I am beginning to feel already that it happened—quite a long time ago. You see, I am getting over it very easily. Now I want you to tell me just what you are going to do."

He felt that he owed her implicit obedience. He answered without hesitation.

"I am going to lay aside my name and position altogether for five years. I have no fancy for being a pauper marquis. I am going to give my solicitor power of attorney to attend to all minor matters for me, and I am going to call myself and be called Mr. Hildyard. I shall take simple lodgings in some unfashionable part, and I shall live on a hundred a year and what I can make by literature. I have already had a desire to do this, even when the necessity was very far away. A man of my position and my order does not get a chance, as a rule. I want to stand on my own feet—a man and a worker like other men—and see how it feels. I have a fancy that I shall find life a larger thing. The richer a man and the older the name he bears here, the more tenacious and the higher are the walls of his environment. I want to break down my walls. I want to get outside and breathe the fresh air."

"You will be disappointed!" she said, calmly. "The world is an ugly place. You do not like ugliness."

"I am beginning to wonder whether I know what ugliness really is—the truth about it!" he answered. "At any rate, I am nauseated with the beauty which is born simply of elegant surroundings, and living in beautiful places. I want to get beauty from the plain things of life—from what the world calls ugliness."

"You will fall in love with your landlady's daughter!" she said, calmly.

"If I do, I shall certainly marry her!" he answered. "I shall not be prejudiced against my landlady's daughter or her kind in any way. I am going to constitute myself a unit of the democracy."

"Well, I shall envy you," she said. "You are going to escape from your own personality. You are a man, and you can do it."

Her tone was careless, but the light in her eyes fascinated him.

"You look as though you meant what you say!" he exclaimed.

She got up from the chair into which she had flung herself, and came quite close to him. Surely this was a different woman. It was hard to believe in her identity. He would have taken her hand in his, but she calmly ignored his motion.

"Hildyard," she said, "there are some things which you do understand, no doubt, but you do not understand women. Do you imagine that whilst you men sometimes grow weary of the monotony of life, of the dead level of our existence, and try to escape from it—do you imagine that what you feel a woman does not feel? Sometimes, just now and then, a man like you tires of his surroundings, however perfect, aesthetically, they may be. He wants to penetrate further into life, to weep with its sufferers, and rejoice with its happy children. He wants to taste sensations which have not become stale by habit, and pleasures which are not sensuous. Well, let me tell you that for one man who feels that way, there are a hundred women; for one man who suffers, a hundred women are stretched upon the rack. Oh! you are very blind! You and I have lived together for a little while. I have hidden no part of myself from you; yet you have the brutal, the unspeakable effrontery to suggest that I have so little soul as to be content with my life and my pleasures and my courtezanship!"

The word stung him. He held out his hand, but she ignored his interruption and his gesture.

"If you only knew," she continued. "Hildyard, I would rather, I would very much rather be that landlady's daughter of yours. If—if you had only cared for me, the change in our lives would have been nothing. I would have welcomed it, for it would have drawn us closer together. Poverty and homespun gowns would have been a delight; even the suburbanism at which you used to sneer would have been happiness. But you never loved me. You do not understand. You are blind, as all your sex are. You made me your mistress—you have made me hate myself and you. Oh, go away! please go away! I cannot bear it any more!"

"Pauline!"

"No, don't touch me! Don't dare to touch me! Don't come near me! Go!"

His hands dropped to his side, and he went out with bowed head. He was judged with a new judgment, and it seemed to him that the righteous disdain of all her sex had been thundered against him from the pale lips of the woman whom he had left there to her misery. She was right. He had not understood. His new-born enthusiasm had suddenly received a check. It seemed to him then as he walked out into the crowded streets that he would never altogether escape from the memory of that afternoon.

CHAPTER III

If Hildyard had not walked along Piccadilly with unseeing eyes and stunned senses, if that bitter cry had not been ringing in his ears, and that white, stricken face hovering in the air by his side, he would have probably noticed something familiar in the figure of the girl who passed him at the corner of the street, closely veiled and plainly dressed though she was. And if Bertha had been a little less nervous and absorbed in the contemplation of the visit she was about to pay, she too might have looked into his face, and that visit would never have been paid. They passed one another so closely on the pavement that her garments brushed against his, and went their own way—Hildyard to take the first steps towards his emancipation; Bertha to stand upon the steps of the little house in Mayfair which he had that moment quitted.

Mrs. Stanley Owston was at home, but she was not receiving anyone. Struck, however, by something unusual in this visitor's aspect, the man volunteered to take her name. A few minutes later she was standing face to face with the woman whom she had come to see.

Bertha's lodging in London was a humble one, and this first glimpse of luxury, toned down into elegance by the mastery of perfect taste, was like a glimpse of a new world. The little perfumed room with its inexpressible daintiness was a revelation—the toilette of the woman, too, who rose to greet her with a certain languor of expression and mien not in any way assumed, was unlike anything she had ever seen before. She looked into the white, beautiful face wearing once more its mask of studied indifference, and her heart grew faint. Yet the voice which welcomed her was not unkind.

"You have come, then. Won't you sit down?"

Bertha shook her head.

"I have not come to stay," she said. "You know what I want. Will you tell me?"

"Sit down first!"

Bertha obeyed her. The voice was like music, but the gesture was imperative.

"I am glad you have come. I want to have a little talk with you. First of all, tell me, is it true that you have lived upon that little island all of your life—that you have had no friends your own age, no schoolfellows—that you know nothing whatever of the world?"

"It is true."

"And now you have come away without your guardian's knowledge. You came to London, of all places in the world, alone—and friendless. Isn't that so?"

"Yes."

"Won't you tell me how you succeeded in finding a home here, and what you are doing?" Bertha looked up. She did not recognize the still tone of the woman. There was an indefinable change. Something electrical and sympathetic passed between them.

"I was weary of my life on the island, and my guardian said things to me which nearly broke my heart. I got away on a fishing smack, and came to London. At Charing Cross I took a cab, and told the man to go to Chelsea. I had heard Andrew speak of artists living at Chelsea, and I knew nowhere else. I found lodgings there at the house of a German, Herr Dowe! He is a musician, and he has been very good to me. I earn a little money. That is all."

There was the rustle of soft silk upon the floor. Bertha looked up quickly. Mrs. Owston was sitting on a low ottoman by her side. Surely it was not the same woman.

"My little girl," she said, softly, "you have done a very brave but a very foolish thing. Now I want to speak to you about what you asked me yesterday. A certain person came to stay upon the island with your guardian. You want to know his address? You want to find him out?"

"He said that he should come back to the island," Bertha whispered, with her eyes fixed upon the floor. "He will keep his promise. He will go there and I shall have left. I want him to know."

"Is he—very much to you, then?"

"Yes."

The woman looked away and sighed. The bitterness of this thing seemed somehow suspended. Afterwards would come for her the shame, the humiliation, the sorrow. What of that? For her there was no future. But for the girl—her—

She covered her face with her hands, yet no tears came. There was a horror in her heart, all around her, which no tears could lighten. To concentrate her mind upon it was impossible. Had ever sin brought so bitter a harvest?

"My child," she said, softly, "I am an old woman to you. You are living in a world of which you know nothing, and amidst dangers of which you never dream. If you had—if you had—a mother—to tell you all about these things, you would see life differently."

"I do not want to see life differently!" Bertha said softly. "It is beautiful as it is—at least, it might so easily be beautiful."

A hand was laid softly upon hers. She felt suddenly weak. She hated the woman no longer. She was not afraid of her any more.

"My little girl, if you plucked a handful of beautiful berries and raised them to your lips, would you not thank the voice which whispered 'poison'? Sometimes this world is a very beautiful place—sometimes what looks so beautiful is poison and death. Those who have eaten can at least warn others while the poison is in their veins. And, child—don't move away from me—I have eaten them. I have sinned."

There was sudden silence in the little shaded room. The sounds of the streets below came to their ears like the muffled undernote, a background to the intense stillness. Then the girl turned quickly round and laid her arms upon the other's neck.

"I will listen to whatever you wish to tell me," she whispered.

Bertha walked homeward in the dusk with flushed cheeks and bright eyes, and a new seriousness in her gait. But more than once a faint smile played around her lips.

"She does not know him," she said, softly. "He is not like that. She cannot know him, really."

And back in that little boudoir, whose soft luxury and delicate sensuousness were in themselves so suggestive of the worshippers of Mammon, a woman was on her knees, praying. Her white, passionate face looked up through the twilight to the faintly clear sky—the murmur of the great city fell no longer upon her ears.

"Lord," she prayed, "I am a sinner, and for myself I seek no pardon. But for her—if she be indeed my child—save her. Grant that if the berries come within her reach, she may never pluck them. For she has no mother."

CHAPTER IV

Hildyard's new-born enthusiasms were not easily damped. They survived alike the grave expostulations of his man of business and the ridicule of his friends. They survived too that terrible hour in Mayfair when for a time all life had seemed black, and a certain note of conscience-stricken sadness had become woven into all his thoughts of the future. Yet in a way it was the memory of that phase in his life which had nerved his hand to cut away all the old ties and work out his complete emancipation. There should be no more of that sort of thing. His sense of the moral degradation of it was curiously potent. He judged himself with a hard and severe judgment. His new life was to be free of all this. Only when he had satisfied himself by the rigid penance of a year's or even two years' hard work and poverty, would he permit himself to look beyond—to definitely place before him a certain hope with regard to the future.

He found some lodgings in Bute Street, Chelsea. They were in a back street, dark, and rather smelly. There was an arrangement of stuffed birds under a glass shade on the sideboard, and the furniture was padded with slippery horsehair, very hard and shiny. The young person who waited on him had a large black fringe, and wore a red stuff dress, and a hat with a feather in it on Sundays. On the whole, there was a distinctly democratic air about the place, and Hildyard was satisfied. He brought a ready made blue serge suit and a deerstalker hat, and ostentatiously smoked a pipe in the streets. Then he called upon the editor of a small weekly journal to which he had been an occasional but anonymous subscriber, and as "Mr. Hildyard, of Bute Street, Chelsea," secured some work to do. There was not in reality any hurry about it, but he took it straight back to his rooms, ordered a pot of strong tea, trimmed his lamp, and with his pipe in his mouth, set to work with an air of unusual satisfaction. This, after all, was the real thing.

He had been writing for about an hour, when the pen suddenly slipped from his fingers and rolled unregarded down the sloping front of his desk on to the floor. He caught at the sides of the table as though he were falling, and for a moment or two there was a loud humming in his ears, and the horsehair chairs seemed to be chasing one another around the room. Then he recovered himself, and began to mutter that he was a fool. The unspoken words died away upon his lips. He heard it again distinctly. It was the wailing of a violin.

He sat quite still, absorbed in a concentrated effort at listening. The walls of his parlour faded away, and he looked out upon a little stretch of smooth green turf, bordered by flowering rhododendron shrubs and darker pines.

The soft murmuring of the sea crept like a deep undernote to the lighter music to his ears. A faint breeze touched his pale cold cheeks—she was there, leaning against the tree, with her dark eyes lifted to his, her lips parted in that wonderful smile. So she had played him to her side across grey seas which girt her island home. But here—in this dreary London lodging-house—oh, the thing was absurd. He ground his heel into the thin carpet, and asked himself what had become of his common sense.

Presently he became calm. The music had ceased, and there was no sound in the house. He got up and stood in the middle of the little room.

"This is fate," he said to himself. "I shall find her."

He went out on to the landing, and after a moment's hesitation climbed the stairs, and knocked at the door of the room immediately above his own. There was no answer. He turned the handle and walked in.

The room was empty, but it showed signs of recent occupation. It was furnished even more barely than his, but there was a vase of homely flowers upon the table, and the crochet antimacassars had been removed from the worn furniture. There was some music on the side-board, and a tea tray. Whoever had been there had recently gone out.

He staggered downstairs again, and threw himself back in his easy-chair. The bell was within his reach. He stretched out his hand and pulled it furiously.

The young person came in. She was a little annoyed, for she had been flirting with the milkman, and the ring had disturbed her. Besides, she was beginning to look upon this first-floor lodger as a flat. He had a habit of not appearing to see her when she was in the room.

"What is it, please," she asked, sharply.

He roused himself. "Some one was playing the violin just now," he said. "Can you tell me who it was?"

Her face expressed the disgust she felt at having been summoned on such an errand. She answered him brusquely.

"Young lady on the second floor above yourn. She don't play much, but, of course, if you object, mother'll speak to her."

"Object! I never dreamed of objecting," he answered, emphatically. "Can you tell me her name?"

She regarded him suspiciously. "Miss Mallalieu, she calls herself. She plays in the orchestra at some theatre. She won't be back now till half-past eleven. Was that all you rang for?" she added, impudently.

He hesitated. No, he could not ask this young woman. He would find out the truth for himself.

"That is all, thanks," he answered. "I am sorry to have troubled you."

She closed the door and departed without a word. Hildyard was left alone.

He never knew how he spent the evening. At eleven o'clock he opened his door. At half-past he stood there, pale and despairing. At a quarter to twelve there was a light step, and a rustle of a woman's dress upon the stairs. She must pass his door. He opened it wide, and stood in the door-way.

She was almost past him when she glanced up, and he caught a glimpse of a pale, thin face, and a pair of sad, lustreless eyes. Then her violin case slipped from her fingers, and fell with a crash upon the floor. She gave a little breathless cry, and the old fire flashed into her eyes.

Hildyard knew then that he had attained a new sensation. He took her into his arms, and closed the door of the sitting-room.

CHAPTER V

She was faint and trembling, but very happy in a disjointed sort of way. Her face seemed suddenly to have lost its thinness and pallor, and her eyes were very soft and bright. He led her gently to his easy-chair, and knelt down by her side.

She glanced around the room. It was like her own, only a little better furnished. Then she looked up at him. He was wearing the blue serge suit, and appearing to be very much at home.

"It isn't really true, then?" she exclaimed, with a little sigh of relief. "She told me that you were someone very rich and very great. She seemed to think that you could not possibly care for me."

"She lied, then!" he answered, sternly. "Who was it?"

"It was the woman who took you away from me. I saw her in the park. She told me that. But she has been very kind to me. She meant it all kindly."

"I do not understand," he said. "When did you see her?"

"I went to her house; she asked me to. She made me tell her all about myself."

"You have been to her house! She was kind to you!" he repeated, bewildered.

"Very. I shall never forget it. And she is very unhappy herself too. Yet she did not speak of that. She was afraid for me—because I was living alone. She spoke of you, too."

He looked away from her.

"She spoke to you of me?" he said, huskily.

"Yes, she advised me not to think of you, not to try and find you. I wanted to see you—to tell you that I was here. She seemed to think that you were a very dangerous person to know. But then she didn't understand, did she?"

She smiled up at him faintly. His hands closed upon hers.

"No, she did not," he answered, quietly. "She did not tell you anything else about me, then?"

"Nothing else."

He released her hands and went and stood by the window. Pauline had spared him, and he had not deserved to be spared. There was a curious dimness before his eyes. The girl's voice seemed to come from a long distance.

"After you left the island, it was miserable. I cannot tell you how miserable it was. He had one of his worst fits—for days he would not speak to me, and when he did speak he was cruel. So at last I ran away; I could not help it. You brought the light into my life, and when you went away I could not live there. The solitude was killing me. And then, poor Andrew!"

"What of him?"

"He is dead. He died soon after you left the island. He was dying all the time. I never knew it."

"And you—what have you been doing?" he asked.

"I had a little money, and an old man who is the husband of the landlady here was very good to me. He got me an engagement in the orchestra at the theatre where he plays. In the evenings I have gone there, and in the daytime I have spent a good many hours looking for you," she said, naively. "I was afraid that you might go back to the island and find me gone. They gave me a directory at the British Museum, and I looked out all the Hildyards. But there were so many, and I did not know exactly how it was spelt. And, after all, did you want me to go looking for you? When I thought of it I was ashamed. And then," she said, gravely, "there was that other woman. You seemed somehow to belong to her. Tell me. Do you love her? She is very beautiful."

He shook his head.

"No, I do not love her," he said. "I never have loved her. But she was my guest then, Bertha, and she was in a very terrible position. You know that her name is Owston, but you would not know that she was your guardian's wife."

"His wife!"

"Yes; they parted long ago, and when she came with the others for me, she did not expect to see him. It was a terrible meeting for her. She implored me to take her away at once, and I was bound to do so. I owed her that much, at any rate."

She put his hands calmly away from her. A sudden presentiment told him what was coming. His heart sank.

"You and she have been great friends?"

"We have been friends for many years."

She looked at him fixedly. "Hildyard," she said, "I am very ignorant. All that I know of men and women is from books. When you were on the island—just now too—you kissed me. Have you ever kissed that woman?"

"Yes."

She rose from her chair and picked up her violin case. Once more her face was white and strained. The delicate flush had died away. Her lips were trembling.

"Bertha," he pleaded, "forgive me. Since I was on the island I have scarcely spoken to her. Only a few days ago we parted. It was because of you. I have sinned, but when you know more of the world you will see things differently. Forgive me! I love you!"

He would have taken her into his arms, but a flash from her eyes stopped him.

"Don't touch me, please! I do forgive you! I will believe that the world judges those things leniently. But don't touch me! Let me go away."

She was at the door before he could speak. On the way her gown brushed against him. She drew it away with a little shudder. The gesture hurt him like a knife.

"You will not be so cruel," he cried, passionately. "I love you, Bertha—you only. I have never loved any one else."

"Then you have been a hypocrite," she said, coldly.

The door opened and closed. He covered his face with his hands. He was alone!

CHAPTER VI

Early in the morning a note was brought to Bertha by the young person with a fringe. She read it over her apology for a breakfast.

"Bertha, I am going away. Before I leave I must see you. I shall say nothing to offend you, or do anything. But I must see you! Say when I shall come."

The young person had brought the note with a sniff. She removed the breakfast things with a good deal of unnecessary clatter. Bertha did not notice anything. With the letter crumpled up in her hand, she sat looking out of the window—out on to a wilderness of slate roofs and a panorama of chimneys. The depression of it all sent a shudder through her. It was like her life, from which all sunshine seemed suddenly blotted out.

"Any answer to that note, miss?" the young person asked. She had finished clearing away things that had not been used, and was standing at the door, waiting to depart.

Bertha wrote a few rapid words.

"I am going for a short walk at eleven o'clock. If you wish to, you can come with me."

The young person watched them depart from behind the area railing with stern disdain. She did not approve of such goings on, or such sudden familiarities. She watched them until they disappeared, and then, shaking the dust from her mat viciously, went in and shut the door. The action was metaphorical. She resigned all interest in the new lodger.

Hildyard meanwhile was carefully acting up to an idea which had come to him in the middle of a sleepless night. He greeted his companion cordially, but with no trace in his manner of what had passed between them. He walked with her along the embankment, pointing out the different places of interest, talking very much as he would have done to a comparative stranger. Then, finding that she had not seen Westminster, he called a hansom and insisted upon a drive. Despite herself, she enjoyed it. The emotion was new to her; London, touched by the warm spring sunshine, seemed altogether a different place as they were bowled smoothly along the wooden pavements, in and out amongst the crowd of vehicles. He had judged rightly that much of the indignation of the night before would have passed away. So long as he was careful to keep from his voice and manner any note of affection, she was content to be with him. As the morning passed on his heart grew lighter. He was winning a footing. It was all that he desired.

They drove past Westminster Abbey and the Houses of Parliament into

Trafalgar Square, where Hildyard paid the cabman and sent him away. All the while he had been exerting himself to interest her, and had succeeded very easily. As a matter of fact, it was her first glimpse of the picturesque side of London. She could not help being amused. The time had passed like magic. Two o'clock was booming out from St. Martin's Church as they crossed the square.

"Where are we going to now?" she asked.

"To luncheon, of course!" he answered, with a little laugh. "Do you think that I want to starve you?"

He felt in his pocket and found he had a five-pound note. They walked down Pall Mall, and from a side street entered a little restaurant famous for its luncheons. With the *menu* in his hand, Hildyard gave an order which imbued the waiter with a respect not always paid to the wearer of a blue serge suit and a bowler hat in a fashionable part of London. It was served faultlessly. Bertha, to her surprise, found that she was hungry for the first time since she had been in London. Her meals in the little lodging-house had been a horror to her. Apart from the novelty of it, which in itself was charming, the luncheon was a great success.

Afterwards Hildyard turned westwards, overcoming with scarcely an effort the natural objection to being seen amongst his old haunts in his new character. The acquaintances whom he met he either ignored or greeted with a stern reserve which forbade any overtures on their part. Bertha, pale and with an innate distinction which made people, men especially, forget that her clothes were homely and plain, remained altogether unconscious of the fact that they were both the subject of much comment. Hildyard was equally indifferent to it. They spent an hour in a Bond Street picture-gallery, which was to her an hour of perfect happiness. Afterwards they had tea at a famous French confectioner's, where Bertha amused herself by watching the toilettes of the women. Then he called a hansom, and on the way home spoke to her seriously for the first time.

"Bertha," he said, "don't be afraid that I am going to transgress. I have done wrong, and like all wrong-doers I must bear my punishment. But I want you to understand this. Since you played me to you across the water, and I came to your island of Maros, there has been no other woman save yourself in my thoughts. I drew a line there in my life. I rooted up my past and tried to bury it. In a sense I have buried it. I am not going to make love to you. Don't be afraid. What I propose is this. Let us be friends. Let us remain as we have been to-day. I do not want to go away and leave you all alone."

She had retired into herself. Her manner was visibly colder, yet she answered as he desired.

"I am quite willing that we should be friends," she said. "I shall trust to what you say. It is to be as it has been to-day."

He assented, carefully concealing his inward exultation.

"There is one thing," he added. "I wish to be perfectly honest with you. Friends we are to be, and friends we will be—for the present. Until you yourself give me leave, I will not touch your hand or speak to you on any other subject. But I shall never cease to hope. There are three great things in the world, sin, repentance, and forgiveness. I have sinned, and I have repented. Some day I shall hope to be forgiven. I am prepared to wait, if it is necessary, for years, but it will always be there in my heart. I love you, and only you. There can never be anybody else. It is only right to tell you this."

He looked at her and sighed. She had turned very pale again, and her eyes were wet with tears, but they were not tears of yielding.

"I do not think that the old days can ever come again," she said slowly. "It is like a hideous nightmare. You seem to think that when I know more of life I shall judge differently. It is not my judgment at all—it is my feelings. Nothing can ever change those. You could not belong to me at all; you belong to her. When I think—that you have kissed me—I hate myself and I hate you. You had no right to. It was shameful. You ought to go back to her. Even if it was wrong of you to be with her, it was worse to leave her."

He set his teeth hard.

"I have buried the past," he said firmly. "There can be no resurrection. It is you—or no one. Now let it go. Turn over the page. We are friends. Who in the name of wonder is calling at our diggings?"

A victoria and pair, smart and immaculate, were drawn up opposite their shabby little abode. Hildyard frowned as he helped his companion out and dismissed the cabman. He did not doubt but that some of his friends had found him out and were intruding upon his seclusion. But at the door the young person met them with some agitation in her face.

"There's a lady here for you, miss—been here an hour or more. She's waiting in your room."

"What is her name?" asked Hildyard.

The girl produced a square of cardboard, on one corner of which was the impression of a dirty finger-mark. Hildyard took it from her and read,—

"Mrs. Herbert Mallalieu."

CHAPTER VII

For Hildyard the half-hour which followed was an intensely uncomfortable one. Bertha's name was Mallalieu—no doubt, this was some relation of hers who had found her out. He stood by his window looking gloomily into the street. An hour ago he had felt certain of her. Now everything was different. She would be taken away, introduced into a world which could not fail to be fascinating to a girl of her age and humour. All that he had meant to do himself would be done by others. Her attention would be distracted, she would be meeting other men every day. His great opportunity was slipping by. It was execrable ill fortune.

At last came the sound for which he had been listening. They were coming downstairs—both of them. At his door the footsteps halted. There was a knock. He threw it open. Bertha was there, dressed for the street, and by her side a woman, tall, slim, and elderly. She surveyed him calmly through a single eyeglass. Hildyard was thankful that he had not lit his lamp.

"I have come to say good-bye, Mr. Hildyard!" Bertha said, holding out her hand. "This is my aunt! She has come to fetch me. Mr. Owston sent over to her. I am going to stay with her for a little time."

Hildyard bowed to the woman, who was still steadily surveying him.

"This is rather a surprise," he said quietly. "I did not know that you had any relations in London."

The Honourable Mrs. Mallalieu closed her eyeglasses with a sudden snap.

"Miss Mallalieu was scarcely herself aware of it," she remarked coldly. "There were unfortunate differences between my late husband and Colonel Mallalieu. They do not, of course, influence me in the slightest. I am only too thankful to have found my niece."

Hildyard looked away into Bertha's face. What he saw made his heart leap for joy. There were tears in her eyes. Her lips were trembling.

"You have been very kind to me," she said softly. "I shall miss you. You will come and see me, won't you?"

"I shall hope to be allowed to do so," he answered, glancing at Mrs. Mallalieu.

She hesitated for a moment.

"My address is No. 15, Park Lane," she said. "I am at home on Sundays and Wednesdays. Come, Bertha, we must be going. Mr. Hildyard will excuse us, I know."

"You will be sure to come and see me," she said, looking at him, with a shade of entreaty in her face. After all, she was going amongst strangers.

She was very lonely. So her eyes grew soft as they challenged his.

"I shall come—to-morrow," he answered.

He stood at his window and watched them drive off—watched her whirled away into that new world from which he had come. Then he flung himself into an easy-chair with a little laugh. The flavour of the democracy had suddenly palled upon his palate. He looked around his little room and he hated it. Even the work which he had started with so much zeal had lost its savour. It would not bring her any nearer to him now. Life had seldom seemed to him an emptier thing.

Nevertheless, that night and most of the next day he spent writing. On the following afternoon, after leaving his bundle of manuscript in Fleet Street, he called at Park Lane. The ladies were not at home. He tried the next day with the same result. Yet as he was turning away he saw Mrs. Mallalieu and Bertha leaving the house and drive towards the Park.

For three days Hildyard sulked. On the fourth he called upon his favourite sister, the Duchess of Newark. She held up her hands in amazement when he was shown into the room.

"My dear Hildyard," she exclaimed, "I am delighted to see you. Where on earth have you dropped from? I have heard the most extraordinary tales about you. Sit down and let me give you some tea, at once. It is my not-at-home day, fortunately. Excuse me, but how oddly you are dressed."

Hildyard looked down at his blue serge suit and laughed.

"I have had an attack of democracy," he said. "I dare say that it would have developed, but I have fallen in love."

"My dear Hildyard!"

"It is perfectly true. Do you know Mrs. Mallalieu?"

"Yes, but—"

"Oh, no, I am not in love with her. The young lady is her niece."

"Oh, indeed! I have heard of her. A beauty, is she not, and an heiress?"

"I know nothing about her money, but she certainly is a beauty. Will you send them a card for your next crush?"

The Duchess hesitated.

"I must know all about it before I formally aid and abet you," she said. "Come, finish your tea and light a cigarette. I want to know everything."

He told her, if not everything, a good deal. Before he left the cards were sent.

Hildyard walked back to his rooms in better spirits. Perhaps, after all, democracy could get on without him. At any rate it would have to try.

CHAPTER VIII

The Duchess of Newark's receptions were the most popular in London, and Hildyard, who arrived a little late, wandered about the rooms for nearly half an hour without seeing anything of Mrs. Mallalieu or Bertha. Then fortune suddenly favoured him. He came face to face with Bertha talking to his brother-in-law.

At first she evidently did not know him. He had abandoned the garments of Chelsea, and all his old fastidiousness had reasserted itself. He was probably the best dressed man in the room—certainly one of the handsomest, and when he came to a standstill before her, Bertha uttered a little exclamation.

"Mr. Hildyard."

The Duke, hearing his brother-in-law's Christian name, raised his eyebrows and moved off smiling. Hildyard, knowing the house well, led her into a little anteroom.

"Fancy you're being here!" she exclaimed, laughing. "How odd! And how well you look!"

He took her hands into his and looked in her face.

"Bertha, I have a confession to make."

Instantly her face changed, she tried to withdraw her hands, but he held them firmly.

"It is nothing to be ashamed of," he added quickly. "Only I have not been quite honest. I want you to know now. It is about my name. The Duchess of Newark is my sister."

"I guessed that," she answered quietly. "Still I am glad that you told me."

He dropped her hands and looked at her amazed.

"You guessed it?"

"Yes."

Her face had darkened. The shadows of a certain dark memory had closed in upon her.

"I guessed it since you told me—about Mrs. Owston. One day a man told me that she had ruined—the Marquis of Esholt. I did not think then that it was you."

"It was a cruel thing to say," he exclaimed. "It was not true. I alone—my own folly, my own recklessness were to blame. But, Bertha, I am not altogether ruined. For a few years I am poor, but things will come round. I have been an idiot, blind, foolish, wicked, but it is over. I want to start a new life—and you know what else I want. I want you to share it."

She looked sadly into his eyes. Her lips were quivering.

"I cannot," she said. "You know I cannot."

"I know nothing of the sort," he answered fiercely. "What do you think men are, Bertha? They are not saints; you know nothing of life. I have sinned, but who is there without sin?"

"You could not belong to me," she cried. "There is another woman who has a greater claim. You gave it her yourself. You cannot take it away."

"It is madness. I do not love her."

"You have loved her. If I did not believe that you had, I would not speak to you—I would not let you dare to speak to me. She loves you still. You belong to her. If your love has grown weak, hers has not."

"I have bidden her farewell. We have parted. Nothing shall drag me back to her."

For a moment there was silence between them. A sound of distant music, blending with the low notes of hushed conversation and the clatter of teacups, floated into their retreat. Bertha shivered, and drew a little further back into the room. A sudden passion mastered him. He drew her, only feebly resisting, into his arms and kissed her lips. She began to cry softly.

"Don't, don't," she moaned, "you are hurting me."

He let her go, but still held her hand. He was pale to the lips. His voice shook.

"She will have other lovers, Bertha," he whispered. "Sooner than touch her hand again I would die. Don't you know that I love you? Don't you know what love is? you—"

"Hush!"

She dried her eyes. The white despair of her face maddened him.

"You do not know. You have not read the papers. She is very ill. It is because you have left her. She loved you, she loves you still. You belong to her. And I love you. I—love you."

He dropped her hand and stood with dogged face and folded arms.

"She is nothing to me now," he said. "I will not go back to her. If you send me away, I will go away for ever. But I will not go to her. I am sick with shame when I think of what has been; there shall be no more of it."

She clasped her hands and looked steadily upon the floor.

"I may be wrong," she said softly. "I know nothing of life. But if it was sin to love her, it seems to me to be still greater sin to desert her. Nothing can alter how I feel about it."

Then there was a long silence. When she looked up, she was alone.

CHAPTER IX

In less than an hour after Hildyard had left the house in Mayfair and had set his face towards Chelsea, Pauline Owston left it too. She came down plainly dressed and followed by her maid, who carried a small hand-bag. In the hall she called the butler and gave him two notes.

"Take a hansom, Groves," she said, "and deliver these two notes immediately. One is to Mr. Ayres, Lord Esholt's solicitor, in Bedford Place, and the other is for Mr. Maddison, at the Novelty Theatre. You had better take that one first, and deliver it into his own hands."

"Certainly, madam."

"And call me a hansom, please."

Groves whistled for a cab, and she stepped into it, followed by her maid.

"Where to, madam?" Groves inquired from the pavement.

She hesitated. As a matter of fact she had not the least idea. In her haste to be out of the house she had not even considered the question of where she should go to. It made so little difference.

"Tell him to drive on slowly," she directed. "I will speak to him again."

In time they arrived at Bloomsbury. She found some cheap lodgings, in a side street, and took them. Then she turned to her astonished maid.

"Céleste," she said, "I am sorry to lose you, but I shall not require you any more. You must leave me here."

"But, madam," Céleste exclaimed with uplifted hands, "you require to be dressed. It is time to start for the theatre. There is no one who can arrange your hair save myself."

"I am not going to the theatre to-night," Pauline answered. "I am not going there any more. You must not ask me anything about it. I cannot tell you. Here are three months' wages. I only ask one thing of you: if any one inquires of you concerning me or my whereabouts, you know nothing. You understand. You know nothing."

"But madam—"

"Good-bye, Céleste; not another word."

The girl went. Pauline was accustomed to being obeyed.

The sudden withdrawl of Mrs. Stanley Owston from the stage created something akin to a sensation. The truth only leaked out piecemeal. For several days the papers were full of her alarming illness. Then hints began to appear, wild rumours were floated about as to her reasons for this abrupt retirement in the midst of her brilliant and wholly unexpected success. It began to be understood that this retirement was a fact accomplished. The Novelty Theatre closed its doors. Mrs. Owston's settlement, her jewels, and the lease of the theatre were handed over to Mr. Ayres on behalf of his client the Marquis of Esholt. Hildyard received this information on his return from the reception at Newark House, and tore the letter into fragments. Meanwhile a Mrs. Harrison, who had taken rooms in a retired street near Bloomsbury Square, and went about very closely veiled, paid a visit to several respectable chemists in the vicinity, and then feigning a slight indisposition, shut herself up in her room.

On the night after her flight she took out her purse and counted her money. She had a little over five and twenty pounds. A twenty-pound note she put aside for a certain purpose, addressed to her landlady. The remaining five pounds, allowing for a liberal fee to the servant who waited upon her, would pay her bill for fourteen days. She paid it in advance, and locked up some little grey powders, collected from the chemists, in a drawer.

One by one the days went by. She never went out, she scarcely left her room. Often she sat for hours together without moving, looking absently out of the window, and thinking very childish thoughts. Once or twice she found her eyes wet. This made her impatient.

The last day came. Towards evening she called for a pen and paper, and wrote:

"My friend," she wrote. "When you have read these lines, burn them. I had meant to leave the world without adieux, and without remark. I changed my mind, not for my own sake, but for yours. I write to you lest you should at any time blame yourself, or think that you were in any way the cause of my—what shall I call it?—removal. That is not so. It would have come to this in any case. I am too utterly and miserably weary of life to continue in it any longer.

"When I left my husband the thing began. I lost hold of my self-respect, and the love which I had expected to be all sufficing flitted away like a moonlight dream. I made a discovery which your set and mine would laugh to hear—that after all there is something in virtue. The flashes of happiness which I have had during these last seven years, have been followed by periods of corresponding depression. With you I was almost happy. Consequently, now that we are parted I am more miserable than ever. I was very near loving you, Hildyard; and if you had cared for me, if this love had come, the shame and darkness in which my soul seemed to dwell would have passed away. But without that love the stain grew blacker and blacker. Ah, I could never make you understand. I will not try. Remember you are not to blame. All that you promised you gave, only you did not understand me, and when you, too, treated me like a paid mistress whose time of hiring had expired, my heart broke. We all have to die, only, as the process is a lingering one, I am going to hasten it a little. And so farewell, my friend. There is a little wine-glass before me in which I will not drink your health. But all good things I wish you and—farewell."

Her pen stopped. She took an envelope and addressed it. Then she leaned back in her chair.

It was five minutes to eight. She would take it at the first stroke of the hour. She drew the wine-glass nearer to her. How swiftly the long hand was travelling. She could almost see it move. Then her eyes grew dim. She could not see distinctly. The room seemed suddenly full of phantoms. There was her husband, leaning over her tenderly—looking into her face as no other man had ever looked—and by his side a little girl. Ah, it was Pauline, with her hair wildly tumbled and her cheeks flushed with running, holding up her lips to be kissed.

A little dry sob nearly choked her. This was torture. Would the hour never come? Ah! there was the click. Desperately her hand clasped the thin stem of the wine-glass. She raised it. Was that a knock? No matter, the hour was striking. She threw her head back and the glass touched her lips. But it did not move. She was paralyzed.

Before her she saw a phantom, that was no phantom—the incarnation of her most poignant memory. The door was wide open—a man stood upon the threshold gazing at her. It was her husband. There was a look upon his face—what did it mean? She must be going mad. The wine-glass slipped from her nerveless fingers and fell with a crash upon the floor. On the carpet was a deep stain.

CHAPTER X

He closed the door and came into the room. She stood quite still, her hands locked in one another, and her eyes fastened upon him. When he spoke his voice sounded like the echo of dead days. She began dimly to wonder whether this was a rehearsal of a new comedy. Was she acting, or was she playing a real part in a scene from her own life? Or had she swallowed the poison, and was this hell?

"I have found you then, Pauline," he said. "Don't look at me like that. I am not here to hurt you."

As soon as he had spoken she recovered herself. She could understand his coming: he probably coveted the pleasure of reviling her. What she could not understand was his tone, and the look on his face.

He came quite close to her and spoke again.

"Pauline," he said, "on the island I lied to you. There was a girl there. I told you that she was your daughter. It was false."

She felt a little faint. The floor rose up beneath her feet—the ceiling was spinning. Only his face was steadfast before her eyes. She clutched at the table and leaned over towards him.

"Not my daughter—not Pauline? Who was she, then?"

"She was the daughter of my old friend, Colonel Mallalieu. He died at war with all his kin, and left me his executor and her guardian."

"Why did you tell me that it was Paul—my daughter?"

"It was a sudden, devilish impulse. When I saw that he—was with her, the idea flashed into my brain. I judged that it would torture you."

"You were right."

He pushed the thick black hair from his forehead. She could see that he was pale and travel-stained.

"I should like," she said slowly, "to ask you a question. You may say that I have no right to ask it—and I have no right. But to-night you looked merciful. Perhaps you will tell me. My daughter Pauline—is she alive?"

"She is alive," he answered. "She is well. I have come to-night from her to you."

An unconquerable agitation mastered her. She shook all over. Her eyeballs were burning, but they were dry. She could not speak. He was standing opposite to her with one hand resting upon the table. There was a purpose in his set face. She listened to him fascinated.

"Pauline has been at school in France," he continued. "I went to see her recently—and I had a shock, I admit it. I had grown into the belief that our past—yours and mine—was dead, that the grave of it was sealed with an everlasting seal, that there could be no resurrection. But I looked into her eyes—they are your eyes—and a strange, new feeling came to me. The burden of these intolerable years seemed to grow lighter. She asked for her mother, and when I was tired of evading her questions, I asked myself, Why should she be for ever motherless? I have come to ask you that, Pauline."

"Stanley! Great God, what is it that you are saying?"

He held up his hand.

"I mean it. She put her arms around my neck and asked for her mother; and I remembered the day when we stood together in the old Rectory garden, hand in hand, and I asked myself, of those dark things that lay between us, whose was the greater fault?"

He was leaning over towards her, pale, but inspired by his own earnestness. She was trembling from head to foot.

"Stanley, you forget—you forget," she moaned. "I—"

He stopped her with a gesture full of dignity.

"I forget nothing," he declared solemnly. "You have sinned. Well, I too have sinned, and my sin was the cause of yours. You came to me as pure as one of God's angels. I was not fit to touch your fingers. That cursed doctrine which makes one law for the man and another for the woman, numbered me also amongst its disciples. The day came when you learned the truth, when you looked into my eyes with an unutterable disgust, and knew me for what I was. You were hard upon me, Pauline, but I should have made allowances. How were you, the motherless daughter of a country clergyman, to look with large eyes and merciful heart upon what must have seemed to you then such mortal sin? You had ideals, and I blasted them. With my own hands I drew aside the veil and showed you what the worst part of a man was like. Even now I can hear the echo of your hard little laugh, as I finished my explanations and excuses. The memory of it has lived with me all these years. It was I, Pauline, who brought the poison into your life. In my heart I know you to be still a pure woman. Give me your hand to-night, and let me take you to our daughter. If you will do this, I have no fear as to the future."

"But—but the world?"

"Imagine the triumph." He laughed with a touch of his old cynicism. "We shall give the world a new sensation, and—you have no idea how like Pauline is to you."

"Stanley!"

Her face shone. She fell into his arms. Then a horrible fear blanched her cheeks. He divined it.

"She shall never know," he whispered. "As I am a man, I swear it."

The door was suddenly opened. A girl, tall and slender, with fair, expectant face, stood on the threshold. She gave one glance into Pauline's face and flew into her outstretched arms.

"Mother! mother!" she cried. "Forgive me, but I could not wait any longer."

"My child!"

Stanley Owston thrust his hands into his pockets and tried to feel like a cynic. On the contrary, he felt like a young man. A weight of years had rolled away. This was happiness.

❧

Hildyard, with a "Bradshaw" in his hand, labouring amidst a roomful of packing-cases, saw a familiar name on the upturned sheet of a society paper, and paused. He read the little notice through with bland amazement.

"Mr. and Mrs. Stanley Owston are leaving England on Saturday by the P. and O. *Elba* for a tour in the East. We learn with pleasure that Mrs. Stanley Owston has completely recovered from her recent illness, although she has no intention of returning to the stage. Mr. Owston, who is a naturalist of distinction, has been entrusted by the Royal Geographical Society with the task of editing their forthcoming treatises on the Flora of Japan and South America, and proposes to spend some considerable time in both of those countries. He will be accompanied by both his wife and daughter."

Hildyard threw away his "Bradshaw" and jumped into a hansom. In ten minutes he was in Mrs. Mallalieu's drawing-room, the paper in his hand. Bertha came to him at once, and without a word he showed her the paragraph. She looked away out of the window.

"I know all about it," she said softly, "I have seen them both."

"It makes—a difference," he faltered.

She flashed a brilliant smile upon him.

"I think—perhaps—it does."

THE END

Mr. Laxworthy's Adventures

E. Phillips Oppenheim

CHAPTER I
The Secret of the "Magnifique"

The man was awaiting the service of his dinner in the magnificent buffet of the Gare de Lyons. He sat at a table laid for three, on the right-hand side of the entrance and close to the window. From below came the turmoil of the trains. Every few minutes the swing doors opened to admit little parties of travellers. The solitary occupant of the table scarcely ever moved his head. Yet he had always the air of one who watches.

In appearance he was both unremarkable and undistinguished. He was of somewhat less than medium height, of unathletic, almost frail physique. His head was thrust a little forward, as though he were afflicted with a chronic stoop. He wore steel-rimmed spectacles with the air of one who has taken to them too late in life to have escaped the constant habit of peering, which had given to his neck an almost stork-like appearance. His hair and thin moustache were iron-grey, his fingers long and delicate. The labels upon his luggage were addressed in a trim, scholarly hand:

Mr. John T. Laxworthy,

Passenger to—,

Via Paris.

A *maître d'hôtel*, who was passing, paused and looked at the two as yet unoccupied places.

"Monsieur desires the service of his dinner?" he inquired.

Mr. John T. Laxworthy glanced up at the clock and carefully compared the time with his own watch. He answered the man's inquiry in French which betrayed no sign of any accent.

"In five minutes," he declared, "my friends will have arrived. The service of dinner can then proceed."

The man bowed and withdrew, a little impressed by his customer's trim precision of speech. Almost as he left the table, the swing door opened once more to admit another traveller. The new-comer stood on the threshold for a moment, looking around him. He carried a much-belabelled dressing-case in his hand, and an umbrella under his arm. He stood firmly upon his feet, and a more thoroughly British, self-satisfied, and obvious person had, to all appearances, never climbed those stairs. He wore a travelling-suit of dark grey, a check ulster, broad-toed boots, and a Homburg hat. His complexion was sandy, and his figure distinctly toward corpulence. He wore scarcely noticeable side-whiskers, and his chin and upper lip were clean-shaven. His eyes were bright, and his mouth had an upward and humorous turn. His initials upon his bag were *W. F. A.*, and a printed label upon the same indicated his full name as:

MR. W. FORREST ANDERSON,
Passenger to—,
Via Paris.

His brief contemplation of the room was soon over. His eyes fell upon the solitary figure, now deep in his book, seated at the table on his right. He set down his dressing-case by the side of the wall, yielded his coat and hat to the attendant *vestiaire*, and, with the pleased smile of one who greets an old friend, approached the table at which Mr. John T. Laxworthy sat waiting.

The idiosyncrasies of great men are always worth noting, and Mr. John T. Laxworthy was, without a doubt, foredoomed from the cradle to a certain measure of celebrity. His method of receiving the new-comer was in some respects curious. From the moment when the swing doors had been pushed open and the portly figure of Mr. Forrest Anderson had crossed the threshold, his eyes had not once quitted the heavy-looking volume, the contents of which appeared so completely to absorb his attention. Even now, when his friend stood by his side, he did not at once look up. Slowly, and with his eyes still riveted upon the pages he was studying, he held out his left hand.

"I am glad to see you, Anderson," he said. "Sit down by my side here. You are nearly ten minutes late. I have delayed ordering the wine until your arrival. Shall it be white or red?"

Mr. Anderson shook with much heartiness the limp fingers which had been offered to him, and took the seat indicated. His friend's eccentricity of manner appeared to be familiar to him, and he offered no comment upon it.

"White, if you please—Chablis of a dry brand, for choice. Sorry if I'm late. Beastly crossing, beastly crowded train. Glad to be here, anyhow."

Mr. John T. Laxworthy closed his book with a little sigh of regret, and placed a marker within it. He then carefully adjusted his spectacles and made a deliberate survey of his companion. Finally he nodded, slowly and approvingly.

"How about the partridges?" he inquired.

"Bad," Mr. Anderson declared, with a sigh. "It was one storm in June that did it. We went light last season, though, and I'm putting down forty braces of Hungarians. You see—"

Mr. Laxworthy touched the table with his forefinger, and his companion almost automatically stopped.

"Quite excellent," the former pronounced dryly. "Don't overdo it. I should think that this must be Sydney."

Mr. Anderson glanced towards the entrance. Then he looked back at his companion a little curiously. Mr. Laxworthy had not raised his head.

"How the dickens did you know that it was Sydney?" he demanded.

Mr. Laxworthy smiled at the tablecloth.

"I have a special sense for that sort of thing," he remarked. "I like to use my eyes as seldom as possible."

A young man who had just completed a leisurely survey of the room dropped his monocle and came towards them. From the tops of his shiny tan shoes to his smoothly brushed hair, he was unmistakable. He was young, he was English, he was well-bred, he was an athlete. He had a pleasant, unintelligent face, a natural and prepossessing ease of manner. He handed his ulster to the attendant *vestiaire* and beamed upon the two men.

"How are you, Forrest? How do you do, Laxworthy?" he exclaimed. "Looking jolly fit, both of you."

Mr. Laxworthy raised his glass. He looked thoughtfully at the wine for a moment, to be sure that it was free from any atom of cork. Then he inclined his head in turn to each of his companions.

"I am glad to see you both," he said. "On the whole, I think that I may congratulate you. You have done well. I drink to your success."

The toast was drunk in silence. Mr. Forrest Anderson set down his glass—empty—with a little murmur of content.

"It is something," he remarked, vigorously attacking a new course, "to have satisfied our chief."

The young man opposite him subjected the dish which was being offered to a long and deliberate survey through his eyeglass, and finally refused it.

"Give me everything in France except the beef," he declared. "Must be the way they cut it, I think. Quite right, Andy," he went on, glancing across the table. "To have satisfied such a critic as the chief here is an achievement indeed. Having done it, let us hear what he proposes to do with us."

"In other words," Mr. Anderson put in, "what is the game to be?"

There was a short pause. Mr. John T. Laxworthy was continuing his repast—which was, by the by, of a much more frugal character than that offered to his guests—without any sign of having even heard the inquiry addressed to him by his companions. They knew him, however, and they were content to wait. Presently he commenced to peel an apple and simultaneously to unburden himself.

"A great portion of this last year," he said, "which you two have spent apparently with profit in carrying out my instructions, I myself have devoted to the perfection of a certain scholarly tome which I feel convinced is my proper environment. Incidentally, I have devoted myself to the study of various schools of philosophy."

"I will take a liqueur," decided the young man whose name was Sydney— "something brain-stimulating. A *Grand Marnier*, waiter, if you please."

"The same for me," Mr. Forrest Anderson put in hastily. "Also, in a few moments, some black coffee."

Mr. Laxworthy did not by the flicker of an eyelid betray the slightest annoyance at these interruptions. He waited, indeed, until the liqueurs had been brought before he spoke again, continuing the while in a leisurely fashion the peeling and preparing of his apple. Even for some time after his friends had again offered him their undivided attention, he continued his task of extracting from it, with precise care, every fragment of core.

"In one very interesting treatise," he recommenced at last, "I found several obvious truths ingeniously put. A certain decadence in the material prosperity of an imaginary state is clearly proved to be due to a too-blind following of the tenets of what is known as the hysterical morality, as against the decrees of what we might call expediency. A little sentiment, like garlic in cookery, is a good thing; too much is fatal. A little—sufficient—morality is excellent; a superabundance disastrous. Society is divided into two classes, those who have and those who desire to have. The one must always prey upon the other. They are, therefore, always changing places. It is this continued movement which lends energy to the human race. As soon as it is suspended, degeneration must follow as a matter of course. It is for those who recognise this great truth to follow and obey its tenets."

"May we not hear more definitely what it is that you propose?" Anderson asked, a little anxiously.

"We stand," Mr. Laxworthy replied, "always upon the threshold of the land of adventure. At no place are we nearer to it than in this room. It is our duty to use our energies to assist in the great principles of movement to which I have referred. We must take our part in the struggle. On which side? you naturally ask. Are we to be amongst those who have, and who, through weakness or desire, must yield to others? Or shall we take our place amongst the more intellectual, the more highly gifted minority, those who assist the progress of the world by helping towards the redistribution of its wealth? Sydney, how much money have you?"

"Three hundred and ninety-five franks and a few coppers," the young man answered promptly. "It sounds more in French."

"And you, Anderson?"

Mr. Forrest Anderson coughed.

"With the exception of a five-franc piece," he admitted, "I am worth exactly as much as I shall be able to borrow from you presently."

"In that case," Mr. Laxworthy said dryly, "our position is preordained. We take our place amongst the aggressors."

The young man whose name was Sydney dropped his eyeglass.

"One moment," he said. "Andy here and I have exposed our financial impecuniosity at your request. It can scarcely be a surprise to you, considering that we have practically lived upon your bounty for the last year. It seems only fair that you should imitate our candour. There were rumours, a short time ago, of a considerable sum of money to which you had become entitled. To tell you the truth," the young man went on, leaning a little across the table, "we were almost afraid, or rather I was, that you might abandon this shadowy enterprise of ours."

Mr. John T. Laxworthy, without being discomposed, which was almost too much to expect of a man with such perfect poise, seemed nevertheless somewhat taken aback. He opened his lips as though to make some reply, and closed them again. When he did speak, it was grudgingly.

"No successful enterprise, or series of enterprises, can be conducted without capital," he said. "I am free to admit that I am in possession of a certain amount of that indispensable commodity. I do not feel myself called upon to state the exact amount, but such money as is required for our journeyings, or for any enterprise in which we become engaged, will be forthcoming."

Mr. Anderson stroked his chin meditatively.

"I am sure," he said, "that that sounds quite satisfactory."

"I call it jolly fine business," the young man declared. "There is just one thing more upon which I think we ought to have an understanding. You say that we are to take our place amongst the aggressors. Exactly what does that mean?"

Mr. Laxworthy looked at him coldly.

"It means precisely what I choose that it shall mean," he replied. "Any enterprise or adventure in which we may become engaged will be selected by me, and by me only. My chief aim—I have no objection to telling you this—is to make life tolerable for ourselves, to escape the dull monotony of idleness, and, incidentally, to embrace any opportunity which may present itself to enrich our exchequer. Have you any objection to that?"

"None," Mr. Forrest Anderson declared.

"None at all," Sydney echoed.

"There are three of us," Mr. Laxworthy went on. "We each have our use. Mine is the chief of all. I supply the brains. My position must be unquestioned."

"For my part, I am willing enough," Sydney remarked. "It's been your show from the first."

Mr. Forrest Anderson, who had dined well and forgotten his empty pockets, laughed a genial laugh.

"I agree," he declared. "Tell us, when and where do we start, and shall our first enterprise be Pickwickian, or am I to play the Sancho Panza to your Don Quixote and Sydney's donkey?"

Mr. Laxworthy regarded his associates coldly. There was a silence, a silence which became somehow an ominous thing. Around them reigned a babel of tongues, a clatter of crockery. Below, the turmoil of the busy station, the shrieking of departing trains. But at the table presided over by Mr. Laxworthy no word was spoken. Mr. Anderson's geniality faded away. His young companion's amiable nonchalance entirely deserted him. Either of them would have given worlds to have been able to dispel the strange effect of this silence with some casual remark. But upon them lay the spell of the conqueror. The little man at the head of the table held them in the hollow of his hand.

"It may be," he said, breaking at last that curious silence, "that no other occasion will ever arise when it will be necessary to speak to you in this fashion. So now listen. You are right to indulge in the urbanities of existence. Keep always the smile upon your lips, if you can, but underneath let the real consciousness of life be ever present. I do not claim for myself the genius of a Pickwick or the valour of a Don Quixote. On the other hand, we are not paltry aggressors against Society, failing in one enterprise, successful in the next, a mark for ridicule and contempt one moment, and for good-humoured sufferance the next. I do not ask you to embark with me as *farceurs* upon a series of enterprises carried out upon the principle of 'Let us do our best and chance the rest.' It is just possible that the fates may be against us, and that we may live together for many months the lives of ordinary and moderately commonplace human beings. I ask you to remember that no sense of danger would ever deter me from embarking upon any adventure which I deemed likely to afford us either diversion, wealth, or satisfaction of any sort whatsoever. We are not pleasure-seekers. We are men whose one end and aim is to escape from the chains of everyday existence, to avoid the humdrum life of our fellows. Therein may lie for us many and peculiar dangers. Adopt, if you will, the motto of the pagans—'Let us eat and drink, for to-morrow we die!' So long as you remember. Will you drink with me to that remembrance?"

Mr. Laxworthy, as he grew less enigmatic in his speech, became, if possible, more whimsical in his mannerisms. He ordered the best Cognac, at which he himself scarcely glanced, and turned with a little sigh of relief to his book. In the midst of this hubbub of sounds and bustle of diners he continued to read with every appearance of studious enjoyment. His two companions were content enough, apparently, to relax after their journey and enjoy their cigars. Nevertheless, they once or twice glanced curiously at their chief. One of these glances he seemed, although he never raised his head, to have intercepted, for, carefully marking the place in his book, he pushed it away and addressed them.

"Our plans," he announced abruptly, "are not yet wholly made. We wait here for—shall we call it an inspiration? Perhaps, even at this moment, it is not far from us."

Mr. Forrest Anderson and his *vis-à-vis* turned as though instinctively toward the door. At that moment two men who had just passed through were standing upon the threshold. One was rather past middle-age, corpulent, with red features of a coarse type. His companion, who was leaning upon his arm, was much younger, and a very different sort of person. He was tall and exceedingly thin. His features were wasted almost to emaciation, his complexion was ghastly. He seemed to have barely strength enough to move.

"They are coming to the table next us," Laxworthy said, in a very low tone. "The address upon their luggage will be interesting."

Slowly the two men came down the room. As Laxworthy had expected, they took possession of an empty table close at hand. The young man sank into his chair with a little sigh of exhaustion.

"A liqueur brandy, quick," the older man ordered, as he accepted the menu from a waiter. "My friend is fatigued."

Sydney took the bottle which stood upon their own table, poured out a wineglassful, and rising to his feet, stepped and accosted the young man.

"Do me the favour of drinking this, sir," he begged. "The service here is slow and the brandy is excellent. I can see that you are in need of it. It may serve, too, as an *apéritif.*"

The young man accepted it with a smile of gratitude. His companion echoed his thanks.

"Very much obliged to you, sir," he declared. "My friend here is a little run down and finds travelling fatiguing."

"A passing malady, I trust?" Sydney remarked, preparing to return to his seat.

"A legacy from a cursed graveyard—South Africa," the older man growled.

Sydney stepped back and resumed his seat. In a few minutes he leaned across the table.

"The Paradise Hotel, Hyères," he said under his breath.

Mr. Laxworthy looked thoughtful.

"You surprise me," he admitted.

"What do you know of them?" Anderson inquired.

Mr. Laxworthy shrugged his shoulders.

"Not much beyond the obvious facts," he admitted. "Even you, my friends, are not wholly deceived, I presume, by the young man's appearance?"

They evidently were. Their faces expressed their non-comprehension. Mr. Laxworthy sighed.

"You must both of you seek to develop the minor senses," he enjoined reprovingly. "Your powers of observation, for instance, are, without doubt, exceedingly stunted. Let me assure you, for example, that your sympathy for that young man is entirely wasted."

"You mean that he is not really ill?" Sydney asked incredulously.

"Most certainly he is not as ill as he pretends," Mr. Laxworthy declared dryly. "If you look at him more closely, you will discover a certain theatricality in his pose which of itself should undeceive you."

"You know who he is?" Sydney asked.

"I believe so," Laxworthy admitted. "I can hazard a guess even as to his companion's identity. But—the Paradise Hotel, Hyères! Order some fresh coffee. We are not ready to leave yet. Anderson, watch the door. Sydney, don't let them notice it, but watch our friends there. Something may happen."

A tall, broad-shouldered man with a fair moustache and wearing a long travelling-coat had entered the buffet. He stood there for a moment looking around, as through in search of a table. The majority of those present suffered his scrutiny, unnoticing, indifferent, naturally absorbed in themselves and their own affairs. Not so these two men who had last arrived. Every nerve of the young man's body seem to have become tense. His hand had stolen into the pocket of his travelling-coat, and with a little thrill Sydney saw the glitter of steel half shown for a moment between his interlocking fingers. No longer was this young man's countenance the countenance of an invalid. It had become instead like the face of a wolf. His front teeth were showing—he had moved slightly so as to give his arm full play. It seemed as though a tragedy were at hand.

The man who had been standing on the threshold deposited his handbag upon the floor near the wall and came slowly down the room. Laxworthy and his two associates watched. Their two neighbours at the next table sat in well simulated indifference, only once more Sydney saw the gleam of hidden steel flash for a moment from the depths of that ulster pocket. The new-comer made no secret of his destination. He advanced straight to their table and came to a standstill immediately in front of them. Both the stout man and his invalid companion looked up at him as one might regard a stranger.

To all appearances Laxworthy was engrossed in his book. Sydney and Anderson watched and listened, but of all the words which passed between those three men, not one was audible. No change of countenance on the part of any one of the three indicated even the nature of that swift and fluent interchange of words. Only at the last, the elder man touched the label attached to his dressing-bag, and they heard his words:

"The Paradise Hotel, Hyères. We shall be there for at least a month."

The new-comer stood perfectly still for several moments, as though deliberating. The young man's hand came an inch or two from his pocket. Chance and tragedy trifled together in the midst of that crowded room, unnoticed save by those three at the adjoining table. Then, as though inspired with a sudden resolution, this stranger, whose coming had seemed so unwelcome, raised his hat slightly to the two men with whom he had been talking, and turned away.

"The Paradise Hotel at Hyères," he repeated. "I shall know, then, where to find you."

The little scene was over. Nothing had happened. Nevertheless, the fingers of the young man, as his hand emerged from his pocket, were moist and damp, and his appearance was now veritably ghastly. His companion watched, with a deep purple flush upon his face, the passing of this stranger who had accosted him. He had the appearance of one threatened with apoplexy.

"One might be interested to know the meaning of these things," Sydney murmured softly.

Their chief looked up from his book.

"Then one must follow—to the Paradise Hotel," he remarked.

"I begin to believe," Anderson declared, "that it is our destination."

"There is no hurry," Laxworthy replied. "Grimes once told me that this room in which we are now sitting was perhaps the most interesting rendezvous in Europe. Grimes was at the head of the Foreign Department at Scotland Yard in those days, and he knew what he was talking about."

A woman, wrapped in magnificent furs, who was passing their table, was run into by a clumsy waiter and dropped a satchel from her finger. Sydney hastened to restore it to her, and was rewarded by a gracious smile in which was mingled a certain amount of recognition.

"You seem fated to be my Good Samaritan to-day," she remarked.

"It is my good fortune," the young man replied. "Can I help you to get a table or anything? This place is always overcrowded."

She motioned with her head to where a *maître d'hôtel* was holding a chair for her.

"It is already arranged," she said. "Perhaps we shall meet in the *Luxe* afterwards, if you are going south."

"You are travelling far?" Sydney ventured to inquire.

"Only to the outskirts of the Riviera," she answered. "I am going to Hyères—to the Paradise Hotel. Why do you smile?"

"My friends and I," he explained, "have met here to decide upon the whereabouts of a little holiday we mean to spend together. We were at that moment discussing a suggestion to proceed to the same place."

She gave him a little farewell nod as she passed on.

"If you decide to do so," she declared, "it will give me great pleasure to meet you again."

"I congratulate you," Laxworthy remarked dryly, as Sydney resumed his seat. "A most interesting acquaintance, yours."

"Do you know who she is?" the young man asked. "I only met her on the train."

His chief nodded gravely.

"She is a Madame Bertrand," he replied. "Her husband at one time held a post in the Foreign Office, under Faure. For some reason or other he was discredited, and since then he has died. There was some scandal about Madame Bertrand herself, and some papers which were missing from her husband's portfolio, but nothing definite ever came to light."

"Madame seems to survive the loss of her husband," Mr. Forrest Anderson remarked, looking at her admiringly.

Laxworthy held up his hand. Almost for the first time he was sitting upright in his chair, his head still thrust forward in his usual attitude, his eyes fixed upon the door. The thin fingers of his right hand were spread flat upon the tablecloth.

"We have finished for the moment, with the Madame Bertrands of the world," he announced. "After all, they are for the pigmies. Here comes food for giants."

The light of battle was in Laxworthy's eyes. The greatest of men have their moments of weakness, and even Laxworthy, for that brief space of time, forgot himself and his pose toward the world. His thin lips were a little parted, the veins at the sides of his forehead stood out like blue cords. His lips moved slowly.

"You can both look," he said. "They are probably used to it. You will see the two greatest personages on earth."

His companions gazed eagerly toward the door. Two men were standing there, being relieved of their wraps and directed toward a table. One was middle-aged, grey-headed, with a somewhat worn but keen face.. The other was taller, with black hair streaked with grey, a face half Jewish, half romantic, a skin like ivory.

"The greatest men in the world?" Sydney repeated, under his breath. "You are joking, chief. I never saw even a photograph of either of them before in my life."

"The one nearest you," Laxworthy announced, "is Mr. Freeling Poignton. The newspapers will tell you that his fortune exceeds the national debt of any country in the world. He is, without doubt, the richest man that was ever born. There has never yet breathed an emperor whose upraised finger could provoke or stop a war, whose careless word could check the prosperity of the proudest nation that ever breathed. These things Mr. Freeling Poignton can do."

"And the other?" Anderson whispered.

"It is chance," Mr. Laxworthy said softly, "which placed a sceptre of unlimited power in the hands of Richard Freeling Poignton. It is his own genius which has made the Marquis Lefant the greatest power in the diplomatic world. It was his decision which brought about war between Russia and Japan. It was he who stopped the declaration of war against Germany by our own Prime Minister at the time of the Algeciras difficulty. It was he who was offered a million pounds to bring the Tsar of Russia to Germany—and he did it. There is little that he cannot do."

"Is he a German?" Anderson asked.

"No one knows of what race he comes," Mr. Laxworthy replied. "No one knows what country is really nearest to his heart. It is his custom to accept commissions or refuse them, according to his own belief as to their influence upon international peace. They say that he has English blood in his veins. If so, he has been a sorry friend to his native land."

"We seem," Sydney remarked, "to have chosen a very fortunate evening for our little dinner here. The place is full of interesting people. I wonder where those two are going."

A *maître d'hôtel,* whose respect had been gained by the lavish orders from their table, paused and whispered confidentially in Mr. Laxworthy's ear.

"The gentleman down there, sir," he announced, "the grey gentleman with his own servant waiting upon him, is Mr. Freeling Poignton, the great American multi-millionaire."

Laxworthy nodded slowly.

"I thought I recognized him by his photographs," he said. "Is he going to Monte Carlo?"

The attendant shook his head.

"I was speaking to him a moment ago, sir," he declared. "Mr. Poignton has been here a good many times. He and his friends are going for a fortnight's quiet to the Paradise Hotel at Hyères."

The *maître d'hôtel* passed on with another bow. The three men looked at one another. Mr. Laxworthy glanced at the clock.

"Sydney," he said, "will you step down into the bureau and find out whether it is possible to get three seats in the train *de luxe?*"

"For Hyères?" Sydney asked.

Mr. Laxworthy assented gravely.

"Certainly," he said. "You might at the same time telegraph to the hotel."

"To the Paradise Hotel?"

Mr. Laxworthy inclined his head.

A black cloud, long and with jagged edges, passed away from the face of the moon. The plain of Hyères was gradually revealed—the cypress trees, tall and straight, the shimmering olive trees with their ghostly foliage, the fields of violets, the level vineyards. And beyond, the phalanx of lights on the warships lying in the bay. The hotel on the hill-side, freshly painted and spotlessly white, stood sharply out against the dark background. The whole world was becoming visible.

Upon the balcony of one of the rooms upon the second floor a man was standing with his back to the wall. He looked around at the flooding moonlight and swore softly to himself. Decidedly, things were turning out ill with him. From the adjoining balcony a thin rope was hanging, swaying very slightly in the night breeze. The young man gazed helplessly at the end, which had slipped from his fingers, and which was hanging just now over some flower-beds. He was face to face with the almost insoluble problem of how to regain the shelter of his own room.

From the garden below came the melancholy cry of a passing owl. From the white, barnlike farmhouse, perched on the mountain-side in the distance, came the bark of a dog. Then again there was silence. The man looked back into the room from which he had escaped, and down at that end of swinging rope. He was indeed on the horns of a dilemma. To return into the room was insanity. To stay where he was, was to risk being seen by the earliest passer-by or the first person who chanced to look out from a window. To try to pass to his own veranda without the aid of that rope which he had lost was an impossibility.

It was already five minutes since he crept out from the room and had let the rope slip from his fingers. The owl had finished his mournful serenade, the watch-dog on the mountain-side slept. The deep silence of the hours before dawn brooded over the land. The man, fiercely impatient though he was to escape, was constrained to wait. There seemed to be nothing which he could do.

Then again the silence of the night was strangely, almost harshly broken, this time from the interior of the hotel. An alarm bell, harsh and discordant, rang out a brazen note of terror. Lights suddenly flashed in the windows, footsteps hurried along the corridor. The man outside upon the balcony set his teeth and cursed. Detection now seemed unavoidable.

The room behind him was speedily invaded. Madame Bertrand, in a dressing-gown whose transparent simplicity had been the triumph of a celebrated establishment in the Rue de la Paix, her beautiful hair tied up only with pink ribbon, her eyes kindling with excitement, received a stream of agitated callers. The floor waiter, three guests in various states of dishabille, and finally the manager, breathless with haste, all claimed her attention at the same time.

"It was I who rang the danger-bell," madame declared indignantly. "In an hotel where such things are possible, it is well, indeed, that one should be able to sound the alarm. There has been a man in my rooms."

"But it is unheard of, madame!" the manager replied.

"It is nevertheless true," madame insisted. "Not two minutes since, I opened my eyes and he disappeared into my sitting-room. I saw him distinctly. I could not recognize him, for he kept his face turned away. Either he has escaped through the sitting-room door and down the corridor, or he is still there, or he is hiding in this room."

"The jewels of madame!" the manager gasped.

"I am too agitated," Madame Bertrand declared. "I tremble in every limb. How can I know whether or not I have been robbed?"

"The pearls of madame," he persisted—"the string of pearls?"

"That is safe," madame admitted. "My diamond collar, too, is in its place."

The manager and two of the guests searched the sitting-room, which opened to the left from the bed-room. Others spread themselves over the hotel to calm the fears of the startled guests, and to assure everybody that there was no fire and that nothing particular had happened. The search was, of necessity, not a long one; there was no one in the sitting-room. The manager and his helpers returned.

"The room is empty, madame," the former declared.

"Then the burglar has escaped!" she cried.

Monsieur Helder went down on his knees and peered in vain under the bed.

"Madame is sure," he inquired, raising his head with some temerity but remaining upon his knees—"madame is absolutely convinced that it was not an illusion—the fragment of a dream, perhaps? It is strange that there should have been time for anyone to have escaped."

"A dream, indeed!" madame declared indignantly. "I do not dream such things, Monsieur Helder."

Monsieur Helder dived again under the valance. It was just at that moment that Madame Bertrand, gazing into the plate-glass mirror of the wardrobe, received a shock. Distinctly she saw a man's face reflected there. With the predominant instinct of her sex aroused, she opened her lips to scream—and just as suddenly closed them again. She stood for a moment quite still, her hand pressed to her side. Then she turned her head and looked out of the French windows which led on to the balcony. There was nothing to be seen. She looked across at Monsieur Helder, whose head had disappeared inside the wardrobe. Then she stole up to the window and glanced once more on to the balcony.

"Madame," Monsieur Helder declared, "the room is empty. Your sitting-room also is empty. There remains," he added, with a sudden thought, "only the balcony."

He advanced a step. Madame Bertrand, however, remained motionless. She was standing in front of the window.

"The balcony I have examined myself," she said quietly. "There is no one there. Besides, I am not one of the English cranks who sleeps always with the damp night air filling their rooms. My windows are bolted."

"In that case, madame," Monsieur Helder declared, with a little shrug of the shoulders, "we must conclude that the intruder escaped through your sitting-room door into the corridor. Madame can at least assure me that nothing of great value is missing from her belongings?"

Madame Bertrand, though pale, was graciously pleased to reassure the inquirer.

"You have reason, my friend," she admitted. "Nothing of great value is missing. The shock, however, I shall not get over for days. After this, Monsieur Helder, you will not banish my maid again to that horrible annexe. Whoever occupies the next room to mine here must give it up. Not another night will I sleep alone and unprotected."

Monsieur Helder bowed.

"Madame," he said, "the adjoining room is occupied by Mr. Sydney Wing, an Englishman, whom madame will perhaps recollect. He is, I am sure, a man of gallantry. After the adventure of to-night he will doubtless offer to vacate his room for the convenience of madame's maid."

"It must be arranged," madame insisted.

Monsieur Helder backed toward the door.

"If madame would like her maid for the rest of the night—" he suggested.

Madame Bertrand shook her head.

"Not now," she replied. "I will not have the poor girl disturbed. After what has passed, she would lie here in terror. As for me, I shall lock all my doors, and perhaps, after all, I shall sleep."

Monsieur Helder drew himself up upon the threshold. He was not a very imposing-looking object in his trousers and a crumpled shirt, but he permitted himself a bow.

"Madame," he said, "will accept this expression of my infinite regret that her slumbers should have been so disturbed."

"I thank you very much, Monsieur Helder," she answered graciously. "Good night!"

Monsieur Helder executed his bow and disappeared. Madame paused for a moment to listen to his footsteps down the corridor. Then she moved forward to the door and locked it. For a few seconds longer she hesitated. Then she walked deliberately to the French windows, threw them open, and stepped on to the balcony.

"Good evening, Monsieur Sydney Wing—or rather good morning!"

The young man gripped for a moment the frail balustrade. It must be confessed that he had lost entirely his *savoir-faire.*

"Madame!" he faltered.

She pointed to the open doors.

"Inside!" she whispered imperatively—"inside at once!"

She pointed to the swinging cord. The young man stepped only too willingly inside the room. She followed him and closed the windows.

"You will gather, Monsieur Sydney Wing," she said, "that I am disposed to spare you. I knew that you were outside, even while my room was being searched. I preferred first to hear your explanation, before I gave you up to be treated as a common burglar."

The young man's courage was returning fast. He lifted his head. His eyes were full of gratitude—or what, at any rate, gleamed like gratitude.

"Oh, madame," he murmured, "you are too gracious!"

He raised her hand to his lips and kissed it. She looked at him not unkindly.

"You will come this way," she said, leading him into the sitting-room and turning on the electric light. "Now, tell me, monsieur, and tell me the truth if you would leave this room a free man and without scandal. When I saw you first you were bending over that table. Upon it was my necklace, my earrings, a lace scarf, my chatelaine and vanity box, a few of my rings, perhaps a jewelled pin or two. Now tell me exactly what you came for, what have you taken, and why?"

The young man held himself upright. He drew a little breath. Fate was certainly dealing leniently with him.

"Madame," he said, "think. Was there nothing else upon that table?"

She shook her head.

"I can think of nothing," she acknowledged.

"To-night," he continued, "you were scarcely so kind to me. We danced together, it is true, but there were many others. There was the Admiral— the French Admiral, for instance. Madame was favourably disposed toward him."

She was a coquette, and she shrugged her shoulders as she smiled.

"Why not? Admiral Christodor is a very charming man. He dances well, he entertains upon his wonderful battleship most lavishly, he is a very desirable and delightful acquaintance. And you, Monsieur Sydney Wing, what have you to say that I should not dance and be friendly with this gentleman?"

The young man was feeling his feet upon the ground. Nevertheless, he continued to look serious.

"Alas!" he said, "I have no right to find fault. Yet two nights ago madame gave me the rose I asked for. To-night—you remember?"

She looked at him softly yet steadily. Then she glanced at the table and back again into his face.

"You told me," he continued, "that the rose belonged to him who dared to pluck it."

"It is a saying," she murmured. "I was not in earnest."

Mr. Sydney Wing sighed deeply.

"Madame," he declared, "I come of a literal nation. When we love, the word of a woman means much to us. To-night there seemed nothing dearer to me in life than the possession of that rose. I told myself that your challenge was accepted. I told myself that to-night I would sleep with that rose on the pillow by my side."

Slowly he unbuttoned his coat. From the breast pocket he drew out a handkerchief and unfolded it. In the centre, crushed, and devoid of many of its petals, but still retaining its shape and perfume, lay a dark red rose.

Madame Bertrand moved a step towards him.

"Monsieur," she cried incredulously, yet with some tenderness in her tone—"monsieur, you mean to tell me that for the sake of that rose you climbed from your balcony to mine, you ran these risks?"

"For the sake of this rose, madame, and all that it means to me," he answered.

She drew a long sigh. Then she held out her hand. Again he raised it to his lips.

"Monsieur Sydney," she said, "I have done your countrymen an injustice all my life. I had not thought such sentiment was possible in any one of them. I am very glad indeed that when I saw your face reflected in the mirror of my wardrobe, something urged me to send Monsieur Helder away. I am very glad."

"Madame!"

She held up her finger. Already the faint beginning of dawn was stealing into the sky. From the farmhouse away on the hill-side a cock commenced to crow.

"Monsieur," she whispered, "not another word. I have risked my reputation to save you. See, the door is before you. Unlock it softly. Be sure there is no one in the corridor when you leave. Do not attempt to close it. I myself in a few minutes' time will return and do that."

"But, Madame—" he begged.

She pointed imploring towards the door, but there was tenderness in her farewell glance.

"To-morrow we will talk," she promised. "To-morrow night, if you should fancy my roses, perhaps I may be more kind. Good night!"

She stole back to her room and sat on the edge of her bed. Very noiselessly the young man opened the door of the sitting-room, glanced up and down, and with swift, silent footsteps made his way to his own apartment. Madame, some few minutes later, closed the door behind him, slowly slipping off her dressing-gown, and curled herself once more in her bed. Mr. Sydney Wing, in the adjoining room, lit a cigarette and mixed himself a whiskey-and-soda. There were drops of perspiration still upon his forehead as he stepped out on to the balcony and wound up his rope.

It was the most cheerful hour of the day at the Paradise Hotel—the hour before luncheon. A swarthy Italian was singing love-songs on the gravel sweep to the music of a guitar. The very air was filled with sunshine. A soft south wind was laden with perfumes from the violet farm below. Everyone seemed to be out of doors, promenading, or sitting about in little groups. Mr. Laxworthy and Mr. Forrest Anderson had just passed along the front and were threading their way up the winding path which led through the pine woods at the back of the hotel. Mr. Lenfield, the invalid young man, was lying in a sheltered corner, taking a sun-bath; his companion by his side smoking a large cigar and occasionally reading extracts from a newspaper. The pretty American girl, who was one of the features of the place, and Madame Bertrand, were missing, the former because she was playing golf with Sydney Wing, the latter because she never rose until luncheon-time. Mr. Freeling Poignton and the Marquis Lefant were sitting a little way up amongst the pine trees. Mr. Freeling Poignton was smoking his morning cigar. Lefant was leaning forward, his eyes fixed steadily upon that streak of blue Mediterranean. In his hand he held his watch.

"I am quite sure," he said softly, "that I can rely upon my information. At a quarter past twelve precisely the torpedo is to be fired."

"Which is the *Magnifique,* anyway?" Mr. Freeling Poignton inquired.

Lefant pointed to the largest of the grey battleships which were riding at anchor. Then his fingers slowly traversed the blue space until it pointed at a black object, like a derelict barge, set out very near the island of Hyères. He glanced at his watch.

"A quarter past," he muttered. "Look! My God!"

The black object had disappeared. A column of white water rose gracefully into the air and descended. It was finished. Lefant leaned towards his companion.

"You and I," he said, "have seen a thing which is going to change the naval history of the future. You and I alone can understand why the French Admiralty has given up building battleships, why even their target practice here and at Cherbourg continues as a matter of form only."

Mr. Freeling Poignton withdrew his cigar from his mouth.

"I can't say," he admitted, "that I have ever given any particular attention to these implements of warfare, because I hate them all; but there's nothing new, anyway, in a torpedo. What's the difference between this one and the ordinary sort?"

"I will tell you in a very few words," Lefant answered. "This one can be fired at a range of five miles, and relied upon to hit a mark little larger than the plate of a battleship with absolute scientific accuracy. There is no question of aim at all. Just as you work out an exact spot in a surveying expedition by scientific instruments, so you can decide precisely the spot which that torpedo shall hit. It travels at the pace of ten miles a minute, and it has a charge which has never been equaled."

Mr. Freeling Poignton shivered a little, as he dropped the ash of his cigar.

"I'd like to electrocute the man who invented it," he declared tersely.

Lefant shook his head.

"You are wrong," he replied. "The man who invented that torpedo is the friend of your scheme and not the enemy. Listen. It is your desire—is it not—the great ambition of your life, to secure for the world universal peace?"

Mr. Freeling Poignton thrust his hands into his trouser pockets.

"Marquis," he said, "there is no man breathing who could say how much I am worth. Capitalise my present income, and you might call it five hundred million pounds. Put a quarter of a million somewhere in the bank for me, and I'd give the rest to see every army in Europe disbanded, every warship turned into a trading vessel, and every soldier and sailor turned into the factories or upon the land to become honest, productive units."

"Just so," Lefant assented. "It may sound a little Utopian, but it is magnificent. Now listen. You will never induce the rulers of the world to look upon this question reasonably, because every nation is jealous of some other, and no one is great enough to take the lead. The surest of all ways to prevent war is to reduce the art of killing to such a certainty that it becomes an absurdity to even take the field. What nation will build battleships which can be destroyed with the touch of a finger at any time, from practically any distance? I tell you that this invention, which only one or two people in the world outside of that battleship yonder know of at present, is the beginning of the end of all naval warfare. There is only one thing to be done to drive this home. No nation must be allowed to keep that secret for her own. It must belong to all."

Mr. Freeling Poignton nodded thoughtfully.

"I begin to understand," he remarked. "Guess that's where you come in, isn't it?"

"I hope so," Lefant assented. "I have already spent a hundred thousand dollars of your money, but I think I have had value for it."

"Say, why don't you treat this matter as we should on the other side?" Mr.

Freeling Poignton demanded. "It's all very well to bribe these petty officers and such-like, but the admiral's your man. Remember that the money-bags of the world are behind you."

Lefant smiled faintly.

"Alas!" he exclaimed, "the admiral belongs to a race little known in the world of commerce. Money-bags which reached to the sky would never buy him. There are others on the ship who are mine, and with the information I have the rest should be possible."

Mr. Freeling Poignton frowned. He disliked very much to hear of a man who denied the omnipotence of money. He felt like the king of some foreign country to whom a stranger had refused obeisance.

"Well, you've got to run this thing," he remarked, "and I suppose you know what kind of lunatics you've got to deal with. Seems to me the most difficult job is for you to get on the battleship at all without the admiral's consent."

Lefant kicked a pebble away from beneath his feet.

"That is the chief difficulty," he admitted. "I was rather hoping that Madame Bertrand might have been of use to me there. She has been devoting herself to the admiral for some days, and last night she got a pass from him, allowing the bearer to visit the ship at any time, with access to any part of it. This morning, however, she declares that she must have torn it up with her bridge scores."

"I suppose she can get it replaced?" Mr. Freeling Poignton suggested.

Lefant hesitated for a moment.

"To tell you the truth," he declared, "my own belief is that the admiral declined to give it to her. Julie hates to admit defeat, however. Hence her little story. That does not trouble me very much, though. My plans are all made in another direction. To-night is the night of the fancy-dress ball here, and the admiral is coming. When he returns to the *Magnifique,* the drawings of the torpedo will be in my possession."

Mr. Freeling Poignton laid his hand for a moment on Lefant's shoulder.

"Marquis," he said, "I've been a little led into this affair by you. Remember, these aren't my methods, and it's only because I see just how difficult it is to make a move that I'm standing in. But let this be understood between you and me. The moment those plans are in your possession, a copy of them is to be handed simultaneously to the Government of every civilised Power in the world, so that everyone can build the darned things if they want to."

"Naturally," Lefant assented. "It is already agreed."

"No favourtism," Mr. Freeling Poignton declared vigorously, "no priority. We steal those plans, not to give any one nation an advantage over any other, but to put every country on the same footing."

"It is already agreed," Lefant repeated.

Mr. Laxworthy and Mr. Forrest Anderson passed along, on their way back to the hotel. Courteous greetings were exchanged between the four men. Lefant watched them with a faint smile: Mr. Laxworthy with a grey shawl around his shoulders, his queer little stoop, his steel-rimmed spectacles; Anderson in his well-cut tweeds, brightly polished tan shoes, and neat Homburg hat.

"That," Lefant remarked, inclining his head toward Mr. Laxworthy, "is exactly the type of English person whom one meets in a place like Hyères, at an hotel like this. One could swear that he lives somewhere near the British Museum, writes heavily upon some dull subject, belongs to a learned society, and has never had to make his own way in the world. He probably hates draughts, has a pet ailment, and talks about his nerves. He makes a friend of that red-faced fellow-countryman of his because he is attracted by his robust health and his sheer lack of intelligence."

"I dare say you're right," Mr. Freeling Poignton remarked carelessly. "What about luncheon?"

It was the night of the great fancy-dress ball at the Paradise Hotel.

Down in the lounge the tumult became more boisterous every minute. Automobiles and carriages were all the time discharging their bevy of visitors from the neighbouring hotels and villas. A large contingent of naval officers arrived from Toulon. The ball-room was already crowded. Admiral Christodor, looking very handsome, led the promenade with Madame Bertrand, concealed under the identity of an Eastern princess. There were many who wondered what it was that he whispered in her ear as he conducted her into the ball-room.

"It was careless of me," she admitted softly, "but I am really quite, quite sure that it was destroyed. It was with my bridge scores, and I tore them all up without thinking. You will give me another, perhaps?"

"Whenever you will," he promised.

"Listen," she continued. "To-night you must not leave me. There is a young Englishman—you understand?"

"To-night shall be mine," the admiral answered gallantly. "I will not quit your side for a second for all the Englishmen who ever left their sad island."

It was a gallant speech, but if Fritz, the concierge, could have heard it he would have been puzzled, for, barely half an hour later, a gust of wind blew back the cloak of a man who was stepping into a motor-car, and his uniform was certainly the uniform of an admiral of the French navy. Through the windy darkness the motor-car rushed on its way to La Plage. The men who waited in the pinnace rose to the salute. The admiral took his place in silence, and the little petrol-driven boat tore through the water.

"The admiral takes his pleasure sadly," one of them muttered, as their passenger climbed on to the deck.

"He has returned most devilishly early," another of them, whose thoughts were in the café at La Plage, grumbled.

The admiral turned his head sharply.

"I shall return," he announced. "Await me."

Most of the officers of the *Magnifique* were in the ball-room of the Paradise Hotel. The admiral received the salute of the lieutenant on duty, and passed at once to his cabin. Arrived there, he shut the door and listened. There was no sound save the gentle splashing of the water near the port-hole. Like lightning he turned to a cabinet set in the wall. He pulled out a drawer and touched a spring. Everything was as he had been told. A roll of papers was pushed back into a corner of this compartment. He drew the sheets out one by one, shut the cabinet quickly, and swung around. Then he stood as though turned to stone. The inner door of the cabin, which led into the sleeping apartment, was open. Seated at the table before him was Mr. Laxworthy.

Lefant was a man who had passed through many crises in life. Sheer astonishment, however, on this occasion overmastered him. His *savoir-faire* had gone. He simply stood still and stared. It was surely a vision, this. It could not be that little old-fashioned man who went about with a grey shawl on his shoulders who was sitting there watching him.

"What in the devil's name are you doing there?" he demanded.

"I might ask you the same question," Mr. Laxworthy replied. "I imagine we are both—intruders."

Lefant recovered himself a little. He came nearer to the table.

"Tell me exactly what you want," he insisted.

"First, let us have an understanding," Mr. Laxworthy answered, "and as quickly as possible. For obvious reasons, the less time we spend here the better. The pinnace which brought you is waiting, I presume, to take you back. In this light you might still pass as an Admiral, but every moment you spend here adds to the risk—for both of us. My foot is on the electric bell, which I presume would bring the Admiral's steward. You perceive, too, that I have a revolver in my hand, to the use of which I am accustomed. Am I in command, or you?"

"It appears that you are," Lefant admitted grimly. "Go on."

"You hold in your hand," Mr. Laxworthy continued, "the plans of the Macharin torpedo, the torpedo which is to make warfare in the future impossible."

Then Lefant waited no longer. He flung himself almost boldly upon the little old man, who to all appearances presented such small powers of resistance. His first calculation was correct enough. Mr. Laxworthy made no attempt to discharge the revolver which he held in his hand. In other respects, however, a surprise was in store for Lefant. His right hand was suddenly held in a grip of amazing strength. The fingers of Mr. Laxworthy's other hand were upon his throat.

"If you utter a sound, remember we are both lost," the latter whispered.

Lefant set himself grimly to the struggle, but it lasted only a few seconds! Before he realised what had happened, his shoulder and the back of his head were upon the table and Mr. Laxworthy's fingers were like bars of steel upon his throat. He felt his consciousness going.

"You are content to discuss this matter?" his assailant asked calmly.

Lefant could only gasp out his answer. Mr. Laxworthy released his grip. Lefant breathed heavily for a minute or two. He was half dazed. The thing seemed impossible, yet it had happened. The breath had very nearly left his body in the grip of this insignificant-looking old man.

"Now, if you are willing to be reasonable," Mr. Laxworthy said, "remember that for both our sakes it is well we do not waste a single second."

Lefant's fingers stiffened upon the roll of papers, which he was still clutching. Mr. Laxworthy read his thoughts unerringly.

"I do not ask you for the plans," he continued grimly. "You want them for your country. I am not a patriot. My country shall fight her own battles so long as they are fought fairly. These are my terms: put back those papers, or destroy them, and pay me for my silence."

"You do not ask, then, for the plans for yourself?" Lefant demanded.

"I do not," Laxworthy replied. "They belong to France. Let France keep them. You have corrupted half the ship with Poignton's dollars, but it was never in your mind to keep your faith with him. The plans were for Germany. Germany shall not have them. If I forced you to hand them over to me, I dare say I could dispose of them for—what shall we say?—a hundred thousand pounds. You shall put them back in their place and pay me ten thousand for my silence."

"So you are an adventurer?" Lefant muttered.

"I am one who seeks adventures," Laxworthy replied. "We will let it go at that, if you please. Remember that you are in my power. The pressure of my foot upon this bell, or my finger upon the trigger of this revolver, and your career is over. Will you restore the plans and pay me ten thousand pounds?"

Lefant sighed.

"It is agreed," he declared.

He turned back to the cabinet, and Laxworthy half rose in his seat to watch him restore the plans. In a few seconds the affair was ended.

"Monsieur the Admiral returns to the ball?" Mr. Laxworthy remarked smoothly. "I will avail myself of his kind offer to accept a seat in the pinnace."

They left the cabin and made their way to the side of the ship where the pinnace was waiting, and the lieutenant stood with his hand to salute. Secretly, the latter was a little relieved to see the two together. Once more the pinnace rushed towards the land. The two men walked down the wooden quay, side by side.

"You will permit me to offer you a lift to the hotel?" Lefant asked.

"With much pleasure," Laxworthy replied, drawing his grey shawl around him. "I find the nights chilly in these open cars, though."

Smoothly, but at a great pace, they tore along the scented road, through a grove of eucalyptus trees, and into the grounds of the hotel whose lights were twinkling far and wide. Lefant for the first time broke the silence.

"Mr. Laxworthy," he said, "the honours of this evening rest with you. I do not wish to ask questions that you are not likely to answer, but there is one matter on which if you would enlighten me—"

Mr. Laxworthy waved his hand.

"Proceed," he begged.

"My little enterprise of this evening," Lefant continued slowly, "was known of and spoken of only between Mr. Freeling Poignton and myself. We discussed it in the grounds of the hotel, where we were certainly free from eavesdroppers. I am willing to believe that you are a very remarkable person, but this is not the age of miracles."

Mr. Laxworthy smiled.

"Nor is it the age," he murmured, "wherein we have attained sufficient wisdom to be able to define exactly what a miracle is. Ten years ago, what would men have said of flying? Fifty years ago even the telephone was considered incredible. Has it never occurred to you, my dear Lefant, that there may be natural gifts of which one or two of us are possessed, almost as strange?"

Lefant turned in his seat.

"You mean—" he began.

Mr. Laxworthy held up his hand. "I have given you a hint," he said; "the rest is for you."

Lefant was silent for a moment.

"Tell me at least this," he begged. "How the devil did you get on to the *Magnifique?*"

They were passing along the front by the ballroom. Admiral Christodor and Madame Bertrand were sitting near the window. Laxworthy sighed.

"The greatest men in the world," he said, "make fools of themselves when they put pencil to paper for the sake of a woman.... Take my advice, Marquis. Destroy that uniform and arrange for an *alibi*. In a few hours' time there will be trouble on the *Magnifique!*"

Lefant nodded. His cocked hat was thrust into the pocket of his overcoat—he was wearing a motor cap and goggles.

"There will be trouble," he remarked dryly, "but it will not touch you or me. As regards Madame Bertrand—"

"She is innocent," Laxworthy assured him. "Nevertheless, a pass on to the *Magnifique* is a little too valuable a thing to be left in a lady's chatelaine bag."

Lefant sighed.

"One makes mistakes," he remarked.

"And one pays!" Laxworthy agreed.

CHAPTER II
The Tragedy of the Flower Farm

Mr. Laxworthy occasionally played golf. He was naturally not a great performer, but he was in the habit of hitting the ball in the centre of his club with marvellous regularity, and, when once on the green, his putting was little short of miraculous. There were other distractions, however, which appealed more strongly to him, and it was simply owing to the persistence of the American girl, who rather posed as having discovered him, that he happened to be on the fifth green at the time when the tragedy at the flower farm was discovered.

"This for the hole, I believe?" Mr. Laxworthy remarked, whereupon he studied the line of his putt, adjusted his spectacles, took up his stance firmly, and holed out from a distance of about seven yards. The American girl made a face at him.

"I don't believe you're as nice as I thought you were," she said rather crossly. "I hate being three down at the fifth. Now, what are all those boys running for, do you suppose?"

Mr. Laxworthy looked steadfastly in the direction toward which she was pointing. At their feet was spread a waving carpet of purple anemones. Through the trees in the adjoining field a sea of violets bent their heads before the soft west wind. About a hundred yards away stood a large bare-looking farmhouse, built of white plaster, with a red-tiled roof and spacious out-buildings. It was towards this that several caddies and one or two of the players were hurrying.

"It is impossible," Mr. Laxworthy declared, "to say what those boys are running for, except to get away from their work. That in itself appears, as a rule, to be a powerful inducement to them."

"My! but it takes a long time for you to say what you want to," the girl exclaimed. "Let's see what the trouble is."

They walked along one of the straight furrows between the beds of violets. The farmhouse was built without any encircling fence in the centre of the field. A little way back, on the left-hand side, was a huge barn. Outside this, a woman stood weeping and wringing her hands, whilst a man, surrounded by a curious group of caddies and several players, was talking loudly and excitedly. One of the residents at the hotel, who knew Laxworthy by sight, turned towards him as they hurried up.

"You don't happen to be a doctor, do you?" he asked.

"I have never practiced medicine," Laxworthy replied, "but I have some knowledge of it. If anyone is ill, I may, perhaps, be of service until a doctor arrives. What is the matter?"

The peasant stepped forward. He was a broad-shouldered, sunburnt man, of medium height, with black moustache and bristling whiskers. In his blue shirt and soiled corduroy trousers, tied up with a piece of rope, he was entirely typical of his class—French, with a dash of the Italian—which betrays itself, also, in his voluble *patois*.

"If monsieur knows anything of doctoring, he may pass inside," he declared. "Otherwise, no one shall enter my barn. I have sent for a doctor, I have sent for the police. What can a man do more? As for me, I shake. I am filled with terror. It is a horrible thing which has happened."

He wiped the sweat from his forehead with his forearm. There was no doubt about it that he was in mortal terror.

"I do know something of doctoring," Laxworthy admitted, answering him in his own tongue. "Who is ill?"

The man stared at him for a moment, speechless.

"Ill! Monsieur has not heard, then? It is a curse which has come upon my household, a curse upon me for my kindness! But last night he came while we were at our evening meal—a tramp, half-starved, shaking with fatigue and thirst. He prayed for work, for food, for a sip of wine. All these I offered. Why not? It is our busy season, and labour is welcome. Why should I not do the poor fellow a kindness? I gave him food and wine. I let him sleep in the barn. To-morrow, I said, he should work in the vine-yard. This morning, to tell the truth, I forgot that he was there until an hour ago. 'The lazy rascal!' I thought, but I took him a mug of coffee. I carried it from the house out here to the barn. I called to him—Giuseppe he told me that his name was. 'Giuseppe,' I shouted, 'wake up and come to your work. Here is coffee and bread.' Then I threw open the door, and behold! Monsieur may enter."

The peasant pushed back the clumsy door of the barn, and Laxworthy passed over the threshold. On a bundle of hay, just inside, with the sunlight falling full upon his ghastly face, a man lay dead. He lay on his side, and the long knife which had passed through his heart had come out behind his shoulder-blade. Mr. Laxworthy turned round.

"Keep these people away," he called out sharply. "Miss Chambers, you had better go home, please. Don't let anyone in here," he added, turning to the farmer. "Don't let anything be moved or disturbed."

They formed a little bodyguard around the outside of the barn. One of the players, who happened also to be an admirer of Miss Chambers, took her away. Laxworthy sank on one knee by the side of the murdered man. For several moments he remained there. The farmer stood a few feet away, watching.

"He came to you last night, and you had never seen him before?" Laxworthy asked.

"But, never!" the man declared. "He is a stranger. If I had known that he was one of those who are doomed, do you think that I would have had him in here?"

"What do you man by 'one of those who are doomed'?" Laxworthy demanded.

The farmer shivered.

"The Camorra," he answered. "It is a crime of vengeance, this. Who can doubt it, indeed? There is the cross upon the cheek."

Mr. Laxworthy nodded slowly.

"What language did the man speak?"

"But the same as our own, monsieur," the farmer replied. "Why not? He came from Marseilles last, he said, but he had lived in Tuscany. He told us that, and that his name was Giuseppe."

"You have not searched him for papers or anything of that sort?" Mr. Laxworthy inquired.

The farmer's negative was almost fierce.

"I have not touched him," he asserted. "I have not been so near the body as you are standing now. I have no fancy for dead men—I!"

"The knife, then, does not belong here?"

The man shook his head.

"Never have I seen it in my life," he declared.

Mr. Laxworthy rose to his feet. There was a noise outside as of an arrival. A motor-car had drawn up in the road. A sergeant of gendarmes and the doctor came hurrying up. Mr. Laxworthy stood on one side.

"They called me," he explained to the doctor, "but you see for yourself. I have not interfered with the position of the body, nor touched the man. It is an affair, I fear, for the police, and not for human aid."

The doctor looked at the knife and held up his hands.

"*Mon Dieu!*" he exclaimed. "*Mon Dieu!* Some fiend has been at work!"

"But this is indeed for us!" the chief of the gendarmes declared, twirling his moustache fiercely. "Make your examination, doctor. Let us have your report as quickly as possible. There is much to be done."

Mr. Laxworthy strolled away over the perfumed field, and found Miss Chambers waiting on the seat by the sixth tee, accompanied by her escort.

"My honour," he remarked, walking on to the tee.

"Are we—shall we go on?" she asked, looking at him in surprise.

"Just as you like," Mr. Laxworthy replied.

"Has anything been found out?"

Mr. Laxworthy shook his head.

"There is nothing much to find out. The poor fellow up there was dead within a few minutes of receiving that blow, which I should say was about twelve hours ago. The doctor is there, and the chief of the police."

"Have they any idea who did it?"

"The farmer speaks of the Camorra," Mr. Laxworthy replied. "Very likely he is right. The peasants all along here are half Italian—a fierce, passionate race. Shall I drive?"

"If you please," she answered, a little subdued.

At the ninth hole they abandoned the game. Mr. Laxworthy was five up and playing with great precision. Miss Chambers declared that she could do nothing but think of the dead man's face, of which she had had a hurried glimpse. On their way to the club-house Mr. Laxworthy asked her a question.

"You are a young lady," he said, "with some powers of observation. Did anything strike you about the face of that man?"

She shivered.

"Nothing except that it was the most hideous thing I ever saw in my life," she declared. "I'm afraid I'll dream of it for months."

Mr. Laxworthy dismissed his caddie and offered his escort to the hotel to Miss Chambers, who, however, refused it.

"I think I'll stay down here for a while," she remarked. "I may feel like practicing a drive or two presently. I hope you'll have another game with me later on, Mr. Laxworthy."

She watched him as he turned away and walked slowly up the path toward the hotel with his hands behind him. She even leaned over the rail of the balcony and looked after him until he had disappeared. When finally she turned away and glanced towards the young man who had strolled up to her side, the colour had left her cheeks.

"That man is absolutely bloodless!" she exclaimed. "He hasn't a nerve in his body. I believe I'm afraid of him!"

Her companion laughed contemptuously.

"He doesn't look very terrifying. Sits about with a grey shawl around his neck, reading *The Quarterly Review* most of the time."

She shook her head thoughtfully.

"Do you know," she said, "I went and talked to him first because I thought he was lonely? I stayed talking to him because he had a sense of humour. I talked to him the next day because I couldn't help it. I shall talk to him again this afternoon, if he'll let me. And I'm afraid of him. I don't think any of us quite understand the sort of person he is."

"That horrid affair has upset your nerves," the young man declared, soothingly. "Let's go and putt."

Mr. Laxworthy found the usual stream of promenaders taking their sun bath and gossiping in little groups in front of the hotel. The news of the tragedy at the flower farm had already arrived, and people were busy discussing it. Mr. Laxworthy, who seldom went out of his way to speak to anyone, paused before the wicker chair of Mr. Freeling Poignton. The latter laid down his paper and greeted him cordially.

"Say, they tell me you were down yonder and saw this poor fellow who's been murdered?" the latter remarked.

"It is quite true," Mr. Laxworthy admitted. "I have seen the body."

Mr. Freeling Poignton clenched his fists. His eyes flashed. His long, lean face was hard and set.

"If I had my way," he declared, "I'd make short ending of any Government who let these dirty, murdering societies flourish. I don't know that I'm much of a man of sentiment, but it does make me wild to think of a fellow-creature being done to death in the night like that."

"Your humanitarian principles," Mr. Laxworthy said, "are well known. Tell me, would you consider it a gratification to them, or the reverse, that the murderer should be discovered?"

"Why, I'm surprised at that question, Mr. Laxworthy," the American answered. "You know very well that I'm great on the sacredness of human life, and that's why I'm dead set against wars and all manner of armaments. But I'm also strong for justice."

"I am pleased," Mr. Laxworthy answered, "to hear you say this. Now, I believe that you could, if you cared to do so, ensure the bringing to justice of this murderer."

Mr. Freeling Poignton had been in the act of lighting his cigar. The match, however, burnt out between his fingers. He looked at Mr. Laxworthy curiously.

"Say, what do you mean by that?" he demanded.

"I mean," Mr. Laxworthy explained, "that, Camorra or no Camorra, if you cared to offer a thousand pounds reward for the arrest of the murderer, he'd be arrested, right enough, before a week is past. A thousand pounds to you is no more than a sovereign to us, but it will buy justice for that poor fellow."

"by God, I'll do it!" Mr. Freeling Poignton declared, rising at once to his feet. "I'll have my secretary telephone to the police right away. I take it you know what you're talking about, Mr. Laxworthy?"

"There is no manner of doubt about that," Mr. Laxworthy replied. "I congratulate you upon your decision, Mr. Freeling Poignton. It is a truly humanitarian action."

Mr. Laxworthy went to his rooms for a few minutes, and strolled in to luncheon a little later. The invalid young man and his companion occupied a table just inside the large dining-hall. Mr. Laxworthy stood for a moment on the threshold, peering around. On his way to his place he paused before the table.

"How is the invalid this morning?" he asked.

The young man looked up quickly. His companion shrugged his shoulders.

"Getting on slowly," he declared, with a cheerfulness which sounded a little forced. "I can't seem to get him to eat enough, and he sleeps wretchedly."

"It is a pity," Mr. Laxworthy answered. "A walk the very last thing at night is what the most modern physicians are all recommending."

Mr. Laxworthy passed on towards his seat. The two men exchanged glances.

"Do you know who that fellow is?" the young man asked suspiciously.

His companion shook his head. "Rather an old woman, I think," he declared carelessly. "I don't know much about him except that he's always got his nose in some learned journal or another."

The young man's eyes were still following Mr. Laxworthy.

"You don't suppose—" he began, and hesitated.

His friend leaned back in his seat and laughed scornfully.

"My dear Philip," he exclaimed, "don't be an ass!"

Mr. Laxworthy made his way to his own table, where his two companions had already commenced luncheon. He took his place and selected his dishes with his usual scrupulous care. He then measured out his whisky and filled up the glass with soda-water.

"We are both of us," Mr. Forrest Anderson remarked, "exceedingly curious."

"As to what?" Mr. Laxworthy inquired.

"As to the nature of your conversation with Mr. Freeling Poignton," the latter replied. "We saw him leave you and hurry into the office with his secretary."

"There need be no secret about that," Mr. Laxworthy declared. "I have induced Mr. Freeling Poignton to offer a reward of one thousand pounds for the arrest of the murderer of that poor fellow who was found dead this morning in an outhouse of the flower farm."

Mr. Anderson and Sydney exchanged bewildered glances.

"But he was only an Italian labourer!" the former exclaimed.

"The crime was dramatic enough," Sydney intervened, "especially if it should really turn out to be the work of the Camorra; but I don't see what there is about it to interest us."

Mr. Laxworthy continued his lunch for a few moments in silence.

"Well," he said at last, "I had some reasons for my interference. In the first place, the man was not an Italian peasant at all. On the contrary, he was an Englishman."

"An Englishman?" Sydney exclaimed.

They both looked at him in amazement.

"Not only an Englishman," Mr. Laxworthy continued, "but an Englishman with whose name and profession I happened to be acquainted. Furthermore, the farmer, who lied to me this morning, knows all about the crime."

"Tell us who he was," Anderson demanded softly. "An Englishman, whose name and profession you know?"

"Decidedly," Mr. Laxworthy replied. "I recognised him directly I saw him lying there, although he had shaved his moustache. His name was John Beggs, and he was an exceedingly clever and unscrupulous detective. You yourselves saw him only a few days ago in the buffet of the Gare de Lyons."

There was a moment's breathless silence. The little scene in the buffet rose up before their eyes. Sydney involuntarily glanced across the room towards the table where the invalid young man and his companion were sitting.

"Have you told anyone?" he asked.

"Not a soul," Mr. Laxworthy answered. "I prefer to let the venom of that reward do its work. There is no one in this world so covetous for gold as a French peasant of his class. For a thousand pounds there are few of them who would not sell their brother's soul. We shall hear news, and before long."

As soon as luncheon was concluded, Mr. Laxworthy, according to his unvarying custom, slept for half an hour. Afterwards, with Forrest Anderson and Sydney, he walked along the dusty road which led to the flower farm. There were a dozen or so people in the garden looking aimlessly about. The door of the barn was closed and a gendarme stood there on duty. Mr. Laxworthy and his companions entered the house, but found nowhere any sign of life. It was not until the former had knocked for some time upon the banisters that the farmer put in a reluctant appearance at the head of the stairs.

"What do you want?" he demanded gruffly.

"I have come to bring you news," Mr. Laxworthy replied. "You remember me from this morning, I am sure! Come down and talk to me and my friends. You will find it worth your while."

The man came down, a little unsteadily. His eyes were red and bloodshot. He had the air of one who had been drinking. He was none the less perfectly sober. He led the way into the kitchen—a strange apartment, with a stone floor, very uneven, and a low, whitewashed ceiling, from which hung many strings of onions.

"News for me?" he muttered. "The good Lord knows I've had all the news I want to-day! What is it then?"

"A wealthy American gentleman, who is staying at the Paradise Hotel,"

Mr. Laxworthy announced, "is going to offer a reward of a thousand pounds—twenty-five thousand francs, mark you—for any information which will lead to the apprehension of the man who murdered that poor fellow out there. Twenty-five thousand francs! Why, it is a fortune."

The man who listened swayed upon his feet. His eyes were protuberant. The breath seemed to come through his lips with a little hiss.

"Twenty-five thousand francs!" he gasped.

"It is a great fortune," Mr. Laxworthy continued. "With twenty-five thousand francs what could a man do here, for instance? Rebuild the place, buy more land, be master where he has been servant. Directly I was told this, you see, I came to you. You should have the best chance of earning that money, my good friend."

"How can I earn it?" the man muttered.

"By giving such information as will lead to the arrest of the murderer," Mr. Laxworthy remarked cheerfully. "It is quite simple, isn't it? You have to think—to try to remember. There has been no examination yet. You have been wise to hold your tongue."

The man's eyes were lit with cupidity.

"It is a wonderful sum," he said softly, as though to himself. "I must talk with my wife about this."

Mr. Laxworthy led the way toward the door.

"We will go now," he announced pleasantly. "I wished to be the first to bring you this news. And, my friend, a word in your ear."

The farmer stooped down. Mr. Laxworthy whispered. Then he passed out after his companions. The man whom they left there stood perfectly rigid for several moments. Then he spat upon the floor.

"He is a devil, that little Englishman!" he muttered to himself.

Mr. Laxworthy returned to the hotel alone shortly afterwards, having left his two friends to play a round of golf. In one of the sheltered seats near the porch the American girl was sitting, surrounded as usual by a little group of her admirers. Directly she saw Mr. Laxworthy she rose to her feet and dismissed them. She came towards him with a most bewildering smile, which failed, however, to elicit any response from Mr. Laxworthy except the faint movement of his fingers towards his cap.

"Mr. Laxworthy," she begged, "are you in a great hurry?"

Mr. Laxworthy deliberately undid his coat and consulted his watch.

"Not for a few minutes," he admitted. "It is now ten minutes to four. I take my tea at a quarter past."

"Please have tea with me," she invited. "I want to talk to you."

"I am much obliged to you," Mr. Laxworthy replied, "but I make my own tea with water which I get sent up from the chemist's and tea which I brought out with me from England."

"I withdraw my invitation," she sighed. "At the same time, if you could spare me five minutes, I should be very glad."

"I will talk with you so far as the small stone terrace there," he said. "There is a seat to the left which is in the sun and out of the wind. If you have anything to say to me, it would be a convenient spot."

"Any place will do quite nicely for me," she replied. "I will not keep you long."

They walked along the broad terrace in front of the hotel, a somewhat incongruous pair—Mr. Laxworthy, in his neat grey suit and broad-toed shoes, his shawl upon his arm, and with his long neck thrust even farther forward than usual; the girl in a white linen dress and a large picture-hat with pink flowers. Mr. Laxworthy led the way to the seat which he had indicated, and arranged the shawl around his neck.

"I am quite ready," he declared.

His companion leaned a little forward.

"Mr. Laxworthy," she began, "there is a matter which has been worrying me, and upon which I want you to give me your advice. I hope you won't think it a liberty, but I am asking you because you seem to lead so thoroughly self-centred a life, and to be so utterly devoid of interest in what is going on around you, that I feel sure that anything you say will be quite impartial. Another reason why I am asking you in preference to anyone else is because you were really the first at the flower farm this morning to see the—the murdered man."

Mr. Laxworthy did not by the twitching of a muscle of his face betray any signs of interest in her speech.

"It's about what happened at the flower farm," she continued, a little hesitatingly. "They are all saying in the hotel that Mr. Freeling Poignton has offered a reward of a thousand pounds for the arrest of the murderer."

"Mr. Freeling Poignton," Mr. Laxworthy remarked, "is a man of strongly marked humanitarian instincts. He values human life very highly. This action of his is entirely consistent with his principles."

"I will tell you exactly what is bothering me," she went on slowly. "I feel that I need not ask you to consider it in confidence. You know what that farmer says—that the man came late at night, while they were having their evening meal? Well, it isn't true—that's all there is about it."

"Not true?" Mr. Laxworthy repeated calmly. "Indeed!"

"I will tell you exactly what happened," she continued. "You know Mr. Lenfield, the young gentleman who has been so ill, and who is here with a friend—Mr. Hamar his name is? Well, yesterday afternoon I went for a short walk with Mr. Lenfield, and we stopped at the farm while he bought me some violets. Every one else was busy, so the farmer and his wife themselves came out to pick them for us, and while we were all there a man got over the fence by the road and came down one of the furrows towards us. He was quite close before anyone took any notice of him. Then the farmer looked up and asked him what he wanted. He answered quite shortly, and then he said something to Mr. Lenfield in English, which I didn't hear, because I had turned to speak to the woman. When I looked round Mr. Lenfield had fainted. We got him some water from the house and he had a brandy flask in his pocket, and he recovered wonderfully quickly. I never thought anything more about the man who had come up, for he seemed to have gone away almost at once. Mr. Lenfield paid for the violets and we walked home together. He is very delicate, of course, and he says that it was just the shock of hearing someone speak whom he had not seen approach, which upset him."

"You think," Mr. Laxworthy asked, "that this stranger who came across the field and spoke to Mr. Lenfield was the man whom we saw dead at the flower farm this morning?"

"I'm not thinking about that at all," she answered. "I'm sure."

"The incident is a singular one," Mr. Laxworthy remarked.

"This is what's bothering me," the girl went on, leaning a little forward from her place. "At luncheon time Mr. Hamar came to me and asked me if I would mind not saying anything about having been with Mr. Lenfield in the afternoon when that man spoke to him. He said that Mr. Lenfield was in such a delicate state of health, and his nerves were in such an awful condition, that if he were called as a witness, or had to identify the body, he would certainly collapse."

"And what reply did you make to Mr. Hamar?"

"I am afraid," she confessed, "that on the spur of the moment, and feeling sorry, as I did, for Mr. Lenfield, I promised not to mention it. Now, I am wondering whether I have done right. Of course, Mr. Lenfield may have fainted from some other cause, but it did seem to me as though this stranger addressed him not in the least casually, but as though they were acquaintances. I've been troubled about it ever since, Mr. Laxworthy, and I decided to ask your advice. What do you think I ought to do?"

Mr. Laxworthy sat quite still for several moments. Then he rose slowly to his feet.

"My dear young lady," he said, "nothing that you can do or leave undone can alter one hair's breadth the course of events which are likely to transpire. My advice to you is to wait."

"You don't think that I am doing anyone an injustice by saying nothing?" she persisted.

"There is no one, at present, under suspicion," Mr. Laxworthy replied, "so there is no one whom your silence can harm. My advice to you, I repeat, is to wait until the time comes."

"I feel sure you're right," she declared, with a little sigh of relief. "It's very nice of you, Mr. Laxworthy, to let me bother you so. I know these things don't really interest you."

They were on their way back to the hotel. Mr. Laxworthy consulted his watch and frowned.

"I have lost count of time to the extent of four minutes," he said irritably. "Good afternoon, Miss Chambers."

Mr. Laxworthy's room looked out at the back of the hotel. He had scarcely seated himself in his customary chair, and made the usual preparations for the enjoyment of his tea, when there was a hurried tap at the door and Mr. Forrest Anderson entered.

"He left the flower farm two minutes ago," Mr. Anderson announced. "You'll see him in a minute or two coming round that belt of trees."

Mr. Laxworthy nodded and adjusted a small but powerful set of binoculars. In a few moments the figure of the flower farmer appeared in the direction indicated. He was coming straight towards the back of the hotel, along a small footpath, walking hurriedly, and more than once stopping to look behind. Suddenly, when within about a couple of hundred yards of his apparent destination, he checked his pace and commenced to saunter. A man was on his way to meet him. Mr. Laxworthy gave vent to an exclamation of annoyance.

"They will be too far away to be of any use to me," he muttered. "Slip down quickly, Forrest, and disturb them. It doesn't matter how. If they see you, they will certainly come nearer to the hotel rather than farther away."

Anderson hurried off. Mr. Laxworthy, through his glasses, watched the meeting of the two men. At first they stood face to face. Presently they sat down on a fallen log. Then Mr. Anderson, strolling along and whistling loudly, disturbed them. The man who had issued from the hotel rose and greeted him respectfully. Mr. Anderson paused for a moment and then went on, away from the hotel, walking in leisurely fashion, and stopping every now and then to admire the view. The flower farmer and his companion rose and came slowly together towards the hotel. At the edge of the kitchen garden they paused, and seated themselves upon a bench almost immediately underneath Mr. Laxworthy's window. They talked, for a time, earnestly, and then parted. Mr. Laxworthy shut his binoculars with a faint smile. He then had his tea moved to Sydney's room, on the other side of the corridor, and settled down to wait for a visitor. In less than five minutes there was a knock at the door. It was the head waiter himself who entered. He closed the door behind him and advanced into the room before he spoke.

"I beg your pardon, Mr. Laxworthy," he said, "But Jean Massen, the man who keeps the flower farm, is here, and wishes to speak to you."

"To me?" Mr. Laxworthy repeated.

The head waiter—a smart, well-groomed little man, whom everybody called Luigi—bowed.

"I was not sure whether you would care to receive him," he said confidentially. "He seems very much agitated, and I believe that his visit has something to do with the fact that you happened to be passing this morning at the time when the body of the labourer was found."

Mr. Laxworthy laid down his magazine.

"I have no objection to seeing the man," he decided. "Pray bring him here yourself. And Luigi?"

"Monsieur?"

"While you are here," Mr. Laxworthy said, deliberately, "I should like to impress upon you the fact that the tapioca pudding which you prepare for me daily was distinctly undercooked this morning. Such an incident as this, Luigi, has a serious effect upon my digestion."

"I am exceedingly sorry, sir," Luigi apologised humbly. "I will speak to the *chef,* and see that it does not occur again."

Jean Massen, sober enough now, was ushered in a few minutes later. He scarcely waited until the door was closed before he commenced his story.

"Monsieur," he declared, "it is not only the thousand pounds reward—it is not only the money. When I think of what has been done, I tremble all over. My wife, too, she has implored me to tell the truth. Monsieur, I come to you because you understand my tongue, and because you first brought me word of that reward, which shows, monsieur," he added, with a cunning gleam in his eyes, "that you had some idea in your head. There is an Englishman here, an invalid, who was with me in the field when the stranger first came. Last night this Englishman came to me."

Mr. Laxworthy nodded slowly.

"Ah!" he remarked. "I noticed that he took a walk."

"He came to me, monsieur, and he told me that the stranger was no peasant, as he seemed, but a man who was his mortal enemy. He offered me so much money that I dare not mention it, if I would take one of my own pruning knives and stab the stranger while he slept. Monsieur, how could I? What I did do was this. I said to him: 'Monsieur, if you have a quarrel with that man, he lies there in my barn, and the affair is none of mine. Settle your differences and my ears are deaf. It is finished.' He left me, monsieur, and he shook like a leaf, but he went out towards the barn, and on the way he picked up one of my pruning knives from the top of a barrel. What he did in that barn, monsieur, who but the good God should tell? But these words which I have spoken are the truth. I come to you for advice. If I go to the chief of police and tell him these things, will that reward be mine?"

Mr. Laxworthy had listened to the farmer's recital, and his face had remained like the face of a sphinx. He made no sign of approval or disapproval. When his visitor had finished his story, however, he asked him a question.

"This, then, Jean Massen, is all that you know of the affair?"

"It is all, monsieur, and more than enough," the man declared, picking up his hat.

"The truth in these matters is the only safety," Mr. Laxworthy said quietly. "Go to the chief of the police and tell him what you have told me. If the Englishman is taken, the reward will be yours."

The man breathed a deep sigh.

"I wish you good day, sir," he said, and left the room.

Mr. Laxworthy, from the balcony, watched him descend the hill and take the path through the woods into Hyères. Then, with a little shrug of the shoulders, he resumed his study of *The Quarterly Review.*

It was in the lounge after dinner that evening that the guests of the Paradise Hotel at Hyères were witnesses of a tragedy unique, perhaps, in the lives of most of them. The band was playing the music of a popular musical comedy. People were standing about in little knots, talking, before settling down to their bridge. Mr. Lenfield, looking very pale and ill, was taking his coffee and liqueur with his friend Mr. Hamar. The American girl was there, and Luigi himself was serving them. Then down the broad passage-way which led through the lounge a sergeant, followed by a gendarme, pushed his way, to the consternation of every one. They were accompanied by an interpreter in plain clothes. They walked straight to where Mr. Lenfield was sitting. The American girl, who saw them first, went pale to the lips. The young man himself sat perfectly still. His eyes were set in a fixed stare, his cheeks were ghastly. The sergeant came to a standstill before him.

"Monsieur," he announced, "it is my duty to arrest you for the murder of a man, whose name is at present unknown, at the flower farm of Jean Massen last night. You will have to come with me."

The young man half rose and then collapsed. Mr. Laxworthy intervened.

"Mr. Sergeant," he said, "in the interest of justice, let me assure you that you are making a mistake. The man of whom you speak was an Englishman, John Beggs, detective, who, unfortunately for him, spent five years of his life in Genoa. This is the man who murdered him. I can furnish you, I believe, with satisfactory proof."

Mr. Laxworthy's hand suddenly fell upon the shoulder of the head waiter. With a crash Luigi's tray of liqueurs fell to the ground. He sprang back.

"It is a lie!" he shrieked.

The gendarme seized him by the arms. Mr. Laxworthy cleared his throat.

"The murdered man, John Beggs," he said, "was responsible for the arrest in Genoa, four years ago, of the uncle of this man, Luigi Cantello. The uncle and his nephew here are both members of the Camorra, and John Beggs, who fled at once to England, has lived since then with a price upon his head. He came out here to watch, I believe, over Mr. Lenfield, with whose affairs I have nothing whatever to do. He came face to face with Luigi Cantello, who was a frequent visitor at the flower farm, and he has paid the penalty. This afternoon Jean Massen, the flower farmer, and Luigi here, met and agreed that, under the circumstances, which were certainly incriminating, the crime could be fixed upon the Englishman, Lenfield, and the reward divided between them. An extraordinary series of accidents has place these facts within my possession."

There was a moment's breathless silence. The sergeant had turned towards Luigi. With a sudden fierce movement the head waiter wrenched himself free. For a second he crouched as though about to spring at Laxworthy. Every one in the lounge sat or stood like frozen figures, dumb and motionless with horror. Only Mr. Laxworthy remained unmoved. Then Luigi apparently changed his mind. A knife flashed in the air. His own death-cry was only partially drowned by the shrieks of the women. Mr. Laxworthy looked down at the prostrate body.

"The man has paid his own debt," he said solemnly.

CHAPTER III
The House of the Woman of Death

Mr. Laxworthy sat in the porch of the Paradise Hotel, with his grey shawl arranged as usual about his shoulders, a volume of philosophy upon his knee, a pencil in his hand, and a notebook on the small round table by his side. It was barely half-past nine o'clock, but the sun was already high in the clear blue sky, and only the faintest of breezes was rustling in the leaves of the olive and cypress trees. A little stream of people was all the time passing from the hotel, out on to the terrace and down the steps to the golf links, but of these Mr. Laxworthy took no notice whatever. His attention appeared to be entirely absorbed by the volume which lay open upon his knee. There was something almost sphinx-like about his studied isolation.

Radiant in her white linen gown and white tam-o'-shanter, the American girl came out of the hotel on her way to the golf links. She alone remained unimpressed by Mr. Laxworthy's obvious desire for solitude. Directly she saw him she made her way to his side.

"Good morning, Mr. Laxworthy," she said quite amiably.

Mr. Laxworthy slowly turned his head. His reply was perfectly polite, but his tone certainly did not invite overtures. The young lady, however, remained absolutely unconscious of his lack of cordiality. She was much too spoilt to believe that any one of the opposite sex could possibly exist to whom her companionship was not agreeable. Besides, she rather prided herself upon being on specially intimate terms with Mr. Laxworthy.

"I was hoping that I should see you this morning," she remarked, drawing up a chair to his side. "There is something I wanted to ask you."

Mr. Laxworthy gave no evidence of any curiosity. His pencil had paused. He seemed, indeed, in the act of making a note in his book. There was nothing about his manner even to indicate that he was conscious of what she was saying.

"It is about Mr. Lenfield," she went on confidentially. "You admitted the other night, in those few wonderful words of yours, that the poor man who was killed had probably come down here on business connected with Mr. Lenfield."

"Did I?" he murmured absently. "I really forget."

She frowned.

"I do not think that you can possibly have forgotten," she declared. "It was very clever indeed of you to find out all those things without trying in the least, and it proves that you must have great powers of observation.

It is for that reason that I have come to ask you a question. Have you any idea as to the nature of the business which the murdered man might have had with Mr. Lenfield?"

Mr. Laxworthy sighed.

"My dear young lady," he protested, "I know nothing about the matter at all. Chance brought a few of those little happenings before my notice, and I felt bound to point them out. For the rest, the whole affair is not one that interests me. So far as I am concerned, it is finished and done with. I am entirely absorbed in my work."

"I know that," she replied calmly: "but I happen to be a little interested in Mr. Lenfield, and I should like to know whether he has ever done anything likely to put him in the power of such men as the person who was killed. That sounds rather involved, but I am sure that you know what I mean."

Mr. Laxworthy kept his place with his forefinger, and turned his head toward the girl.

"What is your interest in Mr. Lenfield?" he asked.

She leaned forward, tapping the tips of her shoes with the golf club which she carried in her hand.

"Not what you think," she replied. "I was sorry for Mr. Lenfield. I found him very agreeable to talk to, and we are very good friends—"

"Then why not ask him yourself?" Mr. Laxworthy broke in ruthlessly.

"I had intended to," she admitted, "but as a matter of fact I have to play golf at ten o'clock, and I believe that Mr. Lenfield is about to leave for a few days."

Mr. Laxworthy sat quite still for several moments.

"Did he tell you that he was going away?" he asked.

She shook her head.

"I happened to find out quite by accident," she said confidentially; "and, to tell you the truth, I thought it a little strange that he had said nothing to me about it. You know, I have seen a great deal of him since he has been here, and when he was quite ill I used to go and sit with him."

"Indeed!" Mr. Laxworthy remarked gravely. "Under those circumstances, I think his unannounced departure a most ungraceful act."

She shrugged her shoulders.

"You can't tell me anything about him, then?" she asked bluntly.

Mr. Laxworthy considered for a moment.

"No," he said slowly, "I can tell you nothing about him. At the same time, if you had come to me and told me that your friendship with him was likely to increase rather than diminish, I might have said—"

"Said what?" the girl interrupted eagerly.

"That it was a pity," Mr. Laxworthy replied, turning back to his book.

"Then you do know something," she persisted. "And what is that you have there underneath that ugly volume of yours? A time-table, I declare! You don't mean to say that you are going off, too?"

"By no means," Mr. Laxworthy assured her. "The time-table I was glancing at merely as a matter of curiosity. I thought it would be interesting to know how long it took to get to Monte Carlo."

"Mr. Lenfield is going to Monte Carlo," she remarked.

Mr. Laxworthy nodded. The affair seemed to be devoid of interest to him.

"You don't want to tell me anything about him, I suppose—is that it?" she asked.

"I really know nothing," Mr. Laxworthy repeated. "You give me credit for both interest and perceptions which I do not possess. My studies, I suppose, have quickened my powers of observation a little, and the facts that helped to solve the mystery of the flower farm were easy enough to put together. So far as regards Mr. Lenfield personally, I do not think that one needs to be a close student of human nature to decide that he is not a person worthy of an unqualified amount of trust."

"This is only your opinion?" she persisted.

"Only my opinion," Mr. Laxworthy admitted. "And, my dear young lady, if you will allow me to call you so, permit me to point out that while I find your society at all times a most charming distraction, you are just now interrupting what I look upon as my most valuable two hours' work of the day."

She rose at once.

"You certainly are the most ungallant person," she declared. "You are exactly what I have read all Englishmen were like, before I came over."

She moved away, and Mr. Laxworthy returned with a little sigh of relief to his labours. Presently the concierge crossed the threshold of the hotel and came out into the sunshine. Mr. Laxworthy, without appearing to glance up or to interrupt his labours, beckoned him to approach.

"Fritz," he said, "the automobile which Mr. Wing ordered is in waiting?"

"But certainly, sir. It has been here for at least an hour."

"Anyone going away by the omnibus this morning?" Mr. Laxworthy asked carelessly.

"Mr. Lenfield and Mr. Hamar, sir," Fritz replied. "They are going to Monte Carlo for a few days."

Mr. Laxworthy went back to his work. About fifty yards away Mr. Lenfield, looking very ghastly and worn, was leaning back in a chair with his friend by his side. Over his shoulder he had glanced more than once at Mr. Laxworthy, reading and writing in his corner.

"I can't stand that man," he muttered hoarsely. "There is something about him that paralyses me. He sits and watches and waits like a spider. He scarcely moves an eyelash, and yet one feels that he sees all the time."

The young man shivered. His companion laughed.

"That's all rubbish, Philip," he declared. "He did you a good turn the other night, anyway."

The young man turned his head slowly. So far, the southern air seemed to have done little towards restoring his health. His cheeks were still hollow, and his colour ghastly. In his deep-set eyes there lurked still, too, the light of an unquenchable fear.

"A good turn," he muttered. "How do I know that? The end was very near—the end of the journey, Hamar. Why not? One wearies, these days."

His friend looked at him reproachfully.

"Philip," he protested, "this isn't like you. Brace up. Remember there is work before us. If you can sit here before we start, and feel your heart wax faint, what will it be when the time comes?"

The young man shrugged his shoulders.

"For a person in my condition," he said, "there is nothing so stimulating as action. It is when we sit here that I grow weak. I have grown to hate the place. That man's eyes follow us everywhere."

Hamar laughed contemptuously.

"A queer, old-fashioned, bent little misanthrope, with spectacles, and a grey shawl around his shoulders, and rubbers if there's a cloud in the sky!" he exclaimed. "You are full of fancies, Philip. Listen. There is the omnibus coming up from the garage. Let us return to the hotel."

The large white motor omnibus came puffing up to the front, and was soon crowded with little groups of guests on their way down to the town. Mr. Hamar and his companion were the only two who had any luggage. Mr. Helder, the proprietor of the hotel, came out to wish them "Good morning."

"It is only for two or three days," Mr. Hamar declared, shaking hands. "You will see that our rooms are undisturbed? I thought that a flutter at the tables might brighten up our young friend."

Mr. Helder who was well aware of certain gossip concerning the events of a few nights ago, bowed gravely. To tell the truth, he had no particular desire for the return of these two guests. On the other hand, they had taken their rooms for a month, and he was powerless.

"I wish you both good fortune, gentlemen," he said. "One hears that the tables are doing badly just now."

The omnibus started off, commencing its circling detour down into the valley. From behind the glass-enclosed space where Mr. Laxworthy sat taking his sun-bath, he watched until it became a speck in the distance. Then he carefully closed his volume, put the notebook into his pocket, and rose to his feet. As though his doing so were some sort of signal, his two friends suddenly appeared upon the scene. Sydney Wing came strolling up the steps from the golf club, smoking a cigarette and swinging a new mashie which he had just bought. Forrest Anderson, with a big cigar in his mouth, came walking briskly down the broad terrace. The three met on the flagged space in front of the porch.

"So our friends have gone to Monte Carlo to try the tables!" Forrest Anderson said thoughtfully.

Mr. Laxworthy looked at the little cloud of dust, now faint in the distance.

"They are gone, I think," he murmured, "to play for larger stakes than Monte Carlo knows of. Is everything ready?"

Anderson nodded.

"The car is round at the back."

"A jolly good one too," Sydney interposed. "A six-cylinder Rochet. I can get sixty miles an hour out of her any time."

"I sincerely trust," Mr. Laxworthy said sharply, "that it will not be necessary for you to attempt any such folly! You can fetch it."

Sydney nodded and passed through the swing doors on his way to the back of the hotel. A few moments later he reappeared in the avenue, driving a large and handsome touring car, which he piloted to the front of the hotel. Mr. Laxworthy permitted himself to be wrapped in a fur coat, although he still insisted upon the shawl around his shoulders. Just as he was stepping in, the American girl came strolling up the steps from the golf course. Mr. Laxworthy hesitated for a moment. The incident perplexed him.

"You have not been disappointed in your match, I trust?" he inquired, with his foot upon the step.

The girl nodded.

"Mrs. Morson doesn't feel like playing this morning," she remarked. "Don't you want to take me for a ride in that beautiful car instead?"

"With pleasure," Mr. Laxworthy replied politely. "Will you come as you are?"

She looked down at her white linen gown, white shoes and stockings, and the tam-o'-shanter which she was carrying. Her hands touched for a moment her bare head.

"How far are you going?" she asked.

"It is one of my peculiarities," Mr. Laxworthy explained, "that when I start for a little expedition of this sort, I never know. If I enjoy it, I shall go on; if I dislike it, I shall come back."

"If I join you," the girl announced, "I shall claim the privileges of my sex and decide when we are to return."

"On the contrary," Mr. Laxworthy retorted, "the privileges of my infirmities and years will survive. You will come back when I choose."

"I was certainly right when I told you that you are not gallant," she decided, smiling at him.

"My dear young lady," Mr. Laxworthy answered, "I never laid claim to such a quality."

"I can see," she declared, "that I am going to be deserted. Did Mr. Lenfield go on the omnibus, do you know?"

"I believe so," Mr. Laxworthy replied. "Mr. Hamar and he left together."

She smiled.

"The poor fellow ought to have some luck at Monte Carlo. He suffers enough in other ways."

Mr. Laxworthy took his place in the car.

"Since you will not accompany us," he said, "we will wish you 'Good morning.'"

"I don't consider that I was pressed to come, you know," she remarked, watching them settle down.

"Young lady," Mr. Laxworthy returned grimly, "it is very certain that if you had desired to accompany us, you would be occupying at the present moment the seat by my side."

"I am not sure," she laughed, "that I like that reputation you give me."

"It leads," Mr. Laxworthy replied, as the car rolled off, "to success in most of the small cross-ways of life."

She waved her hand and watched them disappear. Mr. Laxworthy was busy arranging his spectacles and cap to keep off the glare of the sun.

"What do you think of that young lady?" Anderson asked him curiously.

Mr. Laxworthy touched his spectacles with his fingers to feel that they were perfectly safe, and leaned back in his place.

"A few minutes ago," he declared, "I was inclined to fear that she might have more intelligence than she cared to display. I was even inclined to fear that she might mar to a certain extent the success of our little expedition to-day."

"And now?" Anderson asked quickly.

"On the whole," Mr. Laxworthy pronounced, "I am reassured. I believe that her interest in our doings merely results from the natural inquisitiveness of her race."

Monsieur Rénaultin, estate agent, lessor of villas—furnished and unfurnished—auctioneer and valuer, closed his ledger that morning with a little sigh. For some reason or other things were decidedly flat. The weather was surely all that could be desired. His dusty little office, situated in the main street of Tropez, was flooded with February sunshine. But the visitors came not, or if they came they stayed at hotels, or took villas from their friends without employing the services of an agent. No stranger had passed his threshold for three days. No coroneted or crested letter, demanding an exact list of his desirable Mediterranean residences, had reached him for more than a week. It grew near to midday. One might as well breakfast. So Monsieur Rénaultin closed his ledger, took down a white felt hat from its peg, arranged his necktie, and permitted his mind to dwell upon the occupation which appealed to him more dearly than any other during the day save his dinner. It should be breakfast, by all means. He must endeavour to forget that he had done nothing to earn it. He had carefully closed the door and was standing upon the step leading into the office, when a great touring car came haltingly along the street, the driver looking from left to right. Monsieur Rénaultin was immediately upon the alert. A direction was almost equivalent to an introduction; an introduction might lead to business. He composed his features into a state of amiable interest. He flattered himself, as he stood there swinging his cane and regarding these three perplexed travellers, that if indeed they were in need of directions, they would certainly apply to one who seemed so willing and so able to give them. Apparently he was not mistaken. The car came to a standstill before the door of his office. He stepped forward with a little bow.

"The gentlemen desire?"

"This is Monsieur Rénaultin?" Sydney asked, raising his cap.

Monsieur Rénaultin swept the pavement with his own hat. This was more than he had dared to hope.

"But certainly!"

"We wish to inquire about a villa," Sydney announced.

Monsieur Rénaultin was instantly at his best. The three Englishmen were ushered into his office and comfortably seated in the only three safe chairs. Photographs, drawn eagerly from a large portfolio, were passed from hand to hand. Prices, accommodations, location, were described with picturesque and ample detail, with eloquence impossible to reproduce. They were palaces, these villas which Monsieur Rénaultin had to let; or ideal little dwellings, whose lawns were embowered with roses, with their strip of sand lapped by the Mediterranean; or ensconced in pine-woods whose fragrance was the most delicious, with an air, an atmosphere, sufficient almost to bring the dead to life. The three men listened, appreciative but silent. One photograph, which Monsieur Rénaultin had been on the point of handing out, he retained in his hand. Mr. Laxworthy, who had said little, leaned over and looked at it.

"It is strange, this location," he remarked. "It looks as though it were built into the sea."

"It is the Villa de Cap Frinet," Monsieur Rénaultin explained. "It is reached only from the mainland by a narrow strip of sand, at high tide no more than a passage, beautiful, as monsieur sees, unfortunately not to let at present."

"I like the appearance of the place," Mr. Laxworthy said. "Do I understand that it is let for the whole season?"

"A month ago, monsieur," he declared, "I let it for three months. Curiously enough, although I have received the rent, the tenants have not yet, to the best of my belief, taken possession. They are expected now, I hear, every day."

"It is let to some English people, perhaps?" Mr. Laxworthy inquired.

"Who can tell?" Monsieur Rénaultin replied enigmatically. "You English, nowadays, speak all languages so perfectly. The lady who took it spoke French. There was a trifle of accent, perhaps, but not sufficient to determine her nationality."

"Is the name a secret?" Anderson asked. "The villa rather takes my fancy, too."

"By no means, gentlemen," Monsieur Rénaultin assured them. "The name of the lady was Madame Laichenon. If monsieur is curious, there is this to be told. She was, I should say, a Jewess. However, the villa is let. Monsieur permits me to draw his attention to the most charming and desirable residence upon the whole Riviera, one mile from San Raphael, a perfect gem."

They listened politely, but it was obvious that they were no longer deeply interested. Mr. Laxworthy, upon some excuse or another, pressed a fee into the hand of the reluctant agent, and took particulars of two of the most desirable villas.

"In a day or two," he declared, "we shall return. In the meantime, we will glance at these place on our way to Monte Carlo. You might also give me a card to view the Villa de Cap Frinet. It is possible that the tenants may not stay longer than the three months. I myself am likely to remain here until June."

Monsieur Rénaultin acquiesced promptly and made out the cards. The business of leave-taking followed, a little elaborate from the fact of the unexpected fee, the hope of letting a villa as well, and the faint smell of omelette wafting up the street from the café. However, it was over at last. Monsieur Rénaultin, with a cigarette in his mouth, went gaily down the street, humming to himself. The touring car shot forward, already in its fourth speed. The three men were a little silent.

"If it should be the woman Rachael!" Anderson murmured.

Mr. Laxworthy looked steadily in front of him.

"Who can tell?"

In less than an hour they were compelled to slacken their pace. They were on a road now of wonderful curves, and every few moments brought them to the very edge of the Mediterranean. They skirted little sandy bays, where brown-faced fishermen gazed at them with the stolid wonder of their class. They encircled high walls, which seemed built to preserve jealously the privacy of some dainty villa almost hidden from the outside world. It was like a miniature toy-land, where people might dwell whose souls were in fairyland. One saw no village. All the pressure and commonplace details of actual life were absent. Then the car came to a standstill. Before them was a little avenue with a locked iron gate, and painted upon the wall "Villa de Cap Frinet."

"It is here," Mr. Laxworthy announced.

"It is here," the others echoed.

They did not at once descend. Mr. Laxworthy seemed to be making observations of the locality. Presently he pointed to a hill a short distance ahead.

"We will ascend," he said. "There we can judge."

The car shot forward. In a few minutes they gained the summit of a steep ascent. From there, looking downwards, they could see the villa itself—a strange little white building which seemed, indeed, as though it had risen like a shell from the sea, with a green veranda which almost encircled it. The gardens were on the mainland, and a little walk with a handrail of about fifteen or twenty yards long led to this curious abode. There was a landing-stage, but, so far as they could see, no boat. No smoke issued from the chimneys of the villa. It had, indeed, all the appearance of being, as the agent had assured them, as yet unoccupied. Nevertheless, the three men sat in the car on the brow of the hill, and were for a time undecided.

"Let us consider," Mr. Laxworthy said softly. "We are moving a little in the clouds. A false step just now might result in serious inconvenience to all of us."

Anderson, who had been gazing at the villa through a pair of small field-glasses, laid them down.

"I am convinced," he declared, "that at present, at any rate, the place is empty."

"It has that appearance," Mr. Laxworthy admitted, "and yet, to-day is the twelfth of the month. To-night should be the night of the great appointment. We know well that yesterday afternoon Madame Laichenon played baccarat in the sporting club at Monte Carlo. We also know that our friends left Hyères this morning, so the meeting-place cannot be far distant. To reach here, they would have to go to Cannes and return. My idea is that Cannes was the meeting-place, that from there they would motor here. On that assumption they cannot arrive for two hours and a half. One would imagine that the others would come from Marseilles."

Sydney was listening with knitted brows.

"It is all rather guess-work, isn't it?" he remarked. "It seems rather as though we were stepping into a big thing blindfolded."

"It is my principle," Mr. Laxworthy continued, "to proceed always upon assumptions, provided those assumptions are logical and carefully thought out. I propose, therefore, that, having this card to view the villa which we procured from Monsieur Rénaultin, we forthwith make an inspection of the place. There can be no harm in that, nor very much risk."

"It is agreed," the others murmured.

Sydney backed the car, and they glided down the hill to the iron gate. The padlock resisted their efforts to enter, but Mr. Laxworthy, with a curious little instrument which he took from his pocket, carefully picked the lock. He examined the ground closely.

"At any rate," he said, "no one has passed in by this entrance for several days."

The descent was almost perpendicular, down a narrow and curving drive-way, on either side of which were thickly growing shrubs and trees, which formed almost an arch over their heads.

"At night this will be as black as the Styx," Sydney murmured.

"So much the better," Mr. Laxworthy assented. "It is a veritable tunnel."

They came suddenly out into the sunlight. The garden was a tangled wilderness of beauty. Mimosa and climbing roses had run riot about the place. There was a whole shrubbery of flaming rhododendrons, a tool-house smothered with clematis. The oleander trees were in blossom. From the midst of a great cactus one blood-red flower gave out a strange perfume. Nowhere was there any sign of any human being. They moved on across the overgrown lawn until they reached the water's edge. They were separated now from the villa only by that little strip of passage-way. Mr. Laxworthy held up his hand.

"Be silent!" he ordered.

There was something ominous in his tone. They remained perfectly motionless, still partially obscured beneath the grove of oleanders which fringed the bay. Through the leaves Mr. Laxworthy stood like a figure of stone, with his eyes fixed upon the villa.

"There is someone there," he said at last, softly.

"There is no other entrance," Sydney whispered.

Mr. Laxworthy inclined his head a little on one side. They saw then the stern of a small petrol-driven launch anchored on the other side of the villa, so close under the walls that it had been invisible from the hill.

"It is not only that," Mr. Laxworthy murmured. "Listen."

They all listened intently. The air seemed full of the repose of afternoon.

Little waves which were scarcely more than a tremor broke upon the thin line of shingle. A few bees were humming, but the place was empty of birds. The background of silence was almost unnatural. And then they all heard the sound which had first been heard only by Mr. Laxworthy—the faint, low moaning of a human being in pain or terror.

"We are too late!" Anderson muttered.

Mr. Laxworthy shook his head.

"It is never too late. Come."

He straightened himself and brushed away the protecting branches of the oleanders. Then he drew his grey shawl closely around his shoulders and stepped casually along towards that narrow footpath. With his hand upon the rail he stopped and turned to his companions.

"Everything about this place," he declared enthusiastically, "favours one's desire for seclusion. Think how one could work amongst such surroundings. Who could there be to disturb one! What unwelcome visitors, indeed, could find one out in such a Paradise?"

They took his cue and chattered lightly, but Anderson was a little pale beneath his healthy tan, and the fingers which held the match to Sydney's cigarette distinctly shook. Mr. Laxworthy stepped leisurely along the narrow path. If he saw the white face suddenly flash behind the window-pane, he took no notice.

"Have you said your prayers?" Sydney murmured to Anderson.

Anderson shrugged his shoulders.

"I expect to hear the bullets whiz at any moment," he replied, "but what can one do? The chief knows."

At the end of the narrow walk they stood literally upon a rock. Here and there were little clefts filled up with green and planted with scarlet geraniums. Immediately in front of them was a broad veranda which encircled the whole of the villa. There were indications that the formal entrance was on the other side. Mr. Laxworthy paused to look around him.

"This," he declared, "is perfectly delightful. I wonder if by any chance it would be possible to get inside. Try that window, Sydney."

The young man's hand was already outstretched toward the fastening. Suddenly he stood as though transfixed. No one moved. Distinctly from the other side of the house came the unmistakable sound of a petrol engine.

"They are off, by God!" Anderson muttered.

Mr. Laxworthy led the way around the veranda to the front. A dozen yard already from the landing-stage a man was bending over the wheel of a low, petrol-driven launch. He turned his head to look at them, and even Mr. Laxworthy gave a little cry. The man's face was obscured by a black mask, he was wrapped from head to foot in a white linen overall. It was impossible to even guess what manner of a person he might be. Already the foam was flying into the air as he gathered speed. He turned round, and holding the wheel still in his left hand, raised his right hand to the skies. He ignored altogether the three who were watching him. His eyes sought an open window.

"My word!" he cried. "I have kept my word! You hear, Rachael?"

There was no sound save the beating of the engine of his boat. The three men stood gazing at him from the balcony. And then they heard suddenly the crash of breaking glass above them. Splinters of it fell all around. They looked upwards. Through a great jagged space in the window of the room above, a woman seemed to have dragged herself upon her side. She lay there, raised a little on her left hand, whilst with her right she lifted a long, strange-looking pistol to a resting place on the fancy ironwork of the balcony.

"And what about mine, Henri?" she cried.

There was a blinding flash, a sharp, metallic report, and the dull spit of a bullet in the waves. The man gave a cry and crouched over his wheel. Again and again came the report and the flash.

"A repeating Mauser!" Sydney whispered hoarsely. "By God! she's hit him."

The man gave suddenly a hideous start. Quivering all over, he fell back from the wheel. The boat swung round before he could grip it again. The woman's teeth were parted, her face was set in awful lines, her eyes looked steadily from the end of the barrel of her pistol towards the man at whom she had fired.

"Twelve more!" she cried. "Good-bye, Henri! This is the end. I kiss the bullet."

The man in the boat half jumped up and again he was hit. He staggered, lost his balance, and fell over with a cry. Sydney tore off his coat and waistcoat. The woman looked down and seemed as though she had seen them for the first time. She was laughing. She leaned over the balcony and her voice was soft.

"Do not be foolish, young English gentleman," she called out. "He is dead—dead in many places. Would you dive fifty feet for a corpse? Come up here and I will show you something."

"It is Rachael," Mr. Laxworthy whispered. "She is right, Sydney. The man is scarcely worth saving. Let him alone. Come."

They found the door of the villa open. The little hall inside was all confusion, as though some sort of struggle had taken place there. They mounted the stairs. On the threshold of the front room, Sydney, who was leading, hesitated.

"It is Rachael herself," he muttered, "the woman of death!"

Mr. Laxworthy pushed by.

"She will not hurt us," he declared.

He threw open the door. The woman was still half crouching upon the floor. Her legs were tied together with rope, the end of which was attached to the bed-post. One arm was bleeding with the effort she had made to disengage herself. Nothing remained of that terrible expression with which she had gazed across the bay. She welcomed them with a soft, almost inviting smile. The pistol lay smoking upon the carpet by her side.

"My friends," she said, "your arrival is opportune. I am very glad to see you. You wish to take a villa, perhaps? I see the card in your hand. It is an admirable residence, this: a tranquil, idyllic spot, where nothing happens, where one may rest—as he will rest."

She pointed toward the sea. Mr. Laxworthy came over and cut the cords from about her feet. He looked around the room.

"Madame," he remarked, with a shrug of the shoulders, "you pay your debts in full."

"Monsieur," she said, "it is the custom of my race. If you are amongst those in whose blood is the love of adventure, although indeed you do not seem of that kind, stay with me here for a little while and you shall see other things."

"Thank you," Mr. Laxworthy replied, "we are peaceful Englishmen looking for a villa."

"You lie," she answered. "You are Mr. John T. Laxworthy, the man of peculiar gifts."

"Dear me!" Mr. Laxworthy exclaimed. "You seem to me to be a remarkably well-informed young woman."

She laughed softly. She was standing up now, but she was pale. Anderson was binding her arm with his own handkerchief.

"Listen!" she said. "You have seen the beginning of a tragedy. I owe you something, perhaps, for your timely appearance. You are a man, and one can trust men. Stay here, then, with me and watch for the second part."

"Madame," Mr. Laxworthy answered, "I do not doubt your hospitable instincts, but your method of ridding yourself of undesirable guests appears to me a little arbitrary. I am not sure whether, from your point of view, or from the point of view of those whom we meet here to-night, that we ourselves might not be considered a little *de trop*."

She held out her hand.

"Monsieur," she announced, "I am Rachael. I am not like that man who lies at the bottom of the sea. I have my friends and my enemies, and they know it. I offer you the chance of your lifetime. To-night there will meet here the man whose deeds a short time ago set all London in a panic, and the bloodhounds who have never been wholly off his track. They meet here and in this spot. It should be worth seeing. Stay, then, with me. From now until night there is a truce between us, if you accept it. After that, who shall say?"

Mr. Laxworthy removed his shawl.

"Madame," he replied, "it will give my friends and myself much pleasure to accept the hospitality of your villa for a short time. We have a motorcar outside. Might I suggest that we spend some of the time before evening in taking you with us to San Raphael? There is an agreeable hotel there, and madame must dine."

She swept him a little curtsy.

"Monsieur," she said, "in the heart of every Englishman, even an Englishman of such accomplishments as Mr. Laxworthy undoubtedly possesses, there dwells a foolish and unnatural prejudice in favour of justice. I fear very much that if you and I were to pass a police-station, the memory of that man who was without doubt my victim might render my position a little precarious. I can assure you that there are other things I can do besides revenge my wrongs. I can make an *omelette aux tomates,* I can roast a chicken as few others, I can mix a salad dressing which is immortal, and you will find from my sideboard that my taste in champagne is unexceptionable."

Mr. Laxworthy permitted himself a smile.

"Madame," he declared, "your invitation is too piquant. I speak for myself and my friends. We accept with pleasure your charming invitation. And in the meantime—"

He stooped and picked up the pistol. With deft fingers he withdrew the cartridges. She smiled at him.

"Monsieur," she said, "until to-night it is yours."

CHAPTER IV
The Strange Meeting at the Villa de Cap Frinet

The glass enclosed luncheon-room of the Casino at Cannes was filled almost to overflowing when Madame Bertrand stopped at the head of the little flight of stairs to make some inquiry of the manager, who had stepped forward to meet her. There was to be a polo match in the afternoon, and the opposing teams, with many of their friends, were seated at one long table, which stretched almost the length of the apartment. Elsewhere were many interesting groups. A Russian grand duke was offering hospitality to a lady whose dancing had once been the delight of two continents. A newly married English peer and his Italian wife were being entertained by a lady of the Royal House of Germany. There were Americans galore, a famous French actress and her dramatist, some well-escorted young ladies of musical-comedy fame from London, a well-known English jockey, and a young lady who might have been his wife. And, amongst it all, two highly respectable middle-aged ladies from Boston, who, to the horror of their waiter, had ordered and were actually drinking tea with their *lobster Neuberg*. Madame Bertrand, who was looking quite her best, and towards whom many heads were turned, stood looking down upon this motley scene.

"It is a gentleman alone whom I seek," she announced. "He left a message for me with the concierge—Monsieur Grayes."

The manager turned his head.

"There is a gentleman who sits alone on the other side of the room, madame," he said. "A yard or so farther round the palms there, and you may see him."

Madame Bertrand inclined her head graciously.

"It is he," she admitted. "Conduct me, if you please."

The manager led the way, and Madame Bertrand walked slowly down the room. Her gown of white serge fitted her to perfection. Her dull gold hair was arranged in the latest fashion. Her dark eyes shone luminously from the background of her pale skin. She was, without doubt, a very handsome woman.

"My dear Paul!" she cried, approaching the man who sat alone.

He sprang at once to his feet. He had been sitting with his left shoulder towards the room, looking out the window at the wonderful harbour, at the white sails gleaming on the deep blue sea, at the silver spray which leapt into the sunshine only a few yards below. He was a man of medium height, squarely and compactly built, with strongly marked features and prominent cheek-bones. He wore his black hair parted in the middle and a little long. His jaw, too, was exceptionally powerful, and his whole appearance gave one the impression of great strength. Nevertheless, his voice when he spoke was exceedingly soft.

"My dear Julie!" he exclaimed. "How careless of me that I did not see you! I sat down here instead of waiting above because the rush for tables was so great that I feared they might be tempted to give this one away. It is charming to see you."

She gave him her hand, which he held for a moment in his. Then he helped her off with her coat and remained standing until she had taken her seat.

"Luncheon is already ordered," he told the *maître d'hôtel*. "Be so good as to see that it is served at once. Madame is, I am sure, hungry—perhaps even as hungry as I am."

"You are from Monte Carlo this morning?" she asked.

"This morning," he admitted. "I drove myself, and I was impatient. Once more let me tell you that it is charming to see you again, dear Julie."

She smiled a little bitterly. Perhaps she detected something of the insincerity of the man's words.

"You are very gallant, my dear Paul," she said. "I only wish that you meant half of what you say. What you, of course, are anxious to hear is my news."

"Julie!" he exclaimed reproachfully.

"We women are never so great fools," she continued, "that we do not understand in our hearts, even though sometimes it gives us pleasure to make believe. However, let that pass. I break my journey here to meet you, and I am glad to do it."

"You had my letter, then?"

She inclined her head.

"Everything has happened exactly as you surmised," she told him. "The two people whom you very carefully described left Hyères this morning. They travelled down to the station in the omnibus and I in a small victoria, but we met at the railway station and again at Toulon. They booked to Monte Carlo, but they descended here."

"You speak now," he asked eagerly, "of the stout red-faced man, Hamar, and his invalid friend, who goes by the name of Lenfield?"

"Exactly," she replied.

"Now tell me," he continued. "There is an elderly little man staying at the Paradise Hotel, whose name is Laxworthy—John T. Laxworthy. He has two friends with him—a Mr. Sydney Wing and a Mr. Forrest Anderson. They seem ordinary people enough, but this man Laxworthy appears to interest himself curiously in other people's business. There was a murder at the flower farm at Hyères—rather an interesting little affair, by the by—which he seems to have cleared up to everybody's satisfaction. Who is he?"

"I cannot tell you who he is," Madame Bertrand replied, "but I can tell you this. You may find it interesting. He and both his friends left the Paradise Hotel in an eighty horse-power motor-car twenty minutes after the other two had left for the station."

The eyes of the man who listened were suddenly bright.

"This Laxworthy," he muttered—"is he, too, in the game?"

Madame Bertrand was grave.

"Paul," she said, "I do not know what game it is that you speak of. You keep everything so secret from me. But I can tell you this. Mr. Laxworthy and his friends are not entirely what they seem. They belong more or less to those who seek adventures."

"You know this?" he demanded.

"Assuredly. One of the three stole a paper from my purse. It was a safe conduct to a French battleship, and very nearly resulted in the theft of some valuable papers."

The man tapped on the table for a moment with his forefinger. He seemed to be thinking deeply. Then the service of luncheon commenced and he showed himself to be at once an exacting and scrupulous dietari-an. To all appearances he had little interest in life beside the satisfactory composition of the salad, concerning which he talked so earnestly with the waiter who bent over his chair. Afterwards he made a remark to his companion about the situation of the Casino, the number of people in Cannes, the composition of the American polo team who were to play that afternoon, his own journey from Monte Carlo in a wonderful new racing car built specially to his order. It was not for some time, indeed, that he returned to their former subject of conversation.

"Julie," he said thoughtfully, "I do not understand why all these people should have come together at the Paradise Hotel. So far as regards the two in whom you know I am chiefly interested—Hamar and Philip Lenfield—it was a safe resting-place. They were close to the final rendezvous, they were in touch with everyone of importance. But afterwards I hear that Lefant is there, Freeling Poignton, now this man Laxworthy and his associates."

"It is a matter of chance," she murmured.

"I do not believe in chance," he answered. "The man Laxworthy disturbs me. To-night should be a night of simple issues."

Madame Bertrand sighed as she took an olive from the dish.

"You talk to me as though I understood," she reminded him.

"Dear Julie," he said, "why should you not understand? You and I sit here this morning amongst a cloud of butterflies, whose only thought is to crowd into their short lives as much happiness as possible. For us there are more serious things—for me especially. This young man Philip Lenfield and I have been concerned in the same affairs for the last three years. Others have fallen away. He and I alone remain."

"You are enemies?" she whispered.

"Enemies, without a doubt," the man answered softly. "While we both live, there is danger. To-night will be the end."

"You meet him to-night?"

"At a villa between here and San Raphael," he told her. "The meeting has been fixed for some time. He believes that he has made everything secure. The woman Rachael has gone over to his side. He expects to reach the villa to-night and to find her there, its mistress. I have planned other things. Rachael's day is past. Before we reach the Villa de Cap Frinet, Gassiat will have settled with her."

"The woman whom you loved," Madame Bertrand murmured.

The man looked at her. Throughout the whole of the time, his expression had varied scarcely as much as the flicker of an eyelid. Yet at this moment his eyes seemed to contract, the flesh around his mouth to grow tighter.

"Julie," he said, "where I love, I trust, and where I trust no longer, my love turns to hate. So with Rachael. She was the woman of my heart. I was faithful to her. I trusted her. She shared my destiny. I was ready to walk hand in hand with her to the end. We have been together in great failures and in great triumphs. Yet the time came when she failed me. She thought she saw the beginning of the end. It was in London, a year ago. We were hard-pressed, it is true. Lacroy and Panmur went down. Felix was arrested. We seemed, indeed, stricken to the core. She never believed that I should escape. I was there in London in those days, Julie, with a cordon around me. Every morning the papers declared that within a few hours I must be arrested. Arrested, indeed! When the time came that I was ready to leave England, I walked out of the Grosvenor Hotel with my valet behind me, and saw my luggage piled up on the train, and bought my magazines at the bookstall. I strolled up and down opposite my reserved place until the train started. I talked to my fellow passengers and I made my bow to England as many another. That was the end of all this talk of my arrest. Since then I have lived as I chose, I have done as I chose. The others went down—all save that one man, Philip Lenfield. He only has known. He and I together have seen the others go to their doom. To-night we are to meet."

She looked at him as though fascinated. She had stopped eating, her eyes were almost distended. He, on the other hand, seemed wholly unmoved.

His tone was perfectly matter-of-fact, his manner clam and self-possessed. She sat there and remembered the time when all Europe had rung with his name, when the papers discussed from hour to hour the chances of his capture.

"In that delightful island," he continued, "where I spent some not unprofitable months, they entirely forgot that it was possible for a person of education—shall I say a gentleman?—to associate for his own purposes with the scum of the world. They searched for me all the time as though I were one of the others. Absurd! They ransacked Whitechapel and Houndsditch whilst I read the morning papers in the lounge at the Savoy. To-night my secret will go down to the grave."

"You trust so few people," she murmured. "Why do you trust me?"

He helped himself to wine, thoughtfully and with a careful hand.

"My dear Julie," he said, "some women keep silence through love, but love turns sometimes, through the byways of jealousy, into hate. Therefore, I do not always trust the woman who loves. With you it is fear, and fear is a more terrible thing. I trust always the woman who fears me."

She leaned back in her chair and laughed. The laugher was musical enough, but it was not wholly natural.

"Really," she declared, "you should have been a greater man than you are. If you had started life with different ambitions, who knows to what you might not have reached?"

The man shrugged his shoulders.

"I would not waste a second of my time," he replied, "in profitless thought. Let that pass. Tell me, are you returning to the Paradise Hotel?"

"To-morrow. I go from here to visit some dear friends who have a villa up in the hills. I stay there to-night."

"I will take you there presently," he said. "In the meantime, I have a fancy. Telephone to your hotel and ask whether Mr. Laxworthy and his friends have returned. In all my doings I like certainties, and in my plans for to-day there is no other element of uncertainty save in the doings of that intrusive person."

She wrote out a message and handed it to the *chasseur.* They lingered over their coffee, and presently the reply was brought.

"Madame," the boy announced, "I have spoken with the Paradise Hotel at Hyères. Monsieur Laxworthy and his friends have not returned."

They dismissed him. The man whose name was Grayes sat for some moments in silence. Then he took a cigarette from his case and smoked.

"I have made my plans," he said thoughtfully, "and I have made them with great nicety, but I have made no allowances for any intervention by any outside party. In the villa at the present moment Rachael lies bound and gagged, awaiting my pleasure. Gassiat is her jailer. At six o'clock this evening I shall be there. At half-past six Lenfield and his bull-dog will be there also."

"Why are you so sure," she asked, "that Philip Lenfield and his friend will be there alone? Are you not afraid lest he should betray you?"

The man shook his head.

"Lenfield knows very well that I am on my guard," he replied. "Besides, this is no ordinary struggle. I tell you many things, but I do not tell you quite all. There is one little fact of which I have not spoken, which, while it makes the young man crave for my death as for nothing else on earth, keeps him yet my slave. He is ordered to meet me there, and he will come. He does not know that he is coming to his end."

Madame Bertrand looked out of the window and sighed.

"It is all too complicated for me," she declared. "I do not understand whether this young man Lenfield is a criminal, a detective, or a traitor?"

Her companion smiled as he paid the bill.

"If he were on his trial," he remarked, "he would find it hard to plead 'Not guilty!' to any one of those charges. Let me take you to your friends' house before I start. I have an hour to spare."

"And to-morrow?" she asked.

"To-morrow," he replied, "when you wake, you may say to yourself that Paul Grayes has commenced a new life. To-morrow I sail from Ville Franche for New York."

Circling the mountain side, dropping now to the shore level, climbing sometimes almost to the skies, Paul Grayes, alone in his low, torpedo-shaped, grey automobile, glided away from Cannes over the most beautiful road in Europe, towards the Villa de Cap Frinet. With his eyes riveted upon the wheel and his cap fixed well over his forehead, the man seemed wholly engrossed in his task, driving with firm fingers and graceful sweeps. If indeed the darkening way were lined with ghosts, no signs of their near presence seemed to trouble or discompose him. He drove on towards his goal as one might pass to his home after the day's work. A little company of cheerful peasants wished him good-night, but gained no answer from him. Such banalities scarcely disturbed his thoughts. It was the end to which he moved. Before the night had passed he meant to rid himself of the two remaining persons on earth still possessed of his secret.

As the sun went down behind the hills, with the slightest touch of the throttle he increased the speed of his car. Once or twice he consulted his watch, and it was barely dusk before he flew up the last ascent. Below him were the little bay and the villa. A single light was flickering from one of the top rooms. He looked at it for a moment thoughtfully. He could picture

Rachael lying there, bound and gagged according to his orders, watched over by Gassiat—the man who had never failed him. Slowly and with firm fingers he guided the car down the hill. Under the shadows of the trees which fringed the villa gardens, he brought it to a standstill and looked once more at his watch. He still had plenty of time. He vaulted lightly over the wall and stood for a moment looking around him at the edge of the lawn. Still no one moved—no sign of life came from the villa. Gassiat should have been on the alert. Nevertheless, he had no thought of evil as he rounded the veranda.

Arrived on the seaward side of the villa, he stopped short. He looked down at the landing-stage with surprise. The launch which he had expected to find fastened there was missing. He stepped back and peered into the boat-shed on the landward side. It was empty save for a small, rickety dinghy. For several moments he hesitated. Nerves were a thing he knew nothing of, yet in the trees at that moment an owl was calling, a faint cold breeze was stirring in the leaves of the cypresses. With the gathering twilight he felt a slight chill, and shivered. A queer little premonition of evil seized him for a moment, only to be brushed on one side impatiently. He had made his plans. It was not likely that anything had gone wrong. If Laxworthy or any other had intervened, the lives of twenty men lay within the weapon upon the butt of which his fingers were already clasped.

He retraced his steps to the front door of the villa and stepped boldly inside. At first he could hear nothing. Slowly he mounted the stairs. He had directed that Rachael was to be bound and left in her bedroom to await his coming. He pushed open the door. There was no trace of her there. He tried all the other rooms upstairs. They were empty. There was no sign of Gassiat, there was no sign of Rachael. Still unfalteringly he descended. What this thing might be which had prevented Gassiat from obeying his orders, he could not tell, but he was prepared to face it. He looked in at the little sitting-room. It was empty. Last of all he opened the door of the dining-room, and he began to understand. He stood there upon the threshold, and his fingers were stiff upon the barrel of his murderous weapon. His hand, however, never moved. For the moment it was useless.

The curtains of the room were closely drawn. Seated at the small round table, on which were the remains of what seemed to have been an excellent dinner, were Rachael, Mr. Laxworthy, Mr. Forrest Anderson, and Sydney. The little halo of tobacco-smoke flickered up towards the ceiling. But the thing which interested him most was the unfaltering and steady pointing of the revolver clasped in Mr. Laxworthy's right hand. Mr. Laxworthy's face was set and rigid, his bottom lip was slightly protruded, his eyes gleamed bright behind his spectacles, his grey shawl was carefully arranged at the back of his chair. The long, skinny forefinger of his right hand hung almost lovingly about the trigger of his weapon. One felt that there was not a single chance in a thousand of his failing, under certain circumstances, to make effective use of it.

"My dear Paul, you are a welcome guest!" Rachael exclaimed, turning her head a little. "Take off your coat and sit down. I have done my best to entertain these gentlemen until your coming."

Paul Grayes stood still upon the threshold, and while he stood his brain was working like lightning. Who was this man Laxworthy? An enemy? One who had been on his track from the first? Was he to be bought, or was this indeed the end? Fortune had always been with him—fortune side by side with his indomitable courage. Was this the last trick in the game? He refused to believe it. He shrugged his shoulders ever so slightly and advanced into the room. He did not, however, at once remove his coat.

"If you are friends of my wife, gentlemen," he said, "you are naturally welcome here. At the same time, you will forgive me if I feel that a certain trifling explanation would not be out of place? You, sir, for instance," he added, addressing Laxworthy, "appear to have adopted an original method of arresting my attention."

"Circumstances," Mr. Laxworthy replied coldly, "have made certain demands upon me. I am happy to meet you, Paul Grayes. Sit down here and talk with us."

"I have no doubt," the new-comer remarked, with his eyes upon Mr. Laxworthy's revolver, "that your fingers are steady, but these modern weapons, I must admit, alarm me. Would it be possible to make some arrangement whereby you could be induced to put that murderous-looking toy in your pocket?"

"Certainly," Mr. Laxworthy assented. "Take off your coat. Leave where it is whatever may be in the pockets."

Grayes obeyed without hesitation. He left the coat, however, on the back of another chair, a little nearer to him than to anyone else in the room. Then he drew a chair to the table.

"I lunched too well to grudge you the dinner which you seem to have eaten," he remarked; "but if that is really the *Clicquot '93* I sent over here, which you are drinking, may I be allowed to join you?"

Mr. Laxworthy's revolver was slowly lowered and laid across his knees. Rachael passed the new-comer a glass and Mr. Anderson the bottle.

"So far as regards any explanation of our presence under your roof," Mr. Laxworthy said, "I can give it you, if you will. My friends and I are wanderers upon the face of the earth, with but one end and aim in existence— we seek for adventures, for new sensations. It seemed to me that nothing was more likely to provide these than the meeting to-night between you and the young man who calls himself Lenfield."

Paul Grayes poured himself out a glass of wine and drank it.

"Mr. Laxworthy," he said, "I agree with you. Left to ourselves, that young man and myself, I do indeed believe that that interview might possess great points of interest. If it is your intention to remain purely spectators, then I do not regret your presence. I often feel the inspiration of an audience."

Mr. Laxworthy smiled.

"To-night," he declared, "you have an appreciative one. We are, I can assure you, in the humour for the performance. Our hostess has given us an excellent dinner, cooked so skilfully that even I, who am a martyr to dyspepsia, have no fear for my digestion. Your champagne is excellent, your liqueur brandy I feel has agreed with me. Now tell us, Paul Grayes. In ten minutes, the man whom you must believe, since the breaking up of your band, has been your secret enemy for all these months, will be here. Do you honestly believe that it is to be a fair fight, that he will bring no help—no one to aid him? That it is to be a battle of either wits or arms between you two, and you two alone?"

The man whose name was Grayes smiled.

"My friend," he replied, "I am sure of it."

"It would interest me exceedingly," Mr. Laxworthy remarked, "to become acquainted with the reason for your confidence. Do you mind?" he added quickly. "I am sorry to trouble you, but I do not like that backwards motion of your chair. I seem to you, perhaps, an old man, but let me assure you that my hand is as quick as yours. See."

Mr. Laxworthy's hand was indeed as swift as lightning itself. It flashed across the table, and the next moment the revolver was there, steady and unfaltering. Paul Grayes waved it away. If he were disappointed, he showed no signs of it. Yet the subtle backward motion of his chair had been unmistakable.

"An unnecessary alarm, let me assure you," he declared. "You asked me a question and I was about to reply to it. The young man who passes for the moment under the name of Lenfield could bring none of those myrmidons of justice with whom he has tampered, to face me. There are crimes in England which they will pardon, but there are some for which the rankest informer who ever breathed could never hope for mercy. Lenfield knows well enough that a dozen words from me, and he might as well plead for a new left lung as to escape his fate. Now come, let me know the meaning of this little gathering, let me know to what it points? Is this a plot? Do you know who I am? Do you want blood-money? What have you to do with these men, Rachael? Tell me, where is Gassiat?"

Rachael shook her head sadly.

"Gassiat lies where he deserves to lie," she replied. "For once you were deceived, Paul. He is a faithless servant. He lies at the bottom of the Mediterranean."

Grayes was looking fixedly at the woman. Slowly his lips seemed to draw apart, showing his white teeth. There was a dull glitter in his eyes. Although not a muscle in his body moved, he seemed somehow like an animal preparing to spring. Rachael's eyes met his steadily. She showed not the slightest fear. Her lips, indeed, mocked him.

"Faithful—ah, no!" she murmured. "Gassiat came here by your orders, to keep me company, to watch with me lest your enemy should reach here first. Gassiat, alas! formed some plan of his own, or did he by any chance misunderstand your instruction? He left me tied hand and foot and gagged in my room, and it was not until we heard the approach of these gentlemen here that he could tear himself away."

Grayes bowed across the table.

"Your intervention," he remarked to Mr. Laxworthy, "was, without doubt, well-timed, but still I do not understand why Gassiat lies at the bottom of the Mediterranean?"

"Because his fingers were clumsy in their haste, and because my strength was greater than he imagined," Rachael replied. "I was able to reach one of those admirable little weapons to which you yourself introduced me, and lying on my side I shot him. I shot him twice, not mortally, but trying to escape from my bullets he fell overboard. Gassiat will make good food for fishes."

Then there came a shock for all of them. The voice was terrible enough, but the figure at which they looked was more terrible still.

"Not yet, Madame Rachael! There are first things to be arranged."

The eyes of all of them were glued now upon that weird figure who had stolen barefooted into the room. His appearance was terrible indeed. The sea-stain was still upon his drenched clothes, there were little fragments of seaweed about him. His hair was dank, one shoulder clumsily bound up, a wound still open upon his cheek. Save for the one blood-stain upon his face, his countenance was as white as marble. In his left hand was a small shining revolver, and, though he spoke to the others, his eyes were fixed upon Mr. Laxworthy's.

"Master," he cried, "get up and take your proper place. If one of those men move, I have the strength left to press this trigger."

Mr. Laxworthy, whose hands were upon the table, nodded, and raised his glass to his lips.

"You had better do as he tells you, Mr. Grayes," he said. "It is certainly a most inopportune appearance, but one should play one's part in these little affairs as at the chess-board. A pawn is of no use against a knight. My weapon is upon my knees, but my hand is upon the table. For a man who has spent a certain part of the day under the water, our friend over there seems to have a steady hand."

Already Grayes had possessed himself of his overcoat. He, too, now was armed. Mr. Laxworthy sipped his wine. Sydney's finger seemed to flicker for a moment towards his pocket, and the silence of the room was broken at once by Grayes' still, hard voice.

"A single movement like that, young sir, will be your last!" he cried. "Now stand up, you three."

They all obeyed. Following blindly the cue given them by their chief, they knew that the time for violence was not then.

"Mr. Laxworthy," Grayes commenced, and then stopped short. He held up his hand. No one spoke or whispered. From outside they heard distinctly the trampling of footsteps and the sound of voices. Grayes' eyes were cold and brilliant with a dangerous glitter.

"How many?" he whispered. "Listen."

Apparently he was satisfied. The voices and footsteps passed on to the side of the house.

"Gassiat," he said, "relieve these gentlemen of their weapons."

Mr. Laxworthy stood aside and indicated with his foot where his pistol had slipped to the floor. The others, following his example, did the same. Gassiat piled the weapons upon the sideboard. Then they heard the sound of footsteps in the hall. Grayes moved to the door.

"Will you come this way?" he invited suavely. "We are waiting here."

There was the sound of a cough, a heavy footstep and a lighter one. Mr. Lenfield came in, leaning on the arm of his friend, Mr. Hamar. There was a moment of breathless wonder. Lenfield's first impulse seemed to be to gaze steadfastly, and with a curious, dramatic intentness, only at the man whose voice had summoned him. But Grayes, with outstretched hand, pointed to the others. Lenfield's eyes, as though unwillingly, followed his gesture, and he started violently as he realised who was there.

"You!" he exclaimed. "Mr. Laxworthy!"

Paul Grayes smiled slightly.

"You recognise Mr. Laxworthy and his friends, I perceive," he said. "Let me introduce you, then, to three very interesting gentlemen. What does he call himself, I wonder, this amiable old busybody, who goes about the world with a grey shawl around his shoulders, peering into everyone's affairs, putting his finger into everyone's pie? Is he a Don Quixote or a Macchiavelli? A wonderful trio of conspirators, I think, only I am not quite sure that they would not have done better to have poked about amongst the scandals of the Paradise Hotel rather than to have forced their way here to witness this final meeting between you and me, Philip Lenfield."

Lenfield shook himself free from his companion's support.

"With Mr. Laxworthy or his friends I have nothing whatever to do," he declared calmly. "I do not know how they discovered our trysting-place. They come here, I presume, at their own risk. Let me look at you, Paul Grayes. Stand out of the shadows there. Ah!"

The two men were opposite to each other now, the face of each dimly illuminated by the great lamp. Curiously enough, as they stood there, all that was worst in Lenfield's wasted features seemed to have crept into his face, to match the hard, bestial stare of the man into whose countenance he was gazing so earnestly.

"You see me," Grayes said. "I am unchanged. You and I together have planned some things which have made the world shiver. You never saw me flinch—you never will. The end of those others is written, but for us— for us, Philip!"

Mr. Laxworthy coughed slightly.

"If I might be permitted," he began, leaning a little over the table something after the fashion of one about to make an after-dinner speech.

His words and his manner of saying them seemed so curiously inapt that both men were silent.

"I have not yet had an opportunity," Mr. Laxworthy continued, "of making a suitable apology for my presence here to-night. Believe me, it is not altogether a blundering visit. I am, as you have perhaps heard, a man addicted to the study of philosophy, who now and then steps a little out of his way to notice curious phenomena in human life. A year or so ago all London was thrilled by the doings of a gang of the most desperate criminals who ever defied the police or the canons of our modern civilisation. I will admit that I was hugely interested. I sought to probe some of the secrets of the band. I found them to be composed of a few ruffians whose safety consisted in one axiom: they fed upon one another."

Lenfield started slightly. Both men now were listening. Rachael, too, leaned across the table with a wicked smile upon her lips.

"But this man is wonderful," she murmured.

"Six or seven, was it, perhaps, this little band consisted of," Mr. Laxworthy continued, "and a score or more of murders at their door. For six or seven there is no safety, for, as we all know, a really great criminal is trapped only by the indiscretions or infidelities of his associates. Two men there were with brains. From their hidden places they pointed one by one, with unerring finger, and those other associates went to the grave. The two were left. The time came when one of those two decided that two were too many."

Paul Grayes was leaning across the table now and his hands were twitching. Lenfield, who had at some time or another possessed a sense of humour, smiled faintly.

"Hear him!" he muttered. "Which, Mr. Laxworthy? Which?"

"You, Philip Lenfield, have been hard pressed," Mr. Laxworthy remarked. "Your secret has been fairly well probed. But, fortunately or unfortunately for you, it is the greater man who is most sought. Perhaps he, too, knows that. Perhaps he, too, has heard the distant echo of suspicion, has heard the footsteps of those who are gathering around. Philip Lenfield has not betrayed you," Mr. Laxworthy continued, raising his voice a little. "He came here to-night, intending very likely to carry out your first principles, but he was forestalled. It is I, Paul Grayes, whom you may thank for the fact that your stateroom upon the *Coronia* to-morrow will be empty, that you will embark instead upon a longer and more momentous journey. The man there who calls himself Lenfield knows your secret, but, as I live, no breath of it has ever passed his lips. I, too, know that the man who has baffled the police of every country in the world for nearly two years, the man who made himself infamous for ever under the name—"

Mr. Laxworthy's genius at that supreme moment did not fail him. He had talked until the last possible second. He broke off with his sentence unfinished. No one knew exactly how it was done, no one saw even from whence he procured the missile—but with one lightning-like blow the lamp fell broken upon the ground and the room was plunged into darkness. Before the sound of the crash had died away, footsteps were heard coming from every direction. Through the French window, left carefully unfastened, Mr. John T. Laxworthy, Mr. Forrest Anderson, and Mr. Sydney Wing stole softly out into the night. A cordon of gendarmes opened to let them pass. They took shelter beneath the oleander trees.

"If one could but see inside!" Mr. Laxworthy muttered. "We left the fraction of a second too soon."

Almost as he spoke, a great blinding flash of light, from which leapt scintillations on every side, lit up the whole of the room which they had just quitted. They heard the crashing of glass, they saw the walls crack. They saw Paul Grayes, a pistol in either hand, first firing madly at the spot where Mr. Laxworthy had stood, then leap into the air and fall down, a huddled-up heap. They saw Rachael, with her head buried in her arms; Gassiat lying at her side. Save those three, there was no one in the wrecked room. Then again there was darkness, broken only by the sound of voices as the gendarmes cautiously drew their circle closer.

"What about Lenfield?" Anderson murmured hoarsely.

"He goes free," Mr. Laxworthy answered. "Come."

Softly they stole along the tunnel-like darkness of the avenue. Mr. Laxworthy seated himself in the tonneau of the car, and wrapped his shawl carefully about his shoulders while Sydney lit the lamps.

"We will proceed to-night," Mr. Laxworthy said, "only so far as Cannes.

I have engaged rooms at the Métropole. To-morrow we will go to Monte Carlo. This night-driving makes me nervous."

Sydney took his place at the wheel. Mr. Laxworthy leaned once more forward.

"I insist upon it, Sydney," he said, "that you drive with great care. I am already a little overheated and the night air is treacherous. Besides, these curves are most dangerous."

With a little smile on his lips, Sydney slipped in the clutch. The car glided up the hill and was lost in the shadows.

CHAPTER V
The Vagaries of the Prince of Liguria

Mr. Laxworthy took an intelligent interest in the gambling at Monte Carlo. He found the atmosphere of the rooms unbearable, and he addressed two complaints to the directors concerning the ventilation, which it may be hoped produced their due effect. Apart from these drawbacks, he found the scene interesting. On the day of his arrival he wandered from table to table, keenly interested in watching the different systems of gambling and the physiognomies of the players. It was not until he had been in the rooms for over two hours that he ventured a bet on his own account, which he promptly lost, greatly to his disgust. After that his interest waned for a time, and finally he left the rooms and sat by himself before one of the small round tables of the Café de Paris, where he arranged his shawl about his shoulders and ordered a pot of English breakfast tea.

It was precisely at this moment that Mr. Laxworthy's character as a man of gallantry was finally established. Inside the rooms, half an hour before, he had been dimly conscious of the smile of a woman from the other side of the tables, a good-looking woman, with a mass of red-gold hair, a long lace coat, and a little Pomeranian under her arm. They had brushed against one another at the door, and his apology had been answered a little more graciously, perhaps, than the occasion demanded. She was walking past him now, very slowly, and as she passed she glanced with amusement at Mr. Laxworthy's shawl and teapot.

"Monsieur feels the cold?" she murmured, with a smile.

Mr. Laxworthy rose at once to his feet.

"Without the society of Madame," he replied, raising his hat. "To offer tea, perhaps, to a lady so essentially Parisian would be clumsy, but there are other refreshments if Madame would condescend."

Madame sank into the chair by his side.

"You are without doubt English," she said, smiling up at him, "and very English. But where did you learn to speak my language like that?"

"Madame," Mr. Laxworthy replied, "in my youth I was more a citizen of the world. It is only for the last fifteen years that I have lived in the quiet places. All this is new to me. Pardon. You will permit me to order you something?"

Madame was disposed to take some coffee. She declined a liqueur, however, and Mr. Laxworthy found himself agreeably surprised by her voice and manner.

"It seems strange," she remarked, "to talk with anyone who finds anything new here. For ten seasons I have spent three months of the year here. Can you understand that I am a little weary?"

"You play?" Mr. Laxworthy asked.

She shrugged her shoulders.

"What can one do? I risk a few louis, and if I lose I leave off. It is not at the tables that the big gambling is done in Monte Carlo."

"I have been given to understand," Mr. Laxworthy said, "that a great many people go instead to the Sporting Club."

"There is high play at the Sporting Club," she admitted; "but there are private houses in Monte Carlo where one may see the most extraordinary gambling in the world."

"You interest me," Mr. Laxworthy declared. "I must admit that I find the study of people engaged in gaming particularly interesting. I am, in my small way, a student of humanity, and the effect of gambling upon certain types of character is more than interesting."

"You are amongst those who think," she murmured, looking at him out of her soft brown eyes. "It is a pleasure to talk with you, Monsieur. Here the men are all butterflies. They think and care for nothing except the amusement or the passion of the moment. That is why I like your countrymen. They see beyond."

"Madame," Mr. Laxworthy sighed, "you flatter me."

"Come," she said; "I stopped to talk with you because I found your appearance amusing. Tell me, why do you wear that grey shawl?"

"I am subject to rheumatism about the shoulders," he replied. "Any sudden change of temperature I feel at once. The shawl is a necessity to me."

"Rubbish!" she exclaimed. "A young man like you to talk of rheumatism!"

Mr. Laxworthy felt his spectacles. To be called young by a woman so charming was, after all, not disagreeable.

"Madame," he said, "I am perhaps a year or two older than I appear, but if it affords you pleasure, behold!"

He carefully removed and folded up his shawl.

"You look much nicer now," she declared. "Please go on and tell me about yourself. You are really a stranger here, and you are interested in your fellow creatures?"

"That is entirely my position," he assured her.

"You are alone in Monte Carlo?" she asked.

"With two friends," he replied, "also Englishmen."

For some reason or other she seemed disappointed.

"Neither of them has ever been here before," he went on. "They are both entirely new to this sort of life."

"They are like you—personable?" she asked. "Forgive me, but I ask for a reason."

Mr. Laxworthy pointed them out. They were on the steps of the Casino, looking about them. She raised her *lorgnette* and approved.

"Very good!" she exclaimed. "Now you must give me your card and present your friends. Then, if it pleases you, I shall give you the opportunity of seeing things in this place which may interest you. I have the entrée to a house where play takes place every night for stakes far exceeding anything you can see in the ordinary way. I will take you and your friends there to-night, if you promise that you will not talk about your visit."

"Madame," Mr. Laxworthy assured her, "it is a promise easy indeed for me to make. I never betray a confidence."

"Your friends are coming," she replied. "You shall present me. My name is De Cléry—Madame de Cléry, remember."

"It is not a name, Madame," Mr. Laxworthy declared, "which I shall ever be able to forget."

"I think," she said, "that in your younger days you must have been quite a courtier."

Anderson and Sydney arrived and were presented. Whatever surprise they may have felt at seeing their chief in such company they effectually concealed. Madame had without doubt the power to charm, and for ten minutes or a quarter of an hour they sat together at the little round table, talking gaily. She rose at last almost regretfully.

"We are to meet again to-night," she said. "That will be really something for me to look forward to, for so many of my friends are away just now that I am even a little lonely. At what hour would you care to go? Will eleven o'clock be too early?"

"Your own hour, Madame," Mr. Laxworthy begged. "We could not, I presume, induce you to dine with us first at Ciro's?"

"I shall be charmed," she replied. "About half-past eight, I suppose? Could I trouble you," she added, turning to Sydney with a little smile. "My automobile is there—no, the grey liveries. If you could step across, it would be charming of you."

Sydney hurried across the road, and a moment or two later a handsome automobile, upholstered in white, with chauffeur and footman on the box and a beautiful bowl of pink roses upon the table, drew slowly up. There was a coronet on the panels. Madame stepped inside with a little farewell nod.

"It is *au revoir,* then," she said. "And, Mr. Laxworthy," she added, laughing at him out of the window, "take care of that rheumatism."

The automobile rolled away. Mr. Laxworthy and his friends followed slowly on foot towards their hotel. In accordance with their established custom, neither Sydney nor Anderson asked a single question. Their curiosity, however, was obvious, and Mr. Laxworthy after a preliminary cough, proceeded to gratify it.

"You were doubtless somewhat surprised to see me engaged in conversation with a lady of Madame de Cléry's appearance," he remarked. "I can assure you that she is a perfect stranger to me, both personally and by reputation. I make it a rule to converse amiably with anyone who addresses me, and the lady in question made, I may say, marked overtures. The inference is naturally simple. She desires to profit by our acquaintance. If she succeeds in amusing us a little, why not? One is willing to pay for amusement."

"Isn't this sort of thing just a little dangerous in Monte Carlo?" Anderson ventured.

"Especially with such a thundering good-looking woman," Sydney put in.

"I," said Mr. Laxworthy dryly, "am not susceptible. The undoubted attractions of Madame are not likely to disturb my peace of mind. I go to this house she speaks of. I shall find pleasure in watching men gamble for huge sums, if indeed that is to be seen there, but I do not think that anyone will induce me to wager more myself than I am content to lose as the price of an evening's entertainment."

"So long as we are able to keep to that," Anderson remarked. "The worst of it is, you can never tell where these things will end."

"One hears such strange stories," Sydney added. "A promiscuous acquaintance at Monte Carlo is about as risky a thing as one can think of."

"Well," said Mr. Laxworthy, "for real Scotch caution commend me to you two. Here we are in the very promised land of adventures. We have one offered to us the ending of which, perhaps, may be a little obvious, but which will possess charms, and you two talk caution like a couple of old housewives. Madame de Cléry does us the honour to dine with us this evening, and we shall certainly visit in her company the house she has spoken of. At this hour of the day I do not usually indulge, but I am informed that the cocktails at the bar on my right here are unusually well mixed and form an excellent *aperitif*. We will enter and drink together to a successful and amusing evening."

Madame arrived at Ciro's barely ten minutes late, and justified in every way Mr. Laxworthy's secretly conceived opinion of her. She wore the plainest black evening gown, with only a single ornament suspended from her neck by a band of black velvet. Her hat was a triumph of simplicity. No one who entered the restaurant was of more distinguished appearance, though it was noticeable to the three men as they greeted her that a whisper passed from one to the other of the little groups of diners.

Mr. Laxworthy had selected a table at the corner of the terrace. Madame took her place with a smile of approval, and buried her face for a moment in the cluster of pink roses by the side of her plate.

"You are indeed civilised people," she murmured, smiling at Mr. Laxworthy, who had for the evening discarded his shawl. "Tell me why it is that this is really your first visit to Monte Carlo? You have travelled much in other countries?"

Mr. Laxworthy spoke of South America and other of the places which he had visited. As the dinner progressed, it was clear that Madame de Cléry had changed her opinion of her new friends, and with her altered point of view a certain uneasiness now and then betrayed itself in her conversation and reference to the evening to come. Towards the conclusion of their repast a trifling incident happened, unnoticed by the others but appreciated by Mr. Laxworthy. A little group of three people were leaving the restaurant, a woman and two men, obviously English, and obviously people of some consequence. Ciro himself conducted them to the exit, in order to gain which they had to pass within a few feet of Mr. Laxworthy and his guests. Madame de Cléry had been in the middle of a sentence, which seemed somehow to die away upon her lips. Her fingers were nervously clasped in one another under the table-cloth, her face was suddenly hard and strained. The remnants of her youth and freshness seemed suddenly to have gone. She looked with dull, longing eyes into the face of the woman who passed. Mr. Laxworthy alone saw the recognition, saw the slight drawing away of the new-comer, the frown on the forehead of the tall, good-looking man who brought up the rear of the procession. The little tragedy—one of those of which the world is full—was over. Mr. Laxworthy leaned over the table and talked for a moment earnestly with his two friends. He had forgotten to tell them something of interest. Madame looked across the garden and struggled with her ghosts.

The conclusion of the meal was gay, though most of the conversation lay between Sydney and Madame. As they rose and strolled out, she seemed afflicted by a curious hesitation.

"After all," she said, turning to Mr. Laxworthy, "perhaps it would amuse you more to go into the rooms. There is always plenty to see there, and I have not been in the evening for some time."

Mr. Laxworthy shook his head.

"The rooms will be there another night. Your offer might not be repeated. I have really a fancy to watch this high gambling of which you have spoken. Unless you foresee any difficulty, or embarrassments, let us keep to our original programme."

Madame made no further objection.

"My automobile is at the door," she said. "Come."

"To the Villa des Acacias," Madame ordered briefly.

"Is it far?" Mr. Laxworthy asked.

"About half-way to Mentone," she replied, "on the summit of the hill. It is rather a beautiful place. You should see it in the daytime. Perhaps," she added, "if you all behave very nicely, our hostess may ask us to lunch one day."

They turned towards Mentone, away from the shore, and climbed the great hill. Soon they left the main road and entered a dark avenue, which they circled round and round until suddenly they came into an open space and saw above them the villa, which seemed indeed to be built on the rocks. Though the night was warm, the curtains were apparently all drawn, and only by odd chinks of light could one believe that it was inhabited. As they drew up before the front door, Madame turned round.

"Look!" she said.

"The view," Mr. Laxworthy declared, turning his coat collar up, "is magnificent. I find this chilly breeze, however, a little dangerous."

"You take too much care of yourself," Madame de Cléry murmured. "I perceive, Mr. Laxworthy, that you are afflicted with nerves."

"I have reached an age," Mr. Laxworthy replied, "when a certain amount of care of one's person is necessary. I admit that the view to which you point is one of the most magnificent in the world. I admit that those lights, which seem to be gleaming at our very feet, are like the spangles upon a woman's cloak. I do see that it is possible, even at this hour of the night, to catch the outlines of those white buildings, which throw their shadows into the sea. It is all wonderful, Madame, but it would interest me more just now to see the door open."

"Really," she declared, "I have met no man for a long time so refreshing. Behold!"

The door was opened. A pale-faced man-servant ushered the visitors in. Fronting them was a great bank of hot-house flowers. Softly shaded electric lights hung from the ceiling. The wide hall was crowded with trophies. A second servant was already relieving them of their coats. A third man had thrown open the door of a small room on the left-hand side of the hall.

"We go in here," Madame remarked, handing her cloak to the maid, who seemed to have appeared from nowhere. "At the Villa des Acacias we invert the order of things. It is our hostess who comes to us."

They found themselves in a charmingly furnished little apartment, full of divans, books and papers, water-colours of the vicinity upon the walls, photographs everywhere. A servant was arranging coffee and liqueurs upon the sideboard, but save for themselves the apartment was empty. Madame de Cléry walked restlessly about.

"Our hostess has peculiar ideas," she explained. "I am one of her intimate friends, but she does not permit even me to introduce strangers unless she herself approves. I have telephoned to say that I am bringing you. She will come and talk to us in a minute or two. In all probability she will invite us to watch the baccarat or the roulette. If she does not, there is nothing to be done but to make our bow and depart."

Almost as she spoke the door was opened. The butler who had admitted them stood on one side.

"Madame la Marquise!" he announced.

A woman of striking appearance entered. She was tall and thin, her face was as white as powder and natural pallor could make it. Her hair was grey, her eyes black. With the same breath she seemed young and elegant, elderly and scholarly. When she spoke, her voice was a charm.

"My dear Lucie," she exclaimed, giving both her hands to Madame de Cléry, "this is indeed a pleasure! Present me to your friends."

Madame de Cléry presented them in turn. Each was allowed the tops of her fingers.

"I find in Mr. Laxworthy," Madame de Cléry remarked, "an interesting claimant upon our sympathies. This is his first visit to Monte Carlo."

The lady who had been announced as Madame la Marquise turned and looked at Mr. Laxworthy. For several seconds she said nothing. Mr. Laxworthy, too, preserved silence. In a sense, the moment was significant.

"Mr. Laxworthy has doubtless been a great traveller in other countries?" Madame la Marquise said softly.

"In my younger life, yes," Mr. Laxworthy assented. "Of late years I have not found it amusing to wander far from home. My health requires attention, and my small estate interests me. My two friends here have persuaded me into this trip."

"We must do all that we can to make it pleasant for you," Madame la Marquise replied. "It is charming of you to climb the hill that I may claim from now the pleasure of your acquaintance. Some evenings we play here. It might interest you to watch us. To-night, alas! I am alone."

There was another silence. Madame de Cléry seemed a little discomposed. Mr. Laxworthy's low bow might indeed have been meant to hide his disappointment.

"Mr. Laxworthy," Madame de Cléry said, "is a philosopher. I have found him studying expressions in the gaming-rooms. He makes notes of what he sees. He travels, I believe, with the manuscript of an uncompleted work."

Madame la Marquise nodded slowly in appreciative attention.

"Mr. Laxworthy has indeed the air of a scholar," she remarked. "He will find, I am sure, much in Monte Carlo to interest him."

This time her tone seemed final. The three men glanced at Madame de

Cléry for their cue. There appeared to be nothing left but to take their leave. Madame la Marquise herself led the way to the door.

"You will do me the honour, Mr. Laxworthy?" she said. "I shall send you a card in a few days for one of my small parties. You may find them interesting. You stay here, and at what hotel?"

"For a few days only, Madame," Mr. Laxworthy replied, "at the Hôtel Hermitage."

They were in the hall now, and the butler was already moving towards the front door. Then from the door of the front room a young man, burly, almost corpulent, with flushed face, suddenly appeared. He held out both his hands to Madame de Cléry.

"Ah, Lucie," he cried. "This is delightful! But you were not going?"

Madame de Cléry paused.

"Dear Julien!" she exclaimed. "Indeed, I had only brought these three friends of mine for the pleasure of presenting them to your aunt."

"Absurd!" the young man declared. "Present me also to your friends. We are dull to-night. Monsieur le Prince has drunk too deeply. All the time he asks for more company. We need livening up. Present me to your friends at once. They must join us."

Madame la Marquise stood like a figure of stone while the introductions progressed. The new-comer, his arm through Sydney's would have led them at once to the room from which he had issued, but Mr. Laxworthy hesitated. He turned at once toward his hostess.

"Madame," he said, "it is perhaps your wish that we should pay you a visit at some other time?"

"Monsieur Laxworthy," she replied, "I appreciate your consideration. I will admit that there are circumstances which made me a little reluctant to offer you the hospitality of my rooms this evening—yet, after all, you three are men. I think that you, Mr. Laxworthy, have learned how to take care of yourself in every part of the world. Stay if you will."

Already the little party was crossing the hall. Mr. Laxworthy and his friends were ushered into a room different in every respect from anything they could have imagined. The floor and panelled walls were of light oak. Although a faint perfume of rose-water hung about the place, the ventilation was perfect. There were no pictures upon the wall. The furniture consisted only of divans and a number of chairs. The room was almost T-shaped. At the farther end was a baccarat table, at which three men were seated. At the end nearest to them was a roulette table. Of the men at the other end of the apartment, one was tall, red-faced, with a mass of grey hair. The others were insignificant.

"It is Monsieur le Prince who sits there," Madame de Cléry whispered to Mr. Laxworthy. "One does not introduce here. You play or not, as you choose."

The hostess bent slightly toward Mr. Laxworthy.

"This is what I used to call my music-room," she said, "when I built the villa ten years ago. Since then, alas! music has become a small thing in Monte Carlo. The fever for gambling is everywhere. To keep my friends I have been forced, as you see, to turn it into a room where one may play."

"The necessity seems regrettable," Mr. Laxworthy remarked, "but I find it interesting. It is indeed strange that in one little corner of the world associations seem inevitably to arouse an instinct that often remains dormant in other countries."

The young man, who had been standing on the outskirts of the circle, laughed.

"Perhaps you yourself, Mr. Laxworthy," he said, "are beginning to feel that instinct. Will you play? The Prince there is eager to take another bank at baccarat."

"I prefer to watch baccarat," Mr. Laxworthy answered dryly. "Roulette, if you will."

"Roulette, by all means," the young man declared. "Playing for so short a time, the odds in favor of the bank will almost disappear. The house shall make a bank against the visitors, or the visitors shall make a bank against that house—which you prefer."

"The visitors are in the majority," Mr. Laxworthy replied. "Let the house take the bank."

The young man seated himself at the wheel. He turned round and called up the room.

"Monsieur le Prince," he said, "we play at roulette. Come and stake some of those thousand-franc notes which you have won from me to-night. What do you say, you other?"

They both turned round, men of uninteresting and undistinguished appearance. Monsieur le Prince laughed harshly.

"I will come, perhaps, soon," he cried. "At present I restore my nerves with your excellent brandy."

They saw then that his eyes were bloodshot, and it seemed to Laxworthy and his companions that it was the task of the two who sat with him to keep him quiet.

"To-night," the young man declared, "I have no courage. I limit you to a thousand francs in even chances, fifty francs on the numbers, and a hundred francs any combination. At this infernal game I always lose."

They sat down—Madame de Cléry—with Sydney at her side. Mr. Laxworthy opposite, next the young man who took the part of the croupier and by his side Forrest Anderson. Madame la Marquise hesitated for a moment. Then she went and stood behind Madam de Cléry's chair.

"Madame la Marquise will not be seated?" Mr. Laxworthy asked.

"Roulette wearies me," she replied. "All these games of chance weary me. They are resolved by no laws. One plays eternally and one learns nothing. One has nothing to hope for. If it were not for my friends," she continued, fanning herself lazily, "there should be no play in my house."

They played for a dozen coups or so. The bank won and lost and won again. Mr. Laxworthy was in the act of placing a hundred-franc bill on the space in front of him when the attention of all of them was diverted by an angry voice at the other end of the room. The Prince had risen to his feet. He stood there—a huge, unprepossessing-looking creature, head and shoulders taller than his companions, with bloodshot eyes, puffy cheeks, and protuberant veins.

"Let me alone!" he cried thickly. "If I choose to play, I play, with whom and when I please."

He pushed one of the men who would have restrained him on one side, and came slowly down the room toward them. He walked unsteadily. His shirt-front was stained with tobacco-ash and coffee. His tie was crooked, his hair unkempt. All the time Mr. Laxworthy watched him approach. The Prince eyed them all fiercely.

"Madame la Marquise," he growled, "you would send me home, eh? Not yet! I will play a little with these good people. Afterwards they shall all play baccarat. Julien takes the bank, eh? Then we know what to expect. Still, I will play. A thousand francs on the red, *mon ami*."

He stood glowering at them all. Mr. Laxworthy's eyes scarcely left his face.

"My dear Prince," Madame La Marquise said, "do you realise that you have been here in your present attire since midnight yesterday? To please you, I have found people to play baccarat all through the day. My friends here only play roulette. Take my advice and go home."

"Why should I go home?" the Prince answered roughly. "I have won money here, I like it here, I like all of you except that miserable young Englishman who insulted me. I have a quick method, Monsieur," he continued, turning suddenly toward Laxworthy, "of dealing with those who do not know their place. I find there are many Englishmen who have that fault."

Mr. Laxworthy looked at him steadily through his spectacles, but he neither spoke nor gave any indication of having heard a word he had said. Monsieur le Prince glared at him, red-eyed and truculent.

"You, sir, with the spectacles," he called out, "I speak to you. Do you hear?"

Mr. Laxworthy, who had just won on a number, finished counting his notes. Then he looked up.

"Certainly I hear," he replied. "I wish you would speak in a lower tone. I find your voice disagreeable."

There was a dead silence. Monsieur le Prince struck the table with his fist so that the counters rattled.

"You hear him!" he cried, glancing around. "He finds my voice disagreeable, that miserable little ape with the bent shoulders and the spectacles! A tradesman from England! He finds my voice disagreeable!"

"Not only that," Mr. Laxworthy continued calmly, "but I find your manners beastly."

The Prince glared across the table. Then very slowly he began making his way around it towards where Mr. Laxworthy sat. Mr. Laxworthy sat back and crossed his legs. Julien leaned towards him.

"For God's sake, man, don't irritate him. You know who he is? The Prince of Liguria. He is first cousin to His Majesty. He does what he likes here. I have known him to strangle a man for saying less than you have said."

"He will not strangle me," Mr. Laxworthy declared.

The Prince was standing now over Mr. Laxworthy. Instead, however, of at once attacking him, he pointed to the end of the room.

"Show them, you there, Mark and Dalamores," he called out. "Show them how I treated the young Englishman who grumbled at my naturals. There is another one here who has to be taught his place in a minute. Show them, I say."

Madame la Marquise glided to his side.

"Monsieur le Prince," she begged, "all that I could do I have done. For Heaven's sake, be discreet."

The Prince shook himself free.

"Show them, I say!" he called out in a voice of thunder, "or I'll wring your necks where you sit!"

They rose hesitatingly and pushed the table before which they had been sitting, on one side. Then one saw that on a sofa behind—the sofa upon which the Prince had apparently been sitting—was stretched the figure of a man. Madame de Cléry sprang to her feet and rushed across the room. It was one of the two men who had dined at Ciro's.

"It is Victor!" she cried. "How did he come here? What has happened?"

"For twenty-four hours," thundered the Prince, "I have played baccarat at that table. I have won money, it is true, but I play well. There came tonight that pale-faced Englishman. He spoke of my naturals—there were four following. He asked me a question. There he lies with my answer upon his temple."

Mr. Laxworthy rose deliberately to his feet. He followed Madame de Cléry across the room. Together they bent for a moment over the young man who lay upon the sofa. Then Mr. Laxworthy turned round.

"Madame la Marquis," he asked, "is there a doctor to be found?"

She glanced at the Prince.

"A doctor is not necessary," she said. "The young man will recover presently. If we sent for a doctor, he would expect us to explain."

Mr. Laxworthy came slowly down the room.

"Sydney," he directed, "you will find a telephone in the hall. Telephone at once to a doctor and to the chief of the police."

The Prince threw up his hands and laughed. He stood before the door and raised his huge arms.

"Let me see," he called out, "who will dare to leave this room."

"My friends and I are about to leave it," Mr. Laxworthy replied. "As for you, you will remain here."

The Prince smiled—a very ugly sight. Madame de Cléry came softly down and laid her hand upon Mr. Laxworthy's arm. She was very pale, but she was struggling hard for composure.

"Mr. Laxworthy," she said, "I am sorry that I brought you here. I did not know that the Prince was in the house. Believe me, it is no use sending for the police. While he is here, he must be obeyed. No one will listen to a word against him. His rule here is one of the most impious things in the world. It is a thing to which you must bow. That young man on the sofa is my own cousin, and he is badly hurt. Worse would come of it if we made a scandal."

Mr. Laxworthy quietly disengaged himself.

"All that you say, Madame," he replied, raising his voice, "might well be true if that man were indeed Monsieur le Prince. As a matter of fact, Madame la Marquise, I am surprised that you should for one moment have been deceived. Look at him closely. I tell you that he is no more the Prince of Liguria than I am. His name I have forgotten, but I will tell you this. He is a Swede, not a Russian, and he bears on his right arm the brand of Sing-Sing Prison."

The silence which followed could almost be felt. Then with a roar the man came at Mr. Laxworthy. Within a few feet he pulled up short and staggered back. Mr. Laxworthy's hand was as steady as ever and the muzzle of his revolver was black.

"I remember your name now," Mr. Laxworthy continued. "You are Carl Osterhafen. You were thrown into prison for keeping a gambling den. You declared yourself to be the natural son of a Russian nobleman. It was very likely true. Madame La Marquise," he proceeded, turning towards his hostess, "if this man has won money in your house, he should be compelled to restore it. Make him do so now. Sydney, stop those others from leaving."

Osterhafen's companions had tried to reach the door, but were prevented. Madame la Marquise was shaking with passion.

"Mr. Laxworthy," she said, "I am eternally indebted to you. These two I knew to have once, at any rate, been in the suite of the Prince of Liguria.

They came here yesterday and told me that he was in Monte Carlo, incognito. For him I got up a baccarat party last night. There were others who said that he cheated. He has won three hundred thousand francs, which he has about him, and nothing which I could say or do would induce him to leave the place. Tell me, what should I do?"

"The young man who is Madame de Cléry's cousin," Mr. Laxworthy declared, "is not seriously hurt. Insist upon the return of the three hundred thousand francs, restore their losings to your friends, and let him go. A scandal here will do no one any good."

Osterhafen swayed upon his feet. The rims under his eyes were purple, his face was diabolical.

"I restore nothing!" he cried. "You little devil!"

Once more he seemed about to fling himself upon Mr. Laxworthy, and once more he pulled up short.

"Osterhafen," Mr. Laxworthy said calmly, "I have dealt with more dangerous brutes than you, and I have never failed to shoot straight when the moment came. Put the money on the table and be gone before Madame changes her mind. The scandal, after all, would be little compared with the pleasure of sending you and your two confederates where you belong. It is not for nothing in Monte Carlo that one personates the head of a Royal House and cheats at baccarat."

Osterhafen fell back. His two associates seized hold of him. They talked together rapidly and earnestly. Osterhafen flung upon the floor a great parcel of notes.

"Are you satisfied, Madame?" Mr. Laxworthy asked.

"Indeed I am," she replied. "Let them go."

Someone touched the bell. The butler appeared at the door.

"Monsieur le Prince and his suite will leave for Monte Carlo in the automobile of Madame de Cléry," Mr. Laxworthy announced. "Be so good as to tell the chauffeur to return here after he has deposited Monsieur le Prince at his hotel."

The man bowed and held the door open. The three men passed out. The man who had been hurt was sitting up now, and Madame de Cléry was at his side, bathing his temple. Mr. Laxworthy replaced his pistol carefully and straightened his glasses.

"I was in the middle of the most interesting little coup," he remarked, leading the way to the roulette table. "If it is not imposing upon you, sir, it would give me great pleasure to continue playing while we await the return of the automobile."

Julien sat down at the croupier's chair and spun the wheel with trembling fingers. Madame la Marquise crossed the room to Madame de Cléry.

"Lucie," she whispered, "where did you find him, this wonderful man?"

Madame de Cléry smiled.

"Sitting outside the Café de Paris, drinking English breakfast tea with a grey shawl around his shoulders," she answered.

Madame la Marquise shook her head. She looked at the notes which she held in her hand. She looked at Mr. Laxworthy, intent once more upon his system.

"It is a wonderful race," she declared. "Mr. Laxworthy!"

"Madame?"

Have you, by chance, ever heard the fable of your great Scotsman—Robert Burns—and the spider?"

"Most assuredly, Madame," Mr. Laxworthy replied, without looking up from the board.

"Will you remember," she begged, "that if ever the spider can help, I and my house are at your service? You will not forget?"

"Madame," Mr. Laxworthy assured her, straightening his spectacles for a moment and turning towards her, "I forget nothing."

CHAPTER VI
Mystery House

"Since you went away," the girl declared, "we have been very dull."

"You flatter me," Mr. Laxworthy murmured.

"It is not you that we have missed," she admitted frankly, "so much as events. Nothing has happened—at least in the hotel. You read the papers, I suppose?"

"Never," Mr. Laxworthy declared firmly.

"You strange person!" she murmured. "No end of things have taken place along this coast. The chief of that terrible band of anarchists, who made such a sensation in London a year ago, was run to earth at a little villa near San Raphael here, and blew up himself and his wife and confederate with a bomb."

"Dear me!" Mr. Laxworthy remarked. "I wonder how I missed that."

"Then," she continued, "the papers were full of all sorts of extraordinary rumours about a very clever swindler, who pretended he was the Prince of Liguria, and won a fortune at a private house at Monte Carlo."

"Was he discovered?" Mr. Laxworthy asked.

"He was discovered and forced to restore every penny."

"Anything else?" Mr. Laxworthy inquired.

"Nothing else," she replied, "except that every day I have been hoping you would return."

"You will turn my head," Mr. Laxworthy murmured.

"I do not think, Mr. Laxworthy," she asserted, "that I or any one else in the world could do that. It is not for any personal reason that I am so glad to see you. It is because there is something going on here which I do not understand."

Mr. Laxworthy glanced at the volume which lay upon his knee, and his place in which he was still marking with his forefinger.

"I am afraid," he said, "that if you do not understand it, there is very little chance that I can help. Has Mr. Lenfield withdrawn his attentions, or are all these new admirers of yours becoming troublesome?"

"Mr. Lenfield," she replied, "has scarcely spoken to any one since he returned from his expedition to Monte Carlo. I think that he was taken ill on the way."

"Poor fellow!" Mr. Laxworthy murmured politely.

"Would you mind talking seriously with me for three minutes?" she begged.

"I am all attention," Mr. Laxworthy assured her.

"You remember Mr. Freeling Poignton?"

"Perfectly. He is a multi-millionaire."

"You also remember the Marquis Lefant?"

"Certainly. The man with a Jewish face and a shocking temper."

"Well, the Marquis Lefant and Mr. Freeling Poignton were here together. Last week the Marquis left."

"I have no doubt," Mr. Laxworthy remarked, "that he found the place a little quiet."

"The moment he left," she continued, "Mr. Lenfield and Mr. Freeling Poignton became inseparable."

"A strange combination," Mr. Laxworthy said thoughtfully.

"A few days ago," she went on, "they took the manager's villa in the grounds there. They found their rooms in the hotel uncomfortable for some reason or another."

Mr. Laxworthy followed the direction which she indicated. The villa was a small grey-stone building, situated in the woods, two or three hundred yards away.

"It seems an odd friendship," Mr. Laxworthy remarked, "but in other respects it is quite a sensible proceeding."

"I suppose you are going to think me a shocking busybody," she said.

"On the contrary," Mr. Laxworthy replied, "although I am not particularly attracted by your sex, I do appreciate the gift of observation somewhat highly."

"Very well! The day after they moved in, neither of them turned up to dinner. That seemed quite reasonable, as of course they have a very pleasant sitting-room there. The next day they did not turn up for lunch, and, though the weather was perfect, Mr. Freeling Poignton never came down for his game of golf."

"How long ago?" Mr. Laxworthy asked.

"The day before yesterday," she replied. "Well, during the afternoon I went to the violet gardens, and on my way back I came round by the villa. It is a little out of the way, of course, because none of the paths really pass the villa at all, but—you see, I am quite frank with you—I went that way out of curiosity. Not only that, but as I passed the windows I looked in."

"Dear me," Mr. Laxworthy murmured, "that was very shocking of you! What did you see?"

"I saw nothing at all," she replied. "There was the sitting-room, but it looked as though it has been unoccupied for days."

"That seems rather singular," Mr. Laxworthy remarked. "They can't spend all their time in the bedrooms."

"I have passed three times now," she went on, "and not once has there been any sign of life downstairs."

"Do they come out at all?" Mr. Laxworthy asked.

"They sit out in the sun together for an hour every morning, and once or twice I have seen Mr. Freeling Poignton walking just outside. But the strange thing is, that directly anyone approaches he goes indoors. He seems to have a perfect craze for avoiding everybody."

"He has a reputation of being eccentric," Mr. Laxworthy reminded her.

"He was never unsociable," she protested. "He used to stop and speak to me every morning. Yesterday I saw him just as he was coming out of the villa, and he no sooner caught sight of me than he went straight back again."

"Incredible!" Mr. Laxworthy declared. "What about his secretary and valet, by the by?"

"The secretary is away, and the valet, I believe, has been ill. I know that Mr. Poignton is expecting a new one every day, but he has not arrived yet."

"Where is Mr. Hamar?"

"Gone to England," she replied.

"So that practically the only people sleeping in the villa are Mr. Lenfield and Mr. Freeling Poignton and the former's servant?"

"Mr. Lenfield's servant is there," she assented. "I have seen him once or twice."

Mr. Laxworthy was silent for several moments.

"After all," he said, "there is nothing in the least mysterious in what you have told me. Mr. Freeling Poignton and Mr. Lenfield are living a life of seclusion. That is what they both came to Hyères for. Why not?"

"Yes, but consider the change," she objected. "Until Mr. Poignton and Mr. Lenfield went to the villa, they used both of them to spend nearly all of their time out-of-doors. Mr. Poignton used to play golf, Mr. Lenfield used to like being talked to. Now, all of a sudden, they have shut themselves up. They don't even spend the time in their sitting-room. And they avoid exchanging a single word with anybody."

"From that point of view, what you have told me is certainly odd," Mr. Laxworthy admitted. "Do our engagements admit of your walking with me a little distance?"

"I will walk with you, with pleasure," she declared. "Where shall we go?"

"To the villa," Mr. Laxworthy answered. "Where else?"

"But you have no excuse for going there?" she objected doubtfully.

"I shall find one," Mr. Laxworthy replied.

They walked along the terrace and took the path to the right, which led into the wood and finally to the villa. When they arrived before it, it certainly had a somewhat deserted appearance. Mr. Laxworthy knocked sharply upon the door. There was no reply. He tried the handle without effect. Then he stepped backwards and looked up. There was smoke appearing from the chimney. He knocked at the door again. This time, after a lapse of a few moments, it was cautiously opened by Mr. Lenfield's servant.

"What is it you want?" he asked curtly, almost uncivilly.

"I desire," Mr. Laxworthy said, "to speak with Mr. Lenfield."

"Mr. Lenfield is not in," the man replied, half-closing the door.

"You can give him a message, then, when he returns," Mr. Laxworthy continued. "Kindly tell him that Mr. Laxworthy is back."

"No need, my dear friend, no need at all to announce it," they heard someone say in the background. "One moment."

Mr. Lenfield appeared, coming down the stairs. He walked to the door, but he did not invite Mr. Laxworthy to enter. He was looking shockingly ill.

"I thought I heard your voice," he remarked. "Welcome back again. How goes the work on philosophy?"

"It makes progress," Mr. Laxworthy replied. "I knocked at your door because I understood at the office that you had asked for me during my absence."

"It is true," Mr. Lenfield admitted. "Alas! however, I am forced to confess that my inquiry was one of curiosity only. We missed you from your accustomed table. We were half inclined to fear that you were finding things a little dull here and had moved on."

"Not in the least," Mr. Laxworthy assured him. "So long as there are people, I am sufficiently interested. You have made a change in your abode since I was here."

"Between ourselves," Mr. Lenfield explained, "there were too many people in the hotel who were interested in other people's business. It is a great fault, nowadays. Mr. Freeling Poignton specially resented it, so we decided to come here, where we are free from any sort of espionage."

"An excellent idea," Mr. Laxworthy replied. "Your quarters, too, seem comfortable."

"On some other occasion," Mr. Lenfield promised, "I will give myself the pleasure of asking you to inspect them."

Mr. Laxworthy raised his hat and turned away. A few yards from the house he paused to watch a man who seemed to have come out of the back door and was making his way into the woods.

"There is no doubt," he remarked, "that there are peculiar circumstances connected with the isolation of our friends."

"It is queer," the girl agreed.

"May I ask," Mr. Laxworthy inquired, "if you are a young lady of nerve?"

"Why, I should say I was," she answered, glancing at him curiously. "Why?"

"If you are sure about it," he continued, "I should like to extend our walk a short distance. We will take this path. It leads, I believe, to the quarries they used to work on the other side of the hill."

"Have you any idea in your head about these two men?" she asked bluntly.

"Not at all," Mr. Laxworthy answered. "The association seems to me quite extraordinary. Lenfield was obviously embarrassed, and Mr. Freeling Poignton has developed a new measure of reserve. Quite an interesting little situation, in its way.... This is the walk, is it not, which they call the loneliest round the hotel?"

"Quite the loneliest," she agreed. "Is that why you asked me if my nerves were good?"

Mr. Laxworthy looked all around him searchingly.

"Not altogether," he admitted. "I may have had another reason at the back of my head. Ah!"

She drew a little closer to him. They had climbed some distance into the woods now, and coming towards them along the narrow path was a man of somewhat forbidding aspect.

"What a hateful-looking person!" she murmured. "Thank goodness I am not alone!"

The man slackened his pace. He was looking fixedly at the girl. She laid her fingers upon Mr. Laxworthy's arm.

"I think that I shall scream!" she declared. "It is the man whom we saw coming out of the back of the villa."

"You'll do nothing of the sort," Mr. Laxworthy muttered. "Wait!"

The man passed without addressing them, although both were conscious of a certain hesitation in his manner. No sooner had he gone by, however, than they heard him come to a halt. Mr. Laxworthy turned sharply round. What followed happened so quickly that the girl, who stood on the one side, found herself afterwards scarcely able even to describe it. She had no time even to shriek. She was carried away with wonder. The man, taller by head and shoulders than his frail-looking opponent, sprang at Mr. Laxworthy, dealing him at the same time a savage blow at the side of the head. She saw Mr. Laxworthy take one step backwards, then spring on one side with the ease almost of a professional gymnast. The rest was indescribable, unexplainable. All she knew was that with a sickening crash the man who had assaulted him was lying upon his back, with Mr. Laxworthy's knee upon his stomach, and Mr. Laxworthy's fingers upon his throat. Now the power to scream had come to her, she realised that it was altogether unnecessary. His assailant was entirely at her companion's mercy.

"Now, my friend," Mr. Laxworthy said, "it remains entirely with you whether I summon help and have you conveyed to prison, or whether I let you go."

"But, Monsieur, I was starving! The sight of so much riches, so much prosperity, at the hotel here every day, drives one mad—us, the very poor, for whom there is no labour, no food."

"Capital!" Mr. Laxworthy replied. "Now we will take the rest for granted. The longer you stay here, the more uncomfortable you will be, because, as you see, I intend to tighten my fingers upon your throat every few seconds. What were your instructions with regard to me?"

"But, Monsieur—" the man faltered.

"Rubbish!" Mr. Laxworthy interrupted. "Your instructions from the two men down at Monsieur Helder's villa. Were you to kill me outright or merely to terrorise me?"

"Monsieur—"

Mr. Laxworthy's fingers suddenly tightened their grip. The man's face was growing black.

"I will tell you the truth," he panted. "They offered me a thousand francs to deal with you so that you should keep to your room for a week. If any accident happened, they would help me to escape."

Mr. Laxworthy rose to his feet. He stood away from his formidable opponent without the least sign of nervousness.

"Get up!" he ordered.

The man staggered to his feet. Perhaps the same thought came to him that came to the girl at that moment. She shrank away. Mr. Laxworthy seemed an easy victim.

"If you like to make another effort," Mr. Laxworthy suggested calmly, "I have nineteen other similar tricks, learnt in Japan, which will disarm you quite as easily, only a little more painfully. What do you say?"

The man slunk away. He looked backwards over his shoulder and plunged into the wood. Mr. Laxworthy felt his spectacles and turned to the girl.

"Ah!" he said, "I am glad to see that your nerves are in good order. Having attained the object of our walk, let us descend."

She was trembling all over.

"Mr. Laxworthy!" she exclaimed. "How did you do that? It seemed miraculous."

"My dear young lady," he protested, "you have surely heard of jiu-jitsu? In my younger days I took some lessons, before the science was so common as it is at present. There is no strength, nothing difficult; a little knack—that is all."

"Sometimes," she murmured, "I am almost afraid of you."

"The interesting point," he continued, "is that we have now assured ourselves beyond doubt that Mr. Freeling Poignton and Mr. Lenfield are engaged in some little enterprise or undertaking in the villa of Monsieur

Helder for which they desire perfect seclusion and no interference. It is an undertaking of an unusual sort, from the fact that they fear the scrutiny or observation of any person such as myself, interested in his fellow-creatures, and with a moderate capacity for putting two and two together. I might, perhaps, have been inclined to let them alone but for this clumsy effort of theirs. I think that under the circumstances it rests with us to discover a little more. What do you think, young lady?"

"Oh, I don't know," she answered. "I am still shaking. I am frightened."

"Perhaps, after all, then," Mr. Laxworthy said, with a sigh, "it will be best for me to forget this little incident and proceed with my work."

They were descending now to the terrace. She caught at his arm.

"Look!"

He turned his head toward the villa, but he was too late.

"There was a face at one of the upper windows," she remarked. "Someone watching us."

"I saw them," he replied.

"But you were not looking," she protested.

"Did you hear what my friend Forrest Anderson once called me?" he asked—"the man of Peculiar Gifts. I have rather a curious hearing and rather a curious eyesight. More than once they have been of service to me. I will tell you that the face at the window there belonged to Mr. Freeling Poignton, and, notwithstanding the fact that he is a great philanthropist, I believe that he was absolutely disappointed to see me coming down this path with you unhurt."

"Mr. Laxworthy," she declared, "I was wondering what it is about you that I find so attractive. I think it must be that I never have the least idea whether you are making fun of me or not."

"My dear young lady," he replied, "who is there on earth who would dare to make fun of the latest product of these days—a young woman of your race? I now, with very much regret, am compelled to leave you."

"You are going to write that chapter on philosophy?" she asked.

"Alas, no!" he answered. "On consulting my tablets, a moment or two ago, I discovered that I was engaged to play a rubber of bridge this afternoon. My engagement is due within a few minutes. And you?"

"I am not playing bridge till after dinner," she told him. "I may come and watch you."

"I only hope," Mr. Laxworthy remarked, with a little frown, and peering into the room as they passed, "that my friends have not taken that table in the draughty corner."

The girl was as good as her word. She found Mr. Laxworthy, notwithstanding his professed indifference to the game, playing bridge with three of the most practiced players in the hotel, and she came and sat by his side. When the rubber was over, she leaned over his shoulder.

"I thought you once told me that you would not play this game because it required too much concentration?"

"Quite true," he admitted.

"You know that you played those two last hands faultlessly?"

"There was little room for error," he replied.

"You must have concentrated or you could never have forced those discards at the end. I saw all the hands. It was so obvious to me what you were playing for, and it was so skilfully done."

"So far as concentrating," he said, "it was during that last hand that I made up my mind exactly what is wrong down at the villa."

"Of course you are joking!" she exclaimed.

"On the contrary, I am much more in earnest than usual," Mr. Laxworthy assured her. "Our rubber is over and our friend here, Mr. Goodrich, is going to play a billiard heat. I have sent Sydney for my cap and cape. I should be glad if you would walk with me for five minutes on the terrace in front."

"I should love it," she declared. "These rooms get so stuffy."

They stepped out into the faint violet twilight. Mr. Laxworthy pointed with his stick to the villa.

"To-night," he said, "very soon after dinner, in fact—I am going through every room there. I know beforehand what I shall find. I trust, by the by, young lady, that your affections are not unalterably fixed upon Mr. Philip Lenfield?"

She laughed at him. "Don't be foolish, please! You know quite well that I should never have spoken to him at all, but I was so sorry to see him in such a state."

"A part of your sympathy," Mr. Laxworthy declared, "is certainly misplaced. Lenfield is ill, of course, but it is as much mental disease as physical that is tearing the life out of him. I know the type. I have studied it. After to-night, I am afraid you will see no more of him."

"Is there anything really wrong down there?" she asked.

"Yes," Mr. Laxworthy replied, "there is a great deal wrong."

"Then why don't you do something?" she insisted. "Can't you get the gendarmes to search the place? I saw Mr. Freeling Poignton sitting out in front this morning, talking to Mr. Lenfield. I don't see what they can be doing so very terrible, those two."

"There is a question or two I should like to ask Fritz," he remarked. "Let's hear how much he is willing to tell."

Fritz was standing on the threshold of the hotel doors. It was obvious that at the first mention of the villa he became uneasy.

"Can you tell me," Mr. Laxworthy inquired, "who else sleeps there besides Mr. Lenfield and Mr. Freeling Poignton? Are there any of the hotel servants in the place?"

"They none of them sleep over there, sir," Fritz replied. "Mr. Poignton has had our stenographer down once or twice, during the last few days, to write letters for him."

"So that, as a matter of fact," Mr. Laxworthy remarked, "there are only Mr. Poignton and Mr. Lenfield and the latter's servant who sleeps in the cottage."

"That is all, sir," Fritz replied.

Mr. Laxworthy took out his fountain pen.

"I am anxious to have a short conversation with Mr. Freeling Poignton," he said. "I will write a note, Fritz, and I would like to have you take it down to the villa at once. I shall expect an answer when I come down to dinner."

"The note shall be delivered in a few minutes, sir," Fritz promised.

They strolled away.

"Are you still as confident as ever that there is something wrong?" the girl asked him.

"Absolutely, now," Mr. Laxworthy replied. "I never had any real doubt about it. There is a little tragedy going on down there which I must stop, and very soon."

"When?" she asked him.

"I shall dine at half-past seven," said Mr. Laxworthy. "At twenty minutes past eight I shall go down to the villa."

"Can I come, too?" she begged breathlessly.

"It seems unfair to say no, especially as you seem to have a genuine interest in the affair. You can come, but I shall have to bring Sydney as well, to look after you."

"Is there likely to be any trouble?" she asked.

"One can never tell," Mr. Laxworthy replied.

Mr. Laxworthy spent some little time before dinner studying the *Times* and other English newspapers, a task which he attempted so seldom that he found it difficult to reach the items of news which he desired. Apparently, however, he was fully satisfied when he at last ascended to his room and changed for dinner. There were still, however, one or two matters with regard to the villa concerning which he desired information, and after a due amount of deliberation he rang his bell and asked for Fritz, the concierge, to be sent up to his room. The man, who was just going off duty, presented himself within a few minutes. Mr. Laxworthy took a hundred-franc note from his vest pocket.

"Fritz," he said, "I am going to ask you a few questions. I am not attempting to bribe you, but I never expect to get information for nothing. Put this in your pocket, please, and remember that the questions which I am asking you I am asking in the interests of your master and the hotel."

The man did not hesitate to accept the note.

"There are no secrets about the place that I know of, sir," he remarked. "If you ask me anything which Mr. Helder would not like known, I shall have to tell you so. Except for that, I shall be pleased to tell you anything in my power."

"It is the situation down at the villa which interests me," Mr. Laxworthy said. "Tell me, who waits upon Mr. Poignton and Mr. Lenfield?"

"No one, sir, from the hotel," Fritz replied promptly. "Mr. Lenfield got Mr. Helder's old cook to look after them, and the waiting is done by Mr. Lenfield's servant. Both gentlemen declared that they were very anxious for an absolutely quiet time. Mr. Poignton, as you know, sir, was always a little eccentric."

"Quite so," Mr. Laxworthy agreed. "So that really no one from the hotel goes down there at all."

"No one, sir. We see Mr. Poignton and Mr. Lenfield sitting outside sometimes, but, as a matter of fact, they seem to be leading a secluded life."

"Mr. Hamar has gone to London, I believe?" Mr. Laxworthy asked.

"That is so, sir."

"Mr. Poignton's secretary is, I think you said, at Marseilles?"

"Yes, sir."

"Thank you," Mr. Laxworthy concluded. "You see, the information I required is not very serious, is it? That is all, Fritz."

The man thanked him and withdrew. Mr. Laxworthy descended to dinner, at which meal he was more than ordinarily thoughtful. At the conclusion of the meal, he sent for his cloak and shawl and cap and summoned Sydney.

"We are going," he announced, "for a short stroll. Miss Chambers will accompany us."

"Are we going anywhere particular?" Sydney asked cheerfully.

"We are going to the villa," Mr. Laxworthy replied. "It is just possible that we may have a little trouble there."

Sydney looked surprised.

"Why, there's only Mr. Lenfield and Mr. Freeling Poignton and one servant there," he remarked. "It doesn't seem as though we could find much trouble amongst that lot."

Mr. Laxworthy sighed.

"Life, my dear Sydney," he said, "is full of surprises."

They approached the front door. Mr. Laxworthy tried the handle softly. The door was fastened with a Yale lock. From his pockets he produced a key.

"Come," he said.

The other two followed him into the hall. Mr. Laxworthy opened the door of the sitting-room. Mr. Freeling Poignton was there alone, reading. He looked up with a frown at their entrance. Mr. Laxworthy said nothing. It seemed as though his silence was purposeful.

"What do you want?" the man in the easy chair asked sharply.

Mr. Laxworthy remained silent. The girl, who was beginning to feel the awkwardness of the situation commenced an apology.

"Why, Mr. Poignton," she exclaimed, "we had no idea that we were going to walk in upon you like this. Mr. Laxworthy brought us here. I have no doubt that he will explain. We were afraid you might not be well. It seems so long since we saw anything of you."

"I am quite well," Mr. Freeling Poignton replied curtly. "I do not understand this intrusion at all."

"You understand it moderately well," Mr. Laxworthy said. "By the by, let me tell you at once," he added, "that if you raise your voice there will be trouble. Keep quiet."

"I don't know what you mean," the other murmured.

Mr. Laxworthy shrugged his shoulders.

"You know very well, Mr. Hastings," he replied. "Remember that I saw you when you gave that little performance at the Paradise Hotel the other night. I heard you offer, after your few impersonations of celebrated people, to impersonate anyone in the audience with five minutes' preparation. You have certainly managed, for the last few days, to allay all anxiety as regards the whereabouts of Mr. Freeling Poignton, and I want you to understand now that the game is up."

The man had commenced to shake. Very quietly he did exactly as he was bidden. The girl had drawn a few steps back. She had become pale. Sydney was shaking his head.

"By Jove, though," he murmured, "it's a clever imitation! Why, I've seen him half a dozen times sitting about outside the villa, and I've never doubted for a moment but that it was Freeling Poignton."

The girl clutched Mr. Laxworthy's arm.

"What has become of Mr. Freeling Poignton?" she asked hastily.

Mr. Laxworthy raised his finger.

"Follow me upstairs," he said. "Sydney, you come next. See that Miss Chambers is out of harm's way. I have an idea that Lenfield may be troublesome."

They ascended quite quietly to the first landing. Outside the door of the front room they all paused. Then what little colour remained in the girl's cheeks suddenly faded away. They all heard distinctly the low, terrible moan of a man in pain. Mr. Laxworthy hesitated for barely a second. He tried the handle of the door. It yielded to his touch. All three crossed the threshold.

The room was lit by a single lamp. In shirt and trousers, with untidy hair, a spot of burning colour upon his cheek-bones, Lenfield was standing with both arms outstretched as though he had been interrupted in the middle of a speech. Below him, stretched on a long settee, stripped of its cushions, tied with a hundred pieces of rope—tied at the ankles, the knees, the legs, the chest, everywhere—lay the figure of a man, deathly white. Even as they entered the room they heard his piteous appeal.

"Let me go," he moaned. "You shall have another million—ten, if you will. Let me go—I am dying! Ah! What's that?"

He tried to turn his head toward the door, but the ropes prevented him. Lenfield looked up and recognised them with a howl of rage. He stepped between them and his victim.

"Get away!" he cried. "This is no affair of yours. Be off! Laxworthy, you rat, you miserable, scheming, cursed devil, be off! This is no affair of yours. He is mine, given over to me. If you try to take him away, by God, I'll kill you!"

There was a moment's silence.

"Mr. Lenfield!" the girl gasped. He recognized her.

"You, too?" he cried. "What does it mean? What are you doing here? I tell you that this is a just vengeance—a just vengeance. You none of you know anything about it. I am the man to tell you. I am the man who knows what it means, that he—this that you see here—is a millionaire. I am the one who has lived among the people, and who has seen the thousands and thousands who have starved and sold their health and their lives and their honour and their children's honour, that he may be one of the gods of the earth, a creature with unholy, unwholesome power oozing from the very pores of his skin, with a banking account that would buy life and health and joy for all the thousands who rot in the gutters day by day. Be off! You are interfering in a greater matter than you know of. You come between the vengeance of God and the greatest sinner that ever breathed."

"He is mad!" the girl whispered, and Sydney nodded. But Lenfield, whose hearing was extraordinarily acute, leapt upon the word.

"Mad!" he cried. "Why not? Who could have lived my life and not be mad? Mad? Look at me. That man Laxworthy knows a little about me. Listen! Once I was an East End clergyman. It was there that the seeds of madness were sown. Then I went over to the people. Their cause was my cause. I suppose that was where I lost my reason. I became a socialist, afterwards an anarchist. We had traitors amongst our leaders. I betrayed them. It was for the good of the cause. I went to the police. They called me an informer, but it was those who did our cause harm whom I delivered up. Look at me. It is true. I have been an anarchist, a socialist, I have taken lives, I have trod the borderland of crime so closely that there was never a day when I was certain that the hand would not fall upon my shoulder, too. You know the reason. I am as poor now as I was in those days. The reason is simply this. Hatred for the rich, love for the poor, love for the sufferers, hatred for those who ply the whip. What was it you said?" he cried out, pointing his finger towards the girl. "Mad? I think so. I have felt it coming. But sane enough to plan one last just deed. Look at him," he added, pointing downwards to the man who was writhing under the ropes. "I lured him here. I hired that man downstairs to allay suspicions. In this room he has been for five days. I just kept him alive. Each day he signs a great cheque, which I send to London—not for myself, not one penny. Read the English papers. There isn't a society that labours in the East End that hasn't received, within the last few days, the biggest anonymous subscription that has ever been presented to it. Four hundred thousand pounds have gone out of this room in sight-drafts upon London banks, and found their way to charity within the last five days. To-night he is going to sign a larger one still. To-night—"

Mr. Laxworthy stepped forward.

"Lenfield," he said, "this must finish."

Lenfield sprang upon him like a wild cat. Mr. Laxworthy threw him over with a turn of his wrists. Sydney caught him as he fell and held him to the ground. Mr. Laxworthy was already cutting the cords. He looked around.

"Miss Chambers," he begged, "please run up to the hotel and ask them to send a doctor. Mr. Poignton will probably collapse. Ask Mr. Helder to step down here himself at once. You will do this?"

"Of course," she answered. "Is there nothing I can do for him before I go?"

Mr. Laxworthy looked at her.

"Young lady," he said, "get the brandy flask from the pocket of my coat there, pour a little into a tumbler, and pass it to me."

She knelt by his side, and together they finished their task of releasing the bound man. Mr. Poignton struggled to rise, and failed.

"My God!" he muttered to himself. "That man has been mad for five days. My God!"

He turned over and fainted. Mr. Laxworthy nodded and the girl hurried off. At the door, however, she was met by Mr. Helder and his wife. The alarm had already been given by Hastings. They came trooping up the stairs. Mr. Laxworthy, with his finger upon the pulse of the fainting man, waved them back.

"Lock that madman up," he said, pointing to Lenfield. "There is no real harm done. Mr. Poignton has fainted. He will be better directly."

Mr. Poignton opened his eyes.

"I am better already," he gasped. "Another night would have finished me."

He grasped Mr. Laxworthy's hand....

Mr. Laxworthy and the girl walked back to the hotel together. It was still barely nine o'clock.

"You'll have time for your bridge, after all," Mr. Laxworthy remarked.

She looked at him, and remained silent for several moments.

"Mr. Laxworthy," she said, "I think that you are one of the most wonderful men I ever met. Sometimes I am almost inclined to wonder—"

"To wonder what?" he asked.

"Whether I have not been mistaken in you all this time," she continued doubtfully. "Do you really mean that you stumble upon the solution of all these things? That you have no real interest in them? Are you what you seem to be, or are you really some sort of wonderful detective in disguise?"

Mr. Laxworthy sighed.

"My dear young lady," he said, "you flatter me! I am a man with a moderate amount of common sense, but, as a matter of fact, it as you who suggested most of these little affairs to me in which I have been useful. Run along to your bridge now, and get up and see us off in the morning."

"You are not really going to-morrow?" she cried.

"Our month is up," Mr. Laxworthy replied. "We are going for a time, at any rate. We may come back. Who knows?"

By eight o'clock the next morning Mr. Lenfield had been escorted to a French lunatic asylum; Mr. Freeling Poignton had passed a good night and was on the road to recovery; Mr. Laxworthy, Forrest Anderson, and Sydney Wing were seated in the omnibus on their way to catch the Côte d'Azur Express. The girl, who had never been up so early since she had been at Hyères, came out to see them off. She gave both her hands to Mr. Laxworthy, and she looked at him very sweetly.

"I still think," she murmured, "that you are the most wonderful man I ever met."

"Dear young lady," he replied, "you make me feel—"

"What?" she whispered.

"You make me wonder," he answered, "how long I shall be able to keep away."

She laughed and waved her hand. The omnibus rattled off towards the station.

"And now?" Forrest Anderson asked.

"Ah! And now?" Sydney echoed.

Mr. Laxworthy touched his spectacles.

"You were about to ask a question," he remarked.

"Is it home, or more adventures?" they demanded, almost simultaneously.

Mr. Laxworthy glanced out of the window of the omnibus for a moment at a passing automobile. Then he drew his shawl a little closer around him and settled back in his corner.

"Well," he said, "Fate shall decide for us."

CHAPTER VII
The Flowers of Death

Madame de Cléry raised herself a little on her couch. She moved with difficulty, she had lost all her colour, her eyes were dull and sunken. Mr. Laxworthy himself would scarcely have recognised her at this moment. She was, without a doubt, ill. The man who was paying her this morning visit stood by her side, his grey felt hat still in his hand, his whole appearance one of almost tragical sympathy. He was of a type common enough in Monte Carlo and the Riviera generally—short and inclined to *embonpoint*, but agile in his bearing, with olive cheeks and fiercely curled black moustache. By disposition gay, he was this morning in the depths of despair. He had the air of one who has unwillingly injured a friend. He was, alas! indirectly responsible for this suffering, the sight of which so greatly disturbed him, and, being a person of kindly disposition, he felt it almost as much as the ruin which stared him in the face.

"There is a little man," she said, speaking with difficulty, and in a voice scarcely louder than a whisper, "a little man named Laxworthy. He looks like some funny scientific old fossil. He wears thick glasses, and a shawl around his shoulders when the wind blows from the east. He is at the Paradise Hotel at Hyères. Send for him."

Monsieur Décat was a little perplexed.

"But, dear Madame," he ventured, "who is this Monsieur Laxworthy, and what will he do for me? Why should I send for him? What shall I say?"

Madam de Cléry spoke once more—still with effort.

"He would not admit it," she continued, "but he is a detective, an investigator, whatever you like to call him, an amateur, but an inspired one. He did a friend of mine a great service. Send for him, and if anyone can discover the truth, if anyone can save you, he will."

"I will send for him this morning!" Monsieur Décat exclaimed eagerly. "I will use the telegraph. I will do all that I can to get him here. But if he should refuse?"

"He will not refuse," Madame assured her visitor. "The affair will appeal to him. You must give him a free hand at your restaurant, and remember, whatever you do, keep the police out of it."

Monsieur Décat wiped his forehead.

"Madame," he declared in trembling tones, "if the police intervene I am ruined. Already there is talk. There are empty tables even at dinner time, a thing unheard of. It need only a visit from Monsieur the Chief Inspector and I may close my doors."

"Do as I say, and the police shall not intervene," Madame promised him. "Mr. Laxworthy shall save you."

Mr. Laxworthy came to Monte Carlo, and with him Sydney Wing and Mr. Forrest Anderson. They took rooms at the Hôtel de Paris, and it was not until he had made various arrangements with regard to his residence there, the position of his bed, the temperature of his morning bath, and hung up a thermometer near the window, that Mr. Laxworthy consented to listen to the little man who had met them at the station, and who was eager to tell his story.

"We will talk, if you please, across the way," Mr. Laxworthy decided. "It was indiscreet of you to meet us at the station, but, since you have done so, there is no further objection to our being seen together in public. I will take some tea at the Café de Paris. My friends Mr. Wing and Mr. Forrest Anderson will accompany us. I should like them to hear what you have to tell me."

"As you will," Monsieur Décat sighed, leading the way.

They found comfortable chairs near the promenade and for some moments looked out upon the gay little scene with interest. The sun was shining, and the wind was very soft and balmy. The women who floated by wore light summer dresses and beflowered hats. The men, too, were mostly clad in flannels and straw hats. It was toward the end of the season and continual sunshine seemed to have brought with it a certain air of lassitude reflected in the faces and carriages of the crowd of passers-by.

"A wonderful season you have had, Monsieur Décat," Mr. Laxworthy remarked.

"A wonderful season for others, it is true," Monsieur Décat confessed, "but for me, alas! for me there comes ruin. When I see one of my best clients depart from Monte Carlo, I am overjoyed. I tremble when a friend enters my restaurant."

"You had better tell me your story," Mr. Laxworthy said. "Tell it as concisely as you can. If I want to know more I will ask questions."

"The story is short enough because I know so little," Monsieur Décat declared. "About a month ago the trouble began. One of my clients, an Austrian gentleman, was taken ill at my restaurant. He went pale, he shivered, even before he could be removed he was violently upset in the stomach. The doctor shakes his head and speaks of ptomaine poisoning. But at Décat's *chez Décat*, ah, it is impossible! Who eats at my restaurant eats and drinks of the finest which Europe produces. The man is still ill, but he recovers. The next day the same thing happens again. This time an English gentleman was taken ill. It is singular, but who can blame the house of Décat? Two days pass without event. Then it is a lady—a Spanish lady, the great Quadella."

"How many in all have suffered?" Mr. Laxworthy inquired.

"Eleven," Monsieur Décat replied with a groan. "Last of all, my dear patronne, the best and most charming of my dear lady clients, Madame de Cléry."

"You have, I presume," Mr. Laxworthy asked, "made the obvious investigations?"

Monsieur Décat extended his hands.

"What is there which man could do?" he exclaimed. "My kitchens are like palaces. There is not a utensil in my kitchen which Monsieur would object to have upon his luncheon table. My food is selected as one might select the food for a Pope. To all I say the same thing: 'Give me of the best, and I pay what you ask.' My fish comes from the sea to the kitchen; for my chickens, my eggs, my milk, I have my own farm. Three days ago a great scientist from Paris spent the day with me in my kitchen and my cellars, my larder. He paid me all the compliments a man could pay. Yet the next day it was my dear friend Madame de Cléry who suffered. She ate simply of cutlets and asparagus, with a glass of *Graves*. It is from her bedside that I came to meet you at the station."

Mr. Laxworthy did not appear to be greatly interested.

"What do the doctors say?" he asked.

"Not one the same," Monsieur Décat groaned. "Alas, not one the same! There are all the symptoms, they tell me, of ptomaine poisoning. But there is something else. They contradict one another. Yet this much seems clear. There is some poison about the place, whether it descends from the clouds or rises from the earth like a miasma."

"Are these people who have suffered all of the same class?" Mr. Laxworthy inquired. "Does there seem to be any reason why they should have been selected as victims, either as a matter of constitution, nationality, or from any other cause?"

"It is not possible to connect them in any way with one another," Monsieur Décat declared. "There is, alas! Madame de Cléry herself, there is Quadella, there is an English journalist, a French merchant, an Austrian soldier, an Englishman and his wife, and Monsieur Crèpes, the leader of the orchestra at the Opera House."

"Have you any enemies?"

"Not one in the world. Why should I have enemies? I give to the poor, I am of a generous disposition, I greet my friends with both hands in the streets and I take a *petit verre* when they will. I stand in no man's way."

Mr. Laxworthy became a little more cheerful.

"Come," he said, "this may, after all, grow interesting. No enemies that you know of, eh? Not even a woman?"

"A woman least of all," Monsieur Décat assured his questioner. "I have had *affaires,* it is true. Why not? But always I have been a man of honour, and generous."

"I will dine at your restaurant to-night," Mr. Laxworthy decided.

Monsieur Décat nodded his head with satisfaction.

"It is good, that! You have no fear, then?"

"No fear at all," Mr. Laxworthy answered. "There is only one thing further I shall require of you. Let me have at my hotel by seven o'clock, as nearly as you can, a list of the dishes served to your clients who have suffered in this extraordinary manner."

Monsieur Décat agreed gloomily.

"There is little enough there to help you, Monsieur," he announced. "They vary from *Homard Americaine* to *Rosbif Anglais.*"

Mr. Laxworthy smiled grimly as he rose to his feet.

"One finds help sometimes," he remarked, "in unexpected quarters."

Madame de Cléry consented to receive Mr. Laxworthy when he called upon her about half an hour later. She was still upon her couch and still looking exceedingly ill. Mr. Laxworthy murmured a few words of sympathy as, in obedience to her gesture, he drew a chair to her side.

"Dear Madame," he declared, "the sight of your condition moves me. I am for the first time glad that I came to Monte Carlo."

She attempted a smile.

"You understood, of course, that it was I who persuaded Monsieur Décat to send for you?"

"Perfectly."

"You have talked with Monsieur Décat?"

"I was with him a few minutes ago," Mr. Laxworthy replied.

"He has told you everything? What do you think of the affair?"

"Until, Madame," Mr. Laxworthy answered, "I had the mingled pleasure and unhappiness of raising your fingers to my lips this afternoon, I must confess that it in no way appealed to me. It is at once too simple and too complicated."

"Explain yourself, dear Mr. Laxworthy," she begged.

"In a very few words! Monsieur Décat has, without doubt, an enemy. Either that enemy or his agent is an employee at the restaurant. The dishes have been tampered with out of spite against Monsieur Décat, and not from any personal feeling against the individual who is made to suffer. Monsieur Décat himself, if he is a man of good sense, should be able to lay his finger upon the person who owes him a grudge. But he is like all others. He will not tell. He declared to me that he knew no one in his restaurant or out of it who owed him the slightest grudge."

"For my own part," Madame de Cléry remarked, "I should have considered Monsieur Décat the most popular man of his class in Monte Carlo."

"Precisely," Mr. Laxworthy agreed dryly. "It is just the sort of popularity which breeds envy. However, to-night I dine there. Something may happen. A very slight incident should suffice."

"You are taking a risk," Madame de Cléry reminded him.

"Dear lady," Mr. Laxworthy retorted, as he took his leave, "without risks life would indeed be insipid!"

❧

"I eat," Mr. Forrest Anderson declared, "in fear of my life."

"I am absolutely without appetite," Sydney Wing agreed, helping himself for the second time to *hors d'oeuvres*.

"You distress me," Mr. Laxworthy said, glancing at Sydney's plate. "However, to reassure you, I think that to-night you have very little to fear."

"Something has been done?" Forrest Anderson asked.

Mr. Laxworthy sighed.

"Only a few very crude and obvious precautions," he answered. "One feels humiliated to make use of them, but the necessity is urgent. Another case of illness and I believe our friend Monsieur Décat would go out of his mind. We have stationed one of the *maître d'hôtel*, in whom Décat states that he has implicit confidence, in the kitchen amongst the chefs, and two others at the angles of the stairs leading from the kitchen. The whole of the food of the place is now under surveillance from its raw state to the moment it is served. It is not the way to catch the culprit, but it certainly lessens the risk we run."

"It seems a pity," Sydney wing remarked, "that we couldn't have had one open night. It doesn't give you a chance, sir."

Mr. Laxworthy pursed his lips.

"The elucidation of an affair like this," he declared, "is almost invariably a matter of accident. I am not sure that I blame Monsieur Décat. Look around us. When we were in Monte Carlo last, one had to order a table two days beforehand in order to dine here in comfort. To-night the place is nearly half empty."

Mr. Laxworthy's words were certainly true. The restaurant was a handsome room decorated in white and gold, with an annexe on the terrace looking out over the gardens. It was famous not only for its superb cookery and wines but for the excellence of its service, its beautiful glass and linen, and the rare skill with which Monsieur Décat seemed always to attract clients of distinction. Even with every table crowded and Monsieur Décat at his wits' end to mollify his unexpected clients, the place seemed always to enjoy a serenity and freedom from distracting noises which made it more than ever attractive. It possessed an individuality which was, without doubt, the hallmark of Monsieur Décat's genius. To be an habitué there was almost equivalent to admittance into a club; to be spoken to by Monsieur Décat as he passed from table to table was in itself a distinction. The change which had come over the place was very evident indeed. Madame, who sat at the mahogany desk making out the bills, wore an air of desperation which she endeavoured in vain to conceal as her eyes rested upon those empty tables. The head waiters, for whom there was now not enough to do, walked disconsolately about, inventing always some excuse or another to inquiring diners who were curious to know what had happened to the place. The waiters themselves were listless. Monsieur Décat's smiles and urbanity when he appeared, a little later than usual, were distinctly overdone. He came at last to the table where Mr. Laxworthy and his companions were seated.

"Monsieur has dined well?" he remarked, with his usual smile and bow. "Everything all right?"

"Your dinner has been excellent," Mr. Laxworthy pronounced.

"The *Chicken Marengo,*" Mr. Forrest Anderson remarked enthusiastically, "was a dream."

"There was never a *Hollandaise sauce* with exactly the same flavour as yours," Sydney Wing insisted.

Monsieur Décat accepted these compliments with the air of one who is used to them, as indeed he was. Then he bent a little lower over Mr. Laxworthy's chair.

"Nothing has occurred to Monsieur?" he whispered anxiously.

Mr. Laxworthy shook his head.

"Not the ghost of an idea," he admitted. "Come back and see us before we leave. If you have any 1811 *Courvoisier* brandy, bring us some when we take our coffee."

"There is no such brandy as mine upon the Riviera," Monsieur Décat declared, as he took his departure. "I shall have the pleasure, then."

The little orchestra of five were playing by request the *Intermezzo* from "Cavalleria Rusticana." Mr. Laxworthy leaned back in his chair and watched them. He watched, too, the dark-haired flower-girl, who was a privileged and nightly visitor at the restaurant, moving with her basket of flowers from table to table. Presently she reached the spot where they were sitting and after a moment's hesitation would have passed on.

"The gentlemen do not care for any flowers this evening?" she murmured.

"On the contrary," Mr. Laxworthy replied. "I should like a bunch of your beautiful lilacs to take across to my room. They tell me, Mademoiselle, that yours are the most beautiful flowers in Monte Carlo."

She smiled at him very slightly, a smile which seemed only to intensify the white sadness of her face. She bent over the sprays of lilacs for a moment. Then she glanced up at Mr. Laxworthy and hesitated.

"Monsieur has paid me so charming a compliment," she murmured, "that I should like him to have my freshest lilac. It is in the basket outside. If Monsieur permits, I will return."

She walked slowly away, the basked under her arm. She was a little lame and walked with the help of a stick. She wore no hat, and she was dressed in the plainest black robe. There was something, in a way, fascinating in her appearance. Sydney Wing gazed after her admiringly.

"She is the saddest-looking thing in Monte Carlo!" he exclaimed.

"She is a young woman of considerable personal attractions," Mr. Laxworthy declared, watching her pass through the door.

"Honest, for her class," Mr. Forrest Anderson pointed out. "A smarter young woman would have jumped at the opportunity of passing off her faded flowers upon three men."

"There didn't seem to be very much the matter with them," Mr. Laxworthy remarked absently.

The flower-girl came back into the room a moment or two later and made her way toward their table. Her little limp was in itself fascinating, and she brought a magnificent bunch of lilacs which she laid by Mr. Laxworthy's side. Mr. Laxworthy handed her a twenty-franc piece.

"Mademoiselle will permit," he begged. "I have never seen more beautiful lilac."

"Monsieur is very good," she answered hesitating. "It is too much."

Mr. Laxworthy shook his head.

"The pleasure, Mademoiselle, of buying it from you and in such delightful surroundings, should count for something," he insisted. "I have a weakness for absolutely fresh flowers. Perhaps to-morrow evening—"

"Monsieur is so kind," she murmured, and passed on with a little smile of assent.

Monsieur Décat returned, himself carrying a bottle of brandy, and followed by a waiter bringing three glasses of huge size and delicately chilled.

"Monsieur has been patronising our little Annette," he remarked. "My clients are all so good to her."

"She seems," Mr. Laxworthy said, "a very pleasing young person."

Monsieur Décat was himself pouring out the brandy.

"They smile at me sometimes," he declared, "because I allow her the run of my restaurant. It is not usual, of course, but she is an orphan and supports herself. It is better for her to sell flowers to such clients as mine than to frequent the cafés."

Mr. Laxworthy smelt his brandy and proceeded to roll it round in his glass.

"A native of Monte Carlo?" he inquired.

"By no means," Monsieur Décat answered. "She came here two years ago with an invalid father. The man had been in prison—a shocking character. He died lately."

"Poor child," Sydney Wing murmured.

"Poor and unfortunate, indeed," Monsieur Décat agreed. "Yet in Monte Carlo it is easy enough to live. Now, Monsieur Laxworthy, I await your verdict. What of my brandy?"

Mr. Laxworthy sipped it with the air of a connoisseur.

"Excellent!" he pronounced. "Marvellous!"

"And for the rest?" Monsieur Décat whispered, a moment or two later.

"One can do nothing but watch," Mr. Laxworthy replied. "Yet I think I can make you a promise. Within two days your little puzzle shall be solved."

Monsieur Décat was half relieved, half incredulous.

"You have seen something, then?" he exclaimed. "You are on the track?"

Mr. Laxworthy shrugged his shoulders. It was his manner of dismissing the subject.

"Tell me now," he begged, "of some of your clients? The stout, red-faced man, for instance, who has just refused to purchase any flowers?"

"A German millionaire," Monsieur Décat whispered. "A manufacturer of clothing, I believe. He spends money here like water. Let me tell you of the others. There are, alas! few of interest to-night, but if, indeed, Monsieur, you speak the truth, all will soon be well again."

Mr. Laxworthy nodded.

"Rest assured, Monsieur Décat," he said, "that all will be well again with you before very long. I have seen enough for one evening. We must try our luck across the way. Will you give orders that the same table be reserved for us to-morrow night?"

"With all the pleasure in the world!"

The restaurant on the following evening was distinctly fuller. Monsieur Décat welcomed his three expected guests with an air almost of triumph.

"Your coming has brought good fortune, Monsieur Laxworthy," he declared, as he walked with them to their table. "Some of my old clients are back again. You behold Monsieur le Duc! The Prince of Reist is coming with a party. Your English Lady Bolsover sits in the corner there with a friend."

"And your German millionaire, I see, returns," Mr. Laxworthy remarked, glancing across the room.

Monsieur Décat elevated slightly his shoulders.

"The gentleman is not ornamental," he said, with an air of apology, "but he spends the money. To-night he entertains Mademoiselle Cora from the

Folies Bergères. Mademoiselle dances divinely!"

Mr. Laxworthy smiled grimly, but he made no reply. They seated themselves at the table and Monsieur Décat hurried away to greet more guests.

"Order what you please without fear," Mr. Laxworthy said, taking up a menu. "To-night we are safe."

Both Forrest Anderson and Sydney Wing glanced at him expectantly.

"They will happen no more, then—these incidents?" the former ventured to inquire.

Mr. Laxworthy ignored the question.

"*Potage petit marmite,* perhaps afterwards some trout, a chicken and salad," he ordered. "The burgundy we will leave to Monsieur Décat."

The atmosphere of the place was indeed changed. Nearly every table was occupied, and there were still people arriving. There was a cheerful buzz of conversation; Monsieur Décat and his little corps of *maîtres d'hôtel* had their hands almost full attending to the wants of their clients. The orchestra played with renewed spirit; the flower-girl had twice to leave the room to replenish her basket. Mr. Laxworthy watched her thoughtfully as she reached once more the table where the German millionaire and his companion were seated. Again the man shook his head curtly, but his companion stretched out her arms.

"All the roses!" she exclaimed. "I will have all the roses!"

The flower-girl set down upon the floor the basket which she was carrying, and began to put together a great bunch of pink roses, which presently she laid upon the table. Then she took a single carnation and turned toward the man. It seemed as though she were offering it for his buttonhole. He assented gruffly. At that precise juncture, Mr. Laxworthy, who had been watching the little scene with interest, leaned across the table.

"Sydney," he said, "as quickly as you can, without making a disturbance, go and touch the flower-girl on the arm. Tell her to come to this table for one moment. I will not keep her longer. See that she comes at once."

Sydney rose promptly and crossed the room. The girl, with a small syringe in her hand, was in the act of spraying the flower when he addressed her.

"Mademoiselle," he whispered, "Monsieur my friend across the room wishes to speak to you without an instant's delay. The matter is one of urgency."

The girl gave a little start, and the flower which she had been holding slipped from her fingers to the floor. She looked across the room to Mr. Laxworthy, who had risen to his feet. Their eyes met. Mr. Laxworthy's face was immovable. The girl began to tremble.

"I will come," she faltered. "I will come at once."

She picked up the carnation from the floor. The man held out the lapel of his coat, but she shook her head.

"It is spoilt, Monsieur," she said. "I will arrange another. In a moment I will return."

She came to Mr. Laxworthy like a child in mortal fear of some unknown punishment. She set down the basket of flowers upon the floor and stood before him.

"Monsieur?" she began timidly.

Mr. Laxworthy looked at her steadfastly.

"Mademoiselle," he said, "it would be well that you offer no more flowers here this evening. If you will leave the restaurant by the terrace end, there are some seats fronting the gardens. Wait for me there. A matter of five minutes, perhaps."

She picked up her basket without hesitation.

"I shall await Monsieur," she murmured.

Mr. Laxworthy sipped his coffee and watched her thoughtfully as she made her way down the room. His two companions were dumbfounded.

"The flower-girl!" Sydney exclaimed softly. "How could you—how could anyone—"

"A little matter of inspiration," Mr. Laxworthy interrupted, "and a few inquiries."

The girl was leaning forward upon her seat, her face half covered by her hands, her eyes, lit now with real terror, gazing forward into the velvety darkness. Mr. Laxworthy seated himself deliberately by her side.

"Mademoiselle," he said, "I am not used to sitting out of doors at this season of the year, so I shall be glad to make our interview a short one. Have you anything to say to me?"

"Nothing, Monsieur."

"Have you no excuses to offer?"

"None."

"Causes always interest me," Mr. Laxworthy continued. "Tell me your story?"

"Why should I?"

"Mademoiselle," Mr. Laxworthy said, more sternly, "with the little syringe which you have in your pocket you have sprinkled flowers with a poisonous compound and afterwards shaken them over the plates of various people, thereby poisoning them. If this was a wanton act, then you deserve, you very richly deserve, the imprisonment which threatens you. On the other hand, if you have anything to say, I am ready to hear it."

"You are not of the police?" she asked, a little timidly.

"I am not," Mr. Laxworthy replied. "I stand not for the law, but for justice."

She turned upon him with a moment's fierceness.

"There is no justice in this world!" she exclaimed bitterly.

"On the contrary," Mr. Laxworthy said, "the laws of justice are as inexorable as the pendulum of life itself. Every crime and every evil deed is paid for. You are the daughter of Senekou, the chemist and anarchist. Is it some evil germ from his madness which lingers in your blood?"

Terror and indignation seemed to struggle together in her face as she leaned towards him in the darkness. Mr. Laxworthy, however, was unmoved.

"He was never mad!" she cried. "They did their best to drive him out of his senses, but he was never mad. They kept him in prison for eight years, imprisonment which was in itself a torture. Then we came here. Monsieur Décat employed him, and one day he found out who he was and dismissed him at a moment's warning. No one else would give him work. He died of starvation. I remain."

"I know your whole history," Mr. Laxworthy remarked slowly; "I have spent some part of to-day in making inquiries concerning you. Now look me in the face and tell me why you have done this thing."

"I did it because I hate Monsieur Décat," the girl replied in a low tone. "I hate his restaurant, and I would like to see him ruined. I hate the people whom I have made to suffer. I hate this whole place and everyone in it. Monsieur, you are of the world, you understand. What do you think this city of sunshine and jewels and gay ladies and wealth—hideous, senseless wealth—must mean to me? I saw him grow thinner and more tired every day. It was starvation he died of."

"Mademoiselle," Mr. Laxworthy said, "you carry on a futile warfare. Your father sinned and he paid his debt. You have sinned, but I will make myself your judge. You have suffered in advance. It shall be enough. You have relatives in France. Leave Monte Carlo to-morrow and seek them out. There is in this envelope sufficient to keep you from becoming a burden upon them. Do you accept?"

There was a change in her face. Its white tenseness had gone, her eyes glowed at him, her lips were trembling.

"Monsieur," she gasped. "You mean—you mean—"

"Mademoiselle," Mr. Laxworthy declared, rising to his feet, "there will be no one to interfere with you; only remember this, the debt is paid. I wish you good fortune, and a happier life."

Mr. Laxworthy turned up his coat collar and moved away. The girl stood for a moment where he had left her, as though she were in some sort of dream. Then, with the basket upon her arm, she disappeared slowly into the night.

A week later Mr. Laxworthy and his two friends lunched at Décat's.

Every table was full, and the placed seemed to have wholly regained its popularity. Monsieur Décat came up to pay his respects.

"Our farewell visit, Monsieur Décat," Mr. Laxworthy announced. "We leave by the three o'clock train."

"I will fetch the brandy," Monsieur Décat replied promptly.

They drank together out of the great glasses.

"Monsieur Laxworthy," the restaurant proprietor said earnestly, "it is true that your visit here has been, in a sense, fruitless. You have discovered nothing. You have failed to solve the mystery of my poisoned guests. Never mind. I am superstitious. Since your arrival things have mended. Once more Décat's is itself again. And somehow I have confidence. Somehow I feel that the trouble will not return. Therefore, Monsieur Laxworthy, I am your debtor. You will always be a welcomed visitor here."

Mr. Laxworthy shook hands with the little man as they departed. Monsieur Décat was inclined to be sympathetic.

"One cannot always succeed, my dear sir," he declared. "One must bear with one's failures. Why should one not believe, even now, that it is you who have frightened away this malefactor?"

Mr. Laxworthy smiled grimly.

"There is reason in what you say, Monsieur Décat," he agreed. "I will console myself."

CHAPTER VIII
The Deserted Hotel

Mr. Forrest Anderson, Mr. Sydney Wing, and Mr. Laxworthy himself were seated side by side on low canvas chairs at the extreme edge of a little strip of sand jutting out into the Mediterranean. About fifty yards behind them was an hotel built of white stone, and with green shutters, and balconies hung with flowers. Save themselves, there was no other human being in sight.

Mr. Laxworthy was reading, with much apparent interest, a volume of philosophy. Sydney Wing was throwing pebbles into the sea. Forrest Anderson was dozing. The day was warm, and the atmosphere relaxing. Sydney Wing threw his last pebble, gave a mighty yawn, and struck.

"Mr. Laxworthy, sir!"

Mr. Laxworthy frowned and continued to read. When he had finished the sentence, however, he carefully marked his place and turned a little in his chair.

"Well?"

Sydney Wing smiled a little apologetically.

"I am absolutely bored to death, sir."

Mr. Laxworthy looked at him steadfastly and sighed.

"It is because you have no mind, young man," he declared severely. "You have no resources. You cannot enjoy solitude. Here we are cut off for a few days from all the distractions of life. There isn't a villa even in sight. Our hotel is practically empty. Instead of congratulating yourself upon having found such a spot, you find yourself bored."

"I admit it," Sydney confessed sadly. "Even a game of golf would cheer me up."

"You shall have it," Mr. Laxworthy promised him. "Within an hour, a motor-car which I have hired for a month will arrive from Monte Carlo. You can drive yourself to Villascure."

"A motor-car!" Sydney murmured, his face lighting up. "For use?"

"Possibly," Mr. Laxworthy replied dryly.

"You said just now, sir, that the hotel was practically empty," the young man went on. "There surely isn't another soul staying there! We have lunched and dined there for three days, and the salon looks like a desert."

"It has a deserted appearance," Mr. Laxworthy admitted thoughtfully.

Mr. Forrest Anderson sat up suddenly in his chair.

"I will tell you something," he said. "There is something uncanny to me about one or two of those closed rooms upstairs. For three days we have not seen a soul except the waiters about the place. There has been no sign of any other guests. Yet sometimes in the corridors I have fancied that I heard unfamiliar voices. Yesterday morning I distinctly saw a face at the window of one of those rooms which they told us were dismantled. I can never pass down the corridor to my room without feeling that there is one living person, at any rate, close at hand."

Mr. Laxworthy regarded his friend with some interest.

"Really," he declared, "this is quite wonderful. I had no idea that you were developing gifts of this order. A man who can divine the presence of a human being behind a closed door is a man of parts, indeed!"

"You can make fun of me, if you like," Mr. Forrest Anderson replied unmoved. "Yesterday I met a waiter with a dinner tray on the landing. Where did he come from?"

"I could have sworn I heard a violin the other night," Sydney put in.

Mr. Laxworthy looked from one to the other.

"You amaze me," he assured them. "You are both of you developing gifts and powers of observation which are perfectly astonishing. Anything else?"

Sydney Wing lit a cigarette.

"Rather getting at us, aren't you, sir?" he remarked. "There's one thing, we're used to surprises. Think how you've treated us this time! You see this queer little hotel from the road, with its very notice-board thrown down, its drive thick with weeds, looking for all the world as though it were entirely deserted, and you insist that it is the one place in the Riviera for which you have been searching. We follow meekly, and have the utmost difficulty in persuading the landlord to give us any rooms at all. Yet here we have stayed for three days, and until this minute I don't think it has occurred to either Anderson or myself to wonder whether our coming was altogether as unexpected as it seemed."

Mr. Laxworthy took up his book.

"There are limits, I perceive, to this newly-developed intelligence of yours," he said dryly. "Tell me, is this the landlord who comes to us from the hotel?"

Both men glanced round.

"It is the landlord," Sydney announced. "Monsieur Dreiche he calls himself, I believe."

"Quite a superior person," Mr. Laxworthy murmured. "One wonders that he is content to remain in such a place."

"I can't think why he doesn't advertise it or something," Sydney remarked. "It's a charming situation, and the hotel isn't badly furnished inside. Why they should let the grounds go to rack and ruin just near the road, licks me."

"Your dawning powers of observation," Mr. Laxworthy whispered, "may lead you to connect this apparent carelessness with a marked reluctance of Monsieur Dreiche to receive us as guests."

"There does seem something queer about it," Mr. Forrest Anderson admitted under his breath.

Monsieur Dreiche came down the boarded way across the shingle, and approached them hat in hand. He was a man of rather less than medium height, stout, with heavy black eyebrows, moustache and imperial. His complexion was sallow, almost yellow, as though he had at some time suffered from jaundice. He walked heavily; his expression was gloomy, not to say anxious. His smile of politeness as he saluted his visitors was, without doubt, forced.

"We were just remarking," Mr. Laxworthy said, "how inexplicable it was that an hotel so charmingly situated as yours should be so neglected."

Monsieur Dreiche sighed.

"An affair of bad luck, Monsieur, I am convinced," he replied. "Even now I come to you with trepidation. I received you here with reluctance, because, Monsieur, it seemed to me scarcely honourable to accept guests in an empty hotel. When, however, I put this before you, you told me that it was solitude for which you were looking. The society of other guests would be distasteful. You gave me to understand, even, that the arrival of other guests would drive you away."

"I do not remember going quite as far as that," Mr. Laxworthy said. "But I certainly have no objection to solitude. We have been spending a few days in Monte Carlo, and we find the rest beneficial."

Monsieur Dreiche looked gloomier than ever.

"I have news for Monsieur," he announced, "of the worst. Nevertheless, it is necessary to tell the truth. I have a party of guests who will arrive to-day. If Monsieur appreciates the solitude of his surroundings—it is finished. These guests who come, they are not, alas! the most desirable. I bring the news with the deepest regret. Monsieur and his friends will doubtless decide to depart."

Mr. Laxworthy took off his spectacles and rubbed them very carefully.

"How many of these guests will there be?" he inquired.

"Five or six, beyond a doubt, perhaps more," Monsieur Dreiche told him sadly. "But for this wretched season I would have denied them. I know well that they are noisy and ill-mannered."

Mr. Laxworthy sighed.

"We will remain for a day or so longer, at any rate," he announced. "We will see what the inconvenience of their coming amounts to. It would be unfair to leave so hastily."

The smile on Monsieur Dreiche's lips was a little sickly.

"There is, alas! another matter, Monsieur," he continued. "These people selected their rooms a month ago. They comprise the suites at present occupied by Monsieur and his friends."

Mr. Laxworthy frowned.

"But it is absurd, this," he declared testily. "We're in possession, and we shall not move—not to-day, at any rate; perhaps not to-morrow. We await events. At your service, Monsieur Dreiche."

Mr. Laxworthy picked up his book and waved his hand. The hotel proprietor very slowly returned to his hotel.

"We're in the way," Sydney Wing murmured.

"I thought that we might be," Mr. Laxworthy assented as he settled himself down once more to read.

Luncheon that day, in marked contrast with its predecessor, was an almost impossible meal. The *omelette* was burned, the cutlets almost raw, and the service abominable. Curiously enough, all this seemed to afford Mr. Laxworthy the utmost satisfaction.

"We're to be starved out," he declared cheerfully. "Never mind. It is only for a day. If anything comes of our little visit here, it will be all over within twenty-four hours or so."

"There is at least bread and butter," Sydney Wing groaned, tapping a roll.

Presently the manager sought them out once more carrying this time an open telegram in his hand.

"Mr. Laxworthy," he began, "I am desolated. But my guests who are coming insist upon the rooms they themselves selected, and so much of my hotel is dismantled that I have no other apartments fit to offer. My friend the manager of the Grand Hotel at Villascure telegraphs me that he will be delighted to receive Monsieur and his friends. Monsieur, I am sure, will find his hotel most comfortable."

"When I go to it I daresay I shall," Mr. Laxworthy replied. "For two days I remain here. That is settled. If you turn us out of our rooms—a course against which I protest most vigorously—it will be necessary for you to find us others."

Monsieur Dreiche turned away, baffled. Mr. Laxworthy had imparted a certain amount of irritation to his manner which seemed wholly in keeping with his appearance. It is without doubt a fact that the hotel proprietor, as he retired disconsolately to his office, had no suspicion that he had anyone else to deal with in this matter than an obstinate, crotchety Englishman.

At about half past ten that evening Mr. Laxworthy and Mr. Forrest Anderson left the smoking-room together. Instead, however, of following his usual custom of retiring for the night, Mr. Laxworthy reached down his coat and shawl.

"The moonlight is wonderful," he declared; "we will walk for half an hour on the sands. Where is Sydney?"

"Out looking the car over," Mr. Forrest Anderson replied.

Mr. Laxworthy nodded approvingly.

"We will fetch him," he said. "There is a way to the garage through the shrubbery."

They found Sydney, who had completed his task, seated outside the garage, smoking.

"Ripping car," he pronounced. "I can get forty out of her, if necessary, even on these roads."

"She is ready to start?" Mr. Laxworthy asked.

"With a turn of the wrist."

"Very good. We will now walk together on that strip of sand by the sea. I have a fancy for that spot, for it is the one place where we could not possibly be overheard."

"You have something to tell us?" Sydney demanded eagerly.

"Less, a great deal, than you are expecting to hear," Mr. Laxworthy replied dryly. "However, the time has come for my confession. You are wondering why I brought you here, you are wondering why I refuse to leave. Frankly, I do not know. I can only tell you this. There is a man hiding here and I can't imagine why. There are some guests expected here to-night connected in some way with this man, and I have no idea why they are coming. The whole affair may be of absolutely no importance. We may have wasted our time here completely. On the other hand, I object to coincidences which I do not understand. Listen."

The three men stood perfectly motionless. The whole of the front of the hotel was dark except for one window at the end of the row, from which came a faint glimmering light. The window was open and through it came floating out softly upon the moonlight stillness a breath of very faint, very sweet music. Someone was playing the violin, playing to themselves very quietly, but with exquisite skill. The music grew and grew, becoming stranger and more passionate with every note. The three men stood entranced.

"Our mysterious neighbour at last," Sydney murmured.

Gradually the music died away. Then there was silence. Something seemed to have passed from the beauty of the night. The perfume of the mimosa was hardly so sweet. Some quality of softness seemed to have gone from the atmosphere and from the stars hung in the cloudless sky and reflected far across the deep blue sea. Mr. Laxworthy drew his shawl a little closer around his shoulders.

"The fellow plays like a magician," he murmured.

"He is surely a great master!" Forrest Anderson exclaimed.

"He is the *chef d'orchestre* at Décat's restaurant, or rather he was until a few nights ago," Mr. Laxworthy replied dryly.

"A *chef d'orchestre!*" Sydney repeated, incredulous. "What on earth is he doing here, then?"

Mr. Laxworthy smiled amiably.

"Precisely the question I ask myself. The man is in hiding. Why?"

"Got into trouble at Monte, I should think," Forrest Anderson suggested. "He's a foreigner, I suppose, and a foreigner who can make music like that must have a temperament. He's probably been using his knife."

Mr. Laxworthy shook his head.

"So far as one could gather from a few casual inquiries," he declared, "the man's character is irreproachable. He has a quieter manner than most of his kind, and has a reputation for being ambitious. Monsieur Décat, for example, made but one complaint of him. He sought, without a doubt, to attract the attention of the wealthy ladies who frequented the restaurant. Décat replaced him with infinite regret. He left Monte Carlo openly. There is not a word spoken against him."

"In my opinion," Mr. Forrest Anderson said, "we are going very soon to find ourselves *de trop* here. It is probably a love assignation which the fellow has come to keep."

"That view of the situation has occurred to me," Mr. Laxworthy confessed. "On the other hand, why this desire on the part of the hotel proprietor to get rid of us? Why this secrecy concerning the man's presence here? Why, too, should these expected guests arrive by water?"

"How do you know that they are going to?" Sydney asked.

"This afternoon," Mr. Laxworthy pointed out, "a new rope has been affixed to that little landing-stage. Since dinner time Monsieur Dreiche has walked down here, looking toward the point, at least a dozen times. These things are not for nothing. The visitors will arrive by water from Monte Carlo."

"After all, it may be only an elopement," Sydney suggested.

"There are many kinds of elopements," Mr. Laxworthy retorted grimly.

The three men presently returned to the house. Their rooms all looked toward the sea and were in line with the one from which the music had issued.

"I must confess," Mr. Laxworthy said, "that the arrival of these guests interests me to such an extent that I shall not retire for the present. I do not imagine that anything will happen to-night, but it would be wise, I think, if you others follow my example."

"Are we likely to want the car?" Sydney inquired.

"One never knows," Mr. Laxworthy replied thoughtfully.

"I'll sleep in her, at any rate," Sydney declared. "If you want me I shall be on hand."

The hours of the night passed peacefully and uneventfully away. The full yellow light faded from the stars, the moon became colourless. The faintest of grey mists hung upon the water. In the east the clouds began to break and a ripple of wind passed across the sea. Suddenly those who watched were rewarded for their vigil. A dark object glided round the point and came rushing in toward the shore. Almost as it appeared the music recommenced. The man in the end room was standing up now. Mr. Laxworthy could see him distinctly, could trace the fierce upward curl of his moustache, the white face, the burning eyes. The tone of his music had changed. It was becoming now a paean of welcome. Then from the boat came a cry. Mr. Laxworthy heard it and smiled. It was one of wonder, but underneath it there was fear. That cry was his justification.

The boat glided up to the landing-stage. The little party disembarked in the glimmering twilight. There were only three passengers, two men and a girl. They came very slowly up the little strip of sand. Then, when they were about twenty yards from the front door of the hotel, a figure suddenly emerged, running towards them. It was the musician.

"Mademoiselle, dear Mademoiselle," he exclaimed with an exaggerated gesture of great joy, "you have come to me! It is the morning of my life, this! I kiss your hands, dear Mademoiselle."

She placed her hands firmly behind her. Even in that dim, ghostly twilight the two men who watched could see that she was tall and fair. Her tone was full of angry contempt.

"Come to you, indeed! You must be mad. I came because they told me that my father was here, that he'd had an accident. Is this a trick?"

The musician pressed towards her.

"Dear Mademoiselle," he pleaded, "it is no trick. It is the call of my heart to yours. No longer could I play at Décat's pining for a word with you, a touch of your fingers. I have had your messages, Mademoiselle; I have seen the light flash from your eyes to my little balcony. But these things are not enough for one of my disposition. They are not enough for one who lives. Mademoiselle, be kind to me, I pray. I am only a poor artist, but there is no one in your great world who could love as I."

"Artist, indeed!" the girl retorted. "I should call you a mountebank! The messages I sent were simply to the maker of music which pleased me for a moment. They had nothing to do with the man. Stand out of the way, please. In your balcony at Décat's you are in your place. Here you annoy me."

The musician stood quivering with rage, his face convulsed with passion.

He looked like some evil thing. The men who stood on either side of the young woman were grinning at his discomfiture.

"Mademoiselle will regret!" he declared fiercely. "I sent her the message we agreed upon," he added, turning a little as though to appeal to the others. "She leaves her yacht to come to me. Now caprice has seized her. Is it that you are a coquette, after all, Mademoiselle? Is it that you have indeed forgotten that next my heart reposes the flower you sent me—the flower which your lips have touched?"

"You are an idiot," the girl declared scornfully. "I'm not sure that you are not also a knave. I insist upon being told whether your message was a trick. Is my father here, or is he not?"

The door of the hotel had opened. It was Monsieur Dreiche who came out. He bowed low to Mademoiselle.

"Mademoiselle will be pleased to enter," he begged. "There are other guests in the hotel, and one fears to disturb them."

The girl did not move.

"Are you the proprietor?" she demanded.

"At your service, Mademoiselle."

"Will you tell me at once whether my father, Mr. Gilbert Powers, is here?"

Monsieur Dreiche shook his head slowly.

"No, Mademoiselle," he replied. "There is certainly no gentleman of that name in the hotel."

She turned to the two men who had brought her from the boat.

"Am I to believe, then," she cried angrily, "that I have been brought here by a trick? These men came to the yacht and told me that my father was lying here, badly hurt. What does it mean?"

There was a moment's complete silence. A very ugly smile had parted the lips of the musician. Monsieur Dreiche's expression of incredulity was excellent. He turned to the man in oilskins who had driven the launch.

"Henri," he asked, "is this true?"

The man shook his head.

"But assuredly not," he answered. "The message which I gave to Mademoiselle was that Antoine awaited her here—Antoine, our brother. I handed her a note from him, begging her to come. A priest, he told her, was arranged for. Mademoiselle unfortunately dropped the note on the deck of the yacht as she descended."

For the first time the girl seemed terrified. She looked around her as though searching for a friendly face, in vain.

"My father is not here!" she gasped. "It is indeed a plot, this!"

Once more the musician approached her. His conceit was so amazing that he had already forgotten the scorn of her words. He bent towards her in the twilight.

"Ah, Mademoiselle," he pleaded, "dear lady of my dreams, forgive me if I have schemed just a little to win so great a happiness. These are my brothers, Henri, who brought you here in the launch, Charles, who owns this hotel. I come to them and I tell them how things are between you and me, how we love, but how impossible it is to meet; that your father is a millionaire, and you, alas! are never alone. We make this little plot between us. It is for the happiness of both of us, dear. Everything has been arranged, the priest is at hand, by to-morrow night we can be in Paris. Then I will play to you all my life, I will teach you new music, I will—"

His sentence ended in a howl of rage. The girl had leaned forward and struck him across the mouth with the palm of her hand. Her eyes were blazing.

"You are a lunatic!" she exclaimed fiercely. "I have smiled at you once or twice because your music pleases me. I sent you flowers one night because I hesitated to give you money. Whatever more you have imagined is simply the result of your stupid vanity. If you are indeed the manager of the hotel, Monsieur," she added, turning to Monsieur Dreiche, "you will order these men to take me straight back to my yacht."

Monsieur Dreiche was silent for a moment.

"Mademoiselle," he said slowly, "pray consider. The note signed 'Antoine, your lover' will be found upon the yacht. You have said hard things to Antoine to-night, but I cannot believe that you mean them all. You are here, the tide has turned, you cannot return. Poor Antoine adores you. Take his hand and be reconciled, Mademoiselle, and let me send for the priest."

"Do you seriously believe," the girl cried furiously, "that I would marry a monkey like that!"

"Mademoiselle," the hotel proprietor replied, making a little sign to the others, "for a young lady in your position, marriage with an artist, even though he be a poor one, is better than—"

"Than what?" she demanded.

No one answered. The two men had drawn nearer.

"Mademoiselle will enter the hotel," Monsieur Dreiche insisted. "We can talk out here no longer. We shall disturb our other guests," he added, with a half fearful glance up at the three open windows beneath which they were standing.

"I refuse to set my foot inside the place," the girl declared.

Monsieur Dreiche gave a little sign. In a moment she was seized from behind. Antoine's hand was upon her mouth.

"Bring her to my room," he ordered. "She shall be tamed."

They had barely dragged her a single yard before they stopped short. Several most amazing things were happening. There was suddenly a low hum of a motor, and Sydney, seated in a grey car, emerged from behind the garage and came sweeping up to the door of the hotel. Mr. Laxworthy and Mr. Forrest Anderson appeared on the threshold. The former came slowly towards the little group, who were standing like stone figures upon the gravel front.

"Monsieur Dreiche," Mr. Laxworthy remarked, "I regret that I cannot possibly remain any longer in a hotel where conversations of such length are carried on at five o'clock in the morning beneath my window."

"Monsieur departs," the hotel proprietor faltered.

"It has occurred to me that, notwithstanding the warmth of her reception, Mademoiselle might care to accompany me," Mr. Laxworthy continued.

She gave a little cry and held out her arms.

"You will save me?" she implored. "You will take me away from this hateful place?"

Monsieur Dreiche put two fingers in his mouth and whistled. Almost immediately several men came stealing out from the house.

"It is a family affair, this," Monsieur Dreiche declared harshly. "You and your friends can go. I am well pleased to have you depart. But the young lady remains."

Antoine struck an attitude.

"If anyone dares to take her from me," he cried, "they shall answer to me for it, if necessary, with their life!"

Mr. Laxworthy had taken up a strategic position with his back to the motor-car. Very slowly his right hand came out of his overcoat pocket. With a yell of terror, Antoine leaped into the air. A bullet had whistled close to his head.

"I only wish to remark," Mr. Laxworthy went on, "that I am accustomed to having my own way, and my pistol is automatic. I have attained, also, a certain proficiency in its use which might easily lead to disastrous results. I think that you had better release the young lady."

The two men who were holding her promptly abandoned their grasp. Mr. Laxworthy with his left hand assisted her into the motor. The little body of men closed in upon them. One man had rushed into the house. Antoine was whispering to his brother in oilskins.

"Monsieur Dreiche," Mr. Laxworthy said sternly, "I have no certain compromise to offer you, but if this young lady takes my advice the affair will remain as it is. If, on the other hand, our departure is interfered with in any manner, there will be reprisals."

Monsieur Dreiche did not hesitate. He stood back and raised his hat.

"A little misunderstanding," he murmured, "a lovers' quarrel, perhaps, which is better finished. Monsieur and his friends will return some day, I trust."

The car swung up the avenue and into the road. The girl, who was gripping Mr. Laxworthy's hand, had begun to sob.

"Tell me who you are," she begged. "How did you come there?"

"I am just an incident," Mr. Laxworthy remarked. "In Monte Carlo I happened to hear a few words pass between that fiddle player and his brother. I saw you in the restaurant, too, and I noticed the way Antoine, as he calls himself, watched you. Let me give you a word of advice, young lady. May I?"

"I was an idiot," she murmured. "Yes, please do!"

"When the music of a person of that class pleases you, remember that it is wiser to let your mankind offer cigars than to send a flower for yourself. Those fiddlers are all eaten up with conceit. They don't understand."

The girl smiled through her tears.

"You know, I believe you are right," she admitted.

CHAPTER IX
The Case of Mr. and Mrs. Stetson

Mr. John T. Laxworthy, Mr. Forrest Anderson, and Sydney Wing were standing together upon the platform at Toulon. Mr. Laxworthy was in one of his most enigmatic moods, and Sydney Wing, who acted always as courier to the little party, was beginning to get a trifle irritable. As yet he had received no precise instructions as to their destination.

"It is fate, beyond a doubt, he admitted, "which has caused the train for Marseilles and Paris to break down at Nice, and fate again which decrees that the *Luxe*, when it arrives, should have to wait here for twenty minutes. But meanwhile, the porter desires to know where we want our luggage registered to."

Mr. Laxworthy drew his shawl a little closer around his neck.

"This Toulon station," he declared testily, "is the draughtiest place in Europe. Every time I spend a few minutes here I am terrified of a chill. I am conscious already of a tickling in my throat. Have you the formamint lozenges, Anderson?"

Mr. Forrest Anderson produced a small bottle from his pocket. Mr. Laxworthy gravely thrust one of the lozenges into his mouth.

"To London, Paris, or Monte Carlo?" Sydney Wing persisted.

It must be confessed that Mr. Laxworthy, considering the reasonableness of the inquiry, treated it with indifference.

"What does it matter?" he asked. "There are adventures everywhere, even, no doubt, in Toulon. Let us cross the line and see the train from Paris arrive. We may, perhaps, see someone who will tell us whether it is raining in London. Other things being equal, why should not climatic conditions influence our destination? Your porter shall receive his orders, Sydney, in a quarter of an hour."

Thereupon Sydney Wing explained to the official in question that Monsieur desired to speak with a gentleman travelling from London, and that after a conversation with him immediate instructions concerting the luggage should be given. This information being accompanied by a preliminary *pourboire* of a substantial nature was accepted as entirely satisfactory, and the three travellers crossed the line.

The *train de luxe* from Paris had just thundered in. Notwithstanding the early hour, a fair number of passengers had already descended. These, however, instead of occupying themselves in the usual manner, by buying coffee or flowers, were standing about talking to one another or to any uniformed official who would stop to answer a question. All the way down the train other passengers, in various stages of deshabille, were to be seen peering curiously from behind cautiously raised blinds. Several of the attendants were talking together with the station-master and another official of the railway company. No less than four gendarmes, accompanied by an inspector, were drawn up opposite a certain compartment of the train.

"Something has happened," Mr. Forrest Anderson, with rare acumen, ventured to observe.

"A man has been killed—probably murdered," Mr. Laxworthy, who had been watching intently the inspector's lips, declared.

"I will go and get tickets and our luggage registered to Monte Carlo," Sydney Wing decided promptly.

The inspector who was in charge of the gendarmes held a little informal court of inquiry upon the platform. Then he disappeared into the train. Presently his head was to be seen from a window. He beckoned to the four gendarmes, who, with the air of men of consequence embarking upon a fateful errand, also mounted the train. Mr. Laxworthy a few moments later followed them. When he reappeared, he was looking a little annoyed. Mr. Anderson, who was drinking a cup of coffee, looked at him questioningly. The news had spread, and quite a surprising number of the blinds had been raised during the last few minutes. The station-master himself was examining the tickets of two or three passengers who had descended.

"Raining hard in London," Mr. Laxworthy announced, gloomily. "Also a fog. Give me another formamint."

"Can't see that that makes any difference to us," Mr. Forrest Anderson remarked cheerfully, producing his little bottle. "It'll be all right at Monte, anyhow."

"It matters," Mr. Laxworthy declared, "because we happen to be going to London."

Mr. Anderson started slightly, but he declined to be surprised.

"Not interested in this little affair, after all then?"

"On the contrary," Mr. Laxworthy replied, "I am very much interested in it. Only it is my opinion that monsieur the inspector, with his corps of gendarmes, is making rather a mistake in going on. Back to London is my idea. We shall see."

"What happened, anyhow?" Mr. Anderson asked.

"Unpleasant affair," Mr. Laxworthy explained, with some relish. "Elderly English gentleman, travelling alone, chloroformed and strangled in his sleeping berth. Not a sound heard. Attendants sleeping both ends of the car all night. Empty pocket-book discovered at foot of bed. Man's name Simonds. Presumptive evidence that he was a bookmaker and was going to Monte Carlo to shoot pigeons."

"Is it known how much money he had with him?"

"Not to any of us," Mr. Laxworthy answered dryly.

"What are the gendarmes doing?" Mr. Anderson inquired curiously.

"Guarding the attendants and the passengers in the adjoining compartments till the train arrives at Nice," Mr. Laxworthy announced. "There the authorities will take the matter over."

"What about the passengers who have descended here?"

"There were only two," Mr. Laxworthy replied. "You can see them over there—the young couple waiting for the Hyères train. The inspector has examined their tickets and asked the man few questions. He has, apparently, no further interest in them."

Mr. Anderson nodded. He rather prided himself on his powers of intuition.

"Honeymooners," he declared positively. "New clothes, new luggage, man looking like a self-conscious ass, girl wearing a thick veil. Look, he's buying her flowers. See him squeeze her hand then?"

"Just a trifle overdone," Mr. Laxworthy remarked critically. "Not bad, though. The telegram will be a good test."

"What telegram?"

"He has arranged to have a telegram calling him back to London, delivered within a few minutes," Mr. Laxworthy replied. "He is looking about for it much too anxiously."

"Do you mean to say that these two are concerned in the murder?" Mr. Forrest Anderson asked in sudden amazement.

"Of course they are!" Mr. Laxworthy answered a little irritably. "Why else should I have pointed them out to you? Let us walk up the platform a little distance—so. Now back again. Watch this man, my friend. Here is psychological interest for you, if you like. Such a chance may never occur to you again. You can study at close quarters the features and deportment of a man who, within the last few minutes, mind—certainly within the last hour—has committed a brutal murder. To a casual observer he seems callous and unconcerned, doesn't he? In reality he is nothing but a quivering mass of nerves and suspicions. Did you see his face twitch then?"

They passed within a few feet of the couple. The man was young, of a little more than medium height, with broad shoulders, a brown moustache, and somewhat florid complexion. His companion was slim and small. Her figure was certainly girlish, but she wore a veil of the pattern affected by travelling Americans, and very little of her face could be seen. She seemed certainly either shy or nervous. Her hands were linked in her husband's arm, and she kept whispering in his ear. They were both well enough dressed, but their clothes were a little obvious in their newness. Their deportment, too, when one studied it closely, was suspicious.

The man's exuberant good spirits were overdone; the girl's timidity was perhaps real, but the reasons for it seemed insufficient. Mr. Forrest Anderson was hugely interested. There was a new reverence in his tone as he addressed his wonderful master.

"Did you notice," he whispered, as they passed down the platform, "how the man's hand was shaking? The cigarette, too, he was pretending to smoke, had been out for a long time."

Mr. Laxworthy nodded.

"An amateur criminal," he decided, "beyond a doubt. Certain to be caught in the long run. How long will it be, I wonder," he continued in a tone almost of annoyance, "before these people who decided upon a criminal career realise that it is absolutely necessary for them to learn the A B C of their craft if they wish for any permanent success in it. It isn't reasonable to suppose that an affair like that"—Mr. Laxworthy waved his hand toward the train—"can be successfully carried through by bunglers."

Sydney came hurrying up with the tickets, and met with a little surprise.

"You will keep one of these," Mr. Laxworthy told him, "and proceed as far as Nice. You can wire us the course of events to the cloak-room, Lyons, and to Charing Cross station. Anderson and I are returning to London."

It was one of the precepts instilled by his instructor into Mr. Sydney Wing that surprise, however natural and reasonable it might be, was an emotion sedulously to be concealed. He handed the two tickets to Mr. Laxworthy.

"You will be able to recover on these, sir," he remarked. "Am I to wait at Nice?"

"Use your discretion," Mr. Laxworthy replied. "I think that you will probably return."

Sydney hurried off to take his seat. In a moment or two the great train rolled slowly out of the station. From where Mr. Laxworthy and his companion stood, they caught a glimpse of the fateful compartment, with its blinds carefully lowered, and at the adjoining windows an impression of the gendarmes. Mr. Forrest Anderson shivered a little.

"Poor fellow!" he muttered. "Off on a holiday, too. It's a brutal thing, this taking of life!"

"I can tell you one thing more sickening," Mr. Laxworthy said slowly, "and that is the intense, awful anxiety of the man who has committed a murder and who fears arrest. The deed seems simple enough when it is planned, the chances of arrest remote. The prize is great. The man, naturally enough, if he is of sporting proclivities, backs himself to take the chance. Then comes the afterwards. The very air seems full of whispers. New horrors are hatched in the brain. A new set of fears is born; a shivering, hideous doubt of every human being poisons life. I am sorry for the lump of clay they are taking on to Nice. If I were in the habit, however, of feeling compassion for anybody, I should be more sorry still for the young man whom they are taking on to London. There's his telegram, just on the point of being delivered. See his clumsy air of surprise. We will proceed to the other side."

"Are you not afraid," Mr. Anderson asked, as they retraced their steps, "that even if we get on the same train they will not leave it somewhere *en route*. Why should they go all the way to London?"

"Because London is the finest hiding-place for criminals in Europe," Mr. Laxworthy replied promptly. "Furthermore, I saw him tell her that they would be in London to-morrow night."

Mr. Laxworthy and his companion obtained seats in the train with some little difficulty. They found themselves, however, in an empty compartment vacated by some passengers descending for Costabelle.

"I wonder where our friends are," Mr. Anderson remarked, as they proceeded to settle themselves down for the journey.

Very soon they were to know. There was the sound of somewhat heated discussion in the next compartment. Suddenly the young man himself appeared in the doorway.

"Are these two seats engaged, sir?" he asked Mr. Laxworthy.

"They are not," Mr. Laxworthy replied.

The young man disappeared and presently ushered in his wife and began to pile up the rack with small articles of luggage.

"Hope we are not disturbing you, sir," he said to Mr. Laxworthy, "but the next carriage was full up, and there was an old Frenchman near the window wouldn't have it moved. Couldn't stick it at any price," added, taking off his hat and wiping his forehead.

"Foreigners are somewhat peculiar with regard to fresh air," Mr. Laxworthy admitted. "I am myself susceptible to draughts, but I am most opposed to anything in the nature of an overheated carriage. Would the young lady care for my seat near the window!"

"Oh, please not!" she exclaimed. "I am quite comfortable here. It's such a relief not to hear all those people chattering a language you don't understand."

The two young people settled down for the journey. They occupied opposite seats on the corridor side of the carriage, and with their heads close together talked a good deal on matters apparently of frivolous import. For some reason or other, the nervousness which they had certainly exhibited on the platform at Toulon had completely vanished. The young man showed no signs of being anything else than what he appeared to be—a commonplace, healthy, middle-class person, probably a manufacturer or professional man from the country. The girl, who looked prettier without her hat, was a veritable type of the suburban belle. In opening her hand-bag to search for a handkerchief, a little show of rice fell upon the floor. Their confusion, the girl's giggle, and the man's half-conscious glance toward Mr. Laxworthy and his companion were perfectly done. Mr. Laxworthy smiled upon them genially and in a few moments all four were in conversation. Their name, it appeared, was Stetson, and they had been married four days. The girl's home had been at Balham, and the man's at Manchester. The names of relatives and friends were freely mentioned. By the time they had passed Marseilles, the quartette were on such terms that Mr. Laxworthy had ordered a bottle of wine and some biscuits to drink the health of the newly-married couple.

"By the by," he remarked, "my friend and I thought we saw you waiting by the Hyères train."

It was the critical moment. Mr. Laxworthy had asked his question with apparently unconscious but subtle suddenness. The embarrassment of the two, however, was tempered with smiles. With a hearty laugh the young man explained.

"We were going to Hyères," he said, "but, to tell you the truth, I've got a mother-in-law who is rather a nuisance to us. It was all we could do to stop her from starting on the honeymoon with us, and just an hour or so ago I had a telegram to say that she had gone on to Hyères and was waiting for us there. We couldn't either of us stick it. We are going to pretend we didn't get the telegram and we are going back to Paris to spend the rest of our time there."

"Poor mother!" the girl murmured. "She'll be fearfully disappointed, but she really is a nuisance."

Mr. Laxworthy commended their plan, and, the wine being finished, he dozed. The young couple went down for lunch early. They left their bags and small luggage scattered about the seats. Mr. Anderson looked at his chief doubtfully. The tragedy of a mistake was a thing which as yet they had never encountered.

"Clever young couple, that," he remarked tentatively.

"They are either," Mr. Laxworthy replied simply, "the cleverest young people I have ever met in my life, or"—his voice shook for a moment; he smothered his hesitation with a cough; it was not a pleasant thing, this, which he had to say—"or," he concluded at last, "I have made a mistake."

Mr. Anderson, who had made up his mind, said nothing. They lunched almost in silence, and on their return surprised their fellow-travellers sitting very close together indeed. The girl hid her face behind a magazine; the man grinned, unabashed. Mr. Laxworthy settled down into his corner with a premonition of disaster.

"At Lyons," Mr. Anderson whispered, "we shall receive a telegram."

Mr. Laxworthy nodded. He was remarkably sparing of speech for the remainder of the journey. He had even given up watching his fellow-passengers. At Lyons the telegram came. He opened it with firm fingers, but he felt beforehand a grim conviction as to its contents. It was dated from Nice a few hours back:

"Attendant of train arrested. Portion of murdered man's property found upon him. Simple case.—SYDNEY."

Mr. Anderson coughed as he handed it back to his chief. Mr. Laxworthy faced the situation boldly. The greatest men in the world had been famous for their mistakes.

"Better get off with us at Paris, sir," the young man suggested, as they drew near the end of the journey. "You and your friend, too. We are going to the Grand Hotel. Proud to entertain you there for a little supper. Our first guests you'd be, eh, Edith?"

The young lady smiled amiably.

"We'd be very glad indeed if you would," she declared. "Henry always liked company. Not that I blame him," she went on hastily. "I'm fond of it myself."

Mr. Laxworthy shook his head regretfully.

"I am sorry," he said. "My friend and I are travelling to London to keep a most important engagement."

"Bad luck!" the young man declared. "Anyway, here's my card," he added, producing one. "I've taken a little house up on Laking Heights, near Manchester. Healthy situation, and near a golf club. Look us up there if ever you come that way."

"I will do so with pleasure," Mr. Laxworthy assured him. "Permit me to offer you my own card," he added, drawing one from his case. "I am rather a bird of passage, but when I am in London I can always be heard of at my club."

"I am a member of the Junior Conservative myself," the young man remarked. "A club in town's always useful, even for a countryman."

His wife tossed her head.

"You gentlemen and your clubs!" she exclaimed. "Let me tell you, Henry, your club isn't going to be much use to you. When you come up to London, I'm coming. I made that bargain with him," she added, turning to Mr. Laxworthy, "before I consented to go and live at Manchester."

"Quite right," Mr. Laxworthy murmured. "I feel sure that your husband's visits to the Metropolis will be more acceptable to him than ever with your charming society."

The train was drawing in to the platform at Paris. They all shook hands. The young man put his head back after their final farewells had been spoken.

"What did you say the French for porter was, sir?" he asked Mr. Laxworthy.

"Mr. Laxworthy stepped out on to the platform and played the part of kindly courier to the young people. He watched them drive off in a cab before he returned to his seat.

"My friend," he said to Anderson, "I am now going to sleep. In the morning let us settle down to forget this little incident. A few days in London will be good for us."

Mr. Anderson agreed, with enthusiasm.

"I shall turn in myself presently," he declared.

The remainder of the journey was uneventful. On the following morning, having collected their luggage, Mr. Anderson presented himself at the cloak-room at Charing Cross, in case there should be any further telegrams from Sydney. He came back to Mr. Laxworthy with two. The first which he opened was unexpectedly long.

"It's in our cipher!" Mr. Anderson exclaimed.

"I have the book here," Mr. Laxworthy remarked. "Let us go into the refreshment room and sit down."

They found a small table and Mr. Laxworthy ordered a glass of milk and an apple. With the book before him, he commenced to decode the message. Except for one startling exclamation from Mr. Anderson, they neither of them spoke till their task was completed. Mr. Laxworthy's fingers, however, trembled slightly as he traced out the last few words. This message, also, was from Nice:

"A thousand congratulations and apologies. Attendant only accomplice. Has made full confession. Murder was committed by famous American criminal, Greenlaw, travelling with young woman, posing as honeymooners. Capture of Greenlaw a veritable triumph. Once more my humble congratulations.—SYDNEY."

Mr. Laxworthy looked at his companion across the table. Mr. Anderson was speechless.

"I asked him once," Mr. Laxworthy said slowly, "whether he had travelled in America. I fancied I caught the suspicion of an accent. What is in the other telegram?"

Mr. Anderson, who had forgotten it, tore open the envelope. They read it together. It was dated from Paris in the early hours of the morning:

"Have just drunk your health at a pleasant little supper party.—MR. AND MRS. STETSON OF MANCHESTER."

"I think," Mr. Laxworthy said, rising, "that we will go round to the hotel now. I shall lie down for an hour or so. I feel that I need rest."

Mr. Laxworthy spent the greater part of his time during the next few days in a state of curious absorption. He did not stir out from the small suite at the Milan which had been reserved for him. Mr. Anderson, who was used to his ways, went to his club for bridge in the afternoons and visited the theatres in the evening. On the third day, Sydney Wing arrived. Mr. Anderson met him at the station and explained the situation. They discussed it gloomily.

"Our chief," Mr. Forest Anderson remarked, as they drove to the hotel, "is suffering from profound mortification. As you know, since our association with him, at any rate, this is his first failure."

"I would have given a good deal," Sydney Wing declared wistfully, "to have seen you four in the railway carriage."

Mr. Anderson smiled grimly.

"It was," he admitted, "the most superb piece of acting I have ever seen. Until all these particulars about the man came out in the newspapers during the last few days, I must admit that the whole affair was absolutely incomprehensible. Now we know that he, too, understands the lip language."

"And many other tricks as well," Sydney remarked. "They say that no one else in the world has been so skilful at disguises. There isn't a reliable description of the fellow in existence."

"I could give a pretty close one," Mr. Anderson grunted. "I sat within a couple of yards of the fellow for the best part of twelve hours."

Sydney shook his head.

"According to those detectives down there, his changes of appearance are almost miraculous."

"Is the identity of the girl known?" Mr. Anderson asked.

Sydney shook his head.

"It is through his *penchant* for women that they hope to catch him some day," he replied. "They say that this last enterprise must have brought him in over ten thousand pounds."

Their cab rolled into the courtyard at the Milan.

"I'm not at all sure," Mr. Forrest Anderson said doubtfully, "whether the chief will see you. However, we must let him know that you have arrived."

They ascended the stairs and knocked at the door of Mr. Laxworthy's sitting-room. Mr. Anderson barely repressed an exclamation of surprise. Mr. Laxworthy was sitting before a table covered with notes and newspapers. A visitor who had very much the air of a detective was just departing. Mr. Laxworthy welcomed his two friends briskly.

"Sit down, Sydney, if you please," he invited. "I have a list here of thirty questions to ask you. Afterwards I shall require to be alone for an hour. Kindly understand that I shall want every moment of your time for the next four days at least."

"Glad to hear it, sir," Sydney replied cheerfully.

Mr. Laxworthy seemed anxious to hear every incident which happened at Nice, and every item of gossip, even the idlest, concerning the man Greenlaw. He made notes of some of Sydney's replies and dismissed him finally with a little wave of the hand.

"I have a little work to do privately," he announced. "At six o'clock I shall want you both. You, Anderson, had better be prepared for a journey. I may want you to go to Paris."

"You are going for Mr. Greenlaw, then?" Mr. Anderson said briskly.

"We are going, without a doubt," Mr. Laxworthy declared, "to assist the police in the capture of a criminal of that name."

Mr. Forrest Anderson left for Paris by the night train, with a sealed letter of instructions in his pocket, not to be opened until he had actually arrived in the city. Sydney Wing was invited to call upon his chief at nine o'clock that same evening. He found Mr. Laxworthy with a letter spread out before him upon the table.

"Come in, Sydney, and close the door," the latter directed. "Anderson has gone, eh?"

"He left by the nine o'clock train, sir," Sydney replied.

Mr. Laxworthy cleared his throat.

"As you may have surmised," he began, "we are interested in the case of this man Greenlaw. My friend John Marlin has been giving me some interesting information. You have heard me speak of John Marlin? He is now deputy-inspector at Scotland Yard."

"I remember him perfectly, sir," Sydney agreed.

Mr. Laxworthy took up a few notes which lay by his side.

"It seems that Scotland Yard has been trying to arrest this man for the last three years, and for the last twelve months, at least, there has been a detective over here from New York, looking for no one else. The fellow has great gifts, without a doubt, but success has made him over-confident. What do you think of this for bravado? It is addressed to Detective Marlin and was delivered to him at Scotland Yard. He brought it to me here only a few hours ago."

Mr. Laxworthy read out the letter:

"My dear Friend Marlin,

"You fellows make me tired. There's no fun to be had over on this side, so I'm off home, and pretty quick, too. You've been after me for three years and I've never had even to hurry to get out of your way. You've seven jobs up against me, most of them 'lifers,' but you're just about as slow as that old dead-head from New York, who has been traipsing after me for the

Lord knows how long! Now see here, I'm a bit of a sport, and I'm going to give you your last chance. There's some money of mine lying in London, and I'm coming over myself to fetch it on Tuesday, May 15th. I shan't tell you by what train, or where I am going to stay, but it will probably be at one of your best hotels. Now do make one last effort. It would really give me a thrill to meet you face to face and read suspicion in your eyes. Come, why should we not take a drink together? I will make an assignation with you. I am very fond of a glass of vermouth before my dinner. Between six and seven each evening I am in London, I shall call either at the bar of the Milan Hotel, the Metropolitan Bar or Fitzhenry's. Shall I say au revoir?—Yours,

"DAN GREENLAW."

"Do you believe that he means to come?" Sydney asked eagerly.

Mr. Laxworthy did not reply for a moment. He appeared to be deep in thought.

"Marlin himself," he said at last, "has not the slightest faith in the letter. He believes it to be a complete hoax. That, however, is not to be wondered at. Marlin's limitations are almost too painfully obvious. He is entirely destitute of a sense of humour. It is one of my theories that without a sense of humour no man can succeed in any profession which brings him in touch with his fellows."

"And you, sir, what do you believe?" Sydney persisted.

"I believe that he will come," Mr. Laxworthy declared. "I have thought this matter out very carefully indeed. I have come to a certain conclusion. I may be wrong. We shall see. On the other hand, if I am right, it will, I must confess, afford me a peculiar satisfaction. I shall not easily forget that journey from Toulon."

"What will there be for me to do?" Sydney asked.

"To-morrow," Mr. Laxworthy replied, "is Tuesday. Marlin, of course, is all for watching trains, and that sort of things. Quite useless, in my opinion. Greenlaw, if he comes, will probably travel by motor-car from some insignificant port. I have some idea of asking you to frequent the bar rooms which he mentions, with the exception of the Milan. I will attend to that myself."

"Are there any descriptions of the man?" Sydney asked. "I know his height, which I suppose he cannot alter—six foot exactly—and they say he is fairly broad, and his natural complexion is florid."

Mr. Laxworthy touched a little pile of papers by his side.

"There are seventeen descriptions here from Scotland Yard," he remarked. "They vary slightly in detail, but they are all much about the same. They are, I imagine, the chief reason for the wonderful confidence which this man Greenlaw displays."

"You can't believe that they are accurate, then?" Sydney inquired. "Yet Anderson's description of the fellow coincided exactly with this."

Mr. Laxworthy nodded thoughtfully.

"Well," he said, "I have an idea of my own. I have mentioned it to Merlin, but he only laughs at me. Nothing remains but for me to test it myself."

"Are there no instructions for me, sir?" Sydney asked.

"None for this evening," Mr. Laxworthy replied. "To-morrow I shall require you to be my companion. We will go round to a few of these bars. To-night I shall retire early. I drank a little Chablis with my lunch which has not wholly agreed with me. I shall not dine this evening."

Mr. Laxworthy, on the following evening, drank vermouth at Fitzhenry's, mixed vermouth at the Metropolitan, and a cocktail at the Milan, without the slightest result. He dined alone, in a very bad temper, went to bed early, and received this letter next morning:

"MY DEAR OLD LADY,"

"So you are in the game, too! It made my heart ache this evening to see you trotting round to these bars and peering into every strange face from behind those disfiguring spectacles of yours. Besides, at your time of life *aperitifs* are extremely bad for the digestion. I can assure you that I felt quite guilty when I saw you struggling with your third.

"Come, now, to-morrow night I will have mercy. We will leave out the Metropolitan. I don't know how it struck you, but I didn't care for the place at all. A very mixed crowd, and I had my doubts of the vermouth. We will visit Fitzhenry's and the Milan only. Who knows but that we may have luck and drink our cocktail together?—Ever yours,

"D. G."

Mr. Laxworthy's eyes sparkled as he read.

"This is indeed worth while," he said to himself. "He has the real instincts, this man."

Mr. Laxworthy showed this letter to several mysterious personages from Scotland Yard, and to Sydney Wing. They all treated it in the same manner. Scotland Yard concentrated upon the Metropolitan, and from six till half-past seven every harmless stranger who drank his cocktail or sherry and bitters there was subjected to a very searching and inquisitive scrutiny. Mr. Laxworthy, on the other hand, obeyed strictly the invitation of his letter. He visited Fitzhenry's first, and after half an hour there drove to the Milan. From the small smoke-room it was possible to see into the American Bar through a glass swing-door. Mr. Laxworthy peered into the room and stood for an instant quite still. A very small and apparently a very young gentleman of Indian extraction was leaning against the counter with a cocktail before him. Mr. Laxworthy turned to Sydney, who accompanied him.

"Sydney," he said, "the thing is finished. You see those two men in the corner of the smoke-room?"

Mr. Laxworthy pointed out two harmless-looking individuals who were talking together upon a settee.

Sydney nodded. At that moment, one of them looked up cautiously. Mr. Laxworthy beckoned to them. They came over at once.

"You will hold this door," he directed in a low tone. "The man for whom we are seeking is inside."

"Let me go in with you, sir," Sydney begged.

Mr. Laxworthy assented. They approached the bar. The young man who was leaning against the counter was dressed in the height of fashion. His silk hat was exceedingly glossy, his shirt front immaculate. He was really very little darker than an ordinary olive-skinned Englishman. He eyed the new-comers a trifle insolently, and turned to his cocktail. Mr. Laxworthy stood by his side.

"Will you give me a cocktail—the same as you have fixed for this gentleman, if you please?" Mr. Laxworthy ordered.

The girl mixed it in silence. As they all three stood there, a somewhat curious change took place in the attitude of the young man. He slipped furtively back from the counter. Mr. Laxworthy turned suddenly towards him.

"My friend," he said, "Daniel Greenlaw, or Mrs. Stetson, or whatever it pleases you to call yourself this evening. I have come to take my *apéritif* with you. Our friends outside can wait. There are so many questions it would interest me to ask you."

Mr. Laxworthy was absolutely prepared, and he was, without doubt, extraordinarily proficient in all the ordinary tricks of wrestling and jiujitsu. Nevertheless, he was lying two seconds later upon his back in the bar. The young man sprang for the door, saw the two figures waiting there for him and hesitated. The moment's hesitation was fatal. Sydney's arms were round him from behind. Even then he struggled like a wild cat, and it took the united efforts of the three men to secure him. Marlin arrived just as the struggle was over. He shook his head doubtfully as he saw their prisoner.

"This isn't Greenlaw," he exclaimed.

Mr. Laxworthy smiled.

"You take him along," he directed, "and I promise you that when he is brought up before the magistrates to-morrow morning I will prove that he is Greenlaw half-a-dozen times over."

Mr. Laxworthy dined that night in the café with Mr. Forrest Anderson, who had returned from Paris, and Sydney Wing. He was in high good-humour.

"I don't see, even now," Mr. Forrest Anderson remarked, "how you guessed the truth."

Mr. Laxworthy sipped his wine with the air of a connoisseur.

"You see," he explained, "the man has been wanted for three years. No one has ever laid their hands upon him. Every description of him is the same. Naturally I began to wonder whether something might not be wrong with that description. I read up all the notes about him that were collected by Scotland Yard, and I noticed that although he had the reputation of having endless women friends, he was invariably accompanied by a small dark woman, especially when any particular startling outrage was on foot. It just occurred to me as both possible and ingenious that the man might have concealed his identity all these years and gone about as his own companion. His Mrs. Stetson was certainly wonderfully done, but there were one or two flaws, and when I came to put everything together I felt pretty certain that my guess was a true one. Marlin and his men were looking everywhere for a big man. I was looking for the real, unknown Greenlaw—a small, dark man in any plausible form of disguise. The fellow's last little piece of bravado will cost him his life."

A porter from outside came up and addressed Mr. Laxworthy.

"I beg your pardon, sir," he announced, "but there is an important telephone message for you from the Charing Cross Hospital."

Mr. Laxworthy rose deliberately from his place and followed the man out of the room. He stepped into the telephone box and held the receiver to his ear.

"Is that Mr. Laxworthy?" a voice inquired.

"Yes?"

"I am Dr. Wendell, of the Charing Cross Hospital," the voice continued. "I am requested to give you a message by a man named Marlin who has just been brought in, badly hurt."

"What is it?" Mr. Laxworthy asked.

"He wishes me to tell you," the doctor continued, "that Greenlaw is free. He has stabbed one policeman and hurt Marlin badly. He escaped from the cab, and so far they have not been able to recapture him. Marlin wants you to be exceedingly careful, as this man Greenlaw, whoever he may be, will probably feel that he has a grudge against you. Excuse me, if you please, I am in a hurry."

Mr. Laxworthy laid down the receiver and went back to his dinner.

"Greenlaw," he announced, "has escaped."

They both stared at him in astonishment. Mr. Laxworthy told the story.

"We shall have to begin all over again," Sydney Wing declared.

Mr. Laxworthy shook his head.

"On the contrary," he pronounced. "I have finished my campaign against Daniel Greenlaw. I am no longer on the side of the authorities. I delivered into their hands a dangerous criminal and they have let him go. Such affairs are dangerous and—unremunerative. It is you who run the risk and Scotland Yard which takes the credit. Our banking account demands a move in other directions."

"You have something in your mind!" Mr. Forrest Anderson exclaimed.

"For one week," Mr. Laxworthy said firmly, "you will both leave me. I shall remain where I am and I wish to be alone. A week from to-day we dine together here. If nothing else has occurred in the meantime, it is possible that on that occasion I may have something to propose."

CHAPTER X
Mr. Greenlaw's Forty Thousand Pounds

Mr. Laxworthy took quite a fancy to the grillroom at the Milan. He followed his usual practice of making friends with the director, who reserved for him always a small table in a retired but advantageous position. Here for several days Mr. Laxworthy lunched and dined, watching with keen interest from behind his concealing spectacles the constant coming and going of one of the most cosmopolitan crowds in Europe. Young ladies from the theatre lunched here with their juvenile escorts, and supped at the same tables later on, in the half light, with more serious admirers. Men of affairs brought their wealthy clients here to complete a deal. The foreign theatrical element was strong, and, rather a curious thread in the tangled skein, there was always a thin little stream of genuine American tourists, with their quaint ways, and Baedekers in their hands. Mr. Laxworthy, from his table against the wall, and with his strange gift of reading the spoken words from the lips of those whom he watched, skirted the edge of more than one romance, peered over the brink into several strange little tragedies, and learnt something of the methods of a very well-known financier. On the fifth morning, towards the completion of his luncheon, an incident occurred which brought him for the first time into actual touch with one of the figures in this peep-show.

A lady entered the restaurant, and, deserting the main passage, began slowly to thread her way through the maze of tables towards the side of the room where Mr. Laxworthy sat. She came so slowly and her appearance was so unusual that nearly everybody turned to gaze at her as she passed. She was tall, slim, and exceedingly dark. Her complexion was absolutely colourless, but it seemed to be more the natural pallor of a woman of some southern race than any evidence of ill-health. She was plainly dressed, but at the height of fashion. There was not a woman there who did not know that her hat and her costume came from the neighbourhood of the Rue de la Paix. She walked, too, with a natural grace which was entirely un-Saxon. All the time her large black eyes swept up and down the corner of the room which she was approaching.

The chief *maître d'hôtel*, who had seen her enter, came hurrying to her side.

"Madame desires a table?" he murmured, with his best bow. "Unfortunately, on this side, as you see, we are full. I will arrange something if madame will be so good as to follow me."

The lady shook her head a little petulantly. She was looking at Mr. Laxworthy's table, by the side of which she was now standing, with the air of a spoilt child.

"I prefer to sit here," she said decidedly. "It amuses me to watch the people, and, as you see, I am alone."

The *maître d'hôtel* shrugged his shoulders.

"But, madame," he protested, "all the tables here, as one can see, are already occupied."

The lady looked at Mr. Laxworthy's disappearing omelette and up at Mr. Laxworthy. He promptly interposed.

"If the lady would like my table," he said, speaking with his usual quiet precision, "it will be at liberty within five minutes. I have already ordered my coffee."

"You are very kind," the lady answered softly. "Your table is just the one I covet. I will certainly wait."

Now in an ordinary case the chief *maître d'hôtel* would have escorted the lady to the small reception room adjoining the restaurant, would have kept his eye upon Mr. Laxworthy's table, have had it speedily rearranged on the departure of Mr. Laxworthy, and have himself fetched madame at the earliest opportunity. It happened, however, that at that precise moment quite his most important client touched him on the elbow. With a word of excuse he hurried away. The lady stood, for a moment, irresolute. Mr. Laxworthy rose to his feet.

"If you will honour me by accepting the vacant seat at my table until the arrival of my coffee," he said, with a little bow, "it will give me great pleasure."

She thanked him with a very soft and very brilliant smile. She deposited her velvet bag and the trifles which she was carrying upon the table, and seating herself, took up the menu. She laid it down almost at once. Mr. Laxworthy was watching her quietly. She looked at him and smiled. He smiled back again. They talked banalities until the arrival of the coffee.

"You do not mind," she asked him, "if I order my luncheon? I am hungry."

"Certainly not," Mr. Laxworthy replied. "If you are fond of omelette, let me recommend the *Omelette Espagnol*. It is excellent to-day."

"Thank you very much," she said, "I will try it."

Mr. Laxworthy's coffee was hot, and they talked more banalities. The question of nationalities arose. Mr. Laxworthy was invited to guess the birthplace of his companion. With commendable chivalry he suggested Paris. The lady smiled.

"I am South American," she told him. "I am over here on business. I have immense estates there which I wish to sell."

Mr. Laxworthy's eyes twinkled behind his glasses. He was beginning to have a genuine admiration for his beautiful companion.

"A very interesting country," he murmured.

"A Paradise," she replied.

"I lived there for some seven years," Mr. Laxworthy remarked.

"In that case," the lady exclaimed, with a little shrug of her shoulders, "I must rearrange the locality of my estates!"

"Ah!" Mr. Laxworthy said softly. "South America is rather a dangerous country. People travel so much, nowadays."

She smiled.

"Of course, you know who I am really? I come from the Royal Opera House at St. Petersburg, and I am going to dance in the ballet at Covent Garden."

Mr. Laxworthy nodded approvingly.

"If you will permit me to say so without impertinence," he declared, "your statement is easily to be believed. You look the part. I scarcely see, however, its practical advantages—at any rate, as compared with your position as a South American lady with immense estates to sell in a city of susceptible men."

Madame poured herself out a glass of claret from the half bottle which she had ordered, and laughed at her companion.

"You live, I perceive, as a recluse," she remarked. "To dance at Covent Garden one requires jewels, beautiful dresses, an electric brougham, a motor-car in which to seek the fresh air. Alas! I have discovered your city, but not your susceptible men."

"Your imagination," Mr. Laxworthy decided, "is excellent, but you lack precision of detail. I never in my life saw a dancer with an ankle and instep like yours."

She sighed.

"They told me," she said, "that you were a man of observation and peculiar gifts. You make me feel quite clumsy."

"Not at all," Mr. Laxworthy insisted. "As a matter of fact, you have an immense advantage over me. Remember, you know all about me, and for some mysterious reason you have accorded me the privilege of your acquaintance. Whereas I haven't the slightest idea who you are or where you come from. I have only my instinct to tell me whether you come, indeed, as a friend or a foe."

"And what does your instinct say?" she asked.

Mr. Laxworthy poured himself out some more coffee.

"Madame," he replied, "look around you. Indulge for a moment, if you will, in a little speculation of a quasi-philosophical nature. There are fifty small parties of men and women lunching in this room. Let us say that half of them are doing so from the pleasure they find in one another's society.

The other half is composed of men and women who are each seeking something from the other. On our right, a gentleman is seeking to sell a patent to a financier. Over there, a German merchant is trying to impress his London agent with the superiority of his goods over all others. The little lady with the black hair behind you is indeed a dancer. She lunches with the manager of a great Variety House, from whom she needs an engagement—on her own terms. We come to ourselves. We, too, are human beings in temporary juxtaposition. It is you who have sought me—not I you. It is not for the pleasure of my society; therefore, it is something else you want."

"Oh, Mr. Laxworthy!" she sighed. "You are much too clever for a poor, inexperienced young woman! The man who sent me here warned me. I fear that you are not even susceptible. I could be very nice to you indeed. I could say all manner of nice things, and look them, and even mean them a little, for that is the supreme art of my sex. Shall I try? Would it be any good?"

"I have been slandered," Mr. Laxworthy declared. "I have not, alas! those personal qualities which attract such attentions as you have suggested, but it is nevertheless a fact that I am exceedingly susceptible. I have drunk two extra cups of coffee for the sole pleasure of sitting here with you."

"I am so afraid," she murmured, "of bestowing my affections where they are likely to be slighted."

"Then supposing," Mr. Laxworthy suggested, "you tell me in what manner I can be of service to you, and from whom you come?"

She leaned a little across the table.

"I come," she said, "from Mr. Daniel Greenlaw."

Mr. Laxworthy showed no surprise.

"I was inclined to suspect," he admitted, "that that was the case. I trust that Mr. Greenlaw is well?"

"He is in excellent health, I believe," the lady replied.

"And enjoying," Mr. Laxworthy continued, "that measure of liberty and control over his actions from which the prejudiced authorities of this country sought to debar him."

"Assisted," she murmured, "by you."

Mr. Laxworthy coughed.

"I," he explained, "am an adventurer, a free lance, one of those whose hobby it is to pore over the mysteries of human conduct. As regards my—er—campaign against Greenlaw, he brought it upon himself. You have probably heard the history of my railway journey with Mr. and Mrs. Stetson!"

She leaned back in her chair and laughed, laughed so that little lines spread from the edges of her eyes, which themselves became for a moment closed.

"And the telegram," she reminded him.

He nodded.

"The telegram hurt," he confessed. "Nevertheless, these little affairs are good for one. I bore Greenlaw no real grudge, but it certainly put me in the field against him."

"You were robbed of your triumph," she said, "but it was not your fault. Somehow, I do not think now that they will ever catch him."

"He appears," Mr. Laxworthy admitted, "to be a man of remarkable gifts."

"He is the most versatile person who ever breathed," she agreed. "To look at, he is as delicate as a girl, but he has the muscle of a Sandow. His body is like flexible steel. Then I do not think that any actor in the world has ever surpassed him in the art of making up."

"I have myself," Mr. Laxworthy said gloomily, "had ocular proof of his capacity!"

She, too, had arrived at the stage of coffee. Mr. Laxworthy ordered liqueurs.

"Ours has been a pleasant chat," he remarked, "but you have not yet told me the object of your coming. I have watched you very closely, and I am quite sure that you have not slipped poison into my coffee. Besides, I do not think that our friend Mr. Greenlaw is that sort of man."

She laughed softly.

"You might at least do me the compliment to believe that I am not that sort of ambassador," she murmured. "Daniel Greenlaw has not the least desire to do you harm. It is, indeed, something in the nature of an alliance which I am here to propose."

Mr. Laxworthy lifted his spectacles for a moment and replaced them.

"I am a man over middle-age," he said, "and I am moderately wealthy. Of my principles I will not speak, but such as they are, although I claim for myself a considerable latitude of action, I am on the side of the law."

"In the enterprise which I am about to propose to you," the lady declared, "you will remain in that very desirable position."

"I am all attention," Mr. Laxworthy assured her.

"It is a matter of money—a great deal of money," she continued. "Less than a year ago, Daniel Greenlaw entrusted a sum of forty thousand pounds to a Mr. Wills, who was a stockbroker in the city. He entrusted it to him without conditions because a man in Mr. Greenlaw's position, as you can readily understand, is obliged to trust someone. Mr. Wills was a man of honour and there was no doubt that, while he lived, not only was the money perfectly safe, but he would have gone out of his way to let Daniel Greenlaw have it, however difficult the circumstances may have been. Unfortunately, three or four months ago Mr. Wills died, and his partners are Jews and very different people to deal with. They need the money in their business, and they have no idea of parting with it if it can be helped. In reply to the indirect applications which have been made to them, they have declined to communicate with or to pay over any money to anyone else except Daniel Greenlaw himself. The police know this, and Messrs. Wills, Lewitt and Montague know that they know it. It is impossible for Daniel to go to the law, but he wants the money."

"Quite an interesting situation," Mr. Laxworthy admitted. "Legally, of course, there are many ways of obtaining payment, but, on the other hand, I can see the difficulty. These men have only to object to the amount or the terms or something, and take the matter into court. Greenlaw cannot appear. Anyone holding an authorisation from him would be cross-examined as to its source."

"I see that you grasp some of the difficulties," the lady remarked. "Now, you may believe this or not, as you choose. My name is Paula Garesworthy. I have seen quite a good deal of Daniel Greenlaw at different times, and I have a most sincere admiration for him."

"Admiration?" Mr. Laxworthy murmured, a little questioningly.

"Precisely," she assented. "The greater part of my life has been spent in Bohemian circles, not only from necessity, but because I prefer their society to any other. Daniel Greenlaw has many friends, although not all of them know his real name. He is a criminal from absolute excess of sporting instinct. He must have excitement at any price. He has no fear of death nor any respect for other people's property."

"Charming qualities," Mr. Laxworthy interposed.

The lady shrugged her shoulders.

"You are a citizen of the world, Mr. Laxworthy," she said. "You in your time must have had some experience of the order of so-called criminal to which Daniel Greenlaw belongs. If so, you must have learnt to regard them with, at any rate, tolerance."

"I have no hard feelings against the man," Mr. Laxworthy admitted. "We have brushed up against one another and honours are even."

"In your favour," she objected. "Daniel only got a laugh out of you, whereas you very nearly ended his career."

"It seems to me," Mr. Laxworthy remarked, "that a great many law-abiding people would have been rather obliged to me if I had. That little affair in the *train de luxe* between Marseilles and Toulon was a trifle cold-blooded, wasn't it? Nothing to be proud of, at any rate."

She shuddered slightly, and lowered her fine eyes from Mr. Laxworthy's face.

"Those are the things," she confessed, "which I do not care to talk about. However, there is one consideration which should always be borne in mind in judging this man. He chose invariably for his victims the unworthy. This fellow Simonds, the bookmaker, was one of the worst characters in London, a man whom I remember Daniel once said that it pained him to see alive. You are not a sentimentalist, Mr. Laxworthy. You would not accord it an equal sin to set your foot upon vermin as to shoot a nightingale."

Mr. Laxworthy signified his approval.

"We might now venture, perhaps, to discuss," he suggested, "the enterprise to which you have alluded?"

"The enterprise is simple enough," she replied slowly. "Daniel Greenlaw wants you to collect his money for him. I have here an authorisation, properly signed and witnessed."

She passed a paper across the table. Mr. Laxworthy studied it carefully and put it into his pocket.

"Does Mr. Greenlaw," he asked, "suggest any scheme whereby I am to profit in this enterprise?"

She shook her head.

"He offers you nothing but the adventure!"

Mr. Laxworthy signed his bill and, with a word of apology, his companion's also. He thereupon rose to his feet.

"My only recompense, then," he remarked, "is to be the pleasure of this luncheon?"

She laughed softly at him.

"Why not of others?" she murmured. "I fancy that we should amuse one another. We both move along the outside paths."

"You will do me the honour, then," Mr. Laxworthy begged, "of lunching with me here a week from to-day at the same time?"

"I shall only regret, dear Mr. Laxworthy," she whispered as they passed down the room, "that it takes seven whole days to make a week!"

Mr. Forrest Anderson was received, a few mornings later, at the offices of Messrs. Wills, Lewitt and Montague with all the consideration due to a prospective client of satisfactory appearance. Mr. Lewitt, who was a small man with thin, dark features, and indications of Semitic amiability, sat at a desk with a telephone on either side of him. He motioned his visitors to an easy chair opposite him.

MR. FORREST ANDERSON,

 Foston Manor,
  Leicestershire,

he read from the card. "Delighted to see you, Mr. Anderson. What can we have the pleasure of doing for you?"

Mr. Anderson glanced around the room as though to make sure that they were alone, and moved his chair a little closer to his companion.

"I have called," he began confidentially, "on behalf of a client of yours—Mr. Daniel Greenlaw."

Mr. Lewitt started and snatched a speaking tube from his desk.

"Excuse me for one moment, sir," he begged. "I should like my partner to be present. Montague," he went on through the speaking tube, "step this way at once, if you please."

Mr. Montague, spruce, well-groomed, dark, oily, also Semitic, appeared almost immediately.

"Close the door, Sam," Mr. Lewitt begged. "Here's this gentleman's card. He has said one sentence only when I whistled for you. He comes on behalf of Mr. Daniel Greenlaw."

Mr. Montague's lips became for a moment pursed.

"What ith his business?" he said quickly. "What doth he want?"

They both looked at their visitor anxiously. Mr. Anderson hesitated for a moment. He spoke in some affected embarrassment.

"I am sure," he said, "that Mr. Greenlaw's fears have no real foundation. However, as you know, Mr. Wills was his friend, and he has only the pleasure of a very slight acquaintance with either of you gentlemen. To put the matter to you plainly, Mr. Greenlaw has been disturbed by rumours as to the stability of your firm."

"Goodneth gracious!" Mr. Montague exclaimed.

Mr. Lewitt only extended his hands in dumb amazement.

"I have heard it said," Mr. Forrest Anderson continued suavely, "that the death of the senior partner will sometimes affect the credit of the most substantial firms. Mr. Greenlaw, let me hasten to assure you, only requires assurances of the safety of his investments with you."

A marked air of relief was immediately apparent in the countenances of the two partners.

"Anything we can do," Mr. Lewitt hastened to say, "we will do. We can, without the slightest difficulty, prove to you the stability of our position. We should not even object to taking you to our bankers. Try one of these cigars, Mr. Anderson, while we discuss the matter amicably."

Mr. Anderson accepted one graciously, and lit it from the match which Mr. Montague offered.

"Mr. Greenlaw's position," he went on, "is a somewhat peculiar one."

The partners laughed outright.

"Very good!" Mr. Montague exclaimed.

"Excellent!" Mr. Lewitt echoed.

"At the same time, gentlemen," Mr. Anderson proceeded, "I am sure you will be relieved to hear that several recent—shall I say affairs?—which have been attributed to Mr. Greenlaw, have been attributed to him quite erroneously."

"Delighted to hear it," Mr. Lewitt declared, perfunctorily. "Let me ask you, Mr. Anderson, is Mr. Greenlaw thinking of withdrawing his money?"

"Not that I am aware of," Mr. Anderson replied. "That, at any rate, is not the subject of my visit."

The faces of the partners again expressed the liveliest satisfaction.

"There ith interest and dividenth," Mr. Montague remarked, "amounting to a considerable sum. Perhapth Mr. Greenlaw would like a cheque or noteth for this?"

Mr. Anderson shrugged his shoulders.

"Mr. Greenlaw," he explained, "is in no need of money. The object of my visit is simply this. Mr. Greenlaw wishes to assure himself of the safety of his capital. He is a peculiar man and he wishes to do so in a manner of his own."

"Very good, very good," Mr. Lewitt murmured softly. "Pray go on, Mr. Anderson."

"Mr. Greenlaw," Mr. Anderson continued, again glancing around the room, "requires ocular demonstration of the safety of his investment, and for that purpose is willing to run a not inconsiderable risk. He proposes to present himself here at half-past twelve next Monday morning."

"What, in thith office?" Mr. Montague exclaimed.

"Exactly," Mr. Anderson agreed. "There is risk, of course, but, as you have doubtless heard, Mr. Greenlaw is the cleverest man at a disguise on the face of the earth. He will come as an elderly gentleman, and he requires to see upon your desk forty thousand pounds' worth of bank notes, or government bonds, payable to bearer and made out in his name."

The two partners looked at one another.

"But surely, Mr. Anderson," Mr. Lewitt protested, "a visit to the bankers' would have an equally satisfactory effect?"

Mr. Anderson shook his head.

"Greenlaw," he said, "is a man of cranky notions. He is also the most obstinate person I ever knew in my life. If I might venture to offer you any advice, I would suggest that you humour him in this matter. Mr. Greenlaw would, of course, expect to pay the commission upon any necessary transference of stock."

Mr. Lewitt rose from his seat.

"If you will excuse me," he begged. "I should like to consult with my partner for a moment."

"By all means," Mr. Anderson agreed.

The two members of the firm left the room. When they returned, in about five minutes, their accustomed sleek amiability was once more visible in their countenances.

"We have dethided," Mr. Montague declared, "to humour Mr. Greenlaw'th whim."

"Mr. Greenlaw," Mr. Lewitt added, "is an old and valued client. We regret the eccentricities of his career, which have prevented our ever making his acquaintance. We shall be delighted to see him on Monday morning at half-past twelve, and will show him his money in Bank of England notes. The commission will be somewhat heavy, but I presume there will be no objection to that. We shall debit it to the account due for interest and dividends."

Mr. Anderson shook hands with both the partners.

"I am sure," he said, "that you have decided wisely."

At precisely half-past twelve on the following Monday morning, Mr. Laxworthy and Mr. Forrest Anderson entered the offices of Messrs. Wills, Lewitt and Montague. They were shown without an instant's delay into Mr. Lewitt's room, where the two partners were waiting.

"This," Mr. Anderson announced, having shaken hands himself, "is Mr. Greenlaw."

"Care to shake hands?" Mr. Laxworthy asked briskly.

"My *dear* Mr. Greenlaw, delighted!" Mr. Montague exclaimed with effusion, holding out his fat white fingers. "Only *too* delighted," he added with *empressement*, "to have the pleasure of meeting at latht tho valued a client!"

"We have often spoken of you," Mr. Lewitt added, also offering his hand, "and I think we may say that we have taken great interest in your investments, Mr. Greenlaw. Mr. Wills was always most particular what he put you in for. Have a cigar?"

Mr. Laxworthy accepted it, smelt I, and thrust it into his waistcoat pocket.

"Where's my money?" he demanded.

"In a moment—in a moment, my dear sir," Mr. Lewitt replied. "Now if you will come over to this table. We thought it best, in order to remove all possible ground for suspicion, to show you the money in Bank of England notes. How do you like the look of these, eh?"

He thumped down two packets of bank-notes upon the table.

"Thomething tholid about that, eh?" Mr. Montague remarked, with his hands in his trousers pockets. "We've arranged it in two pileth, tho that you can count one and Mr. Anderthon the other. Take your time about it. No hurry."

"Perhaps not for you," Mr. Laxworthy retorted. "Can't say I'm too comfortable here myself."

"No need to detain you a moment longer than you care to stay," Mr. Lewitt assured him suavely. "Mr. Montague would only have liked the opportunity of taking you to our bankers. I can assure you, my dear sir, that we could put on the table, of our own money, more than that useful little amount of yours which you are just counting."

"Glad to hear it," Mr. Laxworthy replied. "Can't think why people ever bother to try and make money honestly. You and I know something better than that, eh, Mr. Montague?"

Mr. Montague grinned a little feebly.

"We do not conthider," he began,—

"Twenty thousand pounds in my pile," Mr. Laxworthy interrupted.

"Same here," Mr. Forrest Anderson echoed.

Mr. Laxworthy thrust both bundles of notes into his pocket. Mr. Lewitt started.

"Here!" he exclaimed. "What's that?"

"My money," Mr. Laxworthy announced. "I'm leaving the country. I'm going to take it with me."

Mr. Lewitt stared at him aghast. Mr. Montague hurried up to the scene of action.

"What'th thith?" he demanded. "What'th thith, eh? Not tho fast, if you please, with that money!"

"Why not?" Mr. Laxworthy asked. "It's mine."

Mr. Lewitt turned to Mr. Anderson with outstretched hands.

"This gentleman here," he cried, "told us particularly that you were going to leave the money here—with us, that you only wanted to see it. We've shown it you, it's quite safe, you can have your interest and dividends in cash now, if you like. But the forty thousand pounds has got to stop with us."

"Oh, has it!" Mr. Laxworthy replied. "You'd better try and take it away from me."

Mr. Montague struck the table with his fist.

"I wath in the room myself!" he almost shrieked. "That gentleman there—that friend of yourth—he gave uth hith word that you would not take the money away. We cannot spare it just now, I tell you! It would ruin uth!"

"Sorry," Mr. Laxworthy said, coolly. "Good morning!"

He turned toward the door. Mr. Lewitt leaned over his desk.

"Mr. Greenlaw," he whispered hoarsely, "be wise!"

Mr. Laxworthy turned and faced him.

"What do you mean?"

Mr. Lewitt was exceedingly pale. The hands which continually clasped one another were damp and shaking.

"Mr. Greenlaw," he begged, "now be reasonable. Be reasonable, my dear sir. We cannot afford to let the money go like this. We must protect our own interests. Now, come. If a few thousand pounds—"

"Thank you" Mr. Laxworthy interrupted. "I've no time for silly discussions. I've got my money, and I'm off."

"You don't underthtand!" Mr. Montague exclaimed, wiping the perspiration from his forehead. "We mutht protect our own interaths."

"And I mine!" Mr. Laxworthy answered, turning swiftly around, with his right hand in the pocket of his overcoat.

There was very little cover in the room, but what there was Mr. Montague and Mr. Lewitt promptly took advantage of. Mr. Lewitt slid from his chair on to the ground behind the roll-top desk at which he had been seated. Mr. Montague squeezed himself tightly against the wall, and held out a heavy office chair in front of his face.

"What's the game?" Mr. Laxworthy demanded fiercely. "Have you laid a trap for me?"

The glittering little piece of steel which Mr. Laxworthy held so firmly in front of him seemed to exercise an almost paralysing effect upon the two partners. He reiterated his question.

"Have you communicated with the police? You may just as well answer me. I'll shoot you if you don't."

Mr. Lewitt's head appeared timidly from behind the desk.

"Mr. Greenlaw," he stammered, "we don't want any trouble here. You just leave that money with us, put it down on the corner of the table. You'll get your interest all right. You can't have safer investments."

"It's my money," Mr. Laxworthy declared. "Supposing I insist upon taking it away with me now, what then?"

Mr. Montague moved the chair cautiously from before his face.

"Your money ith ath thafe with us, Mr. Greenlaw," he protested, "ath in the Bank of England."

Mr. Laxworthy's arm swung around—and up went the chair.

"Answer my question," he insisted. "Have you communicated with the police? Am I going to walk into a trap when I leave this room?"

Mr. Lewitt's head and shoulders appeared from behind the desk. He felt much more comfortable whilst Mr. Laxworthy's arm was pointed towards his partner.

"Mr. Greenlaw," he pleaded earnestly, "we have no ill-will against you. We want to see you get away quite safely, but there is always a risk. Take my advice, now, my dear sir, do! Leave that money here and you can go just whenever and wherever you please."

"And supposing I refuse?" Mr. Laxworthy asked.

Mr. Lewitt's head and shoulders disappeared out of sight. Mr. Montague held the chair squarely in front of his face. A voice came from behind the desk.

"For our own protection," it said, "we were compelled to ask a policeman to occupy the anteroom. We shall not communicate with him at all unless—unless we are obliged."

Mr. Laxworthy turned quickly to the door.

"Come along, Anderson," he directed. "These fellows think too much of their lives to play that sort of game."

Mr. Anderson and Mr. Laxworthy walked steadily down the stairs, regardless of the ringing of electric bells, the whistling, and the tumult of voices. Before they were out of the building, however, they heard the sound of pursuing footsteps. A policeman and an inspector in plain clothes were on their heels. Mr. Montague and Mr. Lewitt hung over the banisters.

"That'th your man," Mr. Montague called out. "He'th got forty thouthand pounds of our money. Be careful, he'th got a pithtol!"

Mr. Laxworthy and Mr. Forrest Anderson stood at the door of the motorcar. Detective Marlin stepped out on to the pavement just as the inspector's hand touched Mr. Laxworthy's shoulder.

"You had better explain to these people who I am," Mr. Laxworthy said to Marlin. "They are trying to arrest me. Seem to have got an idea into their heads that I am Daniel Greenlaw."

The inspector and his subordinate recognised Marlin and saluted.

"We are here upon private information, sir," the former asserted.

"No good," Detective Marlin answered, shaking his head. "This gentleman is Mr. John T. Laxworthy. He is personally known to me."

Emboldened by the presence of the guardians of the peace, Mr. Montague and Mr. Lewitt stood on the outskirts of the little group. The inspector turned towards them.

"Some mistake here, sirs," he said. "This gentleman's name is Mr. Laxworthy—friend of Inspector Marlin, one of our chiefs at Scotland Yard."

"He told us himself," Lewitt protested, excitedly, "that he was Greenlaw!"

"He'th got Greenlaw'th money!" Mr. Montague cried, wildly. "He'th got it in hith pocket."

Mr. Laxworthy produced some documents, which he handed to Mr. Marlin.

"Will someone take these excitable gentleman away?" he begged. "You will find there complete authorisation for me to collect the money which they have just paid me."

Mr. Marlin examined the documents upon the pavement.

"So far as I can see," he told Mr. Lewitt, "these papers are absolutely in order. Mr. Laxworthy was fully empowered to receive this money on behalf of Mr. Greenlaw."

"But he thaid that he wath Greenlaw!" Mr. Montague protested.

Detective Marlin shrugged his shoulders.

"It scarcely seems probable," he remarked. "In any case, if you have any claim against Mr. Laxworthy, I can assure you that he is a gentleman of large means, and he is to be found at any time. A matter for civil action only," he added, turning towards the inspector and policeman, who were still standing by.

He stepped into the car, which promptly drove off. Mr. Laxworthy sat in his corner, smiling grimly to himself.

"What I should like to know is," Mr. Marlin said slowly, "where I come in? Are we allies?"

Mr. Laxworthy shook his head.

"Not this time," he replied. "I am thoroughly grateful to Mr. Greenlaw for this morning's amusement. If I can arrange it, he is going to get his money safely."

The detective sighed.

"Then you'd better let me out at the Embankment," he said.

Mr. Laxworthy lunched at his usual table and with his charming companion of a week ago.

"Your friend," he remarked, as he produced the notes—"your brother if one might venture to take note of certain similarities of features—has done well to get his money. Thorough scoundrels, those fellows."

She looked at him admiringly.

"I shall not ask you any questions," she murmured. "You are a wonderful man, Mr. Laxworthy."

"The forty thousand pounds," Mr. Laxworthy continued, "is there upon the table, but tell me how you are going to pass it on to Greenlaw? The notes can be traced, remember."

She smiled.

"I will tell you," she declared. "It was to have been a secret, but with you it does not matter. I buy jewels. There is no one, not even an expert, who understands diamonds as I do. Daniel carries the jewels with him, and when he has an opportunity he sells. As for the notes, they trace them to me. Very well. If through me they can discover Daniel Greenlaw—they are welcome."

Mr. Laxworthy grunted.

"We can't do better than the *Omelette Espagnol*," he suggested, "with Riz Diane, Stilton cheese and coffee to follow."

"Excellent!" the lady decided. "I feel that I am going to enjoy my luncheon immensely!"

CHAPTER XI
The Disappearance of Mr. Colshaw

Mr. Laxworthy was lunching in the grill-room of the Milan Hotel when Sydney Wing passed through the swing doors, escorting a remarkably pretty young lady. He at once conducted his companion towards his chief.

"Mr. Laxworthy," he said, "I want to introduce you to this young lady—Miss Phyllis Thorndyke."

Mr. Laxworthy rose and bowed. A waiter, obeying his gesture, pushed forward a chair, into which the girl—she was little more than a child—subsided.

"Miss Thorndyke," Sydney continued, "is in great distress, and it occurred to me that you might, perhaps, be of assistance to her."

Mr. Laxworthy looked at the young lady for several seconds through his thick spectacles. The result of his observations was entirely in her favour. Her manner was pleasant and unaffected, and her distress obviously genuine.

"I should be very glad indeed to be of any assistance to you, Miss Thorndyke," he murmured. "I have noticed that for the last few days you have been alone."

She made a little effort to recover herself. It was obvious that she was on the point of tears. She was also very pale, and there was a frightened expression in her large, soft eyes.

"It is four days," she said, "since my father left me, to pay a business call in the City. He expected to be back for lunch. That was Thursday morning at half-past ten. I have not seen him since."

"Your father, I presume, is the tall gentleman with the iron-grey hair, whom I have seen in here with you?" Mr. Laxworthy asked.

She nodded.

"We have been staying here for nearly a week," she replied. "You must have seen us together, because we have no friends. I have not spoken to anyone else except the hotel and shop people since we arrived from New York—until," she added, "Mr. Wing was so kind to me."

Mr. Laxworthy glanced at the young man inquiringly.

"There was a little foreign chap who persisted in following Miss Thorndyke about," Sydney explained. "I saw that she was nervous and annoyed and ventured to help her get rid of him."

"Mr. Wing was very good to me," the girl murmured with a grateful glance at him.

Mr. Laxworthy cleared his throat.

"Referring to your father's disappearance," he continued, "this seems to me to be a case in which you should certainly inform the hotel people, and, through them, the police. The ordinary methods in an affair of this sort are always the best. Your father may have met with some slight accident, and in such cases the police are in direct touch with the hospitals."

Silently the young lady drew a thin sheet of paper from a small bag which she was carrying, and passed it across the table. Mr. Laxworthy removed his spectacles and carefully polished them with the corner of his handkerchief. Having readjusted them, he read these few lines of type-written communication:

"In case I am not home for some little time, Phyllis, I am sending you enclosed a note for twenty pounds. Do not mention my absence to any-one. It would do no good and might easily involve me in further trouble. I can only tell you that I hope to be back very shortly. Whatever you do, do not apply to or communicate with the police.—
Your affectionate father,
    "STEVENS THORNDYKE."

The signature was in ink. Mr. Laxworthy tapped it with his forefinger.
"Your father's handwriting?" he asked.
She assented confidently.
"I should know it anywhere," she declared.
Mr. Laxworthy turned the envelope over in his fingers.
"How did you get this?"
"It was found on the hall-porter's desk on the morning father disappeared, about luncheon time. No one knows who brought it or how it got there."
"It is the only communication you have received from him?"
"Absolutely!"
Mr. Laxworthy was silent for a few moments, during which period he continued eating his lunch, whilst Sydney and the young lady whispered together. Finally, Mr. Laxworthy pushed away his plate and ordered coffee.
"Miss Thorndyke," he said, "if I am to be of any service to you, I must ask you some more questions."
"As many as ever you like," she declared, drawing her chair a little closer to his.
"How long have you been in this country?"
"A week to-day. We came on the *Deutschland*."
"Have you any friends at all in London?"
She shook her head.
"Not one. I have never been here before."

"Is this a pleasure trip or a business one on your father's part?"

"I will tell you just what happened," she replied. "I left boarding-school about six months ago. We had an apartment, my father and I, on Riverside Drive. One evening we were out motoring and stopped at a restaurant for some supper. There was a big yellow car which had been just behind ours for over an hour, wherever we went. It drew up, too, at the restaurant, and as my father was talking to the waiter about a table, a man who had been riding in it touched my father on the elbow and give him a note. I didn't like the look of the man at all, but he didn't seem to want any answer. Directly my father had the note between his fingers he drove away. I couldn't help being a little curious about the matter because it seemed such a strange time and a strange way to deliver a message. I did not ask any questions, however, because I could see that my father was very much upset. He drank three cocktails one after the other, a thing which I had never seen him do before, and he was very white and shaken. He told me then, as we were sitting there, that directly we got home I must pack my trunks, as we were going to Europe the next day."

"He gave no reason for this extraordinary haste?" Mr. Laxworthy asked.

"None at all. He was always so grave and silent that it was difficult for me to ask him questions. But I did ask him about the man in the yellow motor-car who brought him the note. Naturally I could not help connecting that with our sudden journey."

"And what did your father say?"

"He told me that it was a message for which he had been waiting for many years. He said it quite quietly, but there were little points of fire in his eyes when he spoke. The next day we sailed for England."

"Did you gather that your father was pleased with the message, or angry, or frightened?"

She thought for a moment.

"I can only say that he was agitated."

Mr. Laxworthy, after a few moments' pause, continued to ask questions.

"What was your father's occupation?"

"I do not know," she answered simply. "He had an office somewhere near Broadway, where he went every morning and stayed there till three or four. He never talked about his business."

"He had no business friends?" Mr. Laxworthy asked.

"We had no friends at all—none except those we met at the Beach or wherever we were, and we just knew our neighbours to nod to."

"There appears to have been all the elements of a first-class mystery about your father's life," Mr. Laxworthy remarked, dryly. "Did you never wonder at his silence concerning his affairs?"

"I had only been home from boarding-school such a short time," she reminded him, "and father always hated being asked questions."

Mr. Laxworthy stirred his coffee thoughtfully.

"What were your impressions as to your father's means?"

"He always seemed to have plenty of money. He gave the housekeeper of our little flat five hundred dollars a month to keep house, and he gave me a hundred dollars a month for my clothes."

"Is there any single person in America to whom one could cable for further information as to your father's business?" Mr. Laxworthy inquired.

"There was a lawyer named Gidgeon," she remembered. "I don't even know his address, though."

Mr. Laxworthy made a note of the name.

"Any one else?"

She shook her head decidedly.

"Your servants?"

"Father paid them off when we started."

"Furniture?"

"It wasn't our own. It went with the flat."

"Do you know anything of your father's history at all?"

"Very little," she replied. "There was really no one to tell me. I know that he used to live a good deal in England and France. I have been in boarding-schools ever since I was a child. My mother died before I could remember."

"You know nothing about her relatives?"

"I have never seen or heard of a relation in my life," the girl assured him.

Perhaps at the recollection of her lonely state, her eyes began to fill with tears. Sydney looked across the table almost indignantly. It appeared to him that his chief's cross-examination was a little unfeeling. Mr. Laxworthy's attitude, to the casual observer, was certainly neither sympathetic nor interested. The girl herself seemed to realise the fact, for, after a glance at Sydney, she rose timidly to her feet.

"Thank you very much, Mr. Laxworthy," she said, "for listening to my story. I am afraid there is nothing you can suggest, is there?"

Mr. Laxworthy motioned to her a little impatiently to sit down again.

"There are several things," he assured her, "which I could suggest. Wait."

The hall porter suddenly appeared, making his way towards them through the maze of tables. He bowed to the young lady.

"This note has just been left for you, Miss Thorndyke," he announced. "I thought you would like to have it at once."

She took it from him eagerly. Mr. Laxworthy beckoned to the hall porter to come a little closer.

"Can you tell us who brought that note?"

"I am sorry, sir, but my attention was distracted for a moment. I was answering the telephone. When I looked round, the note was upon the counter. There were no signs of anyone waiting for an answer."

"In case," Mr. Laxworthy remarked, "this incident should be repeated—that is to say, another note should be brought to Miss Thorndyke in the same manner—I should like you to remember this: there will be a five-pound note to be distributed amongst your little staff out there if you can detain the bearer of any future communication to Miss Thorndyke of this sort."

The hall porter bowed.

"I will certainly give strict orders about the matter, sir," he promised.

He hurried off. Without a word, the girl pushed the sheet of paper towards Mr. Laxworthy. Upon it there was only a single line of typewritten matter:

"I send you twenty pounds. Be careful to obey the injunctions which I have laid upon you."

This time the message was signed with initials only.

"You are absolutely sure, I suppose," Mr. Laxworthy remarked, "that these messages really come from your father?"

"Absolutely certain," she assured him. "That is just the way he always signs the bills here."

"You had better," Mr. Laxworthy suggested, rising, "leave the matter entirely in my hands until to-morrow morning."

"You are really going to try and help me, then?" she asked, her face brightening.

For the first time the lines in Mr. Laxworthy's face relaxed a little. She was certainly rather a pathetic spectacle.

"I shall be glad to do what I can," he promised. "You have set me rather a difficult task, though."

The three of them had risen to their feet together, and they turned now towards the exit from the restaurant. Mr. Laxworthy stood on one side to allow the girl to precede them. She had no sooner, however, taken a few steps than she stopped short. She turned towards Mr. Laxworthy and gripped him by the arm. Her eyes seemed suddenly to have become distended. Her cheeks were paler than ever.

"Mr. Laxworthy," she whispered, "quick! Look! You see that man at the table there—the one with the lady?"

Mr. Laxworthy followed her gesture.

"Yes," he answered, "I see him quite well. What about him?"

"It is the man," she declared hoarsely, "who was in the yellow car! Wait. I shall speak to him."

Mr. Laxworthy pushed her firmly along.

"Miss Thorndyke," he begged, "don't do anything of the sort. If that man is really the one who brought your father the message, it is all the more reason why you should leave me to find out what I can about him. I know something of the woman who is with him."

"But he brought the note!" she protested faintly. "He must know."

"If he is in any way implicated in your father's disappearance," Mr. Laxworthy pointed out, "it is very much better that you should not put him on his guard by showing that you recognise him."

She turned reluctantly away. As they passed out of the restaurant into the little reception room, Mr. Laxworthy suddenly changed both his attitude and his tone. He had the air now of a man who is genuinely in earnest.

"Miss Thorndyke," he said earnestly, "if you really desire me to help you must do exactly as I tell you. You must not think of going back and accosting that man. You must go to your room now at once and stay there for a short time."

She hesitated.

"But I am sure," she objected, "that that was the man in the yellow motor-car. Why shouldn't I go and speak to him? He ought to be able to tell us why my father left America so suddenly."

"Doubtless he could tell us," Mr. Laxworthy assented dryly. "The question is whether he would! I am inclined to agree with you that he may be concerned in your father's disappearance, but if we are to gain any real benefit through your recognition of him, we must keep that fact a secret. Do as I ask you, I beg. Leave me for a time, at any rate, to do the best I can for you."

She sighed as she went away. Mr. Laxworthy and Sydney Wing re-entered the restaurant.

"My young friend," the former inquired, "have you lunched?"

"Excellently," Sydney replied.

"A little unfortunate," his chief sighed, "because one of us has to lunch again. You are younger and your digestion should be more perfect. We will sit here, if you please. Now order whatever you like. I shall drink coffee."

"What are we going to do here?" Sydney asked in a low tone, after having consulted the menu.

"I am going to watch the man whom your little friend Miss Thorndyke believes is concerned in her father's disappearance," Mr. Laxworthy answered. "From here I have an excellent view of him. You recognise, perhaps, the young lady who is his companion? It is just possible that their conversation may be interesting."

They gave the waiter an order. Mr. Laxworthy sipped coffee, Sydney

Wing toyed with a sole. Meanwhile, a few yards away from them, the man talked continually with his companion. It was quite three-quarters of an hour before they rose to go. On their way out, Paula Garesworthy paused at their table.

"Ah, Mr. Laxworthy!" she exclaimed, giving him her left hand.

Mr. Laxworthy rose to his feet.

"My dear young lady," he murmured, "it is charming to see you once more."

She hurried on with a little word of farewell. The man turned to her and asked a question, glancing over his shoulder at Mr. Laxworthy. Then they disappeared. Sydney leaned across the table.

"Well?" he demanded almost breathlessly.

"Nothing much," Mr. Laxworthy admitted. "One or two little points, however, were interesting. The young lady who affected to see me just now for the first time, not only saw me some time ago, but she carefully warned her companion. They have been talking absolute drivel—simply, I am sure, for effect. I feel convinced of this because as I entered the restaurant for the first time, before your protégée had appeared, I read a single sentence upon that man's lips which made me wonder. I put it aside in my mind as being just one of those fragments that one comes across, little detached epitomes of tragedy, so entirely isolated that one simply wonders in curiosity and passes on."

"What were the words?"

Mr. Laxworthy rose from his place a little abruptly.

"'*Power over your enemies, the power of life and death, is worth waiting for, is worth working for!*' What did he mean by that, I wonder? Come."

The two men passed out into the hall. Mr. Laxworthy rang for the lift. Then he came back and discussed with Sydney some trifling matter. Paula Garesworthy and her escort were parting at the door which led into the street.

"You are sure," the latter asked, "that I cannot give you a lift anywhere?"

She shook her head.

"I am going west," she replied, "and you, I imagine—?"

"I am going to the City," he admitted, smilingly. "We poor slaves, you know, must content ourselves with a snatched half hour or so of relaxation."

"Au revoir, then!" she exclaimed, waving her hand.

She watched him drive off. Then she turned round and made her way at once to where Mr. Laxworthy was standing.

"I want to speak to you," she said.

Mr. Laxworthy showed no surprise. He led her to a couch set back in a corner of the place.

"Mr. Laxworthy," she began, "I know your mania for adventure. I know that you go about the world looking always for new things, new adventures, new interests. Nothing has puzzled me more than the fact that you should be interested in the affair of Stevens Thorndyke."

"How do you know that I am interested in his affair?" Mr. Laxworthy asked.

"It was his daughter who was telling you that pitiful story," she reminded him. "You were evidently interested. You re-entered the restaurant upon some excuse. You sat and watched us."

"And why," Mr. Laxworthy inquired, "should I connect you with the affair of Stevens Thorndyke?"

"Because," the girl told him, "that child recognised my companion as the man who had given her father the note at the Claremont Restaurant a fortnight ago, which summoned him to England. Is that not true?"

"It is quite true," Mr. Laxworthy confessed. "Come, this interests me. Will you not tell me, please, a little more about this man, and why he is behaving in such a mysterious fashion?"

She shook her head slowly. She leaned towards him, her hand fell upon his.

"Mr. Laxworthy," she said in a low tone, "I am going to give you some advice, not for my sake but for your own. Look at me. You do believe that I am honest, don't you?"

Mr. Laxworthy obeyed. She was, at any rate, beautiful.

"Yes," he replied, "I believe that."

"Have nothing to do with this affair, then," she begged. "There is nothing in it for you. I give you my word that there is nothing."

"But the child?" Mr. Laxworthy asked. "What is one to do about her?"

Paula Garesworthy rose to her feet and held out her hand.

"I have warned you, Mr. Laxworthy," she said, "because I like you. You must do as you think best."

Mr. Laxworthy escorted his companion to the door. Whilst a taxicab was being fetched for her, he made his little farewell speech.

"You have given me some very useful advice, Miss Garesworthy," he remarked. "Let me reciprocate. I do not know that it is well for a young lady of your age to be seen lunching in a public restaurant with a man who has spent at least seven years of his life in prison."

She stood very still for a moment.

"You know everything!" she murmured.

"I know at least Richard Wardley," he answered.

The taxicab was waiting before the door. She turned towards it.

"Well," she said, "such associations are part of the price I must pay for my Bohemianism, you know. Nevertheless, Mr. Laxworthy," she added, "balance your advice against mine. Believe me when I tell you that there is no danger whatever for me in such companionship, compared with the danger that waits for you if you disregard my warning."

She stepped into the cab with a little farewell wave of the hand. Mr. Laxworthy, after sending off a cable and making an appointment through the telephone, went round to see his friend Mr. Marlin of Scotland Yard.

"I wonder," Mr. Laxworthy asked him, "if you remember anything about the London and South Westminster Bank robbery. It must have been—let me see—about ten or twelve years ago."

Mr. Marlin looked at his questioner curiously.

"Of course I do," he replied. "There were four men concerned in it—Richard Wardley, got seven years—came out some time ago and went into business; Colshaw, four years—changed his name to Thorndyke, and went to America; Proudson, twelve years; and the fourth man we never caught. They shot the manager and got away with a lot of specie. I should think they must have cleared about thirty thousand pounds by it."

"Ah!" Mr. Laxworthy murmured. "Why did Colshaw only get four years?"

Mr. Marlin shook his head.

"I can't give away secrets, you know, Mr. Laxworthy," he remarked, a little dryly. "Why on earth do you want to know?"

"Just curiosity."

His companion grunted.

"Your curiosity generally leads somewhere," he observed. "Queer that you should ask me about this. Proudson came out last week."

"Is that so?" Mr. Laxworthy asked. "I suppose if I wanted five minutes' conversation with him—"

"Oh, I could find him fast enough, if that's what you're after," Marlin interrupted, "or Richard Wardley either, for that matter. So long as we are allies, you understand. I can't have you come poking about amongst my pets unless I am on to the game."

"Quite so," Mr. Laxworthy agreed. "I wish you'd tell me why Colshaw only got four years?"

Marlin scratched his chin.

"Well, he was led into it by the others, for one thing," he explained. "Then there is no doubt that he had the cleverest counsel."

"That may have been it," Mr. Laxworthy assented, amiably. "By the by, Proudson will, of course, be under police supervision for some time?"

"Certainly!"

"And Wardley?"

Marlin shook his head.

"He's clear, long enough ago. I believe he's doing very well in some sort of business. I don't even know his address without referring."

Mr. Laxworthy took off his spectacles and rubbed them carefully.

"Ah, well!" he said, preparing to depart, "I always enjoy a chat with you, Mr. Marlin. I happened to see Wardley at luncheon time, and I suppose that was what brought the affair back into my mind. I remember I sat all through the trial. Very interesting case it was, too. Of course, I can understand why Proudson got twelve years. He was the one who used the revolver, wasn't he? But I can't quite understand the difference between the other two sentences."

"It depends so often," Marlin remarked sententiously, "upon the way the judge looks at these things."

Mr. Laxworthy returned to his hotel. He dined frugally and alone. Towards the end of the meal, a cablegram was brought in to him. It was signed *Gidgeon,* and dated from New York:

"Thorndyke's life here entirely respectable. Enjoyed considerable income from sale of patent calf leather, for which he held agency. Believe he was in trouble in England under name of Colshaw."

Mr. Laxworthy studied this message for some few minutes with an air of satisfaction. Then, having concluded his meal, he sent for his coat and hat and umbrella, and taking a taxicab out to the farther part of Maida Vale, discovered with some difficulty a newly built block of flats in a back street. He consulted a board for some moments and then rang for the lift.

"I wish to go to Miss Garesworthy's flat," he told the lift attendant.

The man stared at Mr. Laxworthy curiously as he opened the gate. He himself was a singularly unprepossessing-looking object.

"It's on the top floor, sir," he remarked. "Step in, please."

Mr. Laxworthy nodded, and, affecting to arrange his tie in the small looking-glass of the lift, kept his eyes fixed upon the attendant. There was some delay in starting. When they had gone up seven storeys, they came to a standstill. The man opened the gate.

"The lift don't go any further, sir," he explained. "I'll show you the way up to Miss Garesworthy's rooms."

Mr. Laxworthy followed his guide up two flights of stone steps. There was about the whole place a sense of emptiness, and as regards the top portion a sense of complete detachment. Since he had entered the building, Mr. Laxworthy had neither seen nor heard any sign of a human being.

"Are any of these flats in the lower part of the building occupied?" he asked the porter.

"One or two, sir," the man replied. "These are Miss Garesworthy's rooms."

Mr. Laxworthy handed him a shilling.

"Thank you very much," he said. "I will ring the bell. You need not wait."

The man, however, did not move. He was a thick, burly-looking person with the physique of a prize-fighter, and small, narrow eyes.

"I said that you need not wait," Mr. Laxworthy repeated, sharply.

"I am waiting to see if Miss Garesworthy is in," the man answered surlily.

The door in front of them was suddenly opened. It was Paula Gareswor-thy who stood there. She looked at her visitor with an expression of amazement, which gradually changed into one of horror.

"Mr. Laxworthy!" she gasped.

"Madame!" he replied, raising his hat.

He stepped quickly across the threshold. Her hands were outstretched as though to push him away.

"I warned you not to come," she cried quickly. "This adventure is not for you. What is happening is justice, and justice only. Steal down quickly. I will make some excuse."

"I am not altogether sure," Mr. Laxworthy answered, "whether that very amiable person behind would allow me to go, even if I felt disposed. As a matter of fact, however, nothing would induce me to leave this place until my mission is accomplished."

There was the sound of a man's voice heard through the open door. Paula Garesworthy gave a little gesture of despair.

"It is too late!" she exclaimed.

Richard Wardley suddenly appeared, standing upon the threshold of one of the inner rooms. He looked across at Mr. Laxworthy with a curious expression.

"Close the door, Paula," he ordered.

She obeyed him. He moved between it and Mr. Laxworthy.

"Perhaps you will be good enough to tell us," he asked quietly, "what you want here?"

Mr. Laxworthy, who seemed to find nothing unusual in the manner of his reception, drew off his gloves and calmly deposited them in his hat.

"I wish," he said, "to have a word or two with Mr. Colshaw. His daughter is getting anxious as to his absence."

Paula looked at him and turned away in despair. Richard Wardley smiled. He was a fat, unhealthy-looking man, and there was something exceedingly unpleasant about his smile.

"You know that he is here, then?" he asked.

"I am quite convinced of it," Mr. Laxworthy replied, cheerfully.

"Have you shared your suspicion with anyone?"

"Not a soul. I am naturally, I am afraid, of a somewhat secretive nature."

"You shall have your wish," Richard Wardley announced. "Come this way."

They all three passed into a little sitting-room, prettily and even daintily furnished. Paula threw herself into an easy-chair and covered her face with her hands. Richard Wardley opened a door beyond.

"This way," he directed.

Mr. Laxworthy followed him into a bedroom, plainly furnished, with only an iron bedstead and a few chairs. Standing against the foot of the latter, with folded arms, was a tall, emaciated man, with hollow cheeks, dead-looking eyes, and grizzled grey hair. A few yards away, Greenlaw was leaning against the wall with a revolver in his hand, as though on guard. Between the two was a horrible sight. A third man was seated in a chair, to which he was bound with cords. There was a gag in his mouth, and his hands were tied together with a rope which seemed to cut into his flesh. His cheeks were deathly pale, his head drooped a little as though he were unconscious. His eyes, however, were wide open, and they told something of the story of the last four days' horror.

"Mr. Laxworthy!" Greenlaw exclaimed with an oath.

Richard Wardley closed the door and stood with his back to it.

"My friends," he said, "we have here an example of the folly of meddling in other people's affairs. Mr. Laxworthy, a man of gallantry, as we all know, has, on the solicitation of our friend Colshaw's daughter, undertaken to find him. Mr. Laxworthy has succeeded. The interesting question now remains—what are we to do with Mr. Laxworthy?"

Greenlaw's face was dark with anger.

"You fool!" he cried to this most unwelcome visitor. "I told Paula to warn you. This is no affair of yours."

"Unfortunately," Mr. Laxworthy replied, taking up a position on the hearthrug, straightening his spectacles and beaming upon them all with a little more than his accustomed amiability, "I was compelled to make it mine."

The man at the foot of the bed spoke. His voice was harsh and menacing.

"You will find it an unfortunate compulsion!"

"I trust not," Mr. Laxworthy answered suavely. "We shall see."

There was a dead silence for several moments. The eyes of the man who was bound in the chair were fastened upon his would-be deliverer. Greenlaw shrugged his shoulders.

"Mr. Laxworthy," he said, "you know who we all are. You know very well that, having discovered us like this, we cannot possibly let you go back. You may think, perhaps, that a block of flats in a populous neighbourhood is a fairly safe place for anyone, especially if they happen to have left a note of their destination behind them."

He looked inquiringly at Mr. Laxworthy, who only shook his head.

"Not a soul," the latter declared cheerfully, "is in my confidence."

Greenlaw looked disappointed.

"You may even," he suggested, "have your friend Mr. Marlin in the vicinity."

His left eyelid twitched very slightly, but Mr. Laxworthy refused to take the hint.

"I am entirely upon my own," he assured them.

Greenlaw frowned. He had somehow or other conceived a liking for this queer-looking little person.

"You are a brave man, Mr. Laxworthy," he said irritably, "but you are also a fool. I would have been glad to have given you a chance of escape if it had been possible. These quarters, let me tell you, have not been carelessly chosen. They were built by friends of ours, they are let only to friends of ours. They have very special features, I can assure you. There are four different ways by which you can be made to disappear from this room, or at any rate from this suite of apartments, into an undiscoverable eternity."

Mr. Laxworthy shook his head.

"Thank you," he said, "I am not proposing to undertake any voyage of discovery of that sort. My mission here is a peaceful one. Contrary to my custom, I have even come unarmed. I see that my friend Mr. Wardley is making strategic movements towards me. I can assure you that it is unnecessary."

He lifted his hands a little way above his head. Nevertheless, the two men closed slowly in upon him. The gaunt man at the foot of the bed once more broke the silence. His voice sounded strangely—he had spoken little during the last twelve years.

"It is an act of justice, this," he declared, pointing towards the man in the chair.

"Not at all," Mr. Laxworthy objected sharply. "It is an act of injustice."

They all three looked at him steadily. Mr. Laxworthy loosened his coat and removed his muffler.

"You will forgive me," he explained, apologetically, "but I find the atmosphere in this room a little warm, and I am subject to chills. To continue. It is because I believe that you—two of you, at any rate—are fair men, and because I believe that you have some sense of justice, that I have come here unarmed, without taking any precautions, and without communicating certain ideas of mine to Mr. Marlin or his friends. That man," he went on, pointing towards the wretched figure in the chair, "is being tortured by you because you believed that it was he who gave the police that valuable information when you were all tried together—except my clever friend Greenlaw here—for the London and South Westminster Bank robbery. You also believe that he has either helped himself to the plunder or knows where it is. You are perpetrating, therefore, what you consider to be an act of justice. As a matter of fact, it happens to be an act of brutal and flagrant injustice."

The gaunt man at the foot of the bed leaned a little forward. Instinctively Wardley shrank back. Across his face there flashed some glam of the horror to come.

"What do you mean?" Proudson demanded hoarsely.

"I mean that the informer was Richard Wardley," Mr. Laxworthy replied. "Colshaw never even received a lawyer in his cell. He never even knew what became of the gold."

Mr. Laxworthy's finger leaped out, pointing unfalteringly at the man whom he denounced. It was a splendid effort and it succeeded. Wardley's nerve failed him. He made one dash for the door. Greenlaw struck him with the butt end of his revolver as he passed, and knocked him half senseless.

"I got seven years!" he shrieked. "Why did Colshaw get four, then, and I seven?"

"It was at your own request," Mr. Laxworthy declared, "that you were not given too light a sentence, because you were terrified of the afterwards. The afterwards has come!"

Proudson was breathing heavily.

"But why," he muttered, pointing to the figure in the chair, "why didn't he tell us?"

"He never knew," Mr. Laxworthy replied. "He never knew that Wardley was the informer. He never had any idea where the money was. He has made his own living in New York. Better undo him, I think."

Greenlaw stood guard over Wardley whilst Proudson removed the gag from the mouth of the man in the chair and loosened his bonds. He was in a state of collapse. Mr. Laxworthy held a brandy flask to his lips.

"Come, be a man," he said, "and I'll take you back to your daughter."

"I'm all right," Colshaw declared, struggling to his feet. "They wouldn't believe me, though—they wouldn't believe me!" he sobbed. "I've been straight all the time. I knew nothing about the money. I never had a penny of it. I made a business and a living in New York. I came back directly I heard that Proudson wanted to see me."

They both took him by the hand.

"I am sorry," Proudson murmured, in a broken voice.

"And I," Greenlaw echoed. "Thank God you took this on, Mr. Laxworthy! Take him away, sir. I'll pass you to our bully outside."

Mr. Laxworthy nodded, and they moved towards the door. Wardley tried to steal to his feet, but Proudson, with a snarl, was upon him.

"We won't ask you how you found these things out, Mr. Laxworthy," he said. "It isn't our business."

"I was at the trial from the beginning to the end," Mr. Laxworthy told them. "I didn't need to look at you three for ten minutes to know who the informer was. All the same," he added, with a slight smile, "if you'd asked me for proofs, I hadn't any. I simply knew."

"The whole thing's a lie!" Wardley cried, struggling to his feet. "It's an invention—a pack of lies!"

Mr. Laxworthy smiled.

"Ten minutes ago," he remarked, "that might have saved you."

Paula sprang from the couch as they passed through the sitting-room. Her eyes were red with tears. She looked at the two men in amazement.

"They have let him go?" she almost shrieked.

"An affair of a substitute," Mr. Laxworthy explained, with a little wave of the hand. "Come and lunch with me one day and I'll tell you all about it."

Mr. Laxworthy found the young lady of whom he was in search sitting with Sydney in one of the public rooms. She sprang to her feet when she saw him coming. Mr. Laxworthy's manner seemed as quiet and self-contained as usual, but the girl was inspired.

"You have found him!" she sobbed.

Mr. Laxworthy handed her the key of her room.

"You will find him up there," he said. "You'd better order a little dinner for him. He's all right, but he will need looking after for a short time."

She was gone before he could finish his sentence. Sydney looked at his chief admiringly.

"Mr. Laxworthy," he declared, "I've got to thank you, too. I don't care whether he's a thief or whatever in the world he is. You've found my future father-in-law."

Mr. Laxworthy nodded approvingly.

"Miss Thorndyke is a remarkably attractive young lady," he said. "I dined early, and I have been amused. We will take a light supper in the grill-room."

CHAPTER XII
Mr. Laxworthy, Debt Collector

Mr. Laxworthy came to a standstill in the centre of the narrow pavement. Although he was certainly not a man given to casual gallantries, it was obvious that he was engaged in watching a young woman now disappearing through the swing doors of a small restaurant on the opposite side of the street. As soon as she had finally passed out of view, he turned and followed her.

The neighbourhood was an unsavoury one, and the restaurant one of the smallest and meanest of its class. The muslin blinds behind the glass door, which Mr. Laxworthy pushed open, were soiled and torn. The restaurant itself was ill-ventilated, dirty, and noisy. The young woman was sitting at a table by herself, holding the menu in front of her face. The tablecloth spread before her was coarse, torn in places, and looked as though it had already done service for many meals. A fork with one of its prongs missing, a knife with a horn handle, a thick tumbler and a battered mustard-pot were its sole ornaments. Mr. Laxworthy, whose presence the young woman was attempting to ignore, tapped with his finger upon the menu.

"Come, come, young lady!" he exclaimed, a little testily. "I have seen quite enough of the back of that soiled bill of fare. In any case, it is of no interest to either you or me, because we are going to lunch elsewhere."

Very slowly she lowered it and looked up at him. She was thin, and there was an expression in her eyes which Mr. Laxworthy had seen once or twice before during his life, associated with different people, an expression which he did not like at all. Her clothes were desperately shabby. She seemed thinner about the neck, and the fingers, which still held the bill of fare, were almost emaciated.

"How do you do, Mr. Laxworthy?" she said, with an attempt at her old manner. "I am sorry that I did not recognise you at once."

"Rubbish!" Mr. Laxworthy replied irritably. "You not only recognised me but you tried to avoid me. You ought to know by now that I am not a man to be avoided. Put on your gloves again, please, and come with me. We are going to lunch somewhere where the odour of other people's meals is not quite so insistent. Waiter," he continued, addressing a miserable specimen of his class who had just shambled up, "I am depriving you of a customer. Here is recompense. Now open the door for us."

The man almost grabbed at the half-crown which Mr. Laxworthy tendered him, and with the coin safely bestowed in his waistcoat pocket, he opened the door with a joyful flourish.

"Many thanks, sare!" he exclaimed. "Good-day, sare! Good-day, madame!"

The girl followed her companion meekly enough out on to the pavement, but when he called a taxicab she protested.

"I cannot go anywhere to lunch with you!" she declared. "It is not possible. I am not prepared."

Mr. Laxworthy was either in a very bad humour or else he had come to the conclusion that kindness was not the weapon by which he could most easily attain his ends. His manner, in fact, was almost gruff.

"Get in and don't be foolish," he ordered. "I can assure you that I have no idea of going to the Ritz or the Carlton. Look at my own muddy boots and shabby hat. I've been tramping about Soho myself for two hours."

For the first time she smiled very faintly.

"What have you been doing here?" she asked.

Mr. Laxworthy almost pushed her into the vehicle, gave an order to the driver and seated himself beside her.

"Looking for adventures," he answered tartly. "I don't believe there is such a thing left in London. I have spent," he proceeded, with an air of one relieving himself of a grievance, "a most unsatisfactory and unpleasant two months. My young friend Wing has got married. I don't know whether you remember my other friend, Mr. Forrest Anderson, but his brother has left him four hundred a year, and he's gone round the world on a Lunn's tour. I have been to Dinard, Ostend, and Cromer, and found each one duller than the other. Not a thing to do; not a thing to occupy a man of my peculiar tastes. I came back to London last week."

"Where are we going now?" she asked a little timidly.

"Young lady," Mr. Laxworthy declared, "if you would get out of that habit of asking questions we should get on better. We are going to Victoria railway station."

"What for?"

"God bless my soul!" Mr. Laxworthy exclaimed. "What do you think we are going there for? Do you imagine I want to take you down to Brighton for the day, or elope with you on to the Continent? We are going there to eat, of course. Best place I know of," Mr. Laxworthy continued, looking out of the window with an air of satisfaction, "to get a wholesome and satisfactory meal, is in the dining-room of a large railway station. Besides, no one will notice my boots."

The girl laughed, faintly, but still it was a laugh.

"You are a man of resources," she murmured. "Your boots, indeed!"

"If I am tactful enough, my dear Miss Garesworthy," Mr. Laxworthy continued, "to ignore the fact that you are not attired with your accustomed elegance, it is at least up to you to try to forget my boots. When it comes to a question of clothes, I miss Sydney. A soft felt hat like the one I am now wearing would have brought tears to his eyes. Here we are. This way, please."

Mr. Laxworthy paid the driver of his taxicab and conducted his companion into the station dining-room, where he ordered, without consulting her in any way, a plain but substantial lunch. He then made a brief visit to the bar, from which he returned, followed by a waiter, upon whose salver reposed two glasses of amber-coloured liquid.

"A wonderful *aperitif*," Mr. Laxworthy explained, "mixed under my personal supervision. Eat a mouthful of roll and drink it down—so!"

Mr. Laxworthy drained his glass and watched carefully while his companion followed suit. Then he selected a particular brand of Burgundy from the wine list which the waiter had produced, and ordered a bottle of it to be served immediately. Somehow or other, he seemed to manage to keep the conversation to trivialities until they were half-way through luncheon. He waited until he saw a little colour in his companion's cheeks, until he noticed that her fingers had ceased to shake or her lips to tremble. Then, without the slightest embarrassment, he began in the most direct way to ask questions.

"You've been having a rough time, haven't you?" he demanded. "Some of the things that have happened to you I suppose you don't care to tell, but I should like to know what became of Wardley?"

For a moment she half-closed her eyes and Mr. Laxworthy was afraid that he had been premature. She raised her glass to her lips, however, and set it down empty. Mr. Laxworthy carefully filled it.

"Do you know anything at all?" she asked him.

"Nothing," he replied. "When I have finished with an adventure, especially one which brings me so near the sphere of influence of my friend Mr. Marlin, I try to forget it as quickly as I can."

"They tortured Wardley," she said slowly. "They treated him like terriers would have done a rat."

"A very infamous scoundrel, Wardley," Mr. Laxworthy declared, sipping his wine.

"Afterwards," she went on, "they shut him up. There are empty rooms there without a single article of furniture. He was in one of these for three days. I used to hear him sobbing and moaning at night. They got the money out of him and I begged them to let him go. Dan would have consented, but Proudson was like a wild animal. He used to take a chair into the room and sit and watch him writhe about and listen to him moan for mercy. When he came out, there was always the same sort of smile upon his lips. I—I couldn't stand it. One night I set Wardley free."

Mr. Laxworthy paused in his lunch. He looked steadfastly across the table at his companion.

"You set Wardley free," he repeated. "What was he to you that you took such a risk?"

"Nothing," she answered, with a low note of passion in her tone, "less than nothing. I hated him. I despised him. I never listened to him for one moment. He would have married me, anywhere, any time. I would have sooner died! But, Mr. Laxworthy," she went on, dropping her voice, "have you ever heard a man in pain sobbing himself to death? Have you ever wakened in the night and heard a low, weird moaning as though a man were being consumed with some awful pain which brought him nearer and nearer every moment to death, so near that already he was peering into the gulf, and the terror of it was in his brain?"

"Don't!" Mr. Laxworthy exclaimed testily. "You'll spoil my luncheon!"

"I set him free," she continued. "He went off like some badly wounded creature, without a word of thanks. He never even stopped, as a dog would have done, to lick my hand. Proudson would have killed me. Dan threw me out on to the streets. He thought that I had done it for Wardley's sake, and bade me go to him. Since then I have mostly starved. I sold my clothes and bought cheaper ones, and I have lived on the difference; it wasn't very much. The few jewels I had were at the flat. I suppose the police have them now."

"What did Wardley do?" Laxworthy asked.

"Gave information at once," she replied. "He informed against Dan, too, for the bank robbery."

"I read the papers every morning," Mr. Laxworthy began. "I don't seem to remember—"

"Nothing has happened yet," she interrupted; "but, in a way it is terrible. Dan is hiding for his life now, and I don't think Proudson means to be taken alive, although there is only this last assault against him. Wardley is half hunter and half hunted. He sits in his house shivering with fear, though he has a police sergeant sleeping in the adjoining room, and burglar alarms on every window. He dare not go to his office, he scarcely dare leave the house."

Mr. Laxworthy smiled.

"Sometimes one is tempted to believe," he remarked, "that justice is one of the natural laws. I have no doubt that Mr. Wardley is having an exceedingly uncomfortable time. By the by, have you communicated with him at all?"

"I have written to him," she replied. "I have some money which I entrusted to him to invest. It was very little, but still it would have made all the difference to me now. He took no notice of my letter. Then I went to his house. He declined to see me."

"A person," Mr. Laxworthy declared, "of most unpleasant and ungrateful disposition."

She shivered a little.

"I hope I may never see his face again," she murmured.

Mr. Laxworthy ordered some coffee.

"I have enjoyed our talk immensely," he said. "It has also interested me very much to hear your story. How much did you say you had entrusted Mr. Wardley with?"

"The amount was one hundred pounds," she replied.

Mr. Laxworthy opened his pocket-book.

"I will buy that debt from you," he decided, counting out some notes. "It will afford me much satisfaction to collect it."

Her face suddenly lit up, but almost immediately clouded over again.

"You would never be able to get it," she said. "I daren't take the money."

"On the contrary," Mr. Laxworthy retorted, "I am very sure indeed that I shall get that money. If you had had claims upon Mr. Wardley of a more tangible character, it would have given me great pleasure to have increased the amount very considerably. On the whole, however, I am pleased to hear the truth as to your relations with him. Permit me."

He pushed the notes across to her. She looked at them, half frightened.

"A hundred pounds," Mr. Laxworthy continued, leaning back in his chair and pressing the tips of his fingers together, "is not a large sum. There are times, as I know, when it appears inexhaustible. As a matter of fact, a hundred pounds will not last you very long. I understand, of course, the peculiar difficulties connected with any claim you might make for your wardrobe, and I think you are quite wise to keep away from those flats altogether. You will have to start, therefore, by buying yourself a complete outfit. I shall require," he proceeded thoughtfully, "one smart tailor gown, at least two evening dresses, and for indoor work you will need several of those blouse sort of arrangements and neat skirts."

"What indoor work?" she gasped. "What are you talking about?"

"Did I forget to mention," Mr. Laxworthy asked, "that you are going to be my secretary? I am sorry."

"You are laughing at me!" she declared.

"Nothing of the sort," Mr. Laxworthy assured her. "For a man of my resources, I must admit that I have been feeling, during the last two months, exceedingly bored. I need a companion."

"But you haven't any work to be done," she protested.

"That is precisely why I need a secretary," Mr. Laxworthy pointed out. "If I have a secretary, I must get some work. If I have a secretary, there is always the necessity of keeping her employed before me. Therefore, I must do something. I must confess that I wonder the idea did not occur to me before. It is a positive inspiration."

She began to laugh softly to herself.

"Perhaps," she said, "the most amusing part of it all is that I should make a very excellent secretary. I started life in a typewriting office."

"I felt it," Mr. Laxworthy murmured. "I felt, somehow, that you were capable. I propose that the rest of the afternoon you devote to procuring your outfit, bearing in mind the fact that the only colours I have a weakness for in evening clothes are a sort of flame colour, for one, and a deep violet-blue for the other; both colours, I should imagine," he added critically, "likely to suit your complexion. If you find that the hundred pounds of your own is insufficient, I will advance a portion of your salary."

"How much am I going to get, please, and how many hours a day do I work?" she asked.

"I shall pay you," Mr. Laxworthy replied, "as much as you are worthy. You must leave the amount to me for a week or two. As regards the rest, you will have to work just as long and as much and as often as I choose. There is nothing regular about my life or my habits, except as regards my meals and my exercise. Do you understand?"

"I understand," she replied meekly.

"So far as this afternoon is concerned," Mr. Laxworthy went on, "I will collect that hundred pounds from Mr. Wardley, if you will be so good as to give me his address."

For a moment she smiled.

"I almost believe," she said, "that you will get it. He lives in rooms at number 10 John Street, Adelphi. It is really a house, but the bottom part is divided into offices."

"At six o'clock precisely," Mr. Laxworthy directed, as he paid the bill and carefully arranged his muffler and overcoat, "you will arrive at the Milan Court. The hall porter will show you the sitting-room in which you will work, and your own apartment. If you should see nothing of me, you may take it for granted that I shall require you to dine with me this evening, and make the necessary preparations. My favourite hour is eight o'clock. You will probably find me in the sitting-room at that time. Is everything quite clear to you?"

For a single moment her lips began to tremble again. Mr. Laxworthy, however, frowned at her so fiercely that she choked back the little sob which had come into her throat.

"I shall be there," she promised him.

Outside they parted with the briefest of farewells. Mr. Laxworthy took a taxicab to Scotland Yard and had a short conversation with Mr. Marlin, from whom he procured a note. He then drove to number 10 John Street, Adelphi, ascended one flight of stairs, and rang the bell of a door upon which a small brass plate was emblazoned with the name of *Mr. Richard Wardley.* The door was opened, after a short delay, by a tall man in plain clothes and unmistakable build.

"Police Sergeant Choppin, I am sure?" Mr. Laxworthy remarked suavely, handing him the note. "This is from Mr. Marlin at Scotland Yard, and is to ensure my getting an interview with Mr. Wardley."

The man took it a little doubtfully.

"If it is from Mr. Marlin, sir," he said, "of course that's different, but Mr. Wardley is unwell, and not seeing anyone at present. You won't mind if I ask you to wait outside, sir?"

"Not at all," Mr. Laxworthy assented, "so long as you don't ask me to wait long."

Mr. Laxworthy waited upon the landing. It was at least five minutes before the door was reopened, and the sergeant motioned him to come in.

"Mr. Wardley is exceedingly upset at the thought of seeing you, sir," he announced. "However, I gave him Mr. Marlin's message, and he couldn't very well do no other. Will you come this way?"

The whole atmosphere of the place was hateful to Mr. Laxworthy. There were nude statues on the hall table, pictures of actresses and music-hall artistes upon the walls, an odour of cheap incense everywhere. The room into which he was presently ushered was even worse. The atmosphere was as heavy as though no window had been opened for a week, heavy of musk and patchouli and other sedentary perfumes. There was scarcely a print or a photograph upon the walls which was not indecent. Richard Wardley, fatter than ever, whiter than ever, more repulsive than ever, lay half-dressed upon a sofa, surrounded by French comic papers and English sporting weeklies. He watched Mr. Laxworthy, as he entered the room, with the eyes of a frightened animal.

"Don't go away, Choppin," he ordered. "What do you want with me?"

Mr. Laxworthy looked around him and at once removed his muffler and his overcoat, which he placed on Police Sergeant Choppin's arm. He then walked to the farther end of the apartment.

"What are you going to do?" Wardley demanded nervously.

"Open a window," Mr. Laxworthy replied tersely. "I wouldn't stay for two minutes in such a beastly atmosphere."

"No one asked you to!" Wardley growled.

"Well, you don't suppose I came for pleasure," his visitor went on, retracing his steps. "Now do you really want this excellent police sergeant to hear what I have to say to you?"

Wardley hesitated. Mr. Laxworthy winked at Police Sergeant Choppin, who slowly withdrew. This unusual visitor swept a chair clear of its encumbrances of periodicals, and seated himself.

"Got your cheque-book handy?" he asked.

Mr. Laxworthy had certainly found means to galvanise the indolent body of Richard Wardley into some show of animation. The latter sat up on the couch and banged the cushion.

"My cheque-book?" he almost shrieked. "What do you mean? You, too? Don't you know how they bled me—those two devils into whose hands you threw me? Thousands they robbed me of! They made me sell bonds, pay in the proceeds, draw cheques, till my brain swam. I tell you I'm ruined! I've no more money! I've no more money. Do you hear? What do you come for at all, you miserable—you—"

The man seemed suddenly to lose his voice. There was something about his visitor's still contemplation of him which seemed to draw that faint spark of courage from his heart.

"Mine," Mr. Laxworthy said, "is a very harmless errand. I want only the hundred pounds which Miss Garesworthy entrusted to you."

"Let her get it from her brother, then," Wardley answered, sullenly. "He's had all my money—he and the brute Proudson."

"On the contrary," Mr. Laxworthy objected, "it seems to me that it was a part of their own money which they were getting back, and not all of that. Do you give me that hundred pounds?"

"No!" the man snarled.

"I am the inventor," Mr. Laxworthy continued patiently, "of a new scheme of compound interest. I will not explain its workings to you—in your present state you would scarcely be able to follow it—but since that last 'no' of yours, the hundred pounds has become two hundred. Now then, do I get that two hundred pounds or not?"

The man on the couch opened his mouth and closed it again.

"I'll give you the hundred pounds to get rid of you," he muttered. "It is only a hundred pounds which she gave me."

"Pity you're a few seconds too late," Mr. Laxworthy remarked. "Two hundred pounds, if you please. You have ten seconds, or thereabouts, before it becomes three."

"I'll pay!" Wardley cried. "Oh, I'll pay!"

He staggered up to his feet and crossed the room—an untidy, miserable-looking object. He sat down at his desk, drew out a cheque-book from a drawer which he unlocked, and wrote out a cheque with trembling fingers. Mr. Laxworthy received it and studied it carefully.

"Quite correct," he said pleasantly, "two hundred pounds. You see, I trust you implicitly, Mr. Wardley. I have no anxiety whatever. I do not ask you to send for the money. I content myself with knowing that if anything should happen to this cheque, the amount will be four hundred."

"The cheque's all right," Wardley declared savagely. "Now you've got it, what else do you want?"

"I want nothing," Mr. Laxworthy assured him. "I am going, in fact, to relieve you at once of my presence. To tell you the truth, although my errand to you has been successful, as I knew it would be, I have not enjoyed my visit in the least. I think you are one of the most objectionable people whom I have ever met in my life; I loathe the atmosphere of your rooms, and I have not the patience to talk with a man who is such a coward that he has to skulk behind the shoulder of a police sergeant because he has enemies. I hope, Mr. Wardley, that we shall not meet again," Mr. Laxworthy added, with his hand upon the door, "unless at any time I have the pleasure of seeing you in the clearer atmosphere and more bracing surroundings of the Old Bailey."

Mr. Laxworthy received his coat and muffler from Police Sergeant Choppin, whom, as was his custom, he tipped lavishly.

"I do not envy you your office, sergeant," he remarked.

"Rottenest job I ever had, sir," the man replied. "All the same," he added with a grin, "it isn't exactly a sinecure. I'm no sort of a detective myself, but I'm pretty certain this house is watched night and day."

Mr. Laxworthy called at the bank and cashed his cheque. Afterwards he spent a few hours at his club, where he played auction bridge with much skill and some pecuniary benefit. Afterwards, following his accustomed routine, he returned to the Milan Court, took a bath and dressed for dinner. At eight o'clock precisely he entered his sitting-room. Miss Garesworthy, in a remarkably pretty evening dress of a deep shade of blue, was sitting before the table making some adjustments to a typewriter.

"Is the colour all right?" she asked, as he entered.

"Exactly the shade," Mr. Laxworthy assented.

"I spent lots of money," she went on, "and I have bought a typewriter."

"I have seen Richard Wardley and collected a little interest," Mr. Laxworthy announced grimly.

He handed her the further hundred pounds. She shook her head.

"Take it, my dear young lady, I beg," Mr. Laxworthy insisted. "To tell you the truth, I am proud of that hundred pounds. So far as I can remember, it is the first money I ever really stole. If you are quite ready, suppose we dine? It is nearly two minutes past eight, and I am accustomed to regularity with my meals."

At nine o'clock that evening, Richard Wardley was discovered lying in a corner of his room with a bullet wound through his heart. Mr. Laxworthy received the news by telephone from Scotland Yard, together with an intimation that, as the last person who had seen the deceased alive, with the exception of the police sergeant who watched over him, he would probably be called as a witness at the inquest. Later in the evening, however,

Proudson was admitted to a London hospital with only a few hours to live, and cheerfully signed a confession of the crime.

"I killed Richard Wardley," he wrote, "because he was one of the basest and lowest creatures who ever crawled upon the face of the earth—an informer, a thief, a bestial creature, living without regard to decency or morals. Knowing myself to be dying, I feel that I leave this world the easier for having rid it of such a person, and while I confess myself guilty of having forced my way into his rooms to-night and shot him through the heart, I neither repent nor regret the act. Before I lay down this pen for the last time, I wish to add that the London and South Westminster Bank robbery was Wardley's affair and Colshaw's and mine only. There was no other person concerned in it, and Wardley's statements to the contrary are lies.

"Signed by JOHN PROUDSON."

Mr. Laxworthy sat for long over his breakfast the following morning, reading this confession and a fuller account of the crime. Every now and then he glanced at his watch. At exactly ten o'clock Miss Garesworthy arrived.

"Am I too soon?" she asked, drawing off her gloves and looking at his breakfast tray.

"Not at all," he replied. "Ten o'clock was the hour. Have you been out already?"

She nodded.

"I went out to buy all the papers. I wanted to read the news. I wanted to know if anything had been mentioned about Dan."

"This fellow Proudson tried to do him a good turn, anyhow," Mr. Laxworthy remarked.

"They will never find Dan," she declared confidently. "There is no one in the world has such gifts as he."

Mr. Laxworthy poured himself out a little more coffee.

"I don't see any use in having a secretary," he grumbled, "who can't come here in time to make your coffee."

"You told me ten o'clock," she reminded him.

"Then make it half-past nine to-morrow morning," he replied, "and take your coffee with me. I suppose you have breakfasted, by the by?"

"Long ago," she assured him. "What about our morning's work?"

Mr. Laxworthy took off his spectacles and rubbed them industriously.

"Ah!" he repeated, "our morning's work!"

"It would be a good plan, I imagine, to start with answering your letters," she suggested briskly.

Mr. Laxworthy glanced down upon the table. The only communication which he had received that morning was an invitation to patronise a new Strand tailor!

"To tell you the truth," he confessed slowly, "I don't seem to be getting much correspondence just now."

"Then what is there for me to do?" she demanded.

Mr. Laxworthy sighed.

"There is no help for it," he said. "You must marry me."

She looked at him, with her notebook in one hand and her pencil in the other.

"Don't be absurd!" she murmured.

"There is nothing absurd about it at all," Mr. Laxworthy retorted brusquely. "I required your services as a companion—I preferred to put it as a secretary. I haven't any work for you. The only thing I can see to do is to marry you. Then, I suppose, you won't want to do any."

Her eyes filled with laughter.

"Really," she said, "I had no idea this was coming. I hadn't contemplated anything of the sort—and yet, it is terribly difficult to refuse so ardent a suitor!"

"Is that a hint?" Mr. Laxworthy asked.

She looked at him from across the table.

"It has just occurred to me that you might take it in that way," she admitted.

Mr. Laxworthy held out his hands.

"At my time of life, too!" he sighed. "Never mind, I ought to find you useful."

"I shouldn't be surprised," she whispered. "You know I, too, am rather fond of adventures."

Mr. Laxworthy pushed the table on one side.

"We'll start one of our own, Paula," he declared.

THE END

A Collector's Bibliography

Daniel Paul Morrison

A COLLECTOR'S BIBLIOGRAPHY OF OPPENHEIM BOOKS

This collector's bibliography expands and corrects the bibliography I first published in the 2004 Stark House Press edition of *Secrets & Sovereigns: The Uncollected Story of E. Phillips Oppenheim*. My thanks to the Oppenheim collectors who wrote to provided helpful bibliographic tidbits.

Compiling a complete bibliography of the works of E. Phillips Oppenheim is a thorny task. To begin with, the sheer number of Oppenheim titles is daunting. In addition, many Oppenheim books were published under different titles in the United States and the United Kingdom. Pirated titles – seven are listed in this bibliography – add further confusion. And then there is the strange problem of phantom titles – titles that were never published but which appear in various catalogs and lists of "Other Works by E. Phillips Oppenheim" printed inside a few of his books. A final difficulty stems from the fact that Oppenheim's career spanned so many years – from the appearance of *Expiation* in 1887 until the posthumous publication of *The Oppenheim Secret Service Omnibus Number One* in 1946. During that period, cataloging standards changed, making certain information available in some years, but not in others.

I believe this bibliography is unique among all that have been published thus far in that it is not primarily a compilation of data collected from catalogs and indexes – a standard method of creating bibliographies. Because there are errors and omissions in even the best catalogs and indexes, a bibliography based primarily on these sources must repeat those errors. In contrast, the foundation of this bibliography is data gleaned from my 400+ volume collection of Oppenheims as well as the 100+ volume collection of Oppenheims at the Firestone Library of Princeton University. Every piece of information gathered from those Oppenheim volumes has been compared with information contained in six important catalogs: *The English Catalogue* (EC), *The American Catalog* (AC), the *Cumulative Book Index* (CBI), the *National Union Catalog, Pre-1956 Imprints* (NUC), the *British Museum General Catalogue of Printed Books* (BM), and the Online Computer Library Center's WorldCat (OCLC). The EC, AC and CBI are compiled from information provided to the catalog editors by publishers regarding books they have published. The massive 754-volume NUC is a compilation of the entire card catalog of the Library of Congress along with catalogs of a number of other American libraries. The British Museum is the UK equivalent of the Library of Congress, and thus the BM is similar to the NUC. The OCLC is a union catalog of more than 52 million items at more than 9,000 libraries world-wide. It is the 21st century digital online version of the NUC.

In cases of a conflict between the catalogs and the first editions, this bibliography follows the first editions, recording any differences in the footnotes. For example, *The American Catalog* lists a November 1909 Little Brown publication date of *Jeanne of the Marshes*, while the first edition bears the date October 1909; this bibliography uses the October 1909 date.

Ellen Wellman and Wray D. Brown (WB) provided important information in their article "Collecting E. Phillips Oppenheim" which appeared in the Summer 1983 issue of *The Private Library*. In compiling this bibliography, I have also consulted the useful list published in Lesley Henderson's *Twentieth Century Crime and Mystery Writers* (CMW).

I use the abbreviation LB to refer to the list of titles published in the back pages of the Little Brown edition of *The Man Who Changed His Plea*. The LB list indicates the year of the first publication of a work in book form.

Novels and Story Collections

Expiation: a Novel of England and our Canadian Dominion. London, J. & R. Maxwell, 1887.

A Monk of Cruta. London, Ward Lock, Dec. 1894; New York, Neely, 1894; as *The Tragedy of Andrea,* New York, J. S. Ogilvie, Sept. 1906.[1]

The Peer and the Woman. London, Ward Lock, May 1895; New York, J. A. Taylor, 1892.[2]

A Daughter of the Marionis. London, Ward and Downey, Sept. 1895; Boston, Little Brown, Sept. 1910; as *To Win the Love He Sought,* New York, D. W. Newton, 1910.[3]

A Modern Prometheus. London, Unwin, Feb. 1896; New York, Neely, 1897.[4]

The World's Great Snare. London, Ward and Downey, 1896; Philadelphia, Lippincott, 1896.[5]

The Mystery of Mr. Bernard Brown. London, Bentley, March 1896; Boston, Little Brown, Sept. 1910; as *The New Tenant,* New York, D. W. Newton, 1910;[3] as *His Father's Crime,* New York, Street and Smith, April 1929.[6]

The Wooing of Fortune. London, Ward and Downey, July 1896.[7]

False Evidence. London, Ward Lock, Dec. 1896; New York, Ward Lock, 1897.

The Postmaster of Market Deighton. London, George Routledge, Sept. 1897.

The Amazing Judgment. London, Downey, Nov. 1897.[8]

A Daughter of Astrea. Bristol, Arrowsmith, Feb. 1898; New York, D. W. Newton, 1910(?).[9]

As a Man Lives. London, Ward Lock, May 1898; Boston, Little Brown, Dec. 1908; as *The Yellow House*, New York, C. H. Doscher, Dec. 1908.[3]

Mysterious Mr. Sabin. London, Ward Lock, Oct. 1898; Boston, Little Brown, Feb. 1905.

Mr. Marx's Secret. London, Simpkin Marshall, April 1899; Boston, Little Brown, Jan. 1916.[10]

The Man and His Kingdom. London, Ward Lock, April 1899; Philadelphia, Lippincott, 1900.[11]

A Millionaire of Yesterday. London, Ward Lock, July 1900; Philadelphia, Lippincott, July 1900.[12]

The Survivor. London, Ward Lock, Feb. 1901; New York, Brentano's, Dec. 1901.

A Master of Men. London, Methuen, Sept. 1901; as *Enoch Strone*, New York, Dillingham, March 1902.

The Great Awakening. London, Ward Lock, June 1902; as *A Sleeping Memory*, New York, Dillingham, Oct. 1902.[13]

The Traitors. London, Ward Lock, Oct. 1902; New York, Dodd Mead, March 1903.

A Prince of Sinners. London, Ward Lock, March 1903; Boston, Little Brown, May 1903.[14]

The Yellow Crayon. New York, Dodd Mead, Sept. 1903; London, Ward Lock, Oct. 1903.

Anna the Adventuress. London, Ward Lock, March 1904; Boston, Little Brown, May 1904.

The Betrayal. New York, Dodd Mead, Oct. 1904; London, Ward Lock, Aug. 1907.[15]

The Master Mummer. London, Ward Lock, April 1905; Boston, Little Brown, May 1905.

A Maker of History. London, Ward Lock, Oct. 1905; Boston, Little Brown, Jan. 1906.

Mr. Wingrave, Millionaire. London, Ward Lock, March 1906; as *The Malefactor*, Boston, Little Brown, Jan. 1907.

A Lost Leader. London, Ward Lock, Sept. 1906; Boston, Little Brown, Aug. 1907.

The Secret. London, Ward Lock, March 1907; as *The Great Secret*, Boston, Little Brown, Jan. 1908.[16]

The Conspirators. London, Ward Lock Sept. 1907; as *The Avenger,* Boston, Little Brown, May 1908.

The Missioner. London, Ward Lock, April 1908; Boston, Little Brown, Jan. 1909.

The Governors. London, Ward Lock, Sept. 1908; Boston, Little Brown, June 1909.

The Ghosts of Society. (Anthony Partridge) London, Hodder and Stoughton, Sept. 1908; as *The Distributors,* New York, McClure, Nov. 1908.

The Long Arm of Mannister.[†] Boston, Little Brown, Oct. 1908; as *The Long Arm,* London, Ward Lock, Jan. 1909.

Jeanne of the Marshes. London, Ward Lock, May 1909; Boston, Little Brown, Oct. 1909.[17]

The Kingdom of Earth. (Anthony Partridge) Boston, Little Brown, May 1909; London, Mills and Boon, Aug. 1909; as *The Black Watcher,* as E. Phillips Oppenheim, London, Hodder and Stoughton, Sept. 1912.

Passers-By. (Anthony Partridge) Boston, Little Brown, Jan. 1910; London, Ward Lock, Feb. 1911; as E. Phillips Oppenheim, London, Lloyd's, March 1918.

The Illustrious Prince. London, Hodder and Stoughton, April 1910; Boston, Little Brown, May 1910.

The Missing Delora. London, Methuen, Sept. 1910; as *The Lost Ambassador, or, the Search for the Missing Delora,* Boston, Little Brown, Sept. 1910.[18]

Berenice. London, Ward Lock, 1910; Boston, Little Brown, Jan. 1911.[19]

The Golden Web (Anthony Partridge) Boston, Little Brown, Jan. 1911; as E. Phillips Oppenheim, London, Lloyd's, Nov. 1918; as *The Plunderers,* as E. Phillips Oppenheim, London, Hodder and Stoughton, March 1912.

The Falling Star. London, Hodder and Stoughton, Feb. 1911; as *The Moving Finger,* Boston, Little Brown, May 1911.

Havoc. Boston, Little Brown, Oct. 1911; London, Hodder and Stoughton, Jan. 1912.

The Double Four.[†] London, Cassell, 1911; combined with *Peter Ruff* and published in US as *Peter Ruff and the Double Four,* Boston, Little Brown, Jan. 1912.[20]

For the Queen.[†] London, Ward Lock, Feb. 1912; Boston, Little Brown, June 1913.

Peter Ruff.[†] London, Hodder and Stoughton, April 1912; as *The Adventures of Peter Ruff*, London, Hodder and Stoughton, Aug. 1916; combined with *The Double Four* and published in US as *Peter Ruff and the Double Four*, Boston, Little Brown, Jan. 1912.

Those Other Days.[†] London, Ward Lock, July 1912; Boston, Little Brown, June 1913.

The Court of St. Simon. (Anthony Partridge) Boston, Little Brown, Aug. 1912; as *Seeing Life*, as E. Phillips Oppenheim, London, Lloyds, 1919.[21]

The Lighted Way. Boston, Little Brown, May 1912; London, Hodder and Stoughton, Sept. 1912.

The Tempting of Tavernake. Boston, Little Brown, Oct. 1912; as *The Temptation of Tavernake*, London, Hodder and Stoughton, April 1913.

The Mischief-Maker. Boston, Little Brown, March 1913; London, Hodder and Stoughton, Aug. 1913.

Mr. Laxworthy's Adventures.[†] London, Cassell, May 1913.

The Double Life of Mr. Alfred Burton. Boston, Little Brown, Aug. 1913; London, Methuen, Sept. 1914.[22]

A People's Man. Boston, Little Brown, Jan. 1914; London, Methuen, Jan. 1915.

The Way of These Women. London, Methuen, Feb. 1914; Boston, Little Brown, Sept. 1915.

The Amazing Partnership.[†] London, Cassell, Feb. 1914.[23]

The Vanished Messenger. Boston, Little Brown, Aug. 1914; London, Methuen, Feb. 1916.

Mr. Grex of Monte Carlo. Boston, Little Brown, Jan. 1915; London, Methuen, Sept. 1915.

The Double Traitor. Boston, Little Brown, May 1915; London, Hodder and Stoughton, March 1918.

The Game of Liberty.[†] London, Cassell, June 1915; as *The Amiable Charlatan*, Boston, Little Brown, April 1916.

The Black Box. New York, Grosset and Dunlap, 1915; London, Hodder and Stoughton, Feb. 1917.

Mysteries of the Riviera.[†] London, Cassell, June 1916.

The Kingdom of the Blind. Boston, Little Brown, Oct. 1916; London, Hodder and Stoughton, July 1917.

The Hillman. Boston, Little Brown, Jan. 1917; London, Methuen, Feb. 1917.

The Cinema Murder. Boston, Little Brown, June 1917; as *The Other Romilly*, London, Hodder and Stoughton, July 1918.

The Pawns Count. Boston, Little Brown, March 1918; London, Hodder and Stoughton, Nov. 1918.

The Zeppelin's Passenger. Boston, Little Brown, Sept. 1918; as *Mr. Lessingham Goes Home*, London, Hodder and Stoughton, April 1919.

The Wicked Marquis. London, Hodder and Stoughton, July 1919; Boston, Little Brown, 1919.[24]

The Box with Broken Seals, Boston, Little Brown, Oct. 1919; as *The Strange Case of Mr. Jocelyn Thew*, London, Hodder and Stoughton, Jan. 1920.[25]

The Curious Quest. Boston, Little Brown, 1919; as *The Amazing Quest of Mr. Ernest Bliss*, London, Hodder and Stoughton, Jan. 1924.[26]

The Great Impersonation. Boston, Little Brown, Jan. 1920; London, Hodder and Stoughton, Oct. 1920.

Aaron Rodd, Diviner.[†] London, Hodder and Stoughton, May 1920.[27]

Ambrose Lavendale, Diplomat.[†] London, Hodder and Stoughton, May 1920.

The Honourable Algernon Knox, Detective.[†] London, Hodder and Stoughton, May 1920.

The Devil's Paw. Boston, Little Brown, Sept. 1920; London, Hodder and Stoughton, May 1921.

Jacob's Ladder. Boston, Little Brown, Feb. 1921; London, Hodder and Stoughton, Aug. 1921.

The Profiteers. Boston, Little Brown, June 1921; London, Hodder and Stoughton, Jan. 1922.

Nobody's Man. Boston, Little Brown, Nov. 1921; London, Hodder and Stoughton, Nov. 1922.

The Great Prince Shan. Boston, Little Brown, March 1922; London, Hodder and Stoughton, Aug. 1922.

The Evil Shepherd. Boston, Little Brown, Sept. 1922; London, Hodder and Stoughton, March 1923.

The Seven Conundrums.[†] Boston, Little Brown, Feb. 1923; London, Hodder and Stoughton, Feb. 1924.

The Mystery Road. Boston, Little Brown, May 1923; London, Hodder and Stoughton, Feb. 1924.

The Inevitable Millionaires. London, Hodder and Stoughton, Oct. 1923; Boston, Little Brown, Jan. 1925.

Michael's Evil Deeds.[†] Boston, Little Brown, Nov. 1923; London, Hodder and Stoughton, April 1924.

The Wrath to Come. Boston, Little Brown, April 1924; London, Hodder and Stoughton, April 1925.

The Passionate Quest. London, Hodder and Stoughton, July 1924; Boston, Little Brown, Oct. 1924.

The Terrible Hobby of Sir Joseph Londe, Bart.[†] London, Hodder and Stoughton, Oct. 1924; Boston, Little Brown, Jan. 1927.

Stolen Idols. London, Hodder and Stoughton, July 1925; Boston, Little Brown, May 1925.

The Adventures of Mr. Joseph P. Cray.[†] London, Hodder and Stoughton, Aug. 1925; Boston, Little Brown, 1927.

Gabriel Samara. London, Hodder and Stoughton, Oct. 1925; as *Gabriel Samara, Peacemaker, Boston*, Little Brown, Oct. 1925.

The Golden Beast. Boston, Little Brown, Feb. 1926; London, Hodder and Stoughton, May 1926.

The Little Gentleman from Okehampstead.[†] London, Hodder and Stoughton, Feb. 1926.

Prodigals of Monte Carlo. Boston, Little Brown, June 1926; London, Hodder and Stoughton, Aug. 1926.

Harvey Garrard's Crime. Boston, Little Brown, Oct. 1926; London, Hodder and Stoughton, Feb. 1927.

Madame.[†] London, Hodder and Stoughton, Jan. 1927; as *Madame and Her Twelve Virgins*, Boston, Little Brown, Jan. 1927.

The Channay Syndicate.[†] London, Hodder and Stoughton, Jan. 1927; Boston, Little Brown, Jan. 1927.

Mr. Billingham, the Marquis and Madelon.[†] London, Hodder and Stoughton, March 1927; Boston, Little Brown, May 1929.

Nicholas Goade, Detective.[†] London, Hodder and Stoughton, April 1927; Boston, Little Brown, Nov. 1929.

The Interloper. Boston, Little Brown, April 1927; as *The Ex-Duke,* London, Hodder and Stoughton, Aug. 1927.[28]

Miss Brown of X.Y.O. Boston, Little Brown, Aug. 1927; London, Hodder and Stoughton, Oct. 1927.

The Light Beyond. London, Hodder and Stoughton, Jan. 1928; Boston, Little Brown, Jan. 1928.

The Exploits of Pudgy Pete & Co.[†] London, Hodder and Stoughton, March 1928.

The Fortunate Wayfarer. Boston, Little Brown, May 1928; London, Hodder and Stoughton, Sept. 1928.

Chronicles of Melhampton.[†] London, Hodder and Stoughton, July 1928.

Matorni's Vineyard. Boston, Little Brown, Oct. 1928; London, Hodder and Stoughton, Feb. 1929.

The Treasure House of Martin Hews. Boston, Little Brown, Jan. 1929; London, Hodder and Stoughton, June 1929.

Jennerton & Co.[†] London, Hodder and Stoughton, Jan. 1929.

The Human Chase.[†] London, Hodder and Stoughton, April 1929.

The Glenlitten Murder. Boston, Little Brown, Aug. 1929; London, Hodder and Stoughton, Oct. 1929.

What Happened to Forester.[†] London, Hodder and Stoughton, Dec. 1929; Boston, Little Brown, May 1930.

Blackman's Wood. Story included with Agatha Christie's "The Under Dog" in *Two Thrillers,* London, Readers Library, 1929.

The Million Pound Deposit. Boston, Little Brown, Jan. 1930; London, Hodder and Stoughton, March 1930.

Slane's Long Shots.[†] London, Hodder and Stoughton, July 1930; Boston, Little Brown, Nov. 1930.

The Lion and the Lamb. London, Hodder and Stoughton, Aug. 1930; Boston, Little Brown, Aug. 1930.

Up the Ladder of Gold. London, Hodder and Stoughton, Jan. 1931; Boston, Little Brown, Jan. 1931.

Inspector Dickins Retires.[†] London, Hodder and Stoughton, Feb. 1931; as *Gangsters' Glory,* Boston, Little Brown, Nov. 1931.

Simple Peter Cradd. London, Hodder and Stoughton, July 1931; Boston, Little Brown, July 1931.

Sinners Beware.[†] London, Hodder and Stoughton, Oct. 1931; Boston, Little Brown, April 1932.

Moran Chambers Smiled. London, Hodder and Stoughton, Jan. 1932; as *The Man from Sing Sing,* Boston, Little Brown, Jan. 1932.

The Ostrekoff Jewels. London, Hodder and Stoughton, Aug. 1932; Boston, Little Brown, Oct. 1932.

Crooks in the Sunshine.[†] London, Hodder and Stoughton, Sept. 1932; Boston, Little Brown, 1933.

Murder at Monte Carlo. Boston, Little Brown, Jan. 1933; London, Hodder and Stoughton, June 1933.

Jeremiah and the Princess. London, Hodder and Stoughton, Jan. 1933; Boston, Little Brown, July 1933.

The Ex-Detective[†] London, Hodder and Stoughton, Sept. 1933; Boston, Little Brown, Nov. 1933.

The Gallows of Chance. London, Hodder and Stoughton, Jan. 1934; Boston, Little Brown, Jan. 1934.

The Man Without Nerves. Little Brown, May 1934; as *The Bank Manager*, London, Hodder and Stoughton, June 1934.

The Strange Borders of Palace Crescent. Boston, Little Brown, Sept. 1934; London, Hodder and Stoughton, Jan. 1935.

The Spy Paramount. Boston, Little Brown, Jan. 1935; London, Hodder and Stoughton, July 1935.[29]

General Besserley's Puzzle Box.[†] London, Hodder and Stoughton, May 1935; Boston, Little Brown, May 1935.

The Battle of Basinghall Street. Boston, Little Brown, Sept. 1935; London, Hodder and Stoughton, Nov. 1935.

Advice, Limited.[†] London, Hodder and Stoughton, Sept. 1935; Boston, Little Brown, May 1936.[30]

Floating Peril. Boston, Little Brown, Jan. 1936; as *The Bird of Paradise*, London, Hodder and Stoughton, March 1936.

Ask Miss Mott.[†] London, Hodder and Stoughton, May 1936; Boston, Little Brown, May 1937.

The Magnificent Hoax. Boston, Little Brown, July 1936; as *Judy of Bunter's Buildings*, London, Hodder and Stoughton, Sept, 1936.

The Dumb Gods Speak. Boston, Little Brown, Jan. 1937; London, Hodder and Stoughton, Feb. 1937.

Envoy Extraordinary. London, Hodder and Stoughton, July 1937; Boston, Little Brown, July 1937.

Curious Happenings to the Rooke Legatees.[†] London, Hodder and Stoughton, Oct. 1937; Boston, Little Brown, March 1938.

The Mayor on Horseback. Boston, Little Brown, Nov. 1937.

The Colossus of Arcadia. London, Hodder and Stoughton, Jan. 1938; Boston, Little Brown, June 1938.

A Pulpit in the Grill Room.[†] London, Hodder and Stoughton, June 1938; Boston, Little Brown, March 1939.

The Spymaster. Boston, Little Brown, Nov. 1938; London, Hodder and Stoughton, Jan. 1939.

And Still I Cheat the Gallows.[†] London, Hodder and Stoughton, Nov. 1938.[31]

Sir Adam Disappeared. Boston, Little Brown, May 1939; London, Hodder and Stoughton, Sept. 1939.

General Besserley's Second Puzzle Box.[†] London, Hodder and Stoughton, July 1939; Boston, Little Brown, Feb. 1940.

Exit a Dictator. Boston, Little Brown, Aug. 1939; London, Hodder and Stoughton, Nov. 1939.

The Strangers' Gate. Boston, Little Brown, Nov. 1939; London, Hodder and Stoughton, Feb. 1940.

The Milan Grill Room: Further Adventures of Louis, the Manager, and Major Lyson, the Raconteur.[†] London, Hodder and Stoughton, Jan. 1940; Boston, Little Brown, 1941.

The Grassleyes Mystery. London, Hodder and Stoughton, July 1940; Boston, Little Brown, July 1940.

Last Train Out. Boston, Little Brown, Nov. 1940; London, Hodder Stoughton, Feb. 1941.

The Shy Plutocrat. Boston, Little Brown, July 1941; London, Hodder and Stoughton, Nov. 1941.

The Man Who Changed His Plea. London, Hodder and Stoughton, March 1942; Boston, Little Brown, April 1942.

Mr. Mirakel. London, Hodder and Stoughton, June 1943; Boston, Little Brown, Oct. 1943.

Burglars Must Dine. London, Todd Publishing Co., 1943.[32]

The Great Bear. London, Todd Publishing Co., 1943.[33]

The Man Who Thought He Was a Pauper. London, Todd Publishing Co., 1943.[34]

The Hour of Reckoning and The Mayor of Ballydaghan. London, Todd Publishing Co. 1944.[35]

Plays[36]

The Money-Spider. (produced 1908).

The King's Cup. [co-written with H. Dennis Bradley] London and New York, Samuel French, 1913. (produced 1909).

The Gilded Key. (produced 1910).

The Eclipse. [co-written with Fred Thompson] (produced at Garrick Theatre, London, 1919).

Omnibus Volumes

The Oppenheim Omnibus: Forty-One Stories by E. P. O. London, Hodder and Stoughton, March 1931.

The Oppenheim Omnibus: Clowns and Criminals. Boston, Little Brown, April 1931. Contains: *Michael's Evil Deeds; Peter Ruff and the Double Four; Recalled by the Double Four;* and *Jennerton & Co.*[37]

Shudders and Thrills: The Second Oppenheim Omnibus. Boston, Little Brown, July 1932. Contains: *The Evil Shepherd; Ghosts of Society; The Amazing Partnership; The Channay Syndicate;* and *The Human Chase.*

The Secret Service Omnibus: Five Full Length Novels of International Intrigue. London, Hodder and Stoughton, Sept. 1932. Contains: *Miss Brown of X.Y.O.; The Wrath to Come; Matorni's Vineyard; The Great Impersonation;* and *Gabriel Samara.*

Spies and Intrigues: The Oppenheim Secret Service Omnibus. Boston, Little Brown, Oct. 1936. Contains: *The Wrath to Come; The Great Impersonation; Gabriel Samara, Peacemaker;* and *Mr. Billingham, the Marquis and Madelon.*[38]

The Oppenheim Secret Service Omnibus Number One. Boston, Little Brown, May 1946. Contains: *Mysterious Mr. Sabin; A Maker of History;* and *The Illustrious Prince.*

Autobiographical

My Books and Myself. Boston, Little Brown, 1922.[39]

The Quest for Winter Sunshine. [travel] London, Methuen, Nov. 1926; Boston, Little Brown, Jan. 1927.[40]

E. Phillips Oppenheim: The Prince of Story Tellers Tells His Own Story. Boston, Little Brown, 1927.[41]

The Pool of Memory. London, Hodder and Stoughton, Nov. 1941; Boston, Little Brown, Feb. 1942.[42]

Collection edited by Oppenheim

Many Mysteries. Selected by E. Phillips Oppenheim. London, Rich & Cowan, May 1933.

Collections containing works by Oppenheim*

My Religion, London, Hutchinson, 1925; New York, Appleton, 1926. Contains an untitled essay by Oppenheim regarding his religious beliefs.

What I Think: A Symposium on Books and Other Things by Famous Writers of To-Day, (ed. H. Greenhough Smith). London, George Newnes, 1927. Oppenheim contributes "How I Write My Books."

The World's One Hundred Best Short Stories [in Ten Volumes]: Volume Three: Mystery, (ed. Grant Overton). New York, Funk & Wagnalls, 1927. Contains "The Bamboozling of Mr. Gascoigne" from *Mr. Billingham, the Marquis and Madelon.*

World's Great Detective Stories. New York, Walter J. Black, 1928. Contains "Mr. Vincent Cawdor, Commission Agent" from Peter Ruff and the Double-Four.

Baffling Detective Stories by Masters of Mystery. New York, Walter J. Black, 1928. Contains "Mr. Vincent Cawdor, Commission Agent" from Peter Ruff and the Double-Four. This volume is a reduced version of World's Greatest Detective Stories.

Two New Crime Stories. London, Readers Library, 1929; as Two Thrillers, London, Daily Express Fiction Library, n.d. Contains "Blackman's Wood" along with Agatha Christie's "The Under Dog."

The Best English Detective Stories: First Series, (ed. Father Ronald Knox and H. Harrington). New York, Horace Liveright, 1929. Contains "Blackman's Wood" which first appeared in Two New Crime Stories.

My Best Detective Story. London, Faber and Faber, 1931. Contains "The Thirteenth Card" from Slane's Long Shots.

Best Detective Stories: First Series, (eds. Father Ronald Knox and H. Harrington). London, Faber and Faber, September 1933. Contains "Blackman's Wood" which first appeared in Two New Crime Stories. This volume is a reprint of The Best English Detective Stories: First Series.

A Century of Spy Stories, (ed. Dennis Wheatley). London, Hutchinson, 1935. Contains "The Phantom Fleet" from General Besserly's Puzzle Box.

The Great Book of Thrillers, (ed. H. Douglas Thomson). London, Odhams Press Ltd., 1935. Contains "The Café of Terror" from Mr. Billingham, the Marquis and Madelon.

My Best Thriller: A Collection of Stories Chosen by Their Own Authors. London, Faber and Faber, 1937. Contains "The Table Under the Tree" from Crooks in Sunshine.

Century of Thrillers: Volume I. New York, President Press, 1937. Contains "The Great Bear" from Jennerton & Co.

The Mystery and the Detective: A Collection of Stories (ed. Blanche Colton Williams). New York, Appleton-Century, 1938. Contains "Christian, the Concierge" from Mr. Billingham, the Marquis and Madelon.

The Second Century of Detective Stories, (ed. E. C. Bentley). London, Hutchinson, 1938. Contains "The Thirteenth Card" from Slane's Long Shots.

My Best Adventure Story. London, Faber and Faber, 1939. Contains "Neap-Tide Madness" from Slane's Long Shots.

Beware After Dark! The World's Most Stupendous Tales of Mystery, Horror, Thrills and Terror, (ed. T. Everett Harré). New York, Emerson Books, 1942. Contains "Two Spinsters" from Nicholas Goade, Detective.

Wag's Hand-Book: Three Hundred Jokes (by E. R. Skeels). London, Werner Laurie, 1942. Oppenheim contributes the introduction.

Three Famous Spy Novels, (ed. Bennett A. Cerf). New York, Random House, 1942. Contains The Great Impersonation.

World's Greatest Detective Stories, The, (ed. Howard Spring). London, Daily Express Publications, 1934. Contains "Seven Boxes of Gold" from Michael's Evil Deeds.

The Avon Book of Modern Short Stories. Toronto, New Avon Library, 1943. Contains "The Gambler's Road," a story which never appeared in an Oppenheim volume.

World's Great Spy Stories, (ed. Vincent Starrett). Cleveland, World Publishing Company, September 1944. Contains "The Little Lady from Servia" from Peter Ruff and the Double-Four.

Biographical and critical works

Overton, Grant. Cargoes for Crusoes. Boston, Little Brown, September 1924. Contains a chapter-length literary and biographical appreciation of Oppenheim.

One Hundred Years of Publishing: 1837-1937. Boston, Little Brown, February 1937. This history of the Little, Brown and Company publishers contains a portrait of Oppenheim and a discussion of his relationship with the publishing house.

Standish, Robert. *The Prince of Storytellers: The Life of E. Phillips Oppenheim.* London, Peter Davies, 1957. This is the only book-length biography of Oppenheim.

Phantom Titles[43]

A Woman's Blindness

The Lesser Sin

The Vindicator

† Short story collection

* I have included only those volumes published during Oppenheim's life.

1 First UK edition of *A Monk of Cruta* was a *Beeton's Christmas Annual*. Many catalogs indicated that *The Tragedy of Andrea* as an alternate title of *A Monk of Cruta*. LB, however, lists it as an entirely separate book. I have not seen a copy of *The Tragedy of Andrea* so I cannot confirm either claim.

2 Taylor edition a paperback and is No. 4 of the Mayflower Library series. It bears a 1892 copyright date but no publication date given. LB indicates that first publication of *The Peer and the Woman* is 1895.

3 *The Yellow House, The New Tenant,* and *To Win the Love He Sought* are three pirate titles first published by C. H. Doscher & Co. AC lists Dec. 5, 1908 Doscher publication of *The Yellow House*. Doscher editions of *The New Tenant* and *To Win the Love He Sought* do not appear in AC or CBI, however Donald W. Newton editions of *The New Tenant* and *To Win the Love He Sought* list a 1910 Doscher copyright date. The Newton editions also do not appear in AC or CBI. Subsequently, P. F. Collier & Sons, New York, published a three-volume set containing: vol. 1) *The Yellow House* and abridged version of *Master of Men*; vol. 2) *The New Tenant* and abridged version of *A Daughter of Astrea*; and vol. 3) *To Win the Love He Lost* and abridged version of *The Great Awakening*. CBI lists a Feb. 1915 publication for the three-volume set. This set has gone through at least three separate editions.

4 Neely edition not listed in AC; Neely edition has 1897 copyright date, but no publication information.

5 AC lists Lippincott edition; EC does not list 1896 Ward and Downey edition, it appears, however, in Yale University Library catalog. LB lists 1900 as the date of publication.

6 Published by Street and Smith as No. 112 in The Adventure Library series.

7 WB notes: "In 1896 the first rare title was presumably published, since it is listed in the English Catalogue of Books for 1890-1897 as *Wooing of Fortune*, 8vo, 304 pp. 8s., Ward and Downey. Some of the *aficionados* do not think that it was ever published but probably rewritten and published under another title. Mr. Nicholas Davies, the English publisher, recently deceased, was the foremost Oppenheim collector and had never heard of a copy."

8 According to WB, "the King or Queen of hard-to-find Oppenheims is *Amazing Judgment* (Downey & Co., 1897). There is a copy in the British Museum and a copy appears for sale about every ten years."

9 AC does not list 1910 Newton edition; it does appear in NUC.

10 CMW lists 1899 Street and Smith edition, but there is no such listing

in AC, OCLC or NUC. CBI lists US first as 1916 Little Brown.

[11] Little Brown edition lists first as March 1906.

[12] CMW lists 1899 publication date for Lippincott edition; AC lists 1900 Lippincott publication date with 1899 copyright date.

[13] Dillingham edition lists Oct. 1902 publication date, while AC lists Nov. 1902.

[14] Little Brown edition lists May 1903 publication date, while AC lists June 1903.

[15] First EC listing is Ward Lock, August 1907; BM lists Ward Lock, 1904, likely a reference to copyright date rather than publication date. AC lists Dodd, October 1, 1904.

[16] LB lists 1908 date of first publication of *The Secret*. AC, however, indicates first publication was by Ward Lock in March 1907.

[17] Little Brown edition lists Oct. 1909 publication date, while AC lists Nov. 1909.

[18] Little Brown edition lists Sept. 1910 publication date, while AC lists Oct. 1910.

[19] CMW lists 1907 Little Brown edition. Little Brown first edition is Jan. 1911, copyright date is 1907. First listing in EC is Sept. 1911 for a cheap edition, however the Ward Lock first edition bears the date 1910, with no month indicated. Additionally, LB lists first as 1907.

[20] CMW lists 1911 Cassell edition. Earliest EC listing is July 1913 for a popular edition, however there are multiple OCLC listings for a 1911 Cassell edition.

[21] *Seeing Life* listed in BM, but not in EC or NUC.

[22] LB lists first as 1913.

[23] Cassell edition bears Feb. 1914 publication date, while EC lists March 1914.

[24] Little Brown edition does not list month of publication.

[25] EC lists publication date for *The Strange Case of Jocelyn Thew* as January 1920 while the book's title page carries a 1919 date.

[26] OCLC has multiple listings of *The Amazing Quest of Mr. Ernest Bliss* with a 1922 publication date. CMW also lists this date. EC, however, first lists this title with the date Jan. 1924. The Little Brown edition does not list month of publication.

[27] CMW lists a 1927 Little Brown edition of *Aaron Rodd, Diviner*, but OCLC and NUC do not list an Little Brown edition.

[28] CMW mistakenly lists the Little Brown publication date as 1926. The copyright date of this work is, however, 1926.

[29] LB lists 1934 publication date, however, the Little Brown first edition of *The Spy Paramount* bears a January 1935 publication date.

[30] LB lists 1936 publication date; EC indicates Hodder and Stoughton edition was published September 1935.

[31] LB lists 1939 publication date; EC lists Feb. 1939 publication date; Hodder and Stoughton first edition, however, bears a Nov. 1938 date.

[32] Title is a 16-page pulp edition of the first story from the UK edition of *Ask Miss Mott*. The US edition of Ask Miss Mott has a different initial story, titled "Miss Mott Intervenes." Reprinted in 1945 by Vallancey Press of London. Listed in BM.

[33] Title is 16-page pulp edition of a story from *Jennerton & Co.* Reprinted in 1945 by Vallancey Press of London. Listed in BM.

[34] Title is 16-page pulp edition of a story from *General Besserley's Puzzle Box*. Listed in BM.

[35] Title is a 16-page pulp edition of two stories from *A Pulpit in the Grill Room*. Listed in BM.

[36] Oppenheim's plays are not listed in AC, EC, NUC, BM or OCLC. I have a copy of *The King's Cup*, but have never seen scripts of the other plays.

[37] The 20 stories listed in this omnibus as the contents of *Peter Ruff and the Double-Four* and *Recalled by the Double-Four* are, in fact, equivalent to 21 stories contained in the Little Brown edition of *Peter Ruff and the Double-Four*. The Little Brown volume is divided into Book One, containing 10 stories, and Book Two, containing 11 stories. There has never been a book published with the title *Recalled by the Double-Four*. In the *Omnibus* edition, the first two stories of the Little Brown edition's Book Two are combined to form a single story, thus accounting for the reduction of 21 stories to 20.

[38] EC lists Oct. 1932 publication date; Hodder and Stoughton first edition carries Sept. 1932 publication date.

[39] Pamphlet reprint of an article from *The New York Times Book Review*.

[40] LB lists 1927 publication date; EC lists Nov. 1926 publication of Methuen edition.

[41] This is a 13-page pamphlet.

[42] EC lists publication date for the Hodder and Stoughton edition as Dec. 1941 while the book itself carries Nov. 1941 publication date.

[43] There are a number of titles that appear on various lists that have not

been located by even the most advanced Oppenheim collectors. It seems that publishers announced the titles before the books were actually published and subsequently published the books under a different title. WB writes: "*A Woman's Blindness* is in a panel listing in *Mr. Marx's Secret (Sheffield Weekly Telegraph*, 1899) though no one has found a copy of it. So, too, *The Lesser Sin* is included in a list of Oppenheims in *The Honourable Algernon Knox, Detective* (Hodder & Stoughton, 1920). If *Lesser Sin* was published, where is it now? The Library of Congress had a card for *The Vindicator* but removed it after it was unable to find the book. We think that it was a reprint of *The Avenger* (Little, Brown & Co., 1908)."

There may be an alternate title for *Mr. Laxworthy's Adventure*. The LOC lists *The Peculiar Gifts of Mr. John T. Laxworthy* (New York, n.p., 1911) but notes that its copy is missing. This alternate title is not listed in OCLC or the NUC. The twelve Laxworthy stories were serialized under this title in *Popular Magazine* from May 15, 1912 through November 1, 1912. *Popular Magazine* was a cheap, story magazine and generally not the first-run publisher of serialized stories. It is likely *The Peculiar Gifts of Mr. John T. Laxworthy* appeared earlier in another magazine or newspaper. The LOC item might be a fan-assembled chapbook of clippings. I have such a chapbook containing the whole of *Miss Brown of X.Y.O.* assembled from newspaper clippings.